Y0-DOM-888

Rainhut®

To CHRIS

Ros

Copyright © 2007 Robert G. Adamson III
All rights reserved.
ISBN: 1-4196-6666-5
ISBN-13: 978-1419666667

Rainhut®

Robert G. Adamson III

2007

Rainhut®

PROLOGUE

"Let me get this straight, you picked the locks on the filing cabinets belonging to the other scientists working on the Manhattan Project?" James paraphrased in disbelief.

"I like cracking locks," the professor said. "So what?"

"Nothing, I guess, but did the thought of treason ever cross your mind?"

"The only spy on our team was a Russian named Klaus Fuchs. How do you suppose they caught him?"

"Well, it's starting to sound like..."

"Forget about that," the professor interrupted. "I just wanted to tell you about the flying saucers."

Nothing was more interesting to James than these one-on-one conversations with his famous, inspirational, profoundly eccentric, Caltech physics professor. *I'm talking with one of the most famous physicists in the world, a Nobel Prize winner, and he wants to tell me about flying saucers?* "To be honest, professor, I'm more concerned with the Manhattan Project and how the bomb was built."

"Okay, some other time then. I thought you might be interested to know that there are no flying saucers. I was bored, so I looked in Oppenheimer's and Bethe's filing cabinets. The security at that place was pathetic." The professor turned and walked from the empty classroom toward the exit, hiding the smile on his face.

He's just leaving? But—"Wait! That's it? Are you talking about *Robert* Oppenheimer? You discovered something in the files of the scientific team leader of the Manhattan Project about *flying saucers?*"

The professor turned back, unable to control his laughter.

"Oh, I get it," James said. "Another one of your pranks. You got me that time, Professor."

Professor Richard Feynman once embarrassed James by complimenting him in front of the entire class. For a professor who was more critical than complimentary, it was an unusual moment. He explained that James had a rare combination of common sense, uncanny intuition, and a quick understanding of anything technical. If it had been any other professor, James would have accepted the complement with a simple thank you, but James slouched in his seat when Feynman called him a "young da Vinci."

"So you think this is a prank? You're so...animated when you're curious."

"You have a way of stirring my curiosity," James said.

"I believe that's my job. Now if you'll be patient, I'll explain. You see, way back in the 1940's, when I was young and working on a fission yield calculation for the bomb, I stumbled onto a plan by the government to implement a UFO disinformation strategy. Think about it, James—atomic bombs, high-flying planes, secret projects; those were dramatic times. The government decided to blame much of the secrecy and strange events on visitors from other worlds, and they've been doing it ever since. It's all just basic reverse psychology."

"So you think all this hype about UFO cover-ups by the government is what they wanted people to think? They intentionally planted a seed of doubt to make people believe they were hiding information about UFO sightings?"

"Yep. Pretty cool, huh?"

"Professor, this is historic! How many people have you told?"

"Well, let's see. Including you, that would be one."

"I'm the only person you've ever told? But why?"

"This is not the kind of thing people like to believe about their own government...and it *has* served a purpose. But I was curious to know what you thought. You have a way of picking up on things that others miss. So what do you think? Is this a prank or just the rambling of a conspiracy nut?"

"Well, just off hand, I'd say neither. It's about energy and defense."

"Oh? Care to elaborate?" the professor asked as he sat on the edge of a desk and folded his arms.

"On a need-to-know basis, some of these scientists would be part of the in-crowd. You, on the other hand, were just a junior physicist, a curious young man who happened to be in the right place at the right time."

"Or the wrong place at the right time," the professor said. "I'm guessing your reasoning goes deeper, as usual."

"A little deeper Professor. I know that Oppenheimer was rumored to be part of a super-secret *Operation Majestic* project assembled for the purpose of exploiting information recovered from alien technology. I found that an interesting coincidence. It makes perfect sense though; aliens hanging around checking up on Earth as we move into the atomic era."

"I suspected from your comments in class that you have considerable knowledge on this subject. So are you one of the UFO believers? You seem to enjoy arguing both sides of everything; I can never tell what your *personal* views are."

James' laugh echoed in the empty room. "No, Professor, I'm pretty agnostic on the subject."

"Ah, we are getting somewhere then. What's the basis of your doubts?"

"That's easy, Professor. If there was actual alien evidence, then why hide it? The story would be too big and the real data too hard to confine. It's not about aliens; it's about human nature. Would you have remained quiet had you known of alien evidence? Besides, aliens smart enough to travel light years just to check up on us are not likely to let themselves get caught. I'm guessing *Majestic* was part of the disinformation plan. Am I right?"

"More than right," the professor said with a wink. "All that I've told you is absolutely true. James, you're the most unconventional student I've ever had by far. You remind me of myself. No, I take that back. You're weirder than I ever was."

"Compliment accepted," James said with a wide smile.

"Promise me you'll never change." The professor stood to leave the room again. "I've had other students more academically talented, but you have the real gift, son—the right stuff. What a life's journey you're in for."

ONE

"How deep is the water?" the woman asked again.

Skyler Anderson, an experienced guide, was hoping she would give up. *What the hell*, he conceded, turning to the woman and brandishing a twisted half-grin. "The Hawaiian islands are some of the tallest mountains on Earth. What you see as the island of Kauai is just the tip of a five-million-year-old mountain lifting its head above water. Here, beyond the reef, recent cliffs have been discovered on the island's ridge that extend to the pacific plate more than 18,000 feet below. That's almost three and a half miles...straight down."

The woman pulled her head back into the boat, as expected, looked around at the others with a simper, and blushed at Skyler. Skyler stood at the helm, completely unaware that his own presence was more disarming to the ladies than his comments about the ocean's depth.

He noticed a young attractive woman at the back of the boat. She stared at him longingly and with no discretion. Her eyes moved up and down his six-foot-two-inch tall, sculptured, and darkened body. Two years ago, when he first came to the islands from his life as a college basketball guard in Colorado, he was white as a ghost. Her gaze stopped at his ocean blue eyes, causing Skyler to respond with a boyishly impish smile.

The other women on the boat noticed the eye contact between Skyler and the flirtatious young lady. After a moment of uncomfortable silence, Skyler ran his fingers through his long black hair and said, "There's a rainbow to your right folks." The group turned to see a flawless 180-degree rainbow hanging just above the shoreline. The lush, green, rain-soaked mountains in the background, along with the surf's rolling mist, blended perfectly through the rainbow's spectrum.

While enjoying the spectacle, a strange, inconceivable transformation occurred. The rainbow dissolved sporadically away like a well-designed visual effect. It fizzled apart from right to left and contiguously restored itself from the same direction.

"Wow, that was cool!" one of the kids yelled.

The surprised spectators were no longer concerned with the threatening depths below. Instead, they focused on the soft skies and the distant waterfall-laden mountain peaks of Mount Waialeale.

That was more than cool, Skyler thought to himself. He had been sailing catamarans along this pristine coastline for two years without seeing anything like that before. He made a mental note to ask his good friend Mike Stranton about dissolving rainbows.

"Did anyone get a picture of that?" he heard someone say.

"Yeah, got a vid," said a teenage boy with red hair and dark freckles. Skyler recognized Tommy, a local *howlie* boy from Kapaa. "I'll copy anyone who buys me a pizza," the boy offered.

"Done," Skyler yelled and gave the youngster a thumbs-up.

Skyler was good at what he did—always considerate of the feelings of his passengers. When he first came to the island, he had been flying tours in a helicopter. His careful handling of the people he was responsible for came from his training as a pilot.

As he monitored each of the tourists, he could tell some were nervous. "Ready your cameras folks. That's Ke'e in the distance. Lots of friendly sea turtles in that area."

At the end of the day, the tired passengers were quiet as they made their way back to the weathered wooden docks. In the distance, a rooster crowed, as if to signal the end of their journey.

Daydreaming to the rhythm of the rocking boat, Skyler sailed on mental autopilot. He loved Kauai, but he couldn't understand the locals' obsession with those wild roosters. When he had first moved to the island, he rented a house in the town of Kilauea. His neighbors were a family of cockfighting rooster growers. He thought Kilauea would be a great place to relax, and it was close to the North Shore helicopter airport where he worked. There was even a nude beach nearby called Secret Beach. The sexy real-estate lady that had rented him the house offered a private tour, presumably part of her North Shore marketing strategy.

He soon discovered that these were not the wake-you-up-in-the-morning kind of roosters. They would scream at the top of their lungs at any time, day or night. The few times they were quiet, it seemed, was when some agent was showing a house in the neighborhood. Skyler eventually escaped to the nearby resort community of Princeville where the owners had enacted a rooster ban.

Movement on the boat snapped him out of his daydreaming. The boat came to a bumpy landing with everyone talking at once. "I love the whole wheat pizzas with sesame seeds," Tommy said. His red, sunburned freckles glowed on his chubby cheeks. "We could share a big one!"

"Sounds good," Skyler said, slapping the boy on the shoulders and helping him out of the boat. "I'll even throw in a drink for my parched shipmate."

"Thanks, man. You rock. I'm signed up for your sailing class in three weeks." Skyler enjoyed giving free sailing lessons to his 'kids' at Nawiliwili Harbor.

"Let me grab my laptop out of the van, then you can copy that rainbow while we chow down," Skyler said.

As they sat together in the noisy little pizza place located in the town of Hanalei's Ching Young Village, they played back the spectacle the boy had filmed from the catamaran. Skyler's first impression was right. This wasn't something he had seen before. He could hardly wait to show this to his friend Strant and find out what the hell caused a rainbow to act like that. He roughed up Tommy's hair, patted him on the shoulder and slipped past a large man almost blocking the exit to the quaint open-air mall. As he walked past the photo shop, one of his passengers waved him in. The still photos he had taken matched those of the video. Skyler accepted several copies and left for home.

Driving up the narrow, winding road from Hanalei, Skyler missed the subtle exit into the Princeville resort community but recovered with a hard—and illegal—U-turn.

He enjoyed living on the cliff's edge, overlooking the blue pacific. The sound of waves crashing against the rocks below was relaxing and a far contrast from the screaming roosters. After running up the stairs to his condo, he turned to see the cute girl in the other building watching him again. Skyler suspected she was older than she looked from a distance. He gave her a friendly wave, but, as usual, she didn't wave back.

He placed his laptop on the kitchen table, plugged his cell phone in for charging, and tossed his clothes as he made his way to shower. When he returned, he flipped open his computer and played the video again. Still curious, he pulled his cell phone from the charger and called his friend Strant.

Mike Stranton was brazen smart. A local surf bum, Strant had once been a successful computer programmer in San Jose, California. He dropped out of the whole Internet Web2 explosion after selling his shares in a start-up company he had helped form. "I just wanted to reap the rewards and move on," he once told Skyler.

"Hey, Strant, can you stop by? I have something very cool to show you."

There was a pause. When Strant replied, he had a twist of mischief in his voice, "Don't tell me, that cute girl is stripping for you again."

"I told you before, she was *not* stripping, just getting ready for the beach or something. Anyway, trust me, you'll find this incredible."

"Okay, Sky. I'll stop on by. But this better be good because I have an important date with the blue bursting sunset."

"Just get your butt over here," Skyler said with feigned seriousness.

Skyler watched the video again and played it back in slow motion. *This is weird,* he thought.

Fifteen minutes later, he heard Strant rumbling up the stairs. He came crashing in, going straight for the fridge, while the screen door slapped shut behind him. After finding what he wanted, he snapped open the beer and flopped down next to his friend.

"What's up," Strant asked as he leaned back on his chair, tilting it to a precarious position.

Strant was dressed casually in baggy blue jeans and a *Red Dirt* shirt. When not surfing, he tied his long sun-bleached hair back into a ponytail. He had a pleasant, clear-skinned face with deep blue eyes. Well conditioned from his daily surfing ritual, he carried himself with confidence. At six feet, he was two inches shorter than Skyler but was of the same, strong-jawed, smart, athletic mold. Together, they made a "dangerous duo," according to local Wahine gossip.

Skyler's black hair was shorter than Strant's, although not by much. He preferred to let it hang loose, just brushing his shoulders in the back. It parted naturally in the middle and wisps of it fell into his eyes. He raked it back with one hand. "Watch this video," Skyler said. "A kid on my tour shot it today."

"Okay, let's see what you have here. By the way, Annie asked about you. How do you do it, Sky? What attracts women like her to you?"

"That's easy. I took an art class in college, and my teacher told me I had the right proportions. She said I had the Golden Ratio. Personally, I think it's my charm."

"You must be talking about the number *Phi,*" Strant said. "It's the old 1.618 theory, the mathematics of beauty. That's a new one from you but I like it. You are kind of purdy, in a goofy sort of way."

"Well, not to rub it in, but she said I was a handsomer version of Tyrone Power. He was a famous actor in the 1930s in case you didn't know."

Strant watched the video twice before he laughed a hardy laugh. "Personally...I think the women just feel sorry for you. Anyway, nice try, Tyrone, but you should show this to someone who hasn't spent the last twelve years in the computer industry. It's pretty good though. Who did the editing?"

"I don't follow," Skyler said as he looked at the video again.

"Who added the cool dissolving effect? That's different, I must admit. I'd say it was produced with a perlin noise filter."

"Hey, Strant, we shot this today on Na Pali. I just want to know if you have any idea how it could happen," Skyler said with a touch of irritation.

"That's easy," Strant said. "It can't. Why the hoax? Who's it for? You need some help making it look more real?"

Skyler peered at Strant while trying to find the words that would put an end to this jostling.

"Strant, more than a dozen people were on the sailboat today. What you are looking at is the same thing they saw. You know I enjoy a good prank as much as the next guy, and I wish it were that simple. A professional photographer was one of the people on the boat. He took a still of the same aberration and had it printed while I was having lunch with the boy that filmed the clip. The prints match the video."

Reaching inside his computer case, Skyler pulled out the photos and tossed them on the table. "I'm no expert here, but it seems that two different cameras capturing the same image would be pretty hard to fake. This is *real*, Strant. I just want to know if you have any idea what could cause it. There are lots of things in nature that are hard to explain at first. You must have some ideas."

Strant watched the video again, began to say something, hesitated, and reached for a pen inside of his pocket.

There was a knock on the door. When Skyler approached, the girl from the adjacent building was standing on the porch. With a closer look, even through the screen, it was obvious that she was noticeably attractive.

"I live over there," she said, indicating with a nod of her head across the parking lot to the buildings on the other side. "My aunt from the mainland was on your tour today. She told me about the weird rainbow and wanted to know if you have any pictures." It took Skyler a moment to remember how to speak.

"Uh, yeah, I have a video and some photos. Probably no big deal, but you can take a look if you want."

The girl pulled open the screen and stepped inside. She moved past while staying close, gently rubbing against him.

Whoa, this girl is attractive! Hey, clean up your act. She's probably too young for you.

"Can I have a beer too?" the girl asked.

"We'll need ID," Strant said, winking at Skyler. "Sky here told me he thought you were pretty cute for a teenager."

The girl swirled around and looked straight at Skyler. "He talks about me? Well, you're safe getting me that beer. I'm twenty-two. I know I look younger, but I would think that by now your friend, Mr. Sky, would have known otherwise."

Skyler was confused. *This was definitely a weird day.*

"I think I'll have one too," he said as he backed up to the fridge. Her sumptuous and arousing green eyes remained fixed on his, making it impossible for him to turn.

She started to speak, changed her mind, changed it again and confided, "I'm sorry for not waving back at you. You probably think I'm a snob, but you saw me naked a while ago and...well, it's just awkward. A girl can't be too careful."

Skyler glanced at Strant and could easily read his mind. He decided to say something clever before Strant did. "Don't worry about it. This is Kauai. Naked is just another version of casual." *That was stupid!* he thought to himself. He all but dropped one of the beers, barely managing to extract them both from the fridge without looking away from the girl.

"So does the pretty, *casual* girl have a name?" Strant asked.

"Anchoret, Anchoret Mills. My friends call me Anchor," she said

"Nice name," Skyler said in a serious voice as he handed her the beer. "Anchoret is Welsh."

"How did you know that?" she asked, looking even deeper into his eyes.

"I also know that Anchoret means loved."

"Well, that's why I didn't wave," Anchor berated. "You're hitting on me. You liked what you saw, you know nothing about me, and now you're hitting on me with this lame approach. You probably memorize the meanings of girl's names for use as pick-up lines."

Skyler glanced at Strant who just shrugged. "I suppose that was a little forward of me, telling you I like your name and all. It's been tough memorizing every name, including a common one like Anchor."

As Skyler stood silent with a small grin and a boyish posture, he gave the impression of a scolded child.

Anchor laughed. "So you're the kind of guy who's hard to stay angry with I'm guessing."

"Bingo!" Strant exclaimed. "I hate that about him."

Skyler nodded toward the fridge. "Can I get you anything else? Cheese cake or something?"

"How did you know I like cheese cake? Have you been stalking me?"

"Cheese cake makes me feel better, especially after I've been acting like a jerk and I feel guilty."

"Okay, let's just get this over with. Do you want to see my tits again?" She started unbuttoning her blouse. "This way we can all be friends instead of uncomfortable strangers."

"No, that's not necessary," Skyler said laughing and lifting his hand to signal her to stop. "I'm sure we can find other ways."

"What? I don't think so. She's right. It's the only way to break the ice," Strant said, disappointed.

Anchor glanced at Strant, who had a serious look of anticipation, and presently back to Skyler who was still laughing. "Oh, I guess you're safe enough. If you boys knew me, you'd know I was completely bluffing. Anyway, you still haven't explained how you know so much about my name. It must be some deep dark secret. At least tell me about your name, Skyler. You wouldn't want to have an advantage over a girl, would you?"

Skyler was taken aback at the change of demeanor. "Beats me. Never thought about my name that much. My mother's name was Mary, and she told me once that she wanted to give me an uncommon name."

"She succeeded. I've never known a guy named Skyler. Where's my cheese cake?" Anchor said, slipping past Skyler and looking into the fridge.

Strant had lost interest now that the strip show was not going to happen. He was drawing something on a piece of paper. "Forty-two degrees needed for a rainbow," he said. "White light is made up of a collection of colors: red, green, orange, blue, and so on. In a rainbow, raindrops in the air act like tiny prisms causing a dispersion of light into its colors. The light enters a raindrop and reflects back out. What we see as the rainbow is reflected light from the sun. The color, or spectrum, is the result of light bending, and different colors bend at different angles. Violet bends at forty degrees and red comes back at forty-two degrees."

"Hey, Strant, give me a break here. I just want to know how the rainbow dissolved."

"Look, turtle brain, what I'm telling you is that every rainbow on Earth starts with red and ends with violet, except this one. This is pretty basic science. It was the first thing that made me think your video was bogus. For this video to be real, something would have to interfere with or further disperse the light again or something, probably on the way back."

"Can I watch the movie?" Anchor said as she sat down next to Strant at the wooden kitchen table that was in need of refinishing.

"Did you see anything else while this was happening?" Strant asked.

"No, nothing," Skyler said.

"Did you feel anything?" Anchor asked, not looking up.

"What do you mean, did I feel something? Why do you ask?"

"My aunt said she felt something different about the ocean."

Skyler sat down and tried to think. He had a good memory. When he had played basketball in college, he would go home and replay the whole game in his mind. He did the same now with the rainbow.

"As I think about it now, there was kind of a...stirring, off to my left in the distance. It was like a large school of dolphins, but not the same, more water churning. It was over fast. As I think back, it did seem odd though." Skyler looked at Strant.

"Great thinking, Sherlock." Strant appeared frustrated. "I really don't think a frantic school of dolphins has anything to do with the rainbow effect. Then again, maybe the dolphins did do it. You know, they like to use their mental sonar to mess with rainbows and confuse the crap out of us humans. They're probably down there right now just laughing their tails off. Well, I'm out of here, dudes. I want to have a friend of mine at the community college look at this. Did you make a copy?"

"Yeah," Skyler said. "I've got a copy on my hard drive. You can take the CD. I burned it while I was talking to the kid."

Strant crashed through the door and rumbled back down the steps. "Call ya later," he yelled.

Anchor smiled at the way Strant left. She went to Skyler, who stood by the window watching Strant climb into his car. "I like your friend. What else did you tell him about me?"

"Hey, look, I'm sorry about that. Strant can be a real bull in a china factory at times. I never said much really. I just thought you were a funny girl, that's all."

"Funny in what way? Funny looking?" Her eyes were penetrating again.

At that, Skyler couldn't resist taking a good look. Anchor was probably five-foot-six with a build like that of a professional model. The clothes she wore were too young for her. They were neat and modest, as if she was trying to avoid attention, but on her it didn't work. Her conservative style only aroused Skyler's imagination; she was stunning. Her soft, dark brown hair fell over her forehead, partially covering her wild green eyes.

She blew the hair from her face but it floated back to its naturally sexy position. Her lips were full and somewhat pouty: another temptation. Skyler focused on her firm breasts and held his eyes on them too long as he remembered her naked.

As he scanned slowly downward, she tilted her tight hips in a sensual movement. When he looked back up, her eyes remained fixed intently on his. She tipped her head to the side as if asking, "Well?"

"Definitely not that," Skyler confessed, trying to avoid further eye contact. *This is ridiculous. With all the girls I've known, I'm suddenly nervous?* "Look, I've had a long day. I need to get out of here and do some mountain biking. You know, stretch my sea legs."

"That sounds fun. Here's your beer back," she said thrusting the can into his hand. "I don't really like beer, but I could use a ride myself. Want some company?"

Half an hour later, they loaded their bikes into the back of Skyler's van and drove south along the sole highway connecting the North Shore of Kauai with the rest of the island. There was a trail on the outskirts of Kilauea leading to the location of a film set that Skyler wanted to explore. An artificial lake survived, apparently built for the production.

"I know where that place is," Anchor said. "The Mormons bought the land and made a historic movie. Turn up the road past that small private school. There's a subdivision there. We can probably park at the top and ride a trail the rest of the way."

They drove up the road heading west toward the mountains and away from the ocean. The ocean view was unrestricted from here. The single highway wasn't visible from this vantage point. From here, an observer had the feeling of being on a remote, non-populated island. After a mile or so, the road ended. There was an old, green, forty-foot water tank fenced in with a *No Trespassing* sign. They pulled over and climbed out of the van.

"The lake is up there," Anchor pointed before leaning over to tie her shoes. Skyler admired how well she fit into her tight bike pants. She turned back suddenly and caught him staring at her ass.

I'm busted, he thought.

Anchor stood, walked toward him, and placed her hands on her hips. "Do you want to jump it?"

"Huh?"

"The fence, do you want to jump it? We can hop over and carry our bikes through the field."

Skyler looked at the fence and the field beyond. "We better not. The farmers around here are damn touchy. They don't like tourists going onto their land. We should find another way."

"Come on, handsome. It's getting late, and I want to see what's up there. We can be across the field in twenty minutes. How can they catch us on our bikes? You really don't strike me as the timid type."

"How can I resist?" he said with a slight chuckle.

They crossed the rugged field through long grass that reminded Skyler of the scene from *Jurassic Park* where hiding raptors picked off the people as they walked. He felt better when they came through the other side and started biking up a dirt road. Anchor was a good technical biker. She had a fast pace and obviously knew what she was doing.

"So where did you go to school?" Skyler asked, expecting some high school in California.

"I graduated from MIT about six months ago," she said, stopping her bike at the edge of the canyon trail. "Look at that forest. I love this island."

"Whoa, did you say MIT? You graduated from MIT?" Skyler was impressed.

"That's right. Why, did you think I was just some dumb chick that likes to show off her boobs...and ass?" She reached for her water bottle, tilted her head, and took a long drink. "Sorry, that wasn't nice," she said at last. "I spent the last four years with my nose in the books. I didn't get out much, so my social skills are a little rough. I love astronomy, but I needed this break for lots of reasons. Our family bought the condo when I was eight, and I fell in love with the island. It's my get-away-from-real-life place you could say. I'm trying to land a job at the House of the Sun. That's the observatory atop Haleakala in Maui."

"So you understood what Strant was talking about. What did you think?"

"Your friend is smart. Everything he said made sense to me."

A flock of noisy ducks came flying low up the canyon and broke about ten yards above their heads. The cylcing pair rode farther up the road until they came to the man-made lake. They left their bikes and walked around for half an hour before coasting back down the road. Anchor seemed more relaxed. For being so smart, she still had a girlish way about her, and the more she relaxed the more it showed.

When they arrived at the field they had crossed earlier, Skyler stopped. He looked down the dirt road to see if it ended at the highway. He could see the red strip turn through a farm and stop at the main road half a mile north of the private school.

"We could coast to the bottom and work our way back up to the van. That way we can avoid being picked off by raptors in the long grass."

"I was just thinking the same thing," she beamed.

When they came to the fork in the road that headed for the highway, there was a problem. A herd of giant dirt-covered bulls with long twisty and pointed horns blocked their way at the intersection.

Anchor vigorously shook her head as she slid to a stop. "What's this, a bull's carfax? We'd better go back."

"You really don't strike me as the timid type. We can fly past those bulls. We can catch them by surprise."

"Why are they so tall?" Anchor asked. "I thought bulls were supposed to be more stocky and short."

"Beats me, but I feel the need for speed. Anytime you're ready."

As the bikers blasted through the herd, the bulls were indeed startled and scattered in several directions. A couple of the bulls chased after them but soon gave up. Skyler slowed as they hooted and hollered at their victory over the long-legged giants of the grass.

He was cruising along, daydreaming, when he noticed Anchor, forty yards in front, waving frantically. He snapped out of his slumber and looked behind. What he saw brought a sober fear. The entire herd of at least fifty bulls was on stampede and closing fast. When he faced front, one of the large beasts came off the hill to his left and flew within a few feet of his lead tire. Skyler made a quick adjustment to avoid dumping the bike.

As he came to the crest of a steep hill, with the bulls in hot pursuit, the dirt road disappeared. He found himself riding down a hill of short grass with no way of knowing what lay beneath. "No boulders please," he heard himself say. He voice commanded his shocks to their highest position and set the bike-brain to its most sensitive level. Having no choice, he pedaled hard, hoping he could ride through the bad bumps.

In high gear, flying down the mountain, he angled toward Anchor. The danger had fallen back, but both bikers kept pedaling until they reached the highway. Peering over their shoulders, they could see the bulls thundering in their direction once more. They hurriedly lifted their bikes over the fence, climbed through, and peddled up the gravel-based side of the highway, happy to be in the safety of mere cars.

They rode back to the private school, dropped their bikes and stared at each other like two escaped bandits.

"You do that sort of thing every day?" asked Anchor, laughing and yelling at the same time.

"What? Do you mean the bulls? They just wanted to play."

"That's funny." She walked toward him and grabbed his shirt; then, not knowing what to do next, she let go and backed up.

"Okay, I'll admit the whole thing was pretty stupid. Why would you let me talk you into that?"

She glared at him. "I had no choice. 'I feel the need for speed.' What was that all about? You took off before I could stop you."

Skyler studied Anchor as she vented her anger. He'd seen that look many times before when something spooked a tourist. "I'm sorry if I frightened you. You don't strike me as the timid type," he said, feeling stupid for using the phrase again.

"Okay, I suppose I deserve that. Honestly, I was more frightened for you than myself. I thought those bulls were going to crush you. How did you manage to escape?"

"Adrenalin. And, I guess by pure luck a Specialized Smart goes faster down hill than a herd of stampeding bulls."

Skyler noticed Anchor's eyes were watering. He walked over and gave her a friendly hug. When she seemed more at ease, he let go and roughed up her hair. They laughed and recanted their absurd and stupid brush with eternity.

"You looked just like Indiana Jones flying over that first hill with the bulls in the background like angry natives."

TWO

The world's most remote landmass, the island of Kauai, is home to Aadheenam, a Hindu monastery on 458 acres of tropical lushness. The estate hosts a number of well-known temples including the San Marga Iraivan. This massive Chola-style Hindu temple was carved from white marble in Bangalore before being shipped to the island piece by piece for assembly. Not so well-known is the existence of an advanced computer data center manned by a group of the monasteries Hindu Monks. Pure and exotic scientific research in this sacred seclusion is the subject of speculation by the few outsiders aware of such activities.

Hinduism is widely believed to be a polytheistic religion because of the many gods and goddesses they worship. Although to be accurate, Hinduism is a monotheistic religion at its core, believing there is but one principle essence, substance, or energy in this universe.

Everything you see has its roots in the unseen world. The forms may change, yet the essence remains the same. Every wonderful sight will vanish; every sweet word will fade, but do not be disheartened, the source they come from is eternal, growing, branching out, giving new life and new joy. Why do you weep? The source is within you. And this whole world is springing up from it.

-    *Jelauddin Rumi, Persian poet*

Accordingly, the Ultimate Reality is a formless, ineffable Divine Ground called "Brahman." He is in the sky, in the rivers, in the plants and trees...even in a single raindrop. He is both visible and invisible at the same time. He is here, and he is there. A riddle? He is above, and he is below. He is with form and without form. Hinduism teaches that at the core of our very being, our "Atman," we are identical with this ultimate reality. All living things are Brahman at their core, and yet nothing in the religion is meant to be taken too literally.

To the understanding Hindu, gods are simply tools to guide us in our attempts to capture the infinite, and help us comprehend that which we cannot comprehend on our own. They help us to uncover our own true essence, Atman, and connect us with the divine, which is Brahman.

The monks of Kauai live in a world of dreamscapes surrounded by an environment so beautiful that reality itself is their joy. Their emphasis is on the here and now, they grapple for their own individual essence or haecceity, rather than living for the afterlife or worrying about the past, or placing all their emphasis on faith.

Acharya Jothinatha treasured his times of solitude spent listening to the sacred Wailua River and gazing upward from the foothills of Mount Waialeale. Acharya had once been a white slave to the Silicon Valley industrial movement before he had freed himself, before he had learned to accept his true self. Acharya left the modern world to become a Hindu Monk. Today he functioned as a humble tour guide.

"Thank you so much for letting us visit your beautiful home," the attractive young woman was saying. "Is it proper to hug a monk?" she asked.

"Not a good idea," the handsome young man with her said.

Acharya bowed slowly. "Is there anything else I can do for you?"

"Thank you. We'll just wander over to your book store," the man replied.

"Anchor, this way. You'll enjoy this," Acharya heard the man say to the young woman as he walked away.

Acharya remembered when the Monks had had little interaction with anyone from the outside. It was Satguru Bodhinatha Veylanswami, a former Guru, who just before his untimely death opened the doors of friendship between the people of Kauai and the Hindus.

Acharya still missed Satguru. He recalled another visitor from the day of the San Marga Iraivan temple dedication. The man was there at the direct request of Satguru himself, yet he seemed surprised to find Satguru in a position of such authority. He told Acharya that he was an old friend of the Guru and that they had once been hippies and ski bums in the Rockies.

"Those were good times," Acharya remembered the man saying. "I'll behave myself and keep my distance as requested, but I'm just telling you that, somehow, my old ski buddy, whatever he calls himself now, is sitting right up there. Apparently, he's become the head of your whole flippi'n church."

Acharya found it interesting that Satguru would have such fond memories of an obviously unenlightened friend from so long ago. Satguru never elevated himself, but he was indeed the Guru, and so Acharya could not confirm what the visitor was saying even though he knew it to be true.

"Sir...sir?" Acharya was jolted back to the present by the voice of the young man he had just left.

Acharya turned to see the young lady as well.

"I'm sorry to trouble you again, but I was wondering if you would mind taking a look at this photograph," the girl asked with apprehension.

Acharya immediately recognized the picture as a view of the Na Pali coast off the North Shore. A nice rainbow had been touched up to add color and interest to the picture.

"That is a wonderful picture. I like the enhancement. It adds surrealism to the photo. We have a number of graphic artists and computers on hand that we use in our art. It is one of my hobbies, along with maintaining our computer network."

"I heard you had computers here," Anchor said. "That's not something I would expect for some reason."

"Oh, yes, we use tools to help understand the metaphysical and provide information. We have our own website, our own publication center and even an on-line daily chronicle."

"Have you ever seen a rainbow that looked like this one?" Anchor asked.

"There is a commonality to all rainbows, but this is most beautiful. Is there a purpose or pattern to the alterations?" Acharya was wondering why the girl was so interested in this photo.

"You'll probably think I'm teasing or being disrespectful, but I assure you I'm not. This is a photograph of a rainbow on the North Shore, as you said, but the photo hasn't been altered."

Acharya looked at the picture one more time and bowed. "It is most likely the result of a flaw in the development of the film. I have seen this kind of thing before. Do you have a reason for seeking my advice?"

"I shouldn't have troubled you. I just thought that perhaps you or one of the other monks might have observed something like this," she hesitated. "This isn't the only picture of this event. There is also a video of the rainbow dissolving in this...well, unusual way. It was seen by many eyewitnesses."

"I see," Acharya said. "Are you Christian?"

"Well, yes," Anchor responded. "I'm a Mormon."

"A Mormon?" the young man interrupted. "A hot Mormon girl-jock with a degree from MIT."

"Later," Anchor glared.

"Sorry, I didn't mean to interrupt," he backed away.

"The prophet Ezekiel describes a cloud in the distance filled with fire that speeds toward and descends upon him. God is seen seated on his throne surrounded by an encircling radiance compared to a rainbow in the clouds and called the glory of the Lord. I believe that is described in Ezekiel 1:4-28. Perhaps you have seen a vision."

"But you are Hindu. Why would you be quoting the Bible and talking of visions?" Anchor asked.

"All religion is significant. I was just proposing a possibility. Was the observance seen by a Christian group?" Acharya was the scientist now, probing for a hidden reason to the alteration of the picture.

"No, not at all. They were just a group of tourists on a catamaran my friend was running."

The young man stepped forward and handed Acharya his video camera. "You can see the video for yourself. Trust me; this wasn't a religious group by any means."

Acharya sat down on a large smooth rock and watched the video. He had tasks that needed attention, but the young couple had captured his curiosity. After he watched the video, he looked again at the photograph.

"I have never seen such an event. I would certainly like to. Have there been others?" he said.

"Not that we know of. Um, there was also a strange stirring in the ocean at the time of this occurrence." Anchor appeared uncomfortable with that disclosure.

The story was a bit far-fetched, but Acharya felt she was sincerely looking for his opinion. He calmed his mind and looked at the picture again. He placed himself at the site and applied his knowledge of computer graphics and nature and Brahman. To the others, he appeared to be falling asleep, but Acharya was in deep meditation, and for the first time, a human intelligence was truly observing what had happened that day.

He brought himself back to his immediate surroundings and looked up at the two young visitors. He reached inside his white robe and pulled out a small enchiridion from which he extracted a plain card. "Here is my e-mail address so that we can stay in contact. I must leave now, but I believe you when you say this is not a forgery. Thank you for sharing this with me."

"So," he heard the girl say coquettishly as he was walking away, "you think I'm hot."

Long before Acharya had become a monk, 'Michael' had been fascinated with space and astronomy. As a young boy he would rise early to watch each and every NASA launch of Mercury and Gemini. Those original astronauts were his imaginary friends, and he knew them well.

He hadn't been at all surprised when Neil Armstrong saved the day by opening the hatch to his Gemini space capsule as it was spinning out of control while orbiting the Earth. Armstrong had demonstrated independent thinking at its best. He had changed the center of gravity of his spacecraft by ignoring the ridged rules and acting on his own. Houston sat by, thinking the mission would end in disaster when the unexpected happened and its commander-on-board brought the spacecraft back under control.

Those were the days of heroes, and Michael had been determined to become an astronaut. The path to space was through the Military, and so he prepared. He had taken the Aviation Selection Test Battery exams and the rigorous physical. He had passed both with flying colors. Following graduation from college, he was to report for Officer Candidate School (OCS). He was young and excited. Headed for the 'Cradle of Naval Aviation,' his first step to the stars would soon begin.

He was close to graduation when the brutal reality of the war became personal. Kyle, a high-school friend, was killed on a helicopter rescue mission to Khe Sanh where another high school friend, Sterling, was entrapped as bait along with 6,000 other marines. Kyle had volunteered to fly as a gunner on rescue missions. On the third attempt at a landing, enemy fire brought down his helicopter.

Michael had one more test to face—a test of conscience. All his hopes and dreams; all his childhood love for space and exploration were at risk. He had wanted to be an astronaut and serve mankind in its greatest adventure ever. Could he ignore the war in order to achieve that end?

"If only the world was different," he had said to his mother. "With all of space to conquer, why are we bombing obscure villages in Southeast Asia? If I become a pilot, I'll be required to attack those people in a war I can't understand." His mother had sat and listened without saying a word.

He remembered his eyes filling with tears as he fought the bitter struggle within. He remembered the early morning flights from the cape, and how his mother would bring him breakfast, smiling at his enthusiasm. He would brag to her that someday he would be an astronaut, one of those with the right stuff. And Michael would have been a great astronaut; he fit the part like a script. The only remaining step was to accept the OCS offer, and when he walked on the moon he would say to his father, "We made it, Dad."

He remembered painstakingly, as if standing outside of his own body, when he heard himself say, "I'm sorry, Mom, it would be so easy, but I can't go."

His mother had hugged him and wiped away the tears, but the sorrow and disappointment would never leave his soul for giving up on what he was born to do. It hurt him to the core.

Later, he became a full-fledged antiwar protester, traveling with the organized and disorganized groups. Hatred for the protesters was vicious in the beginning. One afternoon, a man had grabbed his head, screaming obscenities in his ear from just inches away. He had felt the spit on his face, accused of being a coward and a traitor. *A traitor to himself,* he recalled thinking, *a coward afraid of his own conscience.* Then something unexpected had happened: a metaphysical experience.

All the noise and commotion dissolved. He could no longer feel or hear the man in his face. People were still yelling and pushing; there were teargas canisters and police helmets everywhere, but to Acharya it had become a sea of calmness. He was comforted. A peace came over him and something or someone that really mattered had released his soul from the conflict it was having with itself. *There will be other adventures for you*, he had felt something say.

Since that day, Acharya had been on a quest: a search for clues to the existence of that being, or creator, or entity or whatever it was that had communicated with him. Acharya knew that his so-called metaphysical experience was common, but to him it was completely unexpected and he wanted to know more. His approach was to look to science and out toward space for answers. This was the one path that made sense.

His quest took him down unusual paths. He discovered that over 400 years ago an Italian monk, Giordano Bruno, wrote the following: "In space there are numberless earths circling around other suns, which may bear upon them creatures similar or even superior to those upon our human Earth."

Bruno was burnt at the stake for such views. Based on current scientific evidence, it was clear to Acharya that Bruno had received a bad rap. *How could a monk have known, 400 years ago, that there are other stars systems like ours with revolving planets?*

Two fundamental questions fascinated Acharya: What are the odds of other intelligent life in the universe? And, how long would it take for one of those civilizations to make contact with Earth? These were, of course, common questions among scientists of the day, but to Acharya, intellectual dishonesty seemed to pervade the equations. Acharya found that intellectuals would argue for hours about two sides of an issue without ever really listening to each other or seeing the fundamentally important questions.

One evening, he watched a debate between an evolutionist and a creationist. Both made good and bad points in their own realm, but for some reason they both failed to see the bigger picture. After the evolutionist had done his best to shoot down creationism, Acharya wondered why no one asked where evolution itself came from. Was it created? Can you see the algorithms in evolution? Who wrote the algorithms of evolution? Are cloned animals the result of evolution or creationism?

And while the creationist had made some good points, the obvious question was *why the need* to base their arguments on the negative presumption that all things in this area have already been discovered. Why take the position that we can never learn more? What does that have to do with creationism or evolution?

These kinds of issues, though important, were not vitally interesting to Acharya. What Acharya wanted to know was the answer to what he considered a simple question...a question that both science and religion preferred to sidestep because it was too profound. Acharya wanted to know what was on the other side of the universe, the place from where the universe itself originated. To science, it was not a relevant question because science had no way of obtaining empirical data on this subject. To religion, such a question was beyond human reasoning; we should simply have faith. For both science and religion, we exist in a box, a box we call the universe. This box is both the beginning and the end of everything.

Acharya thought of the two young visitors. They had reminded him of his earlier days. He saw in them a thirst for understanding. They were happy and curious and possibly—something that Acharya had experienced once—in love.

Today, Acharya felt more at peace than at any time in his life, except perhaps for his childhood days when dreams of his future were his present. He had seen another piece to a puzzle that he had pondered for years, another verification of a theory he seldom talked about but often thought to himself. *There is a prodigious problem with the universe.*

He recalled the reasoning with ease. There are some 200 billion stars in our galaxy, and there are at least 100 billion galaxies in the universe. Advanced life on Earth required four billion years to evolve or appear. Add another billion years for the condensation of the sun and the solar system from stellar gas. Now—following the example of the Earth—it is necessary to isolate these other systems with star types that have a constant radius and luminosity similar to the sun. These systems must narrow further to stars cooler than F stars and hotter than late K or M stars.

Acharya enjoyed following the trail of reasoning in search of other life in the universe because the conclusions were so fascinating. His thoughts continued...more limitations and restrictions on other stars. What percentage of single stars has planets? To permit stable planetary orbits, double stars must be close together or vastly far apart. His mind wondered through the numbers and arguments, the so-called science.

With 200 billion suns in our own galaxy, the average rate of star formation over galactic history must have been close to ten stars per year. Inducing from what we know today, we can conclude that one civilization forms probably every ten years. When the universe formed from the Big Bang, nothing much happened for the first five billion years. That left at most ten billion years for the appearance of one billion civilizations.

Acharya knew that leading scientists like Carl Sagan, Frank Draky, I.S. Shklovsky, and Joshua Lederberg, generally had agreed that, conservatively, one million super-civilizations equal or far superior to Earth had formed in the Milky Way galaxy alone, with a mean longevity of ten million years. *They could have just asked Giordano Bruno,* Acharya mused to himself. Of course, this number was probably vastly low and inaccurate because the entire deduction came from our limited knowledge of life forms.

Therefore, the next important question is: with an extreme minimum of one million super civilizations having formed in our galaxy, where is everybody? Why the complete absence of what Shklovsky called the Cosmic Wonders? Enrico Fermi and a group of scientists first proposed the question in the 1940's, since known as Fermi's Paradox.

Today, the Paradox has become even more perplexing. Man has built computers and cloned animals. We are on the verge of creating artificial intelligence. Even if every super civilization that formed turned out to be reluctant space faring worlds, and even if they were complete cowards in the nature of Larry Niven's Puppeteers, they could still have sent computer-controlled spacecraft to do their exploring for them.

Furthermore, artificial intelligence has no life span as we think of it. In a few decades, humans would have the capacity to build and send artificially intelligent, self-replicating spacecraft throughout the galaxy. These man-made systems could essentially infiltrate the entire Milky Way galaxy in a mere 10,000 years, a blink of an eye. In essence, Fermi's Paradox on steroids. A form of this automation concept was first proposed by the mathematician Bracewell-Von Neumann in the 1950's. His population projection was a higher guess of four million years—still a relatively insignificant time span.

Why has there been an over reaching for answers to this basic question? Acharya wondered. *Perhaps the answer is too obvious.* Look for the simplest way to answer the question. Follow the process called Ockham's Razor. One should not increase beyond what is necessarily the number of entities required to explain anything. In other words, keep it simple, stupid.

More words of wisdom and knowledge from the medieval. Fortunately, William of Ockham had the good sense to flee for his life before an issue of condemnation was dispatched from Pope John XXII. Thinking was a dangerous pastime in those days.

Acharya had a theory that would surely have condemned him had he lived in earlier times, the ultimate blasphemy of the ages. A theory so simple that even William of Ockham would have said 'bravo' because it made sense of all the nonsense, and mathematically its viability seemed to approach something near certainty.

Acharya knew that the odds of earthlings being the first intelligence to spring through the galaxy were not feasible. In the vast universe, that possibility was statistically impossible. Yet Sagan and the rest could not be completely wrong because one civilization somewhere had to be the first to take those initial steps to the stars. Acharya loved pondering this, the greatest of all dilemmas, because he had one simple explanation, an explanation that required the mind of a scientific monk to conceive.

THREE

The famous Sleeping Giant Mountain is visible from the narrow highway as you pass by the town of Kapaa. On the other side of the mountain is a quaint little community park called the Wailua Homesteads. Homesteads Park has tennis courts and overhead lights that are accessible any time, even in the middle of the night. Tonight, Skyler was playing a late-night game of tennis with his friend Gary Mason. As usual, they had an entire fan club of noisy spectators who would watch their games tirelessly regardless of how long they played or how late into the night.

Gary was a former college tennis player no longer in the best of shape. He had the beginnings of a paunch belly that shook when he laughed, which was often.

Skyler watched his ace serve spin wide into the chain link fence and take a weird bounce that sent it rolling behind Gary, across the adjacent court, and through a wide opening where it barely missed flattening one of their fans by a few inches.

"Those are brave frogs," Skyler yelled as he ran after the arrant ball. The frogs scattered, but Skyler knew they would return. For some inexplicable reason, the frogs of Kauai could *not* resist the game of tennis, regardless of the mortal threat.

Gary was a funny guy. Skyler's quip about the frogs made him chuckle, but a memory from earlier that day made him laugh aloud. They had been to a meeting earlier with a group of rich people who were into the offbeat concepts of new age, numerology, and even crop circles. They were heavy pot smokers and big on hugs.

The leader of the group, who called himself Mika, was a seashell collector. Mika Zito was bald and religiously wore a white seashell necklace like some kind of trademark. His fake attempts at being casual and friendly often failed; his true nature was that of a hot-headed jerk. Although he would pay Skyler to serve as a tour guide, Skyler was finding it more and more difficult to remain professional and agreeable when Mika would engage in his new age amphigories. Mika had a beautiful home and a collection of amazing necklaces and bracelets made from exotic seashells he had gathered wandering the beaches and snorkeling the edges.

His newest girlfriend, or 'soul mate' as he referred to her, was nice looking. She wore loose see-throughs, had large breasts, never wore a bra and leaned over often. They were talking about getting married, which seemed a bit much for Skyler since three weeks earlier she had invited him on a trip to Peru, and the trip hadn't included anyone else. Skyler had politely refused the first offer, but had to be more blunt the second time she asked.

The soul mate and her enormous and boisterous girlfriend were with a tourist from the mainland named Harry Delighter. They had him nestled between them in a kind of sandwich maneuver. Gary and Skyler had been watching the sexual threesome, while at the same time talking with Mika and wondering if he would be getting upset any time soon with the frolicking of his new bride-to-be. Neither Skyler nor Gary had said anything about the incident, feeling it would have been some kind of politically incorrect taboo for this group.

"Just wondering if you might have noticed the uh... dancing going on today at Mika's?" Gary said, not quite sure how to broach the subject.

"Oh yeah," Skyler said. "I've never been subjected to an orgy quite like that before."

"I knew it was obvious. That Harry Delighter is supposed to be one of Mika's best friends," Gary added.

"Well, I was having a hard time keeping a straight face and talking with Mika while his girlfriend was doing the squeeze with Harry and that big girl."

"Are you referring to the Delighter sandwich?" Gary laughed.

"That's the one. How on Earth could Mika not have noticed that? It was..."

"Disgusting," Gary said, finishing the sentence.

"How could the guy even breathe?" Skyler asked. "He was being crushed by the cow on one side and molested by the girlfriend on the other."

They both laughed so hard they couldn't continue their game. Their little fans seem to enjoy that more than the tennis, making noises that sounded like they might be laughing as well.

Catching their breath, they walked to the center bench, and sat down.

"I was talking with Strant today. He was telling me about your new girlfriend, the stripper."

"Yeah, well, Strant thinks everyone's a stripper. This girl is pretty tame. She's actually got something going on upstairs."

"He says you two have been hanging out together working on some secret project or something."

"Hardly a secret. We've been asking anyone who'll listen to us for an explanation on the rainbow. It's quite a puzzle, but the cool thing is I get to hang with a great girl while solving the mystery of the ages."

"So what's more intriguing, the girl or the mystery?" Gary asked as he bounced a tennis ball near a brave frog that had made its way to the bench.

"I would have to say the girl at this point. I'm meeting her tomorrow for a hike on Na Pali. She's never been swimming behind the Hanakapi'ae Falls."

"A bit of a chilly swim," Gary said. "You sure she's up to it?"

"Believe me; this girl is up to it. Been on the edge with her, and she knows how to handle herself. Should be fun though, listening to her scream."

Suddenly, *Concerto for 2 Violins* filled the air. The frogs did nothing. Skyler jumped and grabbed his cell phone to hear Strant yelling in his ear.

"Speak of the devil," Skyler said, grinning at Gary.

"Can you meet me at the campus tomorrow? I have someone I want you to have a chat with," Strant yelled.

"Can we make it early? I'm hiking Na Pali tomorrow with Anchor."

"How's nine?" Strant said, still yelling as if there was something wrong with his cell phone.

"I'll be there. I'm over at the court right now, kicking Gary's ass and entertaining the frogs."

"Hey, see if Gary wants to come. He might find this interesting. See ya tomorrow," he said and was gone.

Skyler looked over at Gary. "Strant wants us both over at the campus tomorrow at nine. Can you make it?"

"Wouldn't miss it. You bringing the stripper chick?"

"She'll be there. Try to behave yourself," Skyler said as he stood for more tennis. He could hear the fans cheering in the distance, begging for the game to begin again. "I've been spending a lot of time with Anchor. This may sound corny, but I think I've lost interest in other girls. I guess

I'm just tired of hot chicks with their clichés and simple enthusiasms. When you meet her, you'll understand. Unlike us cowards, she would have said something this morning."

"Are you sure? What could you really say or do other than try to keep from laughing?"

"How can I explain? She's not bashful about stating the obvious. She's not cruel, but she doesn't put up with crap. I guess you could say she's honest to a fault, but it's interesting being with a hot wahine you can trust."

"Hey, dude, sounds to me like you're pussy whipped with all this wimpy *I can trust her* talk," Gary said as he walked to the center of the court and smacked the net with his racquet.

"It's not that, bro. I've never even kissed her. I'm not sure where this is headed. It's kind of weird. There's nothing going on yet, but there's this kind of silent connection. Neither of us wants to make the other jealous. I go to bed and wake up thinking about her."

Gary looked at his friend for a long time before saying anything. "She thinks you're a prince, dude—the prince who likes frogs. Where did you say you came from? Are you sure she didn't kiss you into existence?"

"Just serve it up, genius. You're down two sets…as usual."

The most extraordinary thing about the Kauai Community College was the alliance it once had with the NASA Helios project, a solar-powered, remotely piloted aircraft that had set world records for high-altitude flights by non-rocket-powered aircraft. Unfortunately, the solar-powered experimental craft had crashed into the Pacific in June 2003.

The college had a pleasant environment, but not much in the way of academics. They had a small computer science department that taught a few introductory classes and their Liberal Arts department focused mostly on the development of general intellectual capacities for reason and judgment instead of specific vocational targets.

Skyler, Anchor, and Gary were on their way to meet Strant and Byron Shirai from the arts department. They were working their way across a wide grass field past the Learning Resource Center toward the Fine Arts building when two sun-baked, glossy-lipped girls wearing shorts and halter-tops came bouncing up to Skyler. These girls were gorgeous by any standard, but Skyler was hoping Anchor wouldn't notice. "Skyler, you are a bad boy," one of the girls exclaimed as she wrapped around his left arm and cushioned up against him. "We haven't seen you at the beach for ages; it's been almost two weeks," she continued to scold him, somehow managing both a pout and a smile at the same time.

"Oh, hi Annie. I had no idea you're a student here," Skyler said as he glanced at Anchor and tried to wiggle away before the other girl latched on to him as well.

Skyler seldom dated his friends from the beach, but Annie's absorbing smile and sense of humor, along with her great looks and other assets, had proven irresistible to him on more than one occasion. With clumsy language, he introduced the girls to Gary and Anchor as old surf buddies, knowing instantly he was in trouble.

"Yeah, surf buddies that like to ride together," Annie said, glancing up at Skyler with a look she knew drove him crazy.

"Tell me more," Gary couldn't resist.

"Yes, is that some kind of surfing trick?" Anchor interjected as she moved in closer.

"Who said anything about surfing?" the other girl giggled.

Skyler knew he needed to put an end to this and fast because Anchor had one hand on her hip and was staring at the girls in a way he hadn't seen from her before. "Hey girls, it's been fun seeing you again, but we're late for a meeting. Hit the waves for me and give old Blacky a hug." Blacky was a worn-down Labrador retriever that lived somewhere near the Kilauea lighthouse adjacent to Secret Beach. He liked to wander the beaches and was a favorite friend of the surfing crowd, especially the girls.

The girls made Skyler promise he would come to the beach later in the week and happily continued on, but not before spanking him for being such a bad boy.

"Well, that was weird," Skyler said as he walked briskly away, scanning the area for more female friends. "I hardly recognized them in their street cloths. I mean they're usually in their wet suits and stuff."

Gary was silent, close to feeling sorry for his friend, but not quite. Anyone who could attract those girls was not in need of his sympathy. "Hey, there's Strant," he belatedly said.

Skyler waved and picked up the pace, feeling as if he'd crossed a minefield.

"So tell me more about this riding together without a surfboard," Anchor said, not quite ready to let Skyler off the hook. "This is just a wild guess, but I'm thinking she was riding your other board. Is that correct, you bad boy?"

"Holy crap! Now I see what you were talking about last night," Gary said. Realizing his mistake, he crouched over, pulled his head in like a turtle and scuffled away as fast as he could.

Anchor was dead serious now. "You talked about me last night?"

"No! Well, yeah. I was telling Gary that I admired how you like to cut to the chase and just say the obvious. We were laughing about something that happened yesterday and how we were both afraid to say anything," Skyler rambled. "I just told Gary that if you had been there, that you would have called them on it, that's all. Anyway, it's kind of hard to explain."

"It's okay, Skyler. The whole thing with the girl was obvious. Anyway, at least you have good taste in women. She's beautiful."

Before he could answer, another girl came running past, gave Skyler a quick kiss on the cheek and said, "Hi, Sky, see ya at yoga."

Gary circled back around and entered the conversation again. "Wow, the uglies are really out today, huh, Sky?"

"Very funny, Gary." said Skyler, moving off to greet Strant.

"Did you know that some have described liberal arts education as the primary colors of the rainbow?" Byron was saying.

Byron was impeccable for a Kauai college professor. His attire was completely out of place for the atmosphere of the campus. His sharp, unwrinkled suit was expensive and his tie and cufflinks matched his uncommon sense of style and good taste. Nevertheless, it seemed to Skyler that he could have been wearing overalls instead of a classy suit and he would still have exhibited a pompous formality.

Skyler was having difficulty concentrating. Byron was droning on, which didn't help, and he was still a little shell-shocked from the encounter with the girls. He was gazing at Anchor in his daydream state—a sure sign of boredom. She caught him staring and just smiled, but it was enough to snap him back to the present.

There was no point in hiding the fact that he enjoyed the company of the ladies. Yet he hardly thought of himself as a player, and given the right girl, he had no doubt he was capable of total loyalty. He was a good friend to those he respected and admired. He'd gone into battle on many occasions in defense of his friends and family. *Why am I thinking like this?* They had not even kissed, but he was falling for Anchor and he knew it.

"What I enjoy most as a teacher is helping my students learn how to learn through liberal arts." Byron was on his soapbox now. "We, obviously, are not a great technology or science institution. Our successful students will move on to bigger and better things, but the one tool or gift we can give our students is an ability to learn, because with that anything is possible." He looked around waiting for a response but even Strant seemed to be fading.

"When Strant first brought me this video clip," Byron continued, "it was tempting to pass it off as a fake. But later I did what I teach my students every day. Have we collected enough information before reaching a conclusion? Are we solving a problem or just making quick judgments?"

"So what do you think?" Anchor cut in. "What caused the effects?"

"Well, if you think about it, rainbows are simply aberrations. For example, if different colored light fragments with their own different wavelengths fall on to various parts of a lens, it will have an effect on the colors of the final image, or what is known as color aberrations. Basically, light travels in straight lines unless something causes it to change direction. When light encounters different matter, it can change direction through refraction, reflection, and diffraction. I'm sure you have noticed how difficult it is to locate the source of a siren in a big city? That's because the clustered buildings cause the siren's sounds to diffract."

"I've never really noticed that," Gary said. "Never been much of a siren chaser."

"So what's the point?" Skyler asked lazily. "What does this have to do with the rainbow we saw?"

"This may sound farfetched, but I believe it is possible that something passed between you and the rainbow," Byron explained.

"Whoa...there was nothing flying between us then." Skyler was alert now. "There were no airplanes, no birds, nothing."

"Besides, if something passed in front of the rainbow, wouldn't it just block the view?" Anchor asked.

"That's the interesting thing about this theory," Strant said. "Byron thinks that one possible explanation is that something large and invisible would do the trick."

"What?" Gary was out of his chair and looking at the video clip up close. "That makes no sense at all."

"Let's consider the possibilities," Byron said. "There are too many witnesses for this to be a fake, so we can rule out a computer graphics hoax. A separate lens could have been moved in front of the camera, but a different camera captured the same exact scene. That would be impossible to synchronize."

Skyler felt vindicated. "So the only other possibility is that something large passed between the rainbow and both cameras at the same time."

"Okay, let's assume for a minute that some secret stealth aircraft or something from a special air force project passed in front of the rainbow. Now, why was the rainbow altered and not the surrounding mountains or sky?" Anchor argued.

"Now that is the fun part and a great question," Byron said. "The answer is that I don't know for sure, but I have an idea. One of my students said she had seen something that looked like this. It was what she called a spider bow because it was composed of pieces of a rainbow on a large spider web. Turns out, she was right. I did some research and found photos of something called a 'dewbow' formed from dew droplets in a spider web. The spider web dewbow looks strangely like this effect of yours.

Skyler had seen dewbow photos, and in his opinion, they did not look like the smooth rainbow transition he had seen.

"What if a transparent craft of some kind picked up rain residue and passed in front of the rainbow, obviously at the same angle needed to produce the rainbow. That would be feasible because the mountain area on the right is one of the rainiest locations on Earth. What you witnessed was not the rainbow at all, but rather a dewbow of sorts from the craft passing in front of the rainbow.

"Notice how after dissolving from right to left, the rainbow returned back to normal, again from right to left, suggesting something moving in front of the rainbow. This could in theory explain why the only area affected was in front of the rainbow, having something to do with the transparency of the craft and the angle of sight," the professor said.

There was a long pause as they watched the video once more. Skyler subsequently said, "Any other theories? I mean seriously, what kind of a craft could do something like that?"

"Well, the Tibetan Buddhists believe that when a great yogi dies, rainbows appear over the rainhut where the body lies in solitude. When they look inside after a few days, the only trace left of the yogi is hair and nails. Supposedly, the physical body is no more solid and real than the rainbow it becomes. In a way, we are just the stuff of rainbows. At the same time, they believe we are also the rainbow source, the One Clear Light." Byron continued, "So I suppose one theory is that you witnessed the translation or return of an advanced being."

"Mystery solved!" Gary said. "We have a choice between an invisible flying saucer or the spirit of some advanced being rising up to heaven."

"There's always the dolphin theory," Strant broke in. "What if the dolphins created a giant wet web and mentally floated it across the rainbow?"

Anchor walked toward Byron, who was looking a bit dejected. "At least we have a plausible start on a theory that has a basis in reality. We now know that these strange rainbow effects do happen in nature, and that means our bad boy Skyler here isn't just pulling everyone's leg, although he obviously likes legs."

Ouch, Skyler thought, realizing he was still in trouble. Perhaps the Na Pali trail hike today would help.

"So what's next?" Strant asked Byron.

"I'll talk with some of my friends at NASA this afternoon and try to find out if they've seen anything unusual or know of anything we should be aware of."

"Keep me posted. I'll do some research on this dewbow stuff," Strant replied.

Gary beelined for the door. "Well, dudes, I'm out of here. I have a committee meeting. I just saw my ride walk in front of the window. This is fascinating. I can't wait to find out what happens next."

Strant and Byron wandered out the door as well. Skyler was amused at the sight of the two friends leaving. *The odd couple*! He thought.

He turned toward Anchor. "Ready to do some exploring?"

"Yes indeed. I need to clear my head. Seems like the more we learn, the stranger this whole rainbow thing gets." Pausing, her face turned mopish. "Do you think you can make it back to the van without being spanked?"

Skyler had no response so Anchor released her artificial melancholy and smiled. "Let's go!"

FOUR

The Na Pali coastline trail is one of the better hikes in the Hawaiian Islands. Na Pali has it all...panoramic ocean views, tropical forest, rainbows, rugged mountains, ancient ruins, giant waterfalls, and some of the cleanest oxygen-rich air on Earth. Nevertheless, the trail is technical and even dangerous when wet, and it is a rare day in paradise when the trail is not wet.

Skyler drove his van in the direction of the trailhead at Ke'e Beach, where the road ended. Anchor's glossy hair danced over her face, tousled in a changing performance that added to her beauty. There were no land vehicles of any kind along the eleven-mile stretch from Ke'e to Kalalau beach on the other side of the trail. Assuming the parking spots near the beach would be gone, Skyler wheeled into a grassy field a block away.

He was anxious to get moving. "I can't believe you've never hiked to Hanakapi'ae Falls!"

"Well, my family was more into driving than hiking. My aunt refused to hike because of snakes. When she found out there *are* no snakes on Kauai, she came up with other excuses. But I *would* climb down to the beaches around Princeville when I was young. I'd hang around Queen Emma's Bath for hours and let the big waves fling me across the lava pool. Recently, I've been appreciating the magnificence of this island by exploring on my mountain bike."

Skyler pondered that for a minute. "I have to say, though, that some of the centipedes around here are big enough to qualify as snakes. There's a home down the street from my condo named the Dragon House. It's right on the edge of a centipede- infested hollow. Dragons are the local name for centipedes. If they called it the Centipede House, no one would rent it, and I'm quite sure that no one has rented it twice."

Anchor was gathering her hiking gear and appeared to be in deep thought. "People tend to get comfortable regardless of where they live. I was in Honolulu a month ago and took a cab to the University of Hawaii. The cabbie had lived his entire life in Oahu. When I said I was from Kauai, he told me that he would like to travel there some day. *Travel there some day?* I wanted to remind him that it's a twenty-minute plane hop."

"Well, today is your day of discovery," Skyler said with a big smile.

A sensuous deep blue hue in his eyes startled her. The blue had become more prominent for some reason as they approached the ocean. She could easily see why the girls were so fond of him. Yet he didn't act like the typical good-looking-babe-magnet. He had none of the cockiness she found so unappealing. Nor did he spend a lot of time talking about himself like so many of the guys she had met in college. Moreover, in many ways—both good and bad—he was still a boy, and she liked that about him. She suddenly wanted to hug him like the surf girls had done that morning.

As they walked to the trailhead, they could see the tourists sunbathing on the small beach at Ke'e. A handful had made their way across the calm inlet and over the rugged reef to the open ocean, where they were snorkeling.

"Look on the other side of the reef. I can introduce you to some of my friends out there when we get back from the hike. A cool swim is a great way to soothe your sore muscles." Skyler suggested.

"What kind of friends are we talking about? The kind that eat you or the kind you eat?"

"Well, if they like you, there's nothing to worry about. I'm talking about the giant sea turtles. Some of them are over 300 years old. I've come to recognize a lot of them. They each have their own unique look, just like people. You would think their worst enemy would be the sharks, but the sharks only attack the sick turtles for some reason. No, their real enemies are us humans.

"I was down the road by the caves about two months ago when some teenagers were whooping and yelling because they'd captured and killed one of the big turtles. They'd thrown it in the back of their pickup and were jumping on him. I wrote down their license plate and reported them to a friend of mine at the police station near Princeville. It was in the papers. What a pathetic waste to kill a creature like that."

"I'd love to meet some of your green friends when we get back. How long will it take us to get to the waterfall?"

"Not long at your pace. I've loaded my backpack with lots of junk food to keep us moving. It's about two miles to Hanakapi'ae valley and the beach there. It's another two miles inland to Hanakapi'ae Falls. The trail is slippery, lots of wet boulders and tree trunks, so be careful. No bulls on this trail though, so we should be okay."

As they hiked the trail, a magnificent vista formed in front of them. Off in the distance, the fertile steep shoreline cliffs with breaking tides extended for miles. They looked back down to see the beach at Ke'e, where they had come from. The ocean was dark blue outward and light blue near the shore where the white water cap line twisted and turned. The trail was a deep red color, surrounded on each side by green, damp foliage.

Anchor was wearing a loose T-shirt and tight khakis. From his vantage point a pace or two behind, Skyler was turned on just watching her hike. They were less than half a mile into the trail when two girls in shorts and nothing on top came walking past from the opposite direction. In this secluded paradise it was common for girls to hike the trail half-naked.

Anchor turned to get Skyler's reaction. He just smiled and shrugged his shoulders.

"Am I overdressed?" Anchor inquired as they came to a breathtaking lookout point.

"Please don't even think about it. I'm having a hard enough time as it is," Skyler responded.

"Should I take that literally?"

Skyler desperately needed to change the subject. "If we walk down this side trail about fifty yards, there's a big warm boulder we can lay flat on. Looking over the edge, you can sometimes see dolphins playing below."

"Lead the way."

As they wormed their way forward on the flat rock, they could feel the warmth from the sun captured as kinetic energy in the boulder. It was relaxing. When they peered over the edge of the rock, Anchor squealed. A school of dolphins frolicked in a natural bay a hundred yards directly below. Wild dolphins at play in indigenous waters tend to both calm and excite the human soul.

"If only humans could learn to live like that," Skyler said and slid back. "If we lie here too long, it's easy to fall asleep on the warm rock."

"I don't think we've known each other long enough to sleep together." Anchor said as she worked her way backward off the rock. Abruptly, she turned and ran up the trail.

From a distance behind, Skyler could see her remove her T-shirt and bra. She mimicked the girls they had seen earlier by swinging her backpack at her side in a playful manner.

"Hey," Skyler yelled as he moved closer.

She giggled and ran ahead around a curve. When he caught up with her, she was dressed again.

"I just wanted to see what it felt like." She was still giggling.

"I would have liked to see what it felt like as well," Skyler said boldly.

"Oh, Sky, are you making a pass at me? I could use a hug if you don't mind."

She ran forward and embraced him; noticing he was growing hard, she turned and playfully skipped up the trail. "I'm having fun, Skyler; you know how to show a girl a good time."

After hiking mostly uphill for two miles, they started down the steep path toward a beautiful beach in the distant valley. They could see a small group of people playing on the sand and hanging out near the mouth of a river. When they reached the bottom, they worked their way across the narrow river by jumping on large rocks. Skyler was following too close behind and had to perform an acrobatic circle backward in order to avoid knocking Anchor into the river.

Unaware of the close encounter, Anchor walked across the sand to a large clump of boulders on the river's edge and took off her backpack. When Skyler arrived, he sat close and dropped his backpack next to hers. He removed his hiking shoes and socks, careful not to get sand in either. Anchor understood what he was doing and did the same, placing her hand on his thigh for balance. She moved her hand subtly higher and caught his eyes with her own.

Why am I so horny? Skyler agonized.

He pulled away from her and ran through the sand, splashing into the blessedly cool ocean. When Anchor followed, they wandered down the small beach to a cave barrier. Holding hands, they worked their way back to the river.

"That was wonderful!" Anchor said, breathing hard.

After eating a snack filled with carbs, they washed their feet in the cold river to remove any grains of sand before putting their hiking gear back on. The trek up to the waterfall was on a trail that ran parallel to the river, but crossed back and forth a few times from side to side by way of jump boulders. From time to time the waterfall would peek into view. As they approached, the air filled inexorably with the sounds of crashing water.

There was a large rock span a few hundred yards below the base of the waterfall. The river ran right through the middle of the flat stones. Skyler noticed that a burly, middle-aged man had worked his way down off the trail and was hiking along the large smooth rock floor on the far edge of the river. He seemed to be trying to catch up with a group of people that had already traversed the rock expanse and were heading back up to the trail. Skyler knew that many people had lost their lives in this desolate region of the pacific. There would be no ambulance coming to the rescue in the event of an injury out here. He sensed the man was probably moving faster than he should in his situation.

Anchor climbed over the last crest and stood in silhouette, watching the postcard-worthy one-hundred-foot waterfall. She turned and waved Skyler forward before running out of sight.

When he reached the crest, he saw her climbing over large boulders to the pool below the falls. By the time he reached her, she had removed her shoes and shirt, standing in nothing but her khaki shorts and bra, covered with spreading goose bumps.

Skyler approached her and said, "You're magnificent."

"What?" she yelled, unable to hear because of the crashing waterfall.

He moved closer. "I said, how do you like the waterfall?"

"It's incredible. Just look at this place."

A young couple sitting on some rocks a little higher up watched and smiled at Anchor's reaction. The girl waved at Skyler. As he waved back, he was sure he knew her but couldn't quite make the connection.

"Come on, let's go swimming," Anchor said.

As Skyler removed his shirt, he heard Anchor jumping into the pool. And then, there it was...the scream. Despite being on a tropical island, the water here was numbingly cold. She came charging back out of the water, stumbling on the round boulders as she tried to regain her footing.

"You bastard! You didn't say it was that cold," she scolded. "I've found a cure for your problem."

"What problem is that?" Skyler yelled above the white noise, feeling he already knew the answer.

"You know, having a *hard time* with the scantily clad females. Go on, just jump in and get cured!"

The couple on the rocks above laughed, obviously entertained.

Skyler moved in and helped her gain her footing. "Let's swim over and go behind the falls."

"I'm not going back in there. Are you kidding?" She begged for mercy.

"The trick is to stay in. After a while, numbness takes over, and you'll forget the cold."

"Oh, sure! That makes sense! Like I'm falling for that!"

Her animated wiggling made Skyler think she might fall. "Let's go. The longer you stand here and shiver, the harder it will be."

She lunged forward and wrapped her arms around him, pulling herself against his bare chest. "But you're so warm. Can't we just stay here and get cozy?"

As tempting as the offer was, Skyler wasn't taking the bait.

"I'll get you through this. You'll thank me later."

"Not likely," she said, remembering their episode with the giant bulls.

He carefully moved her back toward the falls and held her as they slipped into the shimmering cold pool. She was strong, squeezing him so hard that it hurt. He gradually released himself from her vice-like grip until they were swimming together. Skyler rolled over on his back and looked up. The sight was dizzying.

"Try this," he said. "Lay back and up look at that monster."

"No, don't do that! It's hellish!" she yelped.

They swam to the edge of the waterfall. The powerful force pounded their ears and vibrated their bodies. On the backside of the falls was a small ridge. Skyler climbed up, grabbed Anchor and helped her beside him.

"I can see the people through the waterfall," Anchor exclaimed. "Yes! Look at where we are. Skyler, you really do know how to show a girl a good time."

Watching her there behind the falls of Hanakapi'ae, Skyler wondered about Mika and the people that believed in soul mates. If there was such a thing, he may have found his. On the other hand, maybe he was just horny.

They traversed the area behind the waterfall and came out the other side. They swam for shore, angling toward the spot where they had left their clothes. When they climbed out and sat down, the couple watching the unmutilated adventure clapped enthusiastically. "You're braver than me," the girl shouted to Anchor. Skyler was certain he knew the girl, he just couldn't remember where from.

Finally, it hit him. She was a nurse at the hospital in Lihu'e on the South Shore. He had taken Gary to the hospital for a jellyfish sting once. The nurse had spent time assuring him that his friend was going to be fine.

Anchor and Skyler rested by the pool for a while before hiking back down the trail. When they came to the large flat rock area, Skyler recalled the lone hiker and moved off the trail and through the bushes to get a better view of the area below.

"What are you doing?" Anchor yelled.

"Not sure, just a hunch."

As Skyler scanned the river bed, he noticed something white in the distance. It was behind a group of large rocks clumped on top of the flatbed rock floor. He moved back to the trail, walked down fifty feet, and ventured off the trail again, hoping for a better view.

Still unable to see much he called to Anchor. "Wait here. I'm a little worried that we may have a tourist in trouble." Having worked the coastline as a pilot and guide for two years, spotting potentially dumb tourist activity had almost become second nature to him.

He slid down a cliff using tree branches, roots and rocks to slow his descent. Reaching the slick rock, he ran toward the area of concern. He easily jumped from rock to rock to cross the river. On the other side, he saw a dirty white backpack. As he moved closer, he spotted the man he had seen earlier lying some fifteen feet below in a small crevasse created by water erosion and the surrounding boulders.

When the river rose from the rain, this hole would fill with water. An injured person down there had no chance of survival. The man had managed to toss his backpack up and out of the hole; if he hadn't, Skyler would never have found him.

Skyler was an expert climber. He had no trouble climbing down to the man. "Can you hear me?" Skyler asked.

"Yes, I'm just resting before trying to get out. I think I cracked a rib or two on my left side." The man gasped, obviously in pain. "I was hoping my friends would come back. Can you see them?"

As Skyler knelt down to take his pulse, he responded, "There's no one else around. They probably thought you were in front of them. That happens a lot. How do you feel? Are you experiencing any disorientation?"

His pulse was slow, but steady. "No...I'm just in a lot of pain. I fell off the rocks up there, glanced off that smooth bolder, and cracked my ribs before landing here."

"You don't seem to be in shock, but if you have any internal bleeding that could change quickly. Stay down, I'll be right back."

Skyler climbed back up and waved to Anchor. She couldn't hear him, so he ran across the river again and to the edge of the cliff.

"We have an injured man; he probably has broken ribs from a fall. Go back to the trail and flag down the two people we met by the waterfall when they come by. The girl is a nurse, and I need her help. I'm going back to get this guy out of the hole he's in and back on the trail. We need to get him out of here before dark." She waved to signal she understood and shouted, "Are there any girls on this island you *don't* know?" Ignoring the question, Skyler turned and ran back across the river.

He jumped straight down the eleven-foot crevasse and landed on the sand next to the man. "My name's Skyler. I'll help you get back to the beach. We might be able to get a boat out here if we can get you to the beach before dark." He knew that was a long shot because the motorized rubber zodiac landing boats were illegal on the North Shore to protect the Hawaiian monk seal. There were fishing boats, however, and the possibility of some search and rescue craft from the South Shore Nawiliwili harbor.

"Thank you, son. My name's Andy Pehrson. I'm here from New York with some friends. I can't understand what happened to them."

Skyler studied the man as he decided what to do next. He estimated the man's height to be five-foot-ten. Helping him to his feet, Skyler could tell he weighed in somewhere near a hundred and ninety pounds.

"I'll push you from below as you climb out of this hole."

Skyler literally lifted him up the first five feet of rock. Once his feet were planted on Skyler's shoulders, Andy was able to reach close to the top, but not quite all the way. Skyler grabbed his feet and pushed him up another arm's length.

"I can't pull myself over the top. It hurts too much when I try." Andy was struggling to get his breath, and the fear of falling backward was freezing him in place.

"It'll be easier to go up than try to come back down. Broken ribs hurt like hell, I know, but you can do this, sir. I know you can. We need to get out now because it's starting to rain, and this area is right smack in the middle of a flash flood zone."

Skyler gritted his teeth. He was tiring from holding the man's full weight above his head. Exhaustively, after more prodding and coaxing, the man pulled himself higher and teetered on the upper edge. When the weight lifted completely off his shoulders, Skyler scrambled to the top and grabbed the struggling man by the armpits, dragging him the rest of the way out. Without hesitation, he helped the man up on his feet, lifted his right arm around his own shoulders for support and had him walking...none too soon for the crevasse was already filling with water.

It was slow going, but when they eventually made it to the rock's edge, Skyler could see Anchor and the other couple above the cliff through the mist. He looked for an easier route back to the trail and saw a path further down the slick rocks. The same rocks that had been completely dry just minutes ago were now ankle deep in rising water. When they *did* manage to get back near the trail, Anchor and the others ran forward.

They sat the injured man down and the nurse examined him. His pulse had increased, and he had the symptoms of cracked ribs along with an injured hip, but he wasn't yet experiencing signs of shock. They got the man to his feet and walking once more, but his pain prevented Skyler from moving him as fast as needed.

The injured man was nervous about having anyone other than Skyler help him to walk. Skyler said to the nurse, "You should go on ahead and see if you can arrange for transportation to meet us at the beach. Also, try to find anyone with a flashlight we can borrow, because even if he *is* able to walk all the way out, we're never going to make it before dark. If there are people camped on the beach, tell them what happened and let them know we're coming." The nurse and her companion agreed and headed down the trail at a quick pace.

After an hour, even with Skyler and Anchor's help, the poor man had covered no more than a half-mile. Skyler noticed that his hands were cold and clammy, and he had started rambling. Skyler was worried because the man was probably entering stage two of shock. There was, apparently, some internal bleeding and the lack of proper oxygen to the brain was causing confusion.

Skyler scanned their surroundings. "We need to lay him down and get him warm. He's not going to make it to the beach."

Through the rainy mist and beyond a thicket of trees and brush, Skyler spotted a natural jungle canopy, and beneath the canopy, there appeared to be an old and rugged shelter. Skyler couldn't remember noticing the hut before.

As they worked their way up a side trail toward the shelter, various colors formed, like miniature rainbows among the leaves. Minutes later the colors were gone. When they reached the shelter, they moved inside. The interior was small and open-ended, but the middle of the shelter was completely dry. They were in some kind of rainhut, able to shed large amounts of water and provide shelter for a weary traveler. It was the perfect place to comfort the ailing man. They placed him on the sole bench in the rainhut, covered him with what they had and elevated his feet.

Skyler knew that if Andy didn't improve, if he entered the next stage of shock, his chances of survival were not good. Unfortunately, the man was getting worse. Skyler stood and walked to the edge of the rainhut, while Anchor attended to the man. As he stood in the entrance, he saw movement in the trees some thirty feet away. Ensuingly, an old, thin man came walking straight toward him.

What's this feeble old man doing out here? Skyler thought. *He's probably lost and needs help as well. When it rains, it pours.*

The old man was less than five feet tall and wearing a yellow robe. He approached to within two feet of Skyler and looked at him for over ten seconds before speaking. "May I enter?"

Skyler gestured him in. There was a subtle peacefulness about the old man, a kind of nobility despite his apparent state of poverty.

The old man approached the injured tourist and knelt beside him. Skyler thought he heard him say, "It is sometimes better to let go. You have nothing to fear."

Looking up at Anchor, the old-timer said, "Is this your father?"

Instinctively, Anchor felt the old man knew Andy was not her father. "No, he's a tourist we found injured up by the waterfall."

"Yes, I see," the old man whispered. "What is it you wish for him?"

"What do you mean? I don't understand. I want to help him! Can *you* help him?" Anchor didn't even know why she asked. He was obviously some kind of homeless 'stinky' who had been living in the jungle for who knew how long. There was no way he could help.

Skyler moved closer. "Sir, is there anyone else nearby that could help us?"

"Anyone else? No, there is no one else. I must not stay long. His path has yet to be determined. What is it that you wish for him?"

"What do you think? We want to save his life!" Skyler was becoming emotional and felt insulted by the ridiculous question.

The old man raised his hand. "You are a noble soul, as were your ancestors before you. There are many ways to help. It is sometimes best to let go."

Skyler felt stupid for yelling at the old man. He was obviously just a wandering homeless and senile old man, who probably lived in this rainhut.

"So you wish for him to live despite his sorrow?" the old man continued. "That is the most harmful path."

"He has broken ribs and probably internal bleeding. What he is sorry about is falling and getting hurt," Anchor said.

"Can't you see? His sorrow caused his injury. Will you help heal his sorrow if he lives?" The old man's gaze into Anchor's eyes seemed like a challenge to Skyler.

"Wait here, Anchor. I can't just stand around. I'm going to run for the beach and see if there's any way to get him proper medical attention."

"All right, Skyler, do what you can. I'll stay with him."

Skyler left his backpack in the rainhut and set out for the beach through a mile and a half of rugged and wet terrain. He had run this trail before, but not while it was raining. Regardless, he knew he could make good time, and he was determined to find a way to help save the man. Before starting to run, he turned and took one last look at the strange sight of the rugged rainhut with Anchor and the old transient kneeling over the dying man.

FIVE

Acharya was hoping the story of the unusual rainbow would remain private, but like most mysteries that crop up in small communities, it was fast becoming the subject of superstitious gossip. His friend from the data center had spoken with a Professor Byron Shirai from the college. Apparently, there was some interest from NASA as well. When Shirai found out that Acharya had spoken at length with Skyler, he asked if there was a way they could meet. Acharya had summoned Professor Shirai to Aadheenam for a meeting that was to begin within the hour.

Acharya wandered down to the visitor's center. There was a group of Japanese tourists entering the bookstore. The women were speaking non-stop, obviously excited about something, while the men were quiet and looked exhausted. He noticed an old, tattered-looking man wearing a yellow robe. Acharya immediately recognized the man as Buddhist, but couldn't place his origin. He was speaking with one of the elder Japanese men separate from the rest of the group.

As he came near, the old man turned and nodded in recognition of his presence. Acharya was curious and approached the old man. He bowed and said, "Welcome to our monastery. Do I know you?"

"Is it so obvious? You have come a long way in this lifetime. We have met many times before." An apparent reference to reincarnation, Acharya thought.

"I see. Is there anything I can do for you on your journey? Would you like some food?" The old man appeared to be starving.

"Why yes, thank you. I have not given much thought to that lately."

He walked the old man over to the 'mess hall.' As usual, the monks had prepared a wondrous vegetarian buffet. The old monk smiled with his perfect teeth and helped himself to a small sampling of various items. They sat down at a solid wooden table with thin cushions providing a modicum of relief. Acharya gave the old man time to eat before saying anything. He couldn't shake the feeling that he had met this man before. He was old, feeble, hungry, and common, and yet...there was something about him. It was the same feeling he had had when he was in the presence of Satguru. That was it, the old man reminded him of Satguru in the last days before he died, when he was thin and fragile.

"Are you with friends and family?" Acharya asked with concern.

"Friends? Why yes, *you* are my friend."

"What I mean is, are you alone or do you have friends and family to stay with?"

"I am a traveler...a *Keeper of Mumonkan*. I will not be staying long."

Acharya tried to remember the Zen meaning of Mumonkan, something about a gate. That was it; the paradox jolted his memory—*The Gateless Gate*.

"So you are the Keeper of the Gateless Gate?"

The old man looked up at Acharya and said, "Well put, my friend."

Acharya had no idea what that meant, but his visitor was apparently pleased with his knowledge. "I mean no disrespect, but I am concerned for your welfare," Acharya tried again.

"Oh, I see. Yes, that would make sense. But it is I who am concerned for your welfare, Acharya. Yours is one of the seed and the light. That is for you to learn and experience without distraction."

Acharya was surprised. *How does this old man know my name?* "*Keeper*, may I ask how it is that you know my name?"

"You are on the wall of monks in the portal." The old man smiled even wider, exposing his perfect white teeth again, a complete contrast to the rest of his body with the exception of his clear dark brown eyes.

The wall of monks in the portal? "Oh, you must mean a computer. You saw my picture on our website monitor. What I am wondering, though, is if you are in need of care and shelter?"

"That would be wonderful. But I cannot stay long. Is there a place I could sleep tonight? I do not need much."

Finally, they were getting somewhere. "You can stay with me tonight, and tomorrow we will find you more permanent shelter." Acharya wondered how long the old man had been homeless.

After eating, they walked to Acharya's room. The old man settled slowly onto the couch as if he'd not rested in ages. He was so old and thin, it was amazing he could even walk. Acharya covered him with a blanket and explained that he had a meeting to attend. He would return soon, and they could talk more. The old man closed his eyes and was asleep in an instant.

Acharya quickly identified Byron Shirai in the blue-stripped suit. His friend was right; Byron was the epitome of formality. Acharya approach and bowed. "You are Byron Shirai, are you not?"

"Yes, that is correct. Are you Acharya?"

"I am. It is with much pleasure that I make your acquaintance. Please follow me. We can talk in the garden if that is all right with you."

"Of course," Byron said. "I'll not take long. I appreciate your taking the time to see me."

This is a pleasant man, Acharya thought. His formality seemed to add to his likability somehow.

"You might say I am on a bit of a quest for a friend of a friend," Byron began.

Acharya liked the sound of that already.

"It is my understanding that you have seen the video of the rainbow and have spoken with Skyler Anderson."

"Yes, and with his female companion as well. They were quite interested in my thoughts on the rainbow, but they almost seemed more interested in each other, I must say."

Byron smiled. "I noticed that as well. So what were your thoughts on the rainbow, if you don't mind my asking?"

Acharya paused before answering. "It is an interesting puzzle. But there are many puzzles in this universe—are there not? Are you familiar with the works of Ramanath Cowsik? Some have compared him to Enrico Fermi, one of the twentieth century's greatest scientists, for his ability to bridge the gap between theoretical and experimental physics."

"Yes, I am somewhat familiar with his work, partly because he was a professor of physics in Arts & Science," Byron said. "Didn't he write a paper about the possibility that non-zero masses could account for much of the dark matter in the universe?"

"For a community college professor, you seem to have a good deal of scientific knowledge."

"Well, I didn't actually read the paper, and I probably wouldn't have understood it anyway, but I do like to keep up with theories in physics, astronomy, and cosmology."

"Are you aware that Ramanth Cowsik was Hindu?" Acharya asked.

"No, I wasn't aware of that."

"Many Hindus believe that the universe was spontaneously born at some instant after the previous universe was destroyed, and yet, according to Cowsik, if we discover that we may be living in a quantum cosmological universe, it would not contradict with his spiritual underpinnings because he believes that science and religion are complimentary. The contradictions between science and religion are western cultural concerns. According to Cowsik, science and religion address different kinds of questions, but both pertain to truth and reality—with religion focusing on the inner seeking of truth, and science addressing the world we see through our senses and instruments."

Byron seemed impressed. "You may be surprised to know that I believe in much the same way. It seems to me that conflicts between science and religion are mostly the result of each misunderstanding the other."

The two gentlemen sat on a garden bench and Byron pulled out his laptop, placing on his knees. After booting his system, he opened the movie file of the rainbow. He pointed out how the strange transition effect moved from right to left and restored itself in the same way.

"Yes, I noticed that as well," Acharya said. "My immediate response was to conclude that it was created through video editing. Later I looked more carefully and noticed that the video and still images from both cameras were identical. I do not believe that completely eliminates the possibility of a hoax, but it did give me pause."

"Do you have any idea what might have caused this?" Byron asked.

"It is possible that the aberration is a symptom of a universe that is out of balance, a universe in which unusual things can happen without explanation."

Byron seemed confused. "What do you mean by 'out of balance?'"

"Well, for example, why is there more matter in the universe than anti-matter? According to everything we know, there should be an equal amount of matter and anti-matter. Yet, if that were true, the universe would completely annihilate itself."

Acharya paused for a moment considering his next comment. "But to answer your question, I personally believe the aberration is the residue of a time bubble. Stephen Hawking, once the world's leading theoretical physicist, at first discounted the possibility of time travel, but later he believed it was possible because of his study of black holes."

"So you believe that the effects were the result of changes in the time period of the arrival of the different bands of light? But for what purpose and by whom?" asked Byron.

"I have no way of knowing that...but I did run some computer simulations. By moving a warped time bubble across the rainbow, in effect mixing the pixels, it is possible to simulate the effects. Of course working backward, if you think about any computer transition effect, you are in a way altering time lengths of the original images. In real life, the best way to produce the same thing is to do as you said, mix the time of arrival for light waves, and the easiest way to do that is to just fake it with a computer. I am near certain that the video is not a fake, so the single viable option I can think of is a time alteration of the light dispersion."

Byron indefatigably told Acharya about his dewbow theory. Acharya listened carefully. "As I am sure you already know, the problem with this solution is that it requires too many assumptions about some kind of unknown craft, and it is impossible to reproduce in any computer graphics model."

On the other hand, the problem with Acharya's theory was that it pre-supposed some accidental or intentional manipulation of the rate of arrival of the light waves. This wasn't possible by any known rational standard or scientific method. However, Acharya believed the accepted view of our physical world was wrong.

Acharya stood and bowed. "It would seem that we both have well-thought solutions that are difficult, if not impossible, to defend. This has been a good conversation. I must attend to an old...friend, but I would very much enjoy meeting with you again."

"Yes, definitely," Byron said. "He removed his wallet and extracted a business card. Here is my number at the campus. Please call anytime. Everything I know about science tells me that your idea is impossible, but for some reason I can't wait to present it to my friends, if that's okay?"

"But of course. It is just a theory for you to consider on your quest for the truth."

Acharya turned and headed back to his room. He was eager to attend to the old man. When he entered the room, he was surprised to see him sitting in the kitchen reading secret documents that Acharya had inadvertently left on the table.

"I am sorry, but those documents are private. They are the property of the Hindu church and not for public consumption," Acharya said, as diplomatically firm as possible.

"Yes, I am sure this project must remain well contained within the monastery, but I would like to discuss this briefly with you. I can assure you that I am no spy, and what I have to say is important."

"I cannot discuss this project. As I said, these documents are private and you should not be reading them."

"But I have already read them, completely," the old man said as he handed the papers to Acharya.

Acharya was startled. "What possible interest could you have in this project?"

"Do not be concerned; my sole purpose is to tell you that you should reconsider. It is vital that you participate."

Acharya looked at the papers. He remembered when he first learned of the secret science project funded and protected entirely by the Hindu church and a handful of wealthy contributors. An elite group of scientists from around the globe had formed a team for research into an entirely new form of space travel. Acharya concluded that any possible progress in such esoteric research could not possibly yield results for decades, if ever.

"I will need to report this as a breach of security." Acharya had no intention of reporting this poor old man to anyone. There was no way he could possibly be a threat, but Acharya wanted to let him know that this was important, and that he should at least ask before getting into Acharya's things.

"I am deeply sorry." The old man bowed and spread his hands. "It will not happen again. I know you think me a foolish old man. I will be gone soon."

It was Acharya who felt foolish now. He sat down next to the old man. What possible harm could come from talking to him? It would be like talking to his mother about the space program when he was young. She had no idea what he was talking about, but she enjoyed listening to his youthful excitement.

"I am sorry," Acharya said. "Sometimes I revert to my old ways. It is much too easy to avoid the risk of trouble at the expense of humanity. I received these documents in confidence, and it is important that I honor that trust, but I would like to talk with someone about this. Can you assure me that you will not disclose what you have read to anyone?"

The old man looked at Acharya in a parental manner, as if ready to engage in sonorous oration. Instead, he simply said, "Your secret is safe with me. Tell me, what is troubling you?"

"I am no longer young," Acharya replied. "My thoughts of space exploration are desires I need to set aside for my own inner peace. I have regrets about things in this context that still trouble me. I know this makes no sense to you, but it is painful for me to be involved with this project, especially when I know that they have no chance of success."

"Yes, I understand." The old man moved closer. "The path to inner peace is not the path we would normally choose for ourselves, yet you believe that you are now on that path. However, if a journey of epic adventure would also enable you to serve mankind, would that not bring you comfort? We are each on a sacred adventure after all. Does it follow that enlightenment must come from detachment?"

"What did you say?" *Who is this man?* Acharya wondered.

"I was thinking out loud. It is nothing," the old man said, drawing back.

"You spoke of an epic adventure that would serve mankind. What did you mean?"

"The scientists involved in this project are impressive. From what I have read in your papers, there is certainly some possibility of success. From an old man that has nothing but good intentions, I would hope that you might reconsider. If this leads nowhere, you can blame me. At the very least, it could be fun. I have seen the twinkle in your eyes even in the short time we have been together."

Acharya had to admit that he was curious about the project. What could it really hurt to be involved in some small way?

The next morning, Acharya woke early with a sense of eagerness he hadn't felt in a long time. He walked to the couch to see how the old man was doing before leaving for his usual jog along the river's edge. The blankets he had provided the night before were folded and placed on the couch. There was no sign of the old man beyond a flower sitting on top of the blanket. Acharya assumed that was the old man's way of saying goodbye.

SIX

Skyler ran down the trail, passing several tourists and checking to see if they had a short-wave radio. He was remembering his early days on the islands as he ran. Despite working as a helicopter pilot when he first arrived, he hadn't flown for the last two years. The last time he'd flown he'd been trying to put out a fire in the Kapala Valley on Christmas Day when he came close to losing his chopper while filling a water bucket from a pond. It was a stupid stunt, but the fire was putting lives at risk.

Later, he learned that his best friend, who had been flying that day as well, had died when he crashed his Inter-Island helicopter into the De Mello reservoir while attempting a similar refill. *Two stupid fools just trying to help. The odds had to get one of us.*

As he turned a slippery corner, he brushed past a large man and accidentally bumped a young woman off the trail, sending her sprawling face-first onto a muddy patch of grass. He should have been paying more attention.

"I'm sorry about that," he said trying to help the girl to her feet. "There's a man injured up by the waterfall, and I'm in a hurry to get him help. You don't have a short-wave radio by any chance do you?"

"Get your hands off me, you idiot," the girl screamed.

"Sorry, I uh...should have been more careful." Skyler noticed her well-muscled companion with a military style crew cut coming back down toward him.

"Way to go, asshole. Why don't you try running into *me*?" Skyler backed away from the girl, working his way down the trail a ways. Muscle Boy was obviously not going to let this pass.

"Look, I'm sorry. As I said, there's a man seriously injured up by the waterfall, and he could die if I don't get him help. Is there any chance that you have a ham radio?"

Muscle Boy wasn't finished yet. "You long-haired hippie freaks think you know everything. This is a public trail paid for by the U.S. Government. What the hell do you think gives you the right to run through here like that?"

This isn't going well, Skyler thought. He turned to leave when Muscle Boy reached into his pocked and pulled out a ham radio, placing it on a large rock behind him.

"I'm about to kick your ass. If you still want it when I'm done, you can have my radio. I'm coming over there and knocking you around a little. If you fight back, I'll hurt you bad. Otherwise, I'll just mess you up a little."

"Don't be nice," the girl yelled. "Look what he did to me! Just beat the shit out of him!"

"Did you hear what I said?" Skyler yelled. "There is an injured man! We don't have time for this. We need to help him! I run the catamaran out of Hanalei. Help me out here, and I'll get you a free day pass." If he couldn't appeal to their empathy, perhaps he could depend on their selfishness.

"Did you hear what I said, asshole?" Muscle Boy yelled back. "I don't believe there's anyone injured, but there will be soon. I'm going to make you pay for what you did to my girlfriend."

Skyler realized that this guy was a real macho head case and probably dangerous. Although Muscle Boy, as Skyler had mentally named him, was huge and well conditioned, Skyler wasn't intimidated. He had known fear many times in his life, but he had long ago come to grips with intimidation. He remembered his karate instructor teaching him about the art of self-defense. Skyler had learned early on to embrace fear and control his emotional response to it.

"If you can remain calm and focused, you will have a chance to defend yourself. If you give into your fear, you will forget everything you have learned, and you will flounder," his instructor had explained many times. It made perfect sense to Skyler. What good was the knowledge of defense if you forgot everything when it mattered most?

Skyler had a plan. "If you attack me, I'll embarrass you in front of your girlfriend. Either way, I am taking your radio. You can pick it up at the police station near Princeville where some Somaliland friends of mine will be holding it for you." Skyler was calm and focused.

Muscle Boy was confused for a moment and looked hesitantly at his girlfriend. That was *not* the response he'd expected. However, Skyler needed Muscle Boy to lose control if he was to have a chance against him. Therefore, he decided to dig a little deeper. "This trail was built by the ancient Hawaiians, birdbrain. All the U.S. Government has done is try to screw it up." Turning to the girl, he said with a wink, "You look good in mud. What are you doing with this big ugly slob?"

That did it. Muscle Boy came charging at Skyler full force down the muddy trail. The locals refer to the red mud as Hawaiian ice, and for good reason. Skyler had already found a solid rock hiding below the mud in the middle of the trail. He was bracing his left foot against it in anticipation of what was coming. When Muscle Boy was within three feet, Skyler lunged to the side. At his speed, Muscle Boy kept going...stumbling into a minefield of muddy rocks, sticks, and branches as he was unable to make the turn just behind Skyler.

Skyler moved quickly back up the trail and snatched the ham radio. Next he slipped through the grass and trees to the trail below, where it had 'switch-backed' below them. Unfortunately for Skyler, Muscle Boy was an excellent athlete and had managed to recover. Screaming and swearing, he ran down the trail in hot pursuit. Skyler had the advantage of knowing the trail well, and recognized a turn that was approaching.

He made the necessary adjustments to handle the turn and launched forward again. Muscle Boy hadn't learned his lesson and was again tumbling, this time into a group of rocky ramparts that formed a wall on the side of the trail. With this miscue, Muscle Boy wasn't so fortunate. Skyler heard him hit hard. He remained spread out on the ground, moaning and swearing as Skyler made the next turn and continued down the trail with the radio in hand.

When he was sure he was in the clear, Skyler slowed to a walk and dialed the county-wide emergency frequency using the Sector 2 Hanalei Call Sign. He managed to make contact with an operator and explained the situation. She in turn contacted a police officer. Skyler relayed a message not to bother with a rescue boat because it would be too late. When they called back, he agreed to meet a helicopter on the emergency pad near the beach. "Someone's going to have to pay for this," he heard a voice grumble in the background.

When the chopper arrived, they would use Skyler as a guide and hike back up the trail with stretchers to bring the man back down. Skyler moved off the trail to the somewhat secluded helicopter pad and waited, wondering if Muscle Boy and his muddy girlfriend would pass by soon.

SEVEN

Anchor moved away to control her emotions. The poor man was dying, and there was nothing she could do. As she gazed out upon the vaporous rainforest, she saw the outline of a large wild boar running through the trees. Above the boar was a permeating rainbow. *Now that is an odd sight*, she thought to herself. *It seems natural, but how can it be there?* She felt tears falling down her cheek. She wiped them away and rubbed her eyes, wondering if there was any chance Skyler would be back in time. She gathered herself and turned back to the man, hoping to provide what comfort she could.

To her amazement, the injured man was sitting upright on the bench and looking around. The strange old homeless fellow was missing. She walked forward and noticed flowers spread out on the makeshift pad. *This is weird.*

"Where are we?" the injured man asked. "Did I pass out or something? Where's the young man that was helping me?"

Anchor sat down and reached for his forehead. Next she felt his pulse. "My friend, Skyler, ran for help. You weren't doing well, and he was worried. How are you feeling?" The question was absurd.

He stood, walked a little, and turned around. Anchor noticed the weather was clearing, and the rain had stopped. The man reached for his side. "I hurt my ribs? I remember the nauseating pain from walking. How did you make my side quit hurting?"

"It wasn't me! All we did was cover you up and try to make you warm," Anchor said, piqued. "You have broken ribs and internal bleeding, according to the nurse that examined you. As far as I could tell, you were in severe shock just a few minutes ago. Your skin was blue, and you were unconscious."

"What nurse? I don't see any nurse."

"She was the girl who felt your pulse and examined your ribs after Skyler brought you to safety."

"Oh, her. I didn't know she was a nurse."

Anchor was still visibly upset. "Hey, are you okay?" Andy asked, "You look like you've been crying."

"I'm fine. I was just worried about you. Do you remember the old man dressed in the yellow robe that came into the hut with us?

"No, I only remember trying to walk and your friend helping me and...wait, I do remember an old man dressed in a robe. I was standing on the slick rock watching someone fall backward into a deep hole. He was standing behind me and to my right. We were talking about what was happening, for the life of me I can't remember a word he said, but I do remember him."

Anchor was bewildered. The man who moments ago lay dying was now standing in front of her babbling on about a conversation he had with the old man before he was injured.

"You seem to be walking without pain. Do your ribs hurt at all?"

He reached for his ribs and pushed on them. Afterwards, he bent over several times, raised his hands in the air, and twisted. "It seems like I had some kind of...do-over. I know I fell and was injured but now it never happened. I was given a choice and the second time I didn't fall. Hell, that makes no sense at all, but I'm not hurt anymore, so something happened."

"Perhaps you're still in shock. I really think you should sit back down." Anchor pressed, concerned again.

"Why? I'm okay. I mean I feel great, but it makes no sense unless I was dreaming."

"I think you should sit down, so we can be sure you're alright."

"The odd thing, is that I didn't really care if I fell. I believe that's what I was explaining to the old man. I said it didn't matter because I didn't care anymore. He was talking, but I can't remember a damn word he said."

Anchor reflected for a moment, "I remember him telling me something like that. You must have met him before your accident. You're probably still disoriented from your injury. But I do remember the old guy telling me that you fell because you'd given up and didn't care anymore."

"It's true. Nothing seemed to matter much anymore. It's probably a common story. My wife left me. She said I was boring and that she had to leave. I found out she had been seeing someone else even before she left. I came on this trip with some friends hoping to forget about all of that, but nothing really changed."

Anchor pushed firmly on his shoulder, and the man eventually sat down. "I have no idea what happened here today, but you're one lucky man...I was once devastated by something that happened to me."

Anchor reasoned that if she just kept talking, the man might stay seated. "My dad took me for a long drive, and we talked for hours. What I remember most was that he told me about victims and survivors. We've all had bad things happen to us, but after that, it becomes our choice to be a victim or a survivor. The survivors learn from their experience and become stronger. Victims suffer forever. I don't have a clue how you did it, but I'd say that somehow you've become a survivor."

"You're very kind. I don't know how to repay you. How long have we been here in this shelter?"

"It's been about two hours, I believe. I'm just thrilled that you're doing better. I was feeling guilty because I was unable to help you, and I was afraid that Skyler wouldn't make it back in time. Please tell me that you'll take better care of yourself from now on."

"Well, with people like you and your friend around, it can't be all that bad. If you care enough about me to help the way you have, then the least I can do is care too."

Perhaps the joy of seeing the man doing better was efficacious in forming a bond, but Anchor was feeling genuine friendship for him. "I'm not sure if this is the right thing to do, but if you're feeling up to it, I think we should get you out of here and back to your friends before it gets dark."

"I'm already with a friend," he said. "But let's get going before that old man comes back and scares the crap out of us."

As they walked down the trail together, Anchor kept watching and expecting him to collapse, but he was alert and moving easily without pain or discomfort. They were trekking along at a good pace and talking like old friends.

When they came within view of the beach, Anchor thought she heard someone calling her name. She stopped and looked around. There it was again. "Anchor, up here!" It was Skyler calling to her from an area about a hundred feet above the trail.

She waved with both hands and hopped up and down as Skyler ran toward them. When he was closer, he stopped and stared in disbelief. Alarmed, he ran toward them again.

"Andy, how did you manage to get here? How do you feel?"

"I guess I just needed a rest. I'm feeling a lot better now, thanks to you two."

"But how did you recover so fast? I thought you were a goner. I guess I over-reacted." Skyler patted Andy on the shoulder and lifted his shirt to check the injuries. Satisfied, he reached for the radio and called the police officer he had been talking with earlier.

As Andy and Anchor simultaneously tried to explain what happened, he held up his hand for a moment while he asked the officer to belay the rescue chopper. As expected, the rescue was delayed at least another hour anyway. *Typical*, he thought.

Skyler recounted his run-in with Muscle Boy and the girl. Anchor laughed at his description of the couple. "The two of them wandered past here about an hour ago. They didn't see me waiting at the helicopter landing zone, but I could hear them swearing and complaining as they walked past."

The trio crossed the river on slippery boulders with Skyler on one side and Anchor on the other. They attended to Andy like mother hens. He was clearly embarrassed, but they couldn't help themselves. They hiked up the steep trail, leaving the white, wet beach behind. The trail was increasingly dryer above the valley forest. When they reached the fringe of the windy crest, the trail flattened, and trouble was waiting. Muscle Boy and his girlfriend were sitting on a rock, and they did not look happy.

"We meet again, you hippie asshole," Muscle Boy exclaimed with apparent glee as he bounded to his feet. "Is this the dying man you were telling us about? I knew you were lying."

"I'm really going to enjoy this," the girlfriend said as she eyed Anchor up and down with disgust.

"How you gonna get away this time, wise guy? The trail's dried up, and I won't be falling for any more of your chicken-shit tricks."

A glance at Anchor told Skyler she was irritated by the macho gamesmanship. He knew he would have to defend himself this time. Muscle Boy looked even bigger and wilder as he stood above them in the wind. Skyler signaled Andy to move away as Muscle Boy walked forward with evil intent. He gave Anchor a dirty stare and appeared as if he might go after her first, but changed his angle on his way to Skyler.

Suddenly, there was a loud *whomp!* Muscle Boy bent over, grabbing his crotch and screaming in pain. He rolled on the ground. His face was beet red as he vomited from the groin kick Anchor had delivered.

Andy burst into laughter as the girlfriend came running toward Anchor. She was about to attack when she stopped and thought better of it. "You bitch! What have you done? I'm gonna rip your eyes out!" she yelled.

"Oh please, stuff a rag in it. Your boyfriend here won't be giving you much lovin' for a while, if he ever could."

Skyler was dumbfounded. There was nothing to say. He even wondered if Muscle Boy was in need of medical attention. *Oh, the hell with it*, he thought and tossed the ham radio on the ground next to the heaving Muscle Boy as he walked past. Andy was still laughing as they continued up the trail.

"A friend of mine was raped," Anchor explained, "as we walked home from a late high-school band practice."

Anchor was lucky to get away. For years, she blamed herself for not being able to help her friend. Ensuingly, instead of playing the victim, she decided to study karate. "They have a great Shotokan Karate club at MIT," she explained. "I've spent years getting over the guilt for something that wasn't my fault. But if I'd known then what I know now, perhaps things would have been different that day."

"What a coincidence," Skyler said. "We both know karate. Perhaps we could engage in some friendly hand-to-hand sometime."

"Are you asking me for a role on the mat? Are you sure you're up for that? Oh, sorry, I forgot you've been up all day."

"Not funny, Anchor," Skyler said and bumped her off the trail with his shoulder onto a soft embankment.

"Hey, get a room," Andy said, still giddy from watching the big bully taken down and from his own inexplicable survival.

On the next turn, they ran into the nurse and three rescue volunteers complete with stretcher and full-gear first-aid kits. They stood around for a moment and just looked at each other. Skyler was the first to speak. "I thought I was fast. How did you make it back so soon?" Before they answered, he remembered. He'd met the nurse at the hospital, but he had also seen her on the news. She was one of the female finalists in the world-famous Ironman Triathlon.

Ironman, held in Kailua-Kona, is a grueling race consisting of a 2.4-mile rough water swim, a 112-mile bike race, and a 26.2-mile marathon. He recognized the three men as well, one of them being an Ironman World Champion from Switzerland.

"Anchor," Skyler explained, "our friend the nurse here is Stacy Newby, a world-class athlete. She told me about it at the hospital, but I was in a cloud that day. Stacy and her friends train on these trails. I should have stayed put with you and saved myself all the trouble."

Stacy had already cornered Andy and had him down on the ground for another examination. "Why did you move him?" she scolded. "He was in no condition to be moved, let alone walk this far."

"You'll have to ask Anchor and Andy about that one. Somehow, he recovered enough to hike out on his own. I'm still perplexed. I thought he was seriously injured as well."

"He is injured. I told you he has broken ribs, a possible cracked hip, and probably internal bleeding." The entire rescue team was now working on him. They had removed his shirt and had him on the stretcher.

"I'm not seeing that, Stacy," one of the men said. He was wearing a white T-shirt with writing on the back that read: *Now do you believe I can fix your leg? Yes, I stand corrected.*

Stacy looked puzzled. "Doctor, he had muscle spasms and the ribcage was deformed from a fracture. There was acute upper left abdominal pain, indicating possible spleen rupture, and his breathing was labored. He was unable to walk on his own."

"That's correct," Skyler said. "He was in serious trouble and heading into shock when I left."

Anchor moved to the middle of the group. "He was unconscious and his skin was blue just before he recovered. There was an old man in a yellow robe that I believe might have done something to help him."

Andy was claustrophobic from the attention. He tried to squirm his way free, but to no avail. Each time he tried to get up, he was restrained by Stacy, the doctor, and the other two men.

"Sometimes temporary swelling from a fall can make an injury look worse than it is. Especially when there's mud and such," the doctor said. "Everyone should calm down and look at the positive. You did the right thing. Your friend here is just lucky that he wasn't more seriously injured." He released his pressure on Andy and helped him to his feet over Stacy's objection.

Andy would laugh occasionally on their trek back to Ke'e. "My friends won't believe any of this. You have *got* to let me take you to dinner." That comment and his insouciant manner frosted Stacy, who was still trying to explain things to the doctor.

Andy's friends were waiting in the parking lot and came running when they saw him. Just as Skyler suspected, they had concluded that Andy was in front of them.

Andy invited everyone to dinner at the Blue Dolphin, where they laughed and talked about the day. Andy was right; his friends weren't falling for any of the story. However, for Anchor, what had happened on this day was undeniable. She looked at Stacy, who was still nagging the poor doctor. Anchor knew that Stacy's diagnosis had been correct. Andy had been dying from serious fall injuries. Unlike the others, she had been with him as his condition worsened. There was nothing lucky about Andy's recovery. She would be attending the small LDS church in Hanalei on Sunday morning and giving thanks to a higher power.

"This has been a perfect ending to a day I'll never forget," she told Skyler as they drove back to Princeville in Skyler's van. "I now believe in happy endings."

The soft warm evening air combined with the well-exercised feeling was intoxicating. It was hard for Anchor to leave Skyler that night as they headed in opposite directions from the van to their respective condos. As she was going up the stairs, she stopped and called out, "Hey, Skyler, you pervert, don't get any ideas about watching me in the window. I'm pretty tough ya know."

"Aloha, gorgeous. I'm getting my binoculars and expecting a show," he called back.

"Yeah, dude," a kid from a group of surfers said as he walked past.

❧

Anchor's aunt was waiting up when she entered the condo. "He's been watching you through the window?"

"Oh, Aunt Edie, what's wrong with me? I have a nice guy that wants to marry me and all I can think about is Skyler, a horny girl chaser." Anchor collapsed exhausted onto the couch next to her aunt. She cried as the emotions of the day caught up with her.

"What happened? Did he do something to you?" her aunt asked sternly.

Anchor turned to her aunt and gave her a long hug. "No, Aunt Edie, he did nothing wrong—quite the contrary. He's a perfect gentleman. He's brave and he's strong and...and he's never even kissed me."

"I knew it. He's gay!"

Anchor looked at her aunt, who was wiping away her tears, and laughed.

After a few moments, Aunt Edie was laughing as well. "So you like this guy, I take it. He is pretty sexy. All the girls on the boat were staring at him."

"What?" Anchor asked, as she stopped laughing.

"He's cute. Oh, hell, he's a hunk. That's all I was trying to say."

"Aunt Edie! I've never heard you talk like that."

"Why? You don't think I was young once? I know a sexy guy when I see one."

Anchor took a slow deep breath. "Oh, well, I guess he's kind of cute. He's smart too, and he cares about people."

They stared at each other in silence for a moment before laughing again. "Okay, he's hot," Anchor admitted. "He's so hot that he has me acting like a silly high school girl. He needs to step up and kiss me. If he doesn't kiss me soon, I swear I'll trip him and beat him to the ground! I just want to run my fingers through his thick black hair and squeeze those muscles on his arms that ripple the way they do."

Anchor paused, as if in deep thought. "Oh, great. What should I tell Charles?"

"This sounds serious, dear. Just be careful and don't get too carried away when he does finally kiss you."

"I've been thinking about that. It goes against everything I believe about premarital sex, but I'm just not sure what I would do in the right situation with him. I'm not always good at handling that kind of temptation."

"You'd better get to church on Sunday. That's what I think."

"I will, Aunt Edie. Something amazing happened today. I'll tell you all about it tomorrow."

"All right, sweetheart. You best get some sleep now. If you want, I'll mosey on over there and give him a big smooch just to find out if he's worth all this."

"It looks like we're both smitten by Skyler Anderson," Anchor said as she hugged her aunt again and staggered toward the shower.

EIGHT

It was Sunday morning and Skyler was hanging out on the beach. He was trying to relax and sort things out in his head. Anchor had coaxed and begged him to attend church with her, but he just wanted to stroll the beach and soak up some rays. He told her that perhaps he would meet her at the church around midday for what she called sacrament meeting. Skyler knew nothing about the Mormon religion, and the whole idea made him squeamish.

As he strolled down the beach, he ran into an old big-wave surfer friend everyone knew as Bible Bill. Bill was famous for his ability to garner the attention of unsuspecting tourists and preach to them about humility, his favorite subject. Bible Bill was a self-proclaimed expert on the Bible and religion. He knew so much about the bible, he couldn't be bothered with church. For being so humble and Christian, Skyler found it amusing that he would engage in heated arguments with anyone that was foolish enough to participate.

As much as he loved to preach and argue, Bill would never argue with Skyler. Bill had learned to respect Skyler to the point that he would simply not preach to him. Skyler knew that it had something to do with his friendship with the sea turtles. The two had met while swimming one misty afternoon. Both men were snorkeling and had hooked up with a common bale of turtles.

Skyler had swum up to one of the larger turtles, who was gorging himself on the purple growth in the coral. He had grabbed a handful of the stuff and offered it to the turtle.

To Bill's complete and utter amazement the turtle had gobbled the food directly from Skyler's hand and did so with cautious gentleness.

When they surfaced, Bible Bill was gurgling and babbling about how Skyler must be enlightened or something. Skyler still remembered some of the conversation. "I have been swimming with these turtles for twenty-five years, and I have never, I mean never seen that before. Hell, I've never even heard of these wild turtles accepting food from the hand of anyone. I didn't even know there was anyone else besides myself stupid enough to try and feed them like that. Those turtles could take your entire arm off in one quick snap!"

"I never really thought about it," Skyler said, flopping his way to shore and wondering who this old weird guy was.

He had golden hair, a pug nose, a deep tan and a big round belly that was shaking as he talked. "They seem gentle enough to me, and they really like that purple stuff," Skyler explained.

Bible Bill was flabbergasted and continued, "I can't even begin to explain how significant this is! These turtles have innate knowledge of human behavior. They watch the unsuspecting tourists swimming beside them as the tide is receding. When the water drops, the turtles either try to warn the people they like or move quickly away and laugh as the rubbernecks get splattered on the coral.

"When I first noticed that, I would follow up by talking to the people. I found that the turtles have a perfect record of discerning the jerks from the humble people. In your case, I don't believe they even think of you as human." Since that day, Bible Bill had been a true friend, no questions ever asked. Skyler's ability to hand-feed the giant sea turtles was, to Bible Bill, some kind of divine act. Skyler just thought it was fun.

"Hey, Bill, do you know anything about the Mormons?" Skyler ventured. "I've met this amazing girl. I mean she really has me off balance. Anyway, she wants me to go to the Mormon Church with her; it's the church with the bright blue tile roof."

"I know all about them. They've been trying for years to get me to go to that church. They have these young missionaries that travel in pairs. Every few months or so, a new missionary pair surfaces from different places on the mainland. I'm not sure how they do it, but they invariably manage to track me down and invite me to church. Hey, if you want to go, I'd be happy to tag along. That would be a shocker to them."

Skyler and Bible Bill wandered up to the church and entered the front foyer. Anchor spotted them. She was beaming with happiness. Skyler introduced her to Bible Bill and looked around to see what was going on. A handful of the men greeted them with hardy handshakes and shoulder pats. The men were dressed in suits and ties. Skyler and Bill were wearing shorts and grubby T-shirts with important eloquent messages in faded print.

They moved into the crowded assembly room and found an open side isle toward the back. In the front, a cluster of anxious people sitting around the podium represented many races. *The melting pot of the Pacific*, Skyler thought to himself.

After the initial ceremony of passing the sacrament, Bishop McKay, the person in charge, introduced each of the speakers. It was immediately apparent that none of these people, including the bishop, were professional clergy. These were just a group of nervous, ordinary church members, somehow selected to speak.

Bill leaned into Skyler. "Luck of the draw, I'm thinking."

"Yeah, not sure we'll get our money's worth today," Skyler whispered.

To their surprise though, as each person talked about his or her personal spiritual experience, Skyler and Bible Bill found themselves interested in what each new speaker had to say. This wasn't like anything Skyler had experienced in other churches. He was beginning to see how someone as intelligent as Anchor would enjoy coming here. This wasn't so much a religious lesson as it was the coming together of ordinary people, inspiring each other.

When the meeting was over, some of the men asked Skyler and Bill if it was possible to have a follow-up visit with them and explain more about the Church. Bible Bill was quick on his feet with a response. Skyler had seen Bill in action enough to know when he was being straight with someone. "There isn't much point really," Bill said. "These people are already humble and not in need of my help. My time is best spent on the beaches with the lost tourists from around the world."

To Skyler's surprise, the Mormons weren't offended by his response. He knew it was they who wanted to teach Bill, not the other way around. They simply accepted his statement as a compliment, and one of the men looked at Skyler and said, "What about you, Brother Anderson? Would you be interested in having a couple young men meet with you? It's my understanding that you like working with the youth. If nothing else, I'm sure you would enjoy their company. They're both a long way from home. One of them attended high school in Colorado and would get a kick out of sharing basketball stories with you."

Skyler looked at Anchor, who just shrugged. "You seem to know a lot more about me than I do you. Any idea how that's possible?" Skyler asked.

The man laughed and admitted that he had been talking with Anchor before the meeting. "She is rather fond of you, and in this church we pretty much do what our sisters tell us. The men in our church have the illusion of authority."

"Yeah, pretty much just like the rest of the world," Skyler added.

Skyler gave in and agreed to meet with the missionaries. Anchor said she would prepare dinner for them and was clearly satisfied with the tactics of her friend, or "brother," as she called him.

After saying goodbye to Anchor, Skyler and Bill began their meander down the narrow palm-tree-lined streets back to the beach. "That wasn't what I expected," Bill said to his friend. "I may go there again someday if you decide to go."

"Let me ask you something, Bill. You seem to be somewhat of an expert on religions. How much do you know about the Hindu?"

"Oh, I know all about them," Bill said quickly. "They have it all wrong."

"They have what all wrong?"

"If those dudes really knew what they were doing, they'd be worshiping turtles, not cows."

"Well now, that's an interesting point." Skyler said, seldom surprised by the direction of Bill's reasoning. He had learned long ago to expect the unexpected from Bill.

"But what do you know about the temple and the giant monastery in the hills above Kapaa? Have you ever met with any of the monks?"

"I've been to their bookstore and chatted with some of the monks. I tried to preach to them, but it was like talking to a wall. They're nice enough, but it was hard to tell what they were thinking. They bow and agree with everything, but I had the feeling they thought I was full of crap."

Skyler nodded in understanding. "I met with a monk last week, and he seemed like a sharp guy. Not what you would expect from a monk at all."

"Oh, those dudes are smart. Don't let them fool you. I mean, those monks come from all walks of life, and some of them are upper echelon in the brains department. Hey, come to think about it, I've never seen them surfing. Kind of hard to be spiritual if you never surf. Right, ol' buddy?" They gave each other a high five in acknowledgment of those words of wisdom.

Bill paused for a moment before displaying a serious look. "Actually, I do know a little about that place. The skinny is that there's more going on there than just a bunch of monks building temples. Apparently, these guys have computers, research labs, special factories...the works. They're doing some pretty intense research of some kind. Why are you so interested in that place? Don't tell me you know another girl that's Hindu?"

"No, I have my hands full with Anchor. I'm not thinking about other girls, Hindu or otherwise."

"My advice is that you should become a Mormon/Hindu and reap the rewards of the babes. If anyone on this planet could pull that off, it's you."

"Bill, I think that's the first religious guidance you've ever given me. So after being friends for two years, your advice to me is to become a Mormon/Hindu and get as many babes as possible?"

"No, man, that isn't religious guidance. That's just one surfer to another from the heart."

"Oh, I think I'm starting to see the light." Skyler flashed a grin as two girls in thin bikinis strolled past. They smiled back and covered their mouths as they whispered something to each other.

"Dude, if I was your age and I got those kinds of looks, I think I'd become a Mormon/Hindu."

"Hey, old man, a pair of girls like those back there are borderline death. It's not safe for you to even be thinking in that direction."

"Well, if they die, they die. I can still hang five with the best of them. I'm just like the old timers in the Bible. You ever read about those dudes?"

The two friends from different generations continued down the beach, laughing and enjoying each other's company. They bumped into other friends who were eager to hear surfing stories from one of the sport's original legends. Bible Bill was happy to oblige, never one to disappoint.

As the sun was setting and they strolled back to their cars, Skyler told Bill about his experience with the rainbow and the meeting at the college. Unlike everyone else Skyler had talked with, Bill wasn't surprised at all. He just accepted it at face value as his friend described it.

"I know the whole thing sounds pretty hard to believe," Skyler said, searching for his keys.

"Son, it'd be like disrespecting the tide for me to doubt you. This is the land of magic dragons, and if ever there was a lad in harmony with nature, I'm looking at him right here...right now. I can't wait to hear more, but this old surfer needs to crash." Bill checked the surfboard latching on the roof of his rusty Subaru before flopping heavily into the driver's seat. Skyler smiled and smacked the back of the car. He thought he heard Bill singing, "Fifteen men on a dead man's chest," melded with the Beach Boys coming from his tape player.

NINE

As Skyler opened the door to his van, he noticed a sadhu in a saffron robe, leaning against a tree on the other side of the parking lot. He wore his hair in a graying tight back ponytail with a short knob and his beard dropped straight down below his mustache in the manner of an old west gun fighter.

After a moment, the monk lifted his head. His faced beamed with an amiable, happy smile. Skyler recognized him as Acharya from the monastery. It was unusual for a monk to be out near dark so far from his home. As Skyler approached, Acharya waved and bowed.

"I was standing at the front of the monastery today looking up the Wailua River valley to the west when I noticed a full rainbow stretching across Mount Waialeale, and I was reminded of you. Your friend Strant dropped me off. He said he saw you today on the beach. I was hoping you would still be here."

Acharya seemed different to Skyler, somehow less formal. "I've just been resting and hanging out with friends today. It's good to see you again, Acharya."

"You remembered my name. That is unusual. Do you have a few moments to talk?"

"Sure, where would you like to go?"

"Oh, right here is fine," Acharya said.

"The mosquitoes like to hunt at dusk around here. I think we'd be more comfortable down by the ocean."

"I would enjoy a night walk along the ocean. I was a surfer in my younger days. I used to lie on the beach looking up at the stars and dream of being an astronaut," Acharya said cheerfully.

As they made their way to the beach, Skyler almost forgot he was talking with a Hindu monk. He peered at the robe Acharya was wearing and said, "I met a strange old man two days ago on the Napali coast up by the first waterfall. He was wearing a robe similar to your own, but it was yellow. While helping an injured hiker, we found a shelter by chance, so we went inside to keep him warm. A few minutes later, this old man, about five feet tall, came out of nowhere and approached to the shelter. Is there some kind of remote Hindu camp in that area?"

Acharya stopped and looked directly at Skyler. "No, we have no camps in that area. The robe you are describing could be that of a Buddhist. Did he say anything to you?"

"He just asked politely if he could enter. Then he went to the injured man and knelt down. I didn't stick around. I left for help because I was afraid the guy's injuries were serious. It was a day I'll not soon forget."

"I came looking for you because I wanted to talk with you about your rainbow, but now it seems that we may have something in common to discuss." Acharya had become solemn. "Do you remember anything else about the old man?" he asked.

"My friend Anchor thinks he had something to do with healing the injured hiker. You said we have something in common. Do you know anything about this man?"

"I believe I may have met the same man at the monastery. I thought he was homeless, so I let him stay with me. I was going to help him find shelter, but he left the next day."

"Do these Buddhist monks have some kind of healing knowledge? The tourist was hurt badly. I thought he had at least one broken rib. He was in shock and unconscious when I left. The next time I saw him, he was strolling down the trail with Anchor like nothing had happened. Forgive my ignorance, but are these monks some kind of medicine men or something?"

"No, not usually. They are not trained doctors if that is what you are asking."

Acharya tried to remember his encounter with the monk and any identifying features. "Something that I noticed...he had perfect teeth. I thought that was odd for someone of his age. They did not look like false teeth...but who knows nowadays?"

"Yep, I think we're talking about the same guy. That was one of the first things that struck me about him while he was standing in the rain asking if he could enter. He had a dazzling smile. So did he heal someone for you as well?" Skyler was curious now.

"Not in the normal sense. No bone healing or physical miracles. But he did change my life in a way. I have decided to get involved in a science project of sorts. It involves space exploration. The old man was remarkably persuasive."

Acharya abruptly changed the subject. "I am sorry, but do you think we have ever met before? I keep trying to remember where I know you from."

"I've been having the same thought myself," said Skyler. "As we were driving back down to Kapaa from the monastery, we stopped at Wailua Falls. I remember bugging Anchor about it."

Acharya reverted to his monk style politeness and bowed. "I am again sorry, sir, but I must return home right away. My companions will become worried about me. Would it be too much trouble for you to give me a ride? I would be honored to pay you for your trouble."

"Not a problem." Skyler laughed at the sudden change in character. "It'll give us a chance to try and solve some of these riddles. Oh, and you can drop the 'sir' bit. We're probably old friends from a prior life or something."

"What? Why would you say that? Are you a believer in reincarnation?"

"Uh, I don't think so. I was just trying to relax you," Skyler said, hoping Acharya would de-robotize a little.

"I understand. I will try more to...relax." Acharya smiled.

They drove away from the quaint town and over the narrow bridge crossing the Hanalei River. The old van started its climb up the narrow winding road to Princeville. A car coming down from the opposite direction scarcely missed a befuddled mountain biker who had found himself out after dark in a highly dangerous situation. Skyler squeezed his van off to the side as best he could and honked his horn. The biker scrambled desperately across the road.

"Thanks, man," the biker gasped. "This was getting freaky."

"Just throw your bike in the back of the van and jump in. You were about to become another statistic on one of the most dangerous stretches of highway on the planet. I'll give you a ride, and in return you promise me that you'll never ride or walk this section at night again."

"Right on, dude. Solemn oath. That was precarious. Hey, you guys know where the chicks hang at night around here?"

"My friend here is a monk. He might know." Skyler winked at Acharya.

"A monk? Are there chick monks? Count me in!"

"No, I apologize; I can be of no service in this area. But should you choose to follow the path of abstinence in search of *Brahmacharya*, or sexual purity, I would be more than pleased to guide you in that direction." Acharya winked back at Skyler.

"Do you mean give up chicks? You're funny, dude. I'd be better off getting flattened back there. That is just not righteous."

The biker leaned his arms on the back of Skyler's seat. "I'm staying with friends at the golf resort up there. Can you drop me at the market?"

Skyler pulled into the gas station across from Foodland and filled his van for the trip into Kapaa. He watched the youthful biker coasting over to the market, where he slung his bike into a rack and walked toward the store. On his way in, Skyler spotted Anchor, carefree, walking out of the store with a young man trying to put his arm around her. She turned away quickly and bumped into the accident-prone biker, knocked him into a music stand. She apologized and promptly grabbed her mountain bike from the rack while the biker boy uncovered himself of plastic containers.

Skyler yelled at her before she rode off around the corner with the stranger. Anchor changed direction and pedaled toward him, squashing a frog in the process.

"Oh, yuck, I hate it when I do that!"

This was too much. Skyler could no longer help laughing at Anchor's antics. *Wow, she gets cute when she's flustered.*

"I was just getting my aunt some aspirin. A centipede got her and she's been wailing all afternoon. You'd think she was dying."

The man with Anchor followed on a woman's bike, one of Anchor's spares.

"This is my friend Charles. We graduated from MIT together."

Anchor's friend reached out his hand to Skyler. "Hello, pleased to meet you. I just arrived here today. I've never been to this island before."

The young man had a pleasant smile, was well dressed, and handsome. Stuffed into his right formal sock was his pant leg, apparently for biking purposes.

Skyler was captivated with the man's hair. It appeared frozen in place with hair spray or some kind of varnish. He found himself hoping for rain just to see what would happen. "You staying nearby?"

"He's staying with me...and my aunt of course," Anchor said.

"That makes us neighbors then. You staying long?

"Well..."

"No!" Anchor interrupted. "He has friends in Honolulu."

"To tell the truth, I'm here for Anchor. I want her to come back with me."

Anchor spotted Acharya and hopped off her bike.

"That's the monk we talked to. Ar...something."

"Acharya," Skyler said.

"Oh, yes, Acharya. What's he doing in your van?"

"We've just been talking. He met your old Buddhist friend a few days ago. Kind of an amazing coincidence. He needs a ride back to the monastery."

"Very good to see you again. Nice to meet you as well, sir," Acharya said as he left the van and approached. "Where is it that you will be taking Miss Anchor?"

Skyler turned to look at Acharya. *This is curious. Monks don't usually get personal.*

"We will be going back to my home in Massachusetts. My family lives there," the man said with enthusiasm.

"So, will you be gone long, Anchor?" Skyler was trying to make eye contact with her, but Anchor had her head down and was monkeying with her bike.

"To tell the truth, I've asked Anchoret to marry me in the temple," the young man said with a proud smile.

"Oh, you must be Mormon as well then. Congratulations, Charles, when's the wedding? I'll need to start looking for a new famulus," said Skyler, folding his arms and leaning against the van with false sophistication while Anchor dropped her bike.

"Yes, my congratulations as well," Acharya said with a puzzled look.

"Knock it off, Skyler!" Anchor blurted. "Charles and I are just friends. He's confused about a few things, that's all."

"Confused? It sounds to me like he's pretty clear on what he wants."

"Thank you!" the young man said. "That's what I've been trying to tell her. We were together at MIT for four years, and I'm not sure how I could have been more clear about my affectionate feelings toward her. Recently, she's stopped writing and calling me, so I came looking for her. She's a terrific girl."

"Oh, I agree. She's definitely terrific. I'm on your side, Charles. I'm wondering how you could do more than spend four years of affection and close companionship with someone." Skyler couldn't help liking Charles. Despite the emotions boiling inside, he wanted to rough up the young man's hair, as he had a habit of doing when trying to console someone. Instead, he focused again on the hair's unmoving perfection.

"Okay, that's enough Skyler." Anchor yanked her bike off the ground. "We were friends for four years, Charles. We were not 'together.'"

Charles winked at Skyler, moved closer in a confidential manner before Anchor stopped him.

"Charles, we dated, and we were friends. You're terrific, but I'm not ready to get married to anyone right now. I adore you and I want you to be happy, but I can't marry you."

"I'm not suggesting we get married right away. I just wanted to start making our plans. I've spoken with your Bishop, and your aunt is quite pleased."

"My aunt is pleased? When did you talk to my Bishop?"

Skyler pushed off the van and moved toward the driver's side door. "I think we should leave you two love birds alone," he said. "You obviously have a lot to talk about.

"Oh, no you don't!" Anchor went to the back of the van and tossed in her bike.

"Charles, I really have to go. It's important that I talk with Acharya. I'm sorry. Let's go over this when I get back. I have to leave right now. Will you please take these aspirin back to Aunt Edie?" she said, and shoved a plastic bag into his hand.

"All right," Charles said, unperturbed as he glimpsed at the bag. "I'll be waiting up for you."

Anchor climbed into the back seat of the van and spoke just one word: "Go!"

"Four years with your nose in the books, huh," Skyler said with a touch of irritation in his voice.

"Hey, I was at MIT, not a convent. You couldn't understand. Mormon men have this belief that girls are in school for one reason: to find a husband. In many cases that's true.

"It's maddening. They think they're doing a girl a great favor by offering marriage. It's the proper thing to do, and it's the proper thing to accept. Believe me, a girl could do much worse than Charles. He's honest, smart, handsome, and rich."

"Wow, so what's the problem? What are you waiting for?"

"Nothing when you put it that way. I guess I should just go and marry Charles."

They drove another two miles without a word before Anchor spoke again. "Can we just get off the subject. I'm not marrying Charles even if you to want me to."

"Hey, don't bite my head off. It's okay with me. What about you Acharya?" Skyler couldn't resist a little more teasing.

"Well, yes, that is fine with me as well."

As they glanced at each other, both men were close to laughing, but managed restraint out of fear.

After a while, Anchor forgot about the marriage proposal and was full of questions for Acharya. She quizzed him on the rainbow phenomenon and the old Buddhist monk non-stop until they approached Kapaa.

The low moon was so bright they could make out the silhouette of Sleeping Giant Mountain.

"Can you see the sleeping giant?" Anchor asked. It was a grateful change of subject for Skyler.

"Not me, I'm blind to that one," Skyler said.

"Pull over, pull over!" Anchor yelled. "Acharya, will you please show this desperate soul where the sleeping giant is?"

"As you request," he began. "The Nounou Mountain ridge bears a striking resemblance to a sleeping giant. Look there to the highest point on the left. That would be his forehead or crown. The next point going right is his chin. Look to the right again, and you can see his arms folded."

Suddenly, the long-sleeping giant that once roamed the land, came to life for Skyler. "Hey, thanks guys. Now I can't see anything else. That mountain will never look the same to me again. I liked it better before."

Acharya paused and looked at Anchor for help. "According to folklore, the people of Kauai would discourage invaders by lighting fires on the other side of the mountain, which caused an eerie outline of the giant that could be seen for miles out to sea," Anchor said as she faked a shiver. "I think it adds mystery. I suppose Skyler would prefer a lump of dirt."

They turned up the mountain road to the monastery. The night was soft and clear, and the moon behind the mountain cast a romantic glow on the ocean. Skyler pulled into the parking lot at Wailua Falls and turned off the engine. They sat in silence for a while in the dark. Perfect seclusion and enchanted surroundings had quieted Anchor.

"So just who do you think the old man was?" Skyler finally said.

"Not *who,* but *what.*" Acharya replied.

"Oh, this is getting good," Anchor said and climbed up close. "I knew Mr. Pehrson was hurt bad. That old guy is the only explanation. I mean, let's get real."

"When all else fails, look for the simplest answer," Acharya responded.

"Ockham's Razor," she said.

"Okay," Skyler prodded, "so not who, but what was that old guy?"

"He told me that he was the '*Keeper of Mumonkan.*'"

"What does that mean?" Anchor asked.

"He is the *Keeper* of the Gateless Gate or the Gateless Barrier."

After a moment of complete silence, Acharya spoke again. "Well, clearly neither of you are what the Buddhists would call 'people of realization'; otherwise, you would immediately grasp the point at the slightest mention of Mumonkan...the Gateless Gate."

Acharya peered at them both with feigned disappointment and laughed. "You see, Skyler, my friend, I too have a sense of humor. I didn't really expect you to understand."

Skyler wasn't amused.

"I will try to explain," Acharya continued. "There is a verse from the Mumonkan written by Wu-men, a Zen Buddhist Chinese master." Acharya recounted it for them.

The Great Way is gateless,
Approached in a thousand ways.
Once past this checkpoint,
You stride through the universe.

"Zen is a school of Mahayana Buddhism that asserts that enlightenment can be attained through our own intuition, meditation, and self-contemplation, but not through the words of others. The opposite of faith you might say." Acharya paused to see if they were following his explanation.

"In order to master Zen, you must pass the barrier of the patriarchs by changing your way of thinking. Now, what is interesting is that the barrier of the patriarchs is none other than the Gateless Gate: the Mumonkan of Zen."

Skyler seemed confused, but Anchor was fascinated. "I think I kind of understand. To stride through the universe, so to speak, we must pass this Mumonkan or Gateless Gate barrier. But to do so, we must first find the solution, which we already have inside of ourselves. But if the way of passage is just finding the knowledge we already have, then why is there a need for a keeper of the Gateless Gate?"

"Uh, yeah, that's what I was wondering," Skyler lied.

Acharya looked at Anchor with delight. "You, my dear, have hit the proverbial nail on the head. Let us consider for a moment that what Buddhists think of as inner enlightenment is in fact a physical reality. Science is confused with religion because by focusing so intently on shedding and denying the reality of this world, they periodically find a glimpse of the truth.

"Unfortunately, they are unable to comprehend what they have awakened to and so they mystify it and define it as inner truth. The belief in reincarnation would follow because, in their breakthrough moments, they might remember other lives and even other worlds; in the strict sense, reincarnation is not a rebirth, but instead another journey. Mumonkan is a place that surely exists, a checkpoint that we can cross back through...if we can remember how."

"Are you talking about heaven?" Skyler asked in semi-unison with Anchor.

"Not in the traditional sense." Acharya said, apparently wondering if he was going too far but decided to continue. "I would say it is more like a path that we think of as reality, what the Hindus call *Brahman*."

"Wait!" Skyler interrupted. "Are you saying that if we concentrate hard enough that we can cross this gateless thing into a pseudo reality?"

Anchor answered the question. "He's not saying we enter the pseudo reality through the gate, Skyler. He is saying that we leave through the gate and enter the true reality. The universal gateway is manned by a keeper. The

Keeper of Mumonkan is probably part of some advanced system quite capable of controlling anything in the world in which we live. Is that about right, Acharya?"

"Statistically, it is a strong possibility," Acharya responded.

"All right then." Skyler was becoming animated. "So, to explain the old monk healing the injured hiker and to explain the strange rainbow aberration, one answer is that we're living in some kind of alternate universe that isn't the actual real universe. Does that about sum it up?"

Anchor joined the cause. "And we're just experiencing some kind of made-up game, or matrix or something? It sure seems like a long and cruel game if you ask me."

"Ahh...no. This is not a simple game or a matrix, as portrayed in the movie. There is nothing fabricated or simple about this reality," Acharya said.

Skyler was still animated and even more eager to get to the bottom of this. "But you just said, I think, that we live in a pseudo reality universe that isn't real. So which is it, real or not real? This Gateless Gate stuff makes no sense. There is nothing simple or hockum razor about this."

"That's Ockham's Razor," Anchor teased, stepped out of the car and walked to the handrail overlooking the waterfall. Acharya and Skyler followed.

In the dark shadows on the opposite side of the parking lot, a silent observer lingered.

Acharya grabbed the rail and stretched his weary legs. Skyler and Anchor gathered around the monk like children. The majestic, eighty-foot tiered waterfall roared and glowed in front and below them, made visible by the silvery yellow reflection of the distant sun bouncing off the full moon, light that would have otherwise traveled a much greater distance on its once and forever journey.

"This is such an amazing, unique, and beautiful world," Acharya said. "To think that such a world could have been fabricated is not what I am suggesting. Consider the staggering odds: to think that we are standing here on this amazing world for the first time, a lonely and isolated planet, to be discovered at last by civilizations far more intelligent than ourselves."

"So you think the rainbow and the old monk are signs of some close encounter from another world?" Anchor asked.

"No, my friends, the rainbow and the old man are signs of an ancient civilization that set things in motion. We are the distant descendants of that great civilization that, finally, after eons of false starts, spread through the galaxy like wildfire until it came upon our primitive and desperate world, isolated on the twirling outer arms of the galaxy we call the Milky Way.

"Ours was a world destined for eventual failure and destruction. However, the ancients brought this world into the arena of galactic wonders and ensured its survival. We have the memories of their glorious past. Earth could not have persisted if not for these original bold galactic explorers.

"Then, after untold thousands of years, the history of this world was laid forth with a virtual reality technology so advanced that we can only begin to imagine. The universe as we know it, here and now, is a virtual replicate of the original. We are here on a sacred journey of discovery. Who knows how many ancestral worlds we have visited? To think that we are the originals of anything is statistically next to impossible. Oh, there was an original Earth to be sure. But that Earth is long gone, and we are here to learn of its subtle isolated history, not by mere study, but by entirely living it."

Acharya paused and sought to ease the tension. "But please keep in mind that this is a mere theory from a simple rambling monk."

Something in this theory of Acharya's struck home with Anchor like a bolt of lightning. She thought of the bike ride up to the site of the film location for Legacy II, a film about the Book of Mormon people — her people. Her own church had the largest ancestral database in the world. Work done for their ancestors was dependent on knowledge of their lives, their history. A great work had gone forth in the world to gather that information and make an accurate account of the ancestors.

"It's an amazing theory," Anchor said. "It would certainly explain a lot."

"Well, I'm looking for real answers," Skyler said. "I'm not yet ready to be rescued by some ancient aliens."

"A wise choice," Acharya said. "This is but one theory."

However, Acharya was convinced that an advanced race had visited the original Earth eons ago and had brought her civilization at last. Perhaps it would happen in this dispensation. Perhaps he would find himself engaged in an adventure of magnificence, fulfilling the inexplicable prophesy from his war-protest days. Yet even if the visit did not occur in his lifetime, Acharya believed the waterfall, the Moon, the Earth, and the Universe was some form of incredible Ancestral System. Those inevitable galactic travelers would one day visit this replicate Earth, just as the adventurous Captain Cook had visited the people of Kauai.

Skyler put his arm around Anchor. Acharya gazed into the waterfall while a small, concerned old man in yellow watched and listened from the dark, satisfied in knowing that Acharya was wrong.

TEN

James Stevenson was a rebel. Graduated first in his class from Caltech with a bachelor's degree in Physics, expected to follow in the Stevenson family footsteps, expected to earn his PhD and enter the academic world of teaching and research; James followed the beat of a different drum. Often astonished by the profound failure of change in the scientific approach to important solutions, he found himself complaining more than agreeing. Unable to adapt to the rules and proven methods that would provide him with a good living and a steady job, he bounced around from place to place, never given a real chance to finish his projects. The perceived possibility of success was too hard for anyone to justify once James set off on his alternate and inexplicable paths.

As the computer industry exploded, as breakthroughs in physics were changing the face of the planet, James remained completely unimpressed. He kept a copy of an Addison Wiley book on Electronic Digital Systems he had discovered one day in a remote corner of an off-campus book store. In that old, blue, dusty hardcover from the fifties by R. K. Richards, was the summation of all the Earth's computer technology. James knew that nothing fundamental in computer science had changed in half a century...nothing.

The computers were smaller, faster, cheaper, and networked, but the underlying technology was identical to that which was first produced in the 1940's and 50's by true inventors. Artificial intelligence was just a pipe dream within the current state of computer technology, and James found it amusing when someone would announce his or her new AI advancements.

These dead end solutions, like the internal combustion engine, were nothing but a crutch for humanity to lean on, holding it back like a ball and chain around the neck. Computer science wasn't James' main point of interest, but his comments attracted the attention of a wealthy computer entrepreneur one evening at a party in New York. He'd not spoken with James that night, but he was wise enough and experienced enough to know that James was exactly right—having spent a small fortune on an artificial intelligence start-up flop.

This eccentric business tycoon, in cooperation with the Hindu Church, was assembling a team from the top scientists in the world for the sole purpose of achieving manned space flight *without* government involvement. Unlike high-profile projects, like SpaceShipOne, this team was coming together in complete secrecy. When asked to join the team, James had clear instructions: thinking out of the box wasn't a problem; it was a requirement. The secrecy was an added bonus for James, and the money they offered was like a gift from heaven—James Stevenson was only months away from becoming a new addition to the millions of homeless in America.

Homelessness would not have sat well with his best friend and companion, Data, or his wife, Silvia. Data was a high-maintenance two-year-old black Labrador retriever that wanted nothing more than to be human, and he wasn't about to go hungry for even one day. James accepted the offer and joined the team, where he met a small band of scientists that astonished him with their abilities.

"Data!" James yelled. His dog flew through the trees with his ears flopping and his tail in a spin, making him look like a small black helicopter paused on its side for take off.

Data looked at James with pure anticipation, knowing what might be coming next. "Don't get me!" James yelled and took off as fast as he could back down the trail. At fifty-six, James was in great shape for a man of any age. He was unbeaten in three months at the racquetball club in Lihu'e, and there were plenty of young jocks, including the club pro, desperately trying to take a game from him. Running on the jungle path, however, James knew he had no chance against the black monster hot on his trail.

Knowing he was about to be annihilated, he moved quickly to the side and grabbed a tree, swinging himself around in the opposite direction just in time as a black flash shot past. Data slammed on his breaks and slid on his butt, throwing dust like an explosion.

The escape maneuver only served to make the creature more determined. James dove for a soft patch of grass and seconds prior to the attack yelled, "I give, you win!" Data stopped abruptly, satisfied with his victory, and lay down by his friend, who laughed while trying to catch his breath.

Data had spent too many days in a quarantine kennel on Oahu because of a rabies-free policy on the islands. Free at last, he was beside himself with joy. James had picked him up at the airport that morning and taken him straight to a beach near Kapaa. Data had gone straight for the waves like some surfer just out of school. They were frolicking and running along the beach when an animal control truck drove up and a uniformed officer jumped out and approached them.

"Sorry, no dogs allowed on the beaches," he said, removing a notepad from his hip pocket. "Do you have a license for this dog?"

"Uh, no. I just picked him up at the airport no more than two hours ago."

"Well, I'm going to have to take him in for not having a license," the officer said sternly.

James and Data looked at each other in disbelief. James was quite certain Data had a vocabulary that exceeded that of many humans he had known. They had one of two choices: run and escape or try to reason. Capitulation wasn't an option.

"How much is a dog tag?" James asked.

"Fifteen dollars cash, no checks or credit cards. But I'll need to take the dog in for testing, regardless."

"He's been in quarantine on Oahu. What possible tests could they do that haven't already been done to him?" Data sat down, tilted his head and waited for an answer.

Three noisy boys ran past with their hands full of swimming equipment, and one dropped a fin without noticing. Data jumped up and snatched the fin, ran past the boy, placed it on the ground in front of him, then returned to the same exact spot in front of the officer...still waiting for an answer.

"Did I just see what I think I saw?" the officer asked. "Was he trained to do that?"

James laughed, and Data stood up, wondering what was so funny. "No, he was just being helpful. You would have to know him, but I can tell you that in many ways he's smarter than we are."

"Ho brah...I know you," the officer said, his accent suddenly changing to the partial Hawaiian pidgin. "You're that dude at the gym that no one can put down in racquetball. I was sitting at the table when that hot wahine tried to pick you up. I remember you telling her she was gorgeous, but that you had a wife. Everyone says you should geev'um with her grind, but not me, brah. You showed class. How old are you, dude? You play like you is twenty, but with some gray hair. Come on, let's get da cute dog his license before someone nabs him."

James thanked the officer and promised him a game of racquetball. He and Data drove back to their home on the other side of Sleeping Giant Mountain. Although James was working at the monastery, he preferred living on his own. There were secrecy concerns at first, but after considerable lobbying, the scientists could live where they wanted as long as it was relatively close to the monastery.

With the money they were paying, James could afford a beautiful home, even at the current outrageous island prices. His wife was happy and relaxed for the first time in a long time, and with Data back, James was ready for action. Something about the island was giving him clarity. His work was going well and the other team members were migrating to his project designs.

James kept arguing that following the traditional ways of thinking was a waste of time. "Why are we here?" he asked. "We can't wait thousands of years for the rest of the world to figure this stuff out. If not us, then who? If not now, then when?"

For the first time, James was working with extraordinarily intelligent people who were willing to consider the alternatives. James was able to communicate with this team, and they were making progress. Fully engaged, the team was throwing back ideas that he himself had not even considered. For James, science was finally fun again.

He walked into the research center and slapped down his large red bag on the conference table. It never ceased to amaze him just how beautiful this place was. Each scientist had their own office with giant bay windows looking out into the tropical paradise.

As he opened the bag and began pulling out the contents, one of the scientists came through the door in a rampage. "If we're so smart, why can't we do something about those damn mosquitoes?"

One of the younger scientists went to the whiteboard and started listing possible solutions:

1) Vacuum doors that suck them up if they try to enter the building
2) Worldwide extermination
3) Nanomachines that bite them back
4) A repellent mist that surrounds the research center

"We could do what the Hawaiians do," James suggested, as the exotic list grew longer. "Just develop tougher skin. Haven't you noticed how the natives never complain? You see the tourists scratching, itching, and swearing, but never the Hawaiians. Perhaps there's something in the food."

"Funny, James, this is serious!" the scratching scientist said. "Let's figure something out."

"I was serious. I think we should just do what works, and we should take the same approach to our project. Anyway, I come bearing gifts." He began throwing T-shirts to each of the scientists. On the back of each T-shirt read the word 'Hispaniola,' and below in smaller letters the words 'Team Babylonian.' Farther down, at the bottom of each shirt, were three smaller uppercase letters: 'DTK.'

"I had a rather famous teacher in my early days at Caltech—a professor Feynman. Richard Feynman held the view that there were two kinds of physicists, the Greeks and the Babylonians. I propose we think of ourselves as Babylonians hence forth."

"Hey!" one of the scientists interrupted. "I was just reading about a professor Feynman from Caltech. Is he the same guy that dunked a piece of the rocket booster's O-ring into a cup of ice water right in front of the committee at the Challenger hearings when he couldn't get a straight answer to how the O-ring material reacted at lower temperatures?"

"That's the one," James answered with a smile.

"As I was saying, there are two kinds of physicists. The Greeks are the famous physicists. An example is Euclid, one of the inventors of mathematics. The Greeks, were the ones who invented the concept of theorems and proofs. They were more concerned about systems of axioms and assumptions. The Babylonians, on the other hand, were interested in methods that ultimately worked and described the real world. In other words, the Greeks felt there needed to be a formula that everything fit into and the Babylonians were just focused on the phenomena at hand."

"So why are we the Babylonians? We have some pretty good mathematicians on the team, do we not?" asked one of the senior scientists.

"That we do...but our job is to build an interstellar spacecraft as soon as possible. The Greeks can follow up on our work and try to package our solutions into some nice logical system. But we, gentlemen, need to be the dreamers...the Babylonians. The Babylonian approach is one of imagination, instinct, and intuition. I don't care if we break the rules as long as it works.

"When Feynman dropped that piece of O-ring into the ice water, he was telling the commission something acutely important. He didn't care about the mathematics used by the engineers; he wanted to know why someone hadn't simply tested the material properly. And if they had, where were the results? Feynman was a Babylonian."

"Look," the older scientist continued, "you definitely have our attention with some of your concepts, but what if we're just going off on a wild goose chase and wasting a lot of valuable time and money?"

"If we don't get creative," James responded, "this entire project will fail. We don't have a thousand years, or a hundred years or even decades. We must pursue a new approach to space travel *now*. Besides, how can we fail? If Feynman was right, and there's an infinite number of solutions; we just need to find one."

"All right. But even if we do solve the last remaining problems with your system, how do we make short test flights without attracting attention to ourselves?"

"That's easy," James said. "Think like Babylonians. Size doesn't matter. We build models and test them right here inside the building. Next, we do low altitude model testing outdoors. Eventually, we do a few quick short flights with our ship and astronauts. If all goes well, we send the first humans outside the solar system. We launch the *Hispaniola* in search of the greatest treasures and adventures since man first sailed the seas. It's a long shot of course...but you know we are getting close to solving the final problems. I'm betting on the imagination of Team Babylonian."

ELEVEN

Each year, during the months of December through to April, Humpback whales swim 3,000 miles from Alaska to the warm waters off Kauai, where they play and give birth. Just north of the town of Kilauea, a beach is nestled at the base of a large cliff. On a calm midmorning, Skyler and Anchor climbed down the steep rocky trail and came out on perfect sand. Standing near the edge of the water, the turquoise ocean appeared higher than the beach itself, seemingly defying the laws of nature. In the distance, splashing whales disturbed the ocean's calm.

"Just follow me," Skyler yelled above the breaking surf. "The dolphins are straight out from here."

"I heard there were sharks in these waters," Anchor said, repeating her argument for what was probably the tenth time.

"It's true," he yelled as the wave broke down and the sound subsided. "There are lots of sharks around here, but I'll let you in on a little secret. After all, this *is* Secret Beach," he chuckled. "The sharks stay away from the dolphins. So all we have to do is find the dolphins, and we should be okay."

"Well, what if this is the wrong place, or the dolphins run away from us?"

"They won't. They genuinely enjoy protecting their human friends from the sharks. Just relax, this'll be fun."

A hundred yards from shore, Skyler turned and motioned to Anchor. Dolphins, lots of them, were swimming their way. Moments later, a noisy glimmering pod had them surrounded.

Anchor dove under the water to get a better look. There were five baby dolphins swimming within inches of their mothers in perfect harmony. After a while, the baby dolphins demonstrated courage by trying to jump as well.

"I think those babies are showing off for us!" Anchor yelled, coughing from accidentally breathing water in her haste to explain.

Skyler laughed with joy as he watched Anchor playing with the dolphins. By now he was completely in love with this funny, beautiful, sexy woman. When she smiled, it felt to him like morning sunshine. They had been seeing each other for a month now, and for some reason he still hadn't tried to kiss her. She seemed happier today than ever before. The more she laughed and clapped, the more the babies would show off for her. Unexpectedly, the adults became excited as well, flying through the air and darting around under water. Skyler had never seen them stirred up like this.

He was amazed at Anchor's stamina. After more than an hour, he convinced her to return to shore. When she was satisfied that she had said goodbye to each and every dolphin, they swam for the beach. Skyler made sure Anchor got to dry ground first. Watching her, he pushed through the waist high water to the sand. An unexpected and massive wave crashed into his back and sent him tumbling forward. He came up covered with sand from head to foot.

"You look like the boogie-man," Anchor teased. "Should I run or fight?"

"Just find our backpacks. I'll be right back," he said as he ran like a ghost across the beach toward the waterfall at the cliff's edge.

Reaching the waterfall, he washed the sand from the front of his body and hair, but couldn't remove all the sand from his back. He heard a girl's voice from behind.

"Looks like you got hit by a big one," she said.

He turned around to see a gorgeous, completely naked girl standing in the waterfall with him. "Uh yeah, got burned by that one. Wasn't paying enough attention."

"You need any help getting the sand off your back? I've got a sponge. I'll wash yours if you'll wash mine."

"Okay," said Skyler.

After helping each other, he thanked the friendly girl and ran back to the beach where Anchor was sitting...and unfortunately for him, watching. He plopped down onto the blanket with a big smile. "I'm starved."

Nothing but silence—his clue that something bad was coming.

"What was that all about?" asked Anchor with an onerous glare.

"What?" Skyler answered nonchalantly and kicked at the sand with his bare feet.

"The naked girl you just spent the last ten minutes washing, that's what. Who is she, another one of your pseudo surfing buddies?"

"Oh her...never seen her before."

"Well, you would know that for sure, wouldn't you? Not much of her you haven't seen now."

More silence.

"Oh, look there goes a naked hunk to the waterfall. I should probably run over and wash my hair too," said Anchor.

Skyler glanced up and recognized the jock strutting his way to the falls. *What an idiot that guy is*, he thought to himself.

"I know him. His name is Steve Cubin. I'd introduce you, but he's not your type."

"How would you know? He looks like my type from here. So, all-knowing-one, what kind of guy *would* be my type?"

"Your type would be someone like me, strong, loyal, and brave...with clothes on."

"I see, so my type is a boy scout who never kisses girls, but loves to stare at their naked bodies. Is that right? Sounds like a psycho to me. I think I prefer Mr. Cubin."

She jumped up and marched through the deep sand toward the waterfall. Skyler followed and grabbed her arm.

"What are you doing?" she protested. "My destiny awaits."

"I just wanted to clear something up. The guy I was describing does like to kiss."

"I doubt that," she said, pulling away, but found herself swiftly spun back. Skyler's vivid ocean blue eyes locked on hers and she knew she was about to be kissed.

He pulled her hard into his arms and their lips melted together. Then, as if on cue, a group of happy locals began playing *This Magic Moment* by the Drifters, on their sound blaster. Skyler looked up at the people who clapped and smiled in appreciation for the show.

"Skyler, with that kind of hidden talent, why did you wait so long?" Anchor said as the background music continued. "You're more than my type. Except for the wet clothes, you're everything I want." Then she kissed him again.

They played on the beach until the afternoon, laughing at how long it had taken to admit their feelings for each other. Without remembering the climb, they found themselves back up the cliff at Skyler's van where old Blacky was resting in the shade. Some of the most expensive plantations on the island surrounded Secret Beach. Any animal from this wealthy neighborhood was off-bounds to the dogcatchers. Skyler found a treat, which he kept just for these occasions, and gave it to the old dog, who managed to wiggle his tail and pull the treat under his chin like a squirrel saving up nuts.

As he watched the old dog with fondness, Skyler smiled and thought about the girls he had known over the years. If he had expressed his love to any other girl the way he had for Anchor, they would be spending the night together. However, Skyler knew that was too much to hope for with Anchor.

Looking out on the ocean, the whales had calmed down and the dolphins were gone.

"I need to stop by Strant's place, just up the road, and check on his fish. He asked me to baby-sit his cottage for a few days while he's on the mainland."

"Okay, I'm in no hurry. Does he have an aquarium or something?"

"Yeah, you could say that," Skyler said, wondering what Anchor would think of this place.

They got in the van and left the dirt field for the paved road. Skyler soon turned off and approached a large gated entry, where he punched in the pass code. The gate opened and he drove through, continuing on around a circular drive toward a large home perched square on an ocean bluff.

"Is this the 'cottage' you're babysitting for Strant?"

"Sorry, that's what he calls it for some reason. He likes to play down the fact that he's a multimillionaire. The first time he brought me here, we were both grubby. This wasn't what I was expecting either. I thought he was just a poor surf bum. Hard to know the difference around here."

"Looks like I picked the wrong guy to hook up with," she said, as she reached over and ran her fingers through his hair.

"I used to land my helicopter right over there on that round pad. I'd occasionally fly tourists in just for the fun of it. I'd tell them I needed to stop by the house and pick up my messages."

Upon entering the home, Anchor gasped. "This is breathtaking!" With two stories, the upper level was visible from below through an exotic wire railing. The open living room was painted white, offset with a dark shiny hardwood floor covered in the middle by a thirty-foot Persian rug. On the rug were three large tan sofas with metallic red pillows for accent. The massive coffee table was hardwood with an embedded blue rock surface. Several pillars extended from floor to ceiling, breaking up the panoramic ocean views. Dozens of well-placed live plants greened up the interior design with a natural feel. "How big is this 'cottage'?"

"I believe Strant told me it was around 10,000 square feet. It has a great Jacuzzi if you have time to check it out."

"Just try to drag me away. Why does he want you to stay here? He could rent this place for a fortune."

"You're right about that. He used to rent it out and sleep in a tent on the beach. Eventually, he became tired of the hassle. Now, he just wants to make sure someone he trusts is on the premises when he's gone. I told you he was smart; he made a fortune selling his ownership in a community website...Stage something."

Skyler let Anchor climb the ladder to the top of the massive aquarium and throw in the fish food. Anchor ran through the house barefoot like a little girl, squealing at each new discovery. "Want any company tonight? My aunt is gone now, and all I have is a quiet condo with old food in the fridge to go home to. I can sleep on one side of the house, and you on the other. We can use phones to talk to each other."

"I'd like that. It's kinda weird staying here alone anyway. I usually stay in the smallest bedroom and pretend I'm in a condo."

"I'm famished," said Anchor.

Solid dark oak kitchen cabinets surrounded a pink counter top. A colorful Hawaiian photo hung on the wall behind the stove. Above the stove sat a gigantic swooping air vent. They scavenged the kitchen and fixed themselves a gourmet meal of fresh salad, charcoaled ahi, and organic wine.

After dinner, they wandered upstairs to the recreation room where they dozed off watching an old black and white Chaplin movie on the fifty-inch digital screen. When they awoke, Anchor dragged Skyler through the house again so they could pick out their bedrooms.

After a quick shower, they met in the Jacuzzi where they splashed and kissed. Anchor giggled and teased, but backed off each time Skyler tried being too friendly. She knew she was driving him crazy; hell, she was driving herself crazy. Skyler climbed out first and started for his room. With the steamy mist coming off his solid tanned body, he turned back and said, "If you get scared, you know where to find me."

"Why would I be scared? Is there someone around here I should be afraid of?"

"Just trying to be a good host...that's all."

Skyler heard her say something else in response, but he had already left the room. He needed to regain his composure, not sure what was going on. If he ignored her, she would get cozy, but when he tried to hold her, she would move away. He knew she had mixed feelings, and it was best if they both had some down time away from each other.

His bedroom carpeting was pure white. A single wall-sized window looked out on the ocean cliffs to the north with the dark silhouette of the mountains in the distance. It was both eerie and relaxing. He skimmed through the drawers for something to wear, but could find nothing. Most of the bedrooms in the home were seldom-used guest rooms. In frustration, he flipped off the lights, dropped his trunks at the base of the bed and climbed naked under the covers.

The sheets were made from a familiar silk, but nothing like the bedding in Skyler's condo. He felt both covered and naked at the same time. For some reason, it made him want to stretch and roll around like a little boy.

"What are you doing?" He hadn't realized Anchor had followed him.

She picked up his swimming trunks from the white carpet, carried them to the bathroom and hung them on the top of the shower stall.

"It's these sheets. I think I must have had sheets like these when I was a kid. I like to roll around and stretch on them."

"Sounds fun, can I try?" she asked.

"Not a good idea. I'm not wearing much." He felt stupid for stating the obvious.

"What do you mean, not much? What's under there?" she asked.

"Under where?"

"Underwear...oh, that's too bad, I was kind of hoping for nothing." Anchor tossed back her hair as somehow the moonlight managed to capture her perfect, bikini-clad form.

His mind was spinning, and it took him a while to follow the play on words. She was still teasing him.

"You're welcome to try it if you want, but it works best without any kind of 'wear.' You should run to your room and give it a shot," he said, resorting to some teasing of his own.

"Okay, good idea."

She removed her wet bikini in front of him, turned and hung it on the shower stall in the bathroom.

Entering the moonlit room again, she stood naked long enough for Skyler to feel himself getting aroused. Then with one word, "Bye," she left the room.

Skyler wanted to run after her, but he knew how absurd that would be in his current condition. While he was trying to decide what to do next, Anchor came back into the room.

"Well isn't that just bad luck. My sheets aren't the same as yours. Now what should I do?"

"Damn, I guess I'll have to share," Skyler said, pulling back the sheets and patting the bed.

"Such a gentleman," she said, slipping under the covers.

She stretched and rolled sensuously until Skyler grabbed her and pulled her to him. They held each other and kissed for a long time before making love. Skyler could still hear and feel the waves crashing in his mind. It was a common lingering sensation after a long day at the ocean. He was moving with the motion of the sea, gentle but continuous and he could hear Anchor gasping and moaning beneath him.

"I shouldn't be doing this," she whispered in his ear.

Skyler hesitated for a moment, but then she said out loud, "Don't stop! Don't you dare stop!"

The ocean waves left his mind, and they made love with a desperate passion.

TWELVE

Following their daily six a.m. worship, the monks of Kauai's Hindu monastery sit together for an hour of meditation. Afterwards, they sing and receive guidance from the abbot. On this day, Acharya was having difficulty concentrating. He was becoming more involved, even obsessed, with the secret project in the capacity of both advocate and skeptic.

The project, though exciting, was completely absurd. How could a small group of scientists with limited resources hope to achieve what the most powerful nations of the world could only dream of accomplishing? The Americans were building systems at enormous expense for their trek to Mars, yet their noble and well-funded goal paled in comparison to the aspirations of the Babylonian project.

Acharya was impressed with the team of scientists and engineers, but he felt this small group of the world's brightest had no chance of actual success. To Acharya, this was nothing more than a remote exercise in futility. Nevertheless, he couldn't wait to get back to the center.

He was acting more like a team member and less like a monk each day. He couldn't resist the thought that just perhaps there was a glimmer of hope that they could achieve some form of space travel. Even for that, he was willing to risk his life, but he couldn't help but think manned flight to an adjacent star system was impossible for this team.

Eventually, of course, interstellar flight would happen after an advanced civilization bestowed the technology upon Earth's inhabitants. Acharya knew that the odds were heavily with him on that subject and that even this amazing team of overachievers would not win the septillion-dollar lottery.

While at the center one evening, Acharya pulled James aside with his questions. "It's not about money or resources, Acharya. It's about finding a better way," James responded.

"I agree, James. We have no hope of accomplishing anything on this island if we approach this problem like everyone else in history has done." Acharya loved his conversations with James Stevenson. He had never met anyone like James, and Acharya wasn't easily impressed. "But what if we set our goals lower? What if we could just be satisfied with orbital flight? Given our resources, that would be a magnificent achievement."

"Acharya, we aren't here to achieve what has already been done. I need you to show a glimpse of optimism. Think of this as another Enlightenment Era. We must dare to know." James smiled and walked away.

Acharya wanted to ask what James meant when it struck him. He felt his knees wobble. *How does he do that to me?* Acharya wondered. James was referring to the motto by Immanuel Kant: "Dare to Know," popular during the enlightenment period of Western history. Now, Acharya understood the meaning of the small letters 'DTK' printed on the Babylonian T-shirts. For some reason he had never thought to ask.

From that day hence, Acharya was a full member of the team. In his mind, there was still no chance of success, but at least he was going to be part of the effort. Acharya spent less time in his pursuit of inner peace and more time working with the scientists.

Acharya's job was to make suggestions for the destination of the first flight. James called it his prerogative as captain. It was a brilliant stroke of politics by James, and Acharya knew it. How could he possibly be negative about ever getting off the ground when he was in charge of the flight plan? Acharya's other assignment was to help find a pilot. He studied the biographies of over a thirty candidates, and he was meticulous in his research.

Sometimes, though, he found himself laughing at the thought of his introductions. *Hi, my name is Acharya. I am a monk, and I am working on interstellar flight. We will be traveling to a nearby galaxy soon. I would like you to be the pilot of the expedition.* The thought was so funny that Acharya once burst out laughing in his morning meditation session, which ended his continuing participation. Acharya missed the meditations with his friends, but out of respect for the others, he never returned, preferring instead to meditate in solitude or focus on his work.

As days passed, Acharya was spending more time with Skyler and Anchor. They would spread out on the beach at night looking up at the stars. Acharya thought he knew the night skies, but after a few occasions on the night beach with Anchor, he quickly realized that he was just a good amateur astronomer.

Indubitably, one night Anchor became curious. "Why so many questions, Acharya? I'm getting the feeling there's some big secret you're keeping from us."

"I'm just amazed at your knowledge of Astronomy, and I can't seem to get enough." Acharya wasn't good at lying.

The trio soon enlisted Strant to their company and began flying his plane out of Lihu'e once a week. Skyler and Strant enjoyed turning the controls over to Acharya, even though he was no longer a licensed pilot. Acharya loved his adventures with his new friends.

The weather around the island could sometimes turn dangerous and deadly without much warning. It was at those times that both Strant and Acharya would quickly hand the controls over to Skyler. Once, they found themselves caught in a torrent of heavy rain while Strant was flying. Skyler changed places with Strant as the downpour dropped the small plain like a rock. Most other pilots would have lost the craft, but Skyler made the recovery seem easy with his aggressive maneuvers. Strant was sick and threw up on the front passenger seat of his expensive plane, all the while thanking Skyler profusely for saving their lives and his plane.

"In my younger days, I flew with some of the best test pilots in the world," Acharya gasped as he tried to recover from the spinning in his head. "Skyler, you are the best pilot I have *ever* had the privilege of knowing. You have the instinct of a bird."

"I don't know about that, but I sure love the way this baby handles."

Anchor sat pale-faced next to Acharya, looking at Skyler in stunned appreciation. "Let's not do that again," she exclaimed.

༄

The next evening, Acharya made up his mind to tell James about his friend Skyler. "I would like you to meet a friend of mine. I may have found our pilot, and he lives right here on Kauai."

"What are his test pilot credentials?" James asked.

"He has none as far as I know. He was a helicopter pilot for a while. He flew out of the North Shore, taking tourists for joyrides." Acharya sometimes lost his monk style of talking when he was with his close friends.

"So why would we turn over control of the most import mission in the history of the world to a local helicopter pilot?"

Acharya understood James well enough to realize that the question had nothing to do with what he really wanted to know.

"Skyler can fly anything. He saved our lives the other day in a piece of flying that was...well, difficult to explain. He is the best natural pilot I have ever seen. I have no idea if he would be interested, but we can trust him. I just want you to meet him."

Acharya walked to James' house where a large glass of guava juice and Sylvia's homemade bread were waiting. Afterward, Sylvia gave both James and Acharya a ride to Nawiliwili Harbor, where Skyler was teaching a sailing class. They met up with Anchor on the dock. Acharya introduced James and left with Sylvia to a woman's charity club meeting that Acharya had promised he would attend.

James and Anchor stood alone on the dock trying to make small talk while they watched Skyler and his students sailing on the far side of the harbor. Their conversation turned to astronomy, and to Anchor's delight she found someone with a scientific background, an engaging personality, and endless curiosity. Thirty minutes later, they were both oblivious to their surroundings as they talked of the mysteries of the universe.

One of Skyler's students, while clowning around, had broken the mast of his small training boat. Skyler managed to hitch a tow with a harbor patrol boat, but getting his students back to shore had put him in a sour mood. As he crept to shore with the rope tow, he could see Anchor talking with a man. He had forgotten that he was to meet with a friend of Acharya today, and Anchor's animated and happy attitude spurned a touch of jealously. She was paying no attention to Skyler or his students.

When they reached shore, Skyler instructed the students to begin breaking down the boats; he would be right back. He walked up the dock toward Anchor, still unnoticed, and let his emotions get the best of him. "Hey, dude, you seem to be having a good time with my girlfriend."

"Who says I'm your girlfriend?" Anchor responded and latched on to James' arm in mock simulation of the college surfer girls that had done the same thing to Skyler. Skyler did not look happy, and James could see a storm brewing.

"I kiss you a few times at Strant's house, and now suddenly I'm your girlfriend? You've probably told all your friends about me." She grabbed James even tighter.

Skyler took off his hat and slapped it on his thigh. As he opened his mouth to say something else, James laughed. He dragged Anchor up with him and put his other arm around Skyler.

"What the...?" Skyler said surprised. *Kind of hard to pick a fight with this guy*, he thought.

"Acharya was right," James said. "You kids *are* in love."

Anchor immediately burst free. "I'm not in love with him." Rounding on Skyler, "What have you been telling Acharya?"

"Nothing, I haven't told anyone that we had sex," said Skyler.

"Ouch! Bad move, son," James said.

At last, the two men noticed they were still embraced. They separated while trying to appear cool. For some reason that made Anchor laugh. "Why quit hugging on my account?"

"Oh, hey, sorry man. You must be James. Acharya said you were an old guy. You look pretty good to me. I mean..."

"Wow, Skyler. Is there something you need to tell me?" Anchor teased.

"Hey, cut it out. I've had a bad day. One of my students busted up his boat, and I have to pay for it. If you'd been paying attention, you would have noticed me being dragged in by the patrol boat. I have to get back and make sure they don't do any more damage."

"You need some help?" James asked, winking at Anchor.

"Yeah, that would be great. It won't take long, and then we can talk."

As they approached the student sailors, the boy who had broken the boat was still apologizing. Skyler didn't respond, instead, he walked through the scattered boats offering suggestions and instructions. The boy followed a few steps, but reluctantly went back to his broken boat.

James and Anchor helped the students tear down the gear. Next, they helped wind up the ropes, and stack the small boats. After the dejected boy returned to his boat, the students became noisy, happy, and full of questions.

Eventually, the boy summoned the courage to try again. He walked to Skyler and offered yet another apology. Skyler had his head down. He was struggling with a strange knot that one of the female students had 'invented.' Again, Skyler was silent so the boy turned away. Skyler stood and walked toward him. The other students became silent.

Skyler reached out his hand and the boy flinched. Skyler held his hand in position for a moment, then reached further and scrambled the boy's hair.

"It's okay, Bobby. I've got you covered. There's a lesson here. You make me a promise that you will *always* respect your equipment and always—always respect the ocean, and we'll call it square. Do we have a deal?"

"Deal!" the boy said, obviously relieved.

The other students went back to their work, and the noise of their youth returned. Anchor peeked at James and smiled. "I do love him," she whispered.

With the boats stowed away, the students thanked Skyler and dispersed. "While we're here, do you want to go for a quick sail? One of the perks I get for teaching these kids is use of that baby." Skyler pointed to a large and handsome craft.

"Sure, let's do it. I'm not much of a sailor, but it seems I'm in good hands," James agreed.

By the time they crossed the harbor and worked their way out to open sea, Anchor was feeling like a third wheel. There was something natural in the way the two men communicated. She knew Skyler's closest friends, and he was already engaged in the same kind of banter with James.

"Acharya says you're the best pilot he's ever flown with," James yelled above the noise of the wind slapping the sail.

To Anchor's surprise, this opening led to Skyler telling James about his friend who had perished flying a helicopter. Their "quick sail" turned into a three-hour adventure. The two men were tacking the boat so well together that Anchor had only to sit back and enjoy the ride. On the way back, while sailing near the edge of a shallow reef, Skyler slowed the boat. The other side of the reef was deep water.

"What's wrong?" Anchor asked.

"Just wondering why we haven't seen any whales out there. This is a good time for them."

James took the opportunity to stand up and stretch his legs. Skyler noticed the danger too late. A giant whale came up from the deep within ten feet of their boat and slammed his tail, sending a white wash of water over their boat. James flew into the ocean and remained face down. Skyler tossed an inflated lifejacket near his position and dove in. By the time he reached the jacket, James was recovering. Skyler, always cautions, spun him around into a rescue position and lifted his head.

"Gotcha," he said and handed him the jacket.

"I think we found the whale," James choked. "That was a big one."

Skyler waved to Anchor, signaling her that James was all right. "Let's get back before he decides to play again."

They made their way to the boat and climbed in. "Are you okay?" Anchor asked as she mothered James.

"Yeah, thanks to your boyfriend. That was quite a surprise."

"I should have warned you. Whales like to splash the windsurfers near the reef, but not usually larger boats. Still, it's good to be careful."

"Another lesson learned today," James said in reference to the apologetic student. He watched Skyler as he went back to sailing as if nothing had even happened, not looking for any more gratitude. *These are good kids. They need to meet Silvia.*

THIRTEEN

It wasn't long before James and Skyler had become close friends. Acharya knew they would like each other, but this was more than casual acquaintance or friendship. James would often brag about Skyler to Acharya in the manner of a proud father. Anchor had become fond of James as well and he was like a father to both of them. She would run to him and leap in his arms, while Data would bark frantically for her attention, hoping for those magic words: "Don't get me, Data."

After some coaxing, James agreed to fly with Skyler. Even with his limited knowledge, James could tell that Skyler was special. Moreover, Skyler was enjoying flying in a way he hadn't since the death of his best friend.

It had been raining all day on the North Shore. James and Acharya sat in James' office at the research center, watching the downpour through the window into the wet forest. The rain had a relaxing effect on James. He loved the sound. Pressures from the outside world seemed less important when hunkered down in a rainstorm.

"You were right, Acharya. We have found our Neil Armstrong right here on the island of Kauai," James said. "How do you think we should approach him about becoming a Babylonian?"

"The best way is to bring Anchor on board as well. Her knowledge of Astronomy has been an inspiration, and she has been an unknowing source of valuable information already. Her enthusiasm is just what we need to nab Skyler."

"My thoughts exactly. The one problem I'm having is that I'm not emotionally prepared to put our boy in danger."

"I knew that was becoming an issue," Acharya said softly. "We can evaluate the risk once we have something to fly. I know you would not send Skyler, or anyone else, on this mission if you were not convinced we were ready. We can put our A team together and make those life and death decisions once we know for sure what the risk factors are."

"It's not just Skyler. I'll have two good friends putting their lives on the line. I'm not sure this is such a good idea."

Acharya leapt to his feet. "What is happening, James? We have nothing to fly. We have no engineering specifications. We do not even know the nature of our propulsion systems." Acharya paced in front of the window.

"You are one smart monk, Acharya. Calm down and I'll fill you in. I'm not ready to present this to the full team yet, but two of our software developers have made some important breakthroughs. I can tell you that the success of our entire project is dependent on those two programmers."

"You mean Isaac and Alex?"

"Yes, that's right, Isaac and Alex. In reality, the success of the project is dependent on each of the disparate teams, but we can't even get started without the foundation systems from our computer programmers." James was switching into his work mode.

"We need to finish planning our approach with Skyler, but this feels good. I needed to talk with someone else besides the scientists. We should bounce stuff around more often."

James reached for his water. The rain made him thirsty. "From what I've been told, the water on Kauai is some of the cleanest on Earth. I'm not sure why I even bother with this bottled crap."

Acharya knew that James was preparing to explain something complex. He often began his mindbenders by walking across the room or opening a window, anything to buy time while he searched for the words that might give the listener a fighting chance at understanding.

"I have spent more time with Isaac than any of the other scientists," Acharya said. "My background in software engineering gives me a way to at least communicate with him. I have never worked with a computer scientist touting an IQ of 180 before, but Isaac has incredible tolerance. He seems to enjoy explaining his AI database systems to me, even though he knows I am grasping but a glimmer of what he is talking about."

"These two computer gurus live in an abstract world somewhere beyond the understanding of mere mortals," James responded. "What they needed was purpose and guidance, a boost in the right direction, if you will. And boy have they responded." James was clearly excited. "They've assembled a database that reflects the practical engineering capabilities of the human race. This is no Google search engine. This system has an artificial intelligence capable of accepting massive inquiries from an expanding range of categories. It returns a simple Boolean yea or nay at any point. If it can be built by the human race, then it returns true. If not, it returns false."

"I understood that was the direction of their research, but Isaac never explained it quite so directly as that before," Acharya said. "So if one of our other systems made a request for a container that could hold a nuclear fusion reaction, for example, then Isaac's program would return false. Is that correct?"

"That's exactly right. You've chosen a simple and obvious question, but you're on the right track. In evaluating and designing any new product, we have to know immediately if the theoretical is practical. And, we need to know that answer at every stage involving thousands and perhaps even millions of rapid queries. We also have financial and safety constraints. Taking your example again, even if it was possible to construct such a container, the cost can't exceed our budget."

"Have you crosschecked their results for accuracy?" Acharya asked.

"Our boys are no dummies. We've been evaluating system responses for the past two weeks. In fact, they have devised an alternate training and testing system that runs continuously. This thing is fast, smart, and getting smarter. Its rate of failure, even now, is less that one in 500 billion queries. This is a magnificent tool. And on the other side of the equation, our physicists are making great progress as well."

"I am not sure what you mean by the 'other side of the equation,' James...but if you can build it, we will fly it. I say we invite Skyler and Anchor on a tour of the center."

The next morning, James called Skyler. Skyler had emailed some photos and video clips of the rainbow effect to James late the night before.

"Hi, James. Did you get my email?" Skyler asked upon answering the phone.

"Yes, I did. Thank you for putting those together for me." James could see an opening that might help get Skyler's attention. "I'm sending a copy to my team of scientists at the research center in the monastery."

"What research center?" Skyler asked.

"I know I told you I was working on exploration technologies for a company based in California, but that wasn't entirely accurate. I've been required, for security reasons, to keep what I'm actually working on top secret. Yesterday, I received permission to give you and Anchor a tour. You'll need to sign nondisclosure documents, but I believe you'll find this quite interesting."

"Does this have anything to do with the rainbow effect I told you about?" Skyler asked.

"No, but this is a great chance to get your foot in the door and find some real answers from the best team of scientists and engineers on the planet. I know that sounds pretty arrogant, but it's absolutely true. If anyone on Earth can solve your rainbow puzzle, it's this group." James said.

"Have you forwarded my email to any of those people?" Skyler asked.

"I wanted to talk with you first. I'll spend some time today evaluating the photos and video myself. With your permission, I'll copy the team tonight. Can you and Anchor meet me at the monastery at noon tomorrow?"

"Yeah, okay. We were planning to hook up in Kapaa anyway for lunch. I'm sure she'd rather do this. Go ahead and send your partners the rainbow material. If you have any questions, I'll have my cell phone with me. You can also call Byron Shirai, a professor at the college. He's still pretty obsessed with this and has been doing research on his own."

"All right, son. I'll see you and Anchor tomorrow. Let her know we'll be at the center for about three hours."

James grabbed Skyler's photos from the laser printer and barged outside with the screen door slamming behind him. Data was already waiting eagerly for their morning trek up Sleeping Giant Mountain. Once they reached the top, James sat on a large slab of old concrete and beheld the dark blue of the morning pacific. He slipped off his backpack and pulled out the photos.

Many people, including trained photographers, had already examined the photos, so James decided to look, not at the rainbow, but instead at everything but the rainbow. Professor Feynman once told James that what separated him from most of the other brilliant students was his common sense. "Use it often. So few of us have it."

After sequencing through the photos several times, he noticed a small quirk in how the hair on the tourists was flowing in a slightly different direction than their wind-blown clothing. He concluded that static electricity might be the cause. Thinking back on what Skyler and Anchor, and even Acharya, had told him, he couldn't recall any mention of this. *Why would there be so much static electricity on a sailboat?* These really were strange photos! He made a mental note to have his team look into the effects of electromagnetic forces on a rainbow field. He also left a text message for Acharya, asking if he had already considered this possibility.

The next day, James and Acharya met Skyler and Anchor at the entrance to the Hindu monastery. After a fifteen-minute jeep ride, they arrived outside the modern dark-glass research center nestled in a forest field of sugar cane and guava trees. The backside of the building was on the edge of a large tropical forest. Off in the distance, the cloud-covered mountains magnified the primitive atmosphere.

As they entered through a large door, the architecture altered their emotions — the contrast of high-tech rooms and equipment wrapped in large glass windows poised on the edge of a lush tropical jungle had a magical effect.

"James, this place is a scientist's dream! Finally, a research environment where the builders have more on their minds than linear equations," Anchor said as she admired the building.

"We believe environment is critical to the creative process. Our team loves this place. We have fresh cold guava juice waiting in the cafeteria. Then we can take the grand tour."

"You must have read my mind," Skyler said. "I ran on the beach this morning and I'm dying of thirst."

James led his friends from one area of the building to the next. Wonderful abstract art hung on the walls of the sleek interior. A black baby grand piano sat in the upper foyer in front of a window wall. It seemed to float in the air in the midst of a tropical forest. Forty-inch flat-screen monitors were the norm in every office. The place was bubbling with activity as excited men and women hustled about in the open spaces. There were no cubicles anywhere. Anchor was having a great time, and that pleased Skyler more than the tour itself.

Acharya tagged along adding his own comments. "This is our galactic map room. We have created a walk-in map of our near vicinity. You can use these touch-screen lights to zoom and rotate in 3D space."

Anchor jumped on the device and was soon flying through the solar system and out beyond to the triple star system of Alpha Centauri. Her actions were so rapid that it made the others dizzy.

Skyler reached for her hands and said, "Slow down a little. I've flown helicopters through old volcano craters with less tickle in my stomach."

"Oh, sorry. That's a bad habit of mine. I do the same thing with my PC. But this is the best model I've seen anywhere, and I've been to the biggest public planetariums in the world.

Acharya, how can you call this a map of the near vicinity? These star systems are anything but near. How big is this model?"

"We reach out about fifty light years in all directions. Compared to the entire galaxy, this is a near space map." Acharya demonstrated how quickly they could reach the edge of the map.

"The details are amazing. Where did you get your data?"

"From observatories like the one on Maui. And from space telescopes and unmanned probes. Most of what you see here is in the public domain. Notice how the systems get fuzzy when you zoom too close. However, if you want, the computer can speculate...like so. We've assembled this system so we can examine our surroundings easier. Our programmers are some of the best in the world."

Skyler found the complex a curiosity. "Why is this research center inside the Hindu monastery? Most of these people are probably not Hindu. Why the emphasis on outer space? Is this some kind of pseudo religious or astrology research?" Skyler was clearly not as enthusiastic as Anchor.

"Whoa...too many questions for me to remember," James said. "The important thing to know is that this is not a government project. Our support comes from the Hindu church, and wealthy private investors interested in advancing the human race. I wanted to give you the grand tour, but perhaps we should just get right to your questions. Acharya, would you like to explain our purpose here?"

Skyler and Anchor found a large sofa near a strange statue and spread out.

Acharya couldn't help smiling as he prepared to explain the project—the humorous scenario he had anticipated was about to unfold.

"James is in charge of a secret project that, as you can see, is well funded. We believe the long-term survival of the human race is dependent on the success of this project. Although many governments are working on solutions for space travel to the planets in our solar system, none has yet focused seriously on the much more difficult task of traveling to other stars. That is where we come in. We are working on a solution for interstellar space flight."

"It's good you're well funded," said Skyler, "because I'm guessing that will take a very long time."

"More than a long time if we adopted traditional solutions," Acharya said. "Immanuel Kant once challenged western civilization to dare to find answers to the hard questions. We have created a Dare-To-Know chaos-based software system as a tribute to his challenge. I know you love waterfalls, so I will use a waterfall to help explain.

"According to chaos theory, the molecules in a waterfall are free to wander at will; what makes them part of a waterfall is determined by the strange attractions that define the boundaries within their waterfall realm. We have created a software system within our own boundaries that mimic the natural chaos phenomenon. Our realm of restrictions is defined by the engineering capabilities of the human race at this point in time."

"Sorry, Acharya, you've completely lost me. What's the purpose of the system?" Skyler said, looking at his watch.

"I have explained but one side of the system," Acharya said with a shrug. "I am just getting to the good part. The purpose of the DTK system is to cheat nature into giving up a few of her secrets ahead of schedule. We can't wait 10,000 years for the human race to stumble onto the solutions needed for interstellar space travel! For example, our designers have determined that we need a potacitor, along with some other devices. Unfortunately, none of these had yet been invented. Consequently, we created the DTK system to help us invent them.

"The other half of our DTK system has generated over one billion theories on how to create the first device, the potacitor. The chaos half of the system ensures that we do not invent a solution that is impossible for our engineers to build. We have to stay within our engineering waterfall. It also contains the trial and error AI modules to test the other side theories within its strange attractors or constraints."

Anchor stepped between Skyler and Acharya. "Acharya, you sound more like an engineer than a monk. What have they done to you? Anyway, you said none of these devices 'had' been invented," She paused and glanced back at Skyler before asking the obvious question. "Does that mean you've already invented something that could be used for the purpose of space flight?"

"Getting close, we are getting close. That's the reason you're here," James said, fielding the question for Acharya. "We need a pilot to join Acharya on our maiden voyage."

"What! No way!" Anchor said. She grabbed hold of Skyler's arm and tried pulling him away, but Skyler wouldn't budge.

Skyler gently released Anchor's grip and gave her a slight negative nod before turning back to James. "So you want a *test* pilot?"

James said nothing, but affirmed the yes with his expression.

"I've heard enough," Anchor spewed. "Can we please leave?"

"Anchor wait. Just take a little more time. We have more to show you," Acharya pleaded.

Skyler stared into James' eyes, searching for understanding. James was clearly troubled and seemed pleased at Anchor's objections. Skyler placed a hand on his friend's shoulder. "I agree with Acharya. We need to learn more."

There was no satisfaction in James' voice. "All right, let's continue."

FOURTEEN

After six months on the Babylonian project, Acharya could sense something big approaching. While walking toward the research center, Acharya was thinking about the different approaches to self-enlightenment taken by the greatest of all Hindus. In the end though, Acharya realized, each of the different leaders was striving for a common goal, the liberation of human suffering.

Mahatma Gandhi used self-service to others; Ramana Maharshi focused inward toward self-realization; and A.C Bhaktivedants formed an international movement devoted to the service of Lord Krishna, whom he perceived as all-powerful. In a way, Acharya felt that he himself was working for the liberation of human suffering as well.

"Will someone please explain to me how in the hell you did that!" one of the investors was yelling as Acharya entered the crowded room. A small silver ball was floating in the air, and two young scientists were pushing it back and forth between themselves.

"We don't know exactly how it works. Like Thomas Edison and his light bulb, trial and error gave him the results that worked. The difference here is that we had a computer to test millions of possibilities. We got lucky after 400 million failures."

"Are you saying that you just happened to stumble onto a method for blocking gravity?"

"Let me try to explain." James stepped forward. "We're not *blocking* gravity, we're conserving it. It *is* true that in a way we were lucky. We were lucky because the solution just happened to exist in our universe. What makes our approach different is that we focused on technologies for finding stuff.

"Hell, there could be a cure for old age out there, but what good is it if we can't find it. Scientists can spend centuries trying to understand the intricate physics of our potacitor. I don't give a damn. Right now, all we care about is that it *does* work.

"We started our search with an obscure general theory that there are an infinite number of solutions to any physical problem. So we created a software system we call DTK to work with that theory."

"DTK?" the investor asked.

"Dare to Know, in honor of Immanuel Kant," Acharya said, standing within a foot of the floating sphere and poking it with his finger.

"We had our engineers feed mankind's existing construction capabilities into our database," James continued, getting better at giving the DTK elevator pitch. "Using chaos principles, we created an artificial set of strange attractors to keep the system focused on practical solutions, while still remaining free to explore vast possibilities. DTK ramped up by generating one billion random theory speculations, or RT nodes as we call them.

"We found this solution before the computers were half-finished processing the first batch. We basically cheated nature. Instead of waiting several thousand years for someone to stumble on to the solution, as you say, we changed the rules of the game to our advantage."

The investor was beside himself. "Do you have any idea how valuable this technology is? The applications are staggering."

Almost suddenly, the room fell silent as the scientists looked to James for a response. "I'm not sure you understood. As astounding as this device is, we are focused on one goal of which this solution is a part. Beyond that, we all have a pretty good idea just how valuable the DTK system itself is, but we can't lose sight of our original goal. Our team was assembled for the purpose of achieving interstellar flight in this dispensation...and that is what we intend to do."

"Of course, of course. I was only considering the possibilities," the investor said, backing away so others could get a better look at the object floating before them.

"But how?" Acharya asked. "How does it work in principle?" He couldn't take his eyes off the silver blinking sphere floating in front of him.

"What we have, Acharya, is our potacitor," James said. "If you lift any object on Earth, the potential energy of that object can easily be calculated. If you release the object, it falls back to Earth. When you go skiing, you ride the chair lift to the top and then use your stored up potential energy to ski back down. But do you feel any different at the top than you did at the bottom? Where does that potential energy exist? It is an absolute relationship between yourself and the universe around you. Potential energy is even more difficult to explain than electricity. The truth is we don't really know what potential energy is. But like electricity, we can measure it. And now, like electricity, we can store it."

"Cavorite," Acharya said. "In 1901, H.G. Wells wrote a science-fiction book called *The First Men In The Moon* in which the hero uses stuff called 'cavorite' to block gravitational fields. Is that what you have here? Have you discovered cavorite?"

"No, not cavorite. This isn't a gravity shield. It's more like a battery. We considered a shield but rejected it for several reasons. The main reason we wanted this solution was to satisfy one of Einstein's theories. In brief, as an object approaches the speed of light, its mass approaches infinity. We must have a way to ramp up to 80% of light speed without spending months in a gradual acceleration acceptable to the human body. We must also generate a loose rejection shield to protect the craft as it travels through unknown space at near-light speed.

"Now that we have a potacitor, we get to work with this technology in ways that will enable rapid acceleration and deceleration. We also have to find ways to shunt the potential energy generated through acceleration and mass expansion. But gentlemen, I for one believe we can succeed if we 'Dare to Know.'"

"Hear, hear," the group cheered.

Acharya felt as if he was in a dream. The voices faded away and a strange calmness came over him. Acharya knew that it was impossible for Earth to be the first planet in this galaxy to achieve interstellar flight. Yet, here they were, solving problems they shouldn't be able to solve and approaching solutions that just might make it happen. Once before he had experienced this odd feeling of déjà vu. He thought back on his years of meditation, trying so hard to reproduce that experience he had had so many years ago at the war protest. In this moment he could feel the enlightenment happening again.

Why the clarity of future pathways? Was this an illusion or true self-awareness? Acharya had studied, in depth, the life of Maharishi, one of the great modern sages. In a near-death experience, the knowledge of who he was came to Maharishi in an instantaneous flash. As a youth, Maharishi had reached that goal of moksa liberation that Hindus believe takes a lifetime to find. Acharya knew, with certainty now, that he was to embark on a great adventure, but how could he know that? The answer was forming gradually in his mind....

"Acharya...Acharya. Are you all right?" Anchor was pulling on his arm.

Like an explosion Acharya came back to reality. "Oh, yes, I'm...I'm fine. But you should know that Skyler and I have a destiny with the cosmos."

"I'm starting to think we might have a chance as well, but our destiny will be what we make of it." she said.

"No, Anchor, I meant something else. Our journey is inevitable. We will be gone for many years, from your perspective that is."

Anchor gazed fully into the monk's eyes. She saw a deep feeling of concern. She had never seen him like this. Suddenly it occurred to her that he could be right. Even a short trip to somewhere like Alpha Centauri would take years. She would grow older while Skyler was gone.

She ran to Skyler and wrapped her arms around him. "We have to leave!"

"What's wrong?" Skyler asked. The group fell silent waiting for an answer.

"Please, Skyler, this is too dangerous," Anchor pleaded.

James stepped forward. "She's right, son. You've both made great contributions here, but we have other pilots that are better qualified for this project."

Acharya watched as the drama played out, knowing that he and Skyler were already taking their first steps to the stars and nothing could prevent that. But how did he know? If only he could see more. If only he could somehow assure Anchor that everything would turn out well. However, that knowledge was not part of his metaphysical experience. He could see Skyler trying to calm Anchor as a team of the most intelligent people on the planet were floundering for a way to solve this latest problem. Anchor stormed from the building, and one of the most important meetings in human history came to a solemn end.

Sitting by the river that evening, Acharya recalled some of the first lessons from his guru about the Upanishads writings. "Self, or 'Atman,' is the same in all beings," he learned. "You are from Brahman, the Holy Power of the universe, and the identity between Self and the Power leads to moksa, the liberation from the cycle of death and rebirth. It is my task, as your guru, your teacher, to bring to you, my sisya, disciple, this understanding by leading you to the still waters of knowledge."

Acharya opened the paper he was holding and began reading from the ancient parable of the rivers found in the Chandogya Upanishad.

"All these rivers flow, my son, the eastern toward the east, the western toward the west. But they really flow from the ocean and then back to the ocean, once again. Flowing, they become the ocean itself, and becoming ocean they do not say, 'I am this river.' In the same way, my son, even though all creatures have come forth from Being, they know not that they have come forth from Being. Whatever a creature may be here, whether tiger or lion or wolf or boar or worm or fly or gnat or mosquito, they become that Being again and again. For that Being is the finest essence of all this world, and in that Being, every creature has its Self. 'That is reality.'"

This made sense to Acharya, but reincarnation wasn't the same as repetitive life cycles. So why the feelings of déjà vu? Why the certainty of his future? How could he know with certainty his future if it was yet to come?

Acharya felt he was once again close to the answer. He began thinking about the Hindu concept of maya, the magical power with which Brahman both reveals and conceals itself to creation. Anyone who mistakes all that has been created for reality is suffering from a lack of true understanding. The creation is said to be the mere appearance, or maya, created with the power of Brahman. When one is caught up in maya, they are entangled in a delusion that all the created worlds are real.

I accept the principles of maya, so what is wrong? What am I missing? Again, the world around him seemed to slow down and even the sound of the river died away. Gradually the foundation of everything he knew and believed fell apart like the shattering of a large bay window looking out upon the world.

Acharya smiled upon realizing what he had done, what he had remembered. At last, he understood. He had been close to the answer all along. Maharishi had achieved great knowledge, he mused. But he, like Acharya, had been standing on the *edge* of reality, not reality itself. Not surprised, Acharya saw the old Buddhist monk moving up the river toward him with impossible speed.

To an outside observer, the ensuing conversation would have lasted hours, but moments later, Acharya awoke in the dark of night with no recollection of the yellow-clad monk. "What am I doing here? I've fallen asleep! I must get back right away," he said aloud to himself. For the first time, he felt fully committed to the Babylonian project. That was where he needed to apply his energies, not in search of some metaphysical experience from his youthful past.

FIFTEEN

James stared in disbelief as the news conference unfolded. It brought back memories of a private conversation he once had with his Caltech Physics professor, Richard Feynman. If anyone had reason to be suspicious of the news conference, it was James Stevenson.

His famous professor had confided in him one afternoon, and James had never forgotten the conversation. "There are no flying saucers," his professor had told him. In confidence, the professor had explained that flying saucer beliefs were the result of an intentional fabrication of disinformation, and James believed him. They talked at length on two other occasions about the plot. The professor never fully explained why he was confiding in James, but it seemed important to him that James know.

The phone had been ringing for the past hour, but James had no interest in talking with anyone right now. According to the White House, the debate on other intelligent life in the universe was over. The President told the nations of the Earth of an alien life form now based on the far side of the moon. The Earth, according to the President, was on notice to organize into a common government and enter the fold of advanced civilizations.

For security reasons, civilians were restricted from the base or from viewing any of the inhabitants. No civilian spacecraft could approach the moon. The answers to Earth's problems were near at hand, but the aliens insisted that we form a one-world government.

Too appalled to continue watching, he picked up the phone. "James, have you seen the news?" Skyler asked frantically.

"Yep, been watching all morning. The President's making arguments to implement the old Bush Executive Directive 51." *What cosmic irony in that number*, thought James. "Anyway, I've got serious doubts—too many loose ends."

"I had the same feeling. It reminded me of that Powell speech at the UN before the Iraq war. No solid proof of anything, but because it was coming from the White House we all assumed it had to be true. Still, there's no way the President of the United States is making this stuff up. It's too big."

"That's the whole point, Skyler; it's too big to be taken on nothing but faith. I received an email from the board. Our project is on hold. They haven't yet reported the existence of our project to the government, but they're thinking about it. I'm calling Acharya now. Get over here as fast as you can."

As Skyler and Anchor came through the door, Data barked with excitement. They found James and Acharya on the back porch. "The board's position is simple; the purpose of our project is now void, but they're still interested in the DTK system and our potacitor technologies," James was explaining.

"Can they do that?" Skyler asked with frustration. "Can they just shut us down?"

"I have been convinced for a long time that Earth would be visited by advanced beings in my lifetime," Acharya said. "This verifies my feelings, but James is right; why all the secrecy? We need verification, and we need it fast before the whole world falls into step. As an old war protester, I am a firm believer in healthy skepticism."

"I agree," Anchor said. "We know that any space vehicles launched toward the moon will be shot down by the American Moon Defense systems or the aliens, if they exist. But what if we sent a potacitor probe from the Earth in the opposite direction of the moon into deep space, turned it around, and brought it back as the moon revolved into position? We could then approach the backside of the moon from deep space undetected. Not even the aliens would expect that, based on what they know of our technology."

"Can we do that?" Skyler asked with excitement.

Anchor loved the little boy in Skyler. "Indeed we can," she said and kissed him on the cheek.

"She's right," James said. "This would make a great test for our systems. But we need to keep the final destination of the probe to ourselves. As far as everyone knows, we're flying in the opposite direction to avoid any possible discovery of our existence. I'll place Anchor in charge of command and control."

"Now this is getting exciting," she said and gave both James and Acharya a big kiss on the cheek.

Acharya was flustered and embarrassed at first. He hadn't felt the touch of a woman's lips on his skin for a long time. However, Anchor was his friend and as good a friend as he had ever known. "I agree," he said, recovering. Presently he smiled and gave high fives to the others. "This *is* getting exciting...and fun. Let's just hope we don't spend the rest of our lives in prison or hunted by aliens."

James was able to convince the board and the investors to hold off on any disclosures about the project. He made it clear that the technologies behind the project were too valuable and needed more testing before any of their likely competitors discovered that such enormous capabilities were possible. The fastest way to test the potacitor technologies, which the investors were presently obsessed with, was to go forward as planned with the unmanned launch.

Just to be safe, James advised that they launch when the moon was on the opposite side of the Earth. With all eyes on the moon, they could play this to their advantage, he argued. He neglected to tell them that the flight plan called for a return to Earth when the moon had revolved between the Earth and the probe, giving the probe a perfect view of the back side of the moon, and, of course, the alien base camp. No existing spacecraft had the ability to stop on a dime and simply return. Even with the investors understanding of the potacitor, the thought of such a maneuver would never occur to them.

SIXTEEN

Anchor asked Acharya to meet her at the secluded Lumahai Beach on the North Shore. Lumahai was the Nurses' Beach in the famous World War II romance movie *South Pacific*. It had been raining all morning, but Anchor knew the rain was gone for the rest of the day—along with most of the tourists. She laughed when she thought about the tourists running away, not to return until the next day. Little did they know that they were missing the best of Kauai.

"Acharya, what am I going to do?" she pleaded. "Each day I spend with him, the more I love him. I tend to become bored with men after a few months, but with Skyler it's different. I hate being away from him. He's some kind of prince. Have you ever noticed that about him, how he has this...?"

"I have felt a kind of noble majesty in the lad that is hard to describe," Acharya replied politely.

"That's part of what makes me love him, but...oh, Acharya! I want to marry him!"

"That is wonderful," Acharya came to a quick stop. "I am so happy for the both of you. My two best friends are getting married. This is too much joy."

"No, you don't understand, he hasn't asked yet and besides, Skyler isn't Mormon. I have dreamed of being married for time and all eternity in the temple. Mormons believe that families are forever if they're married in the temple and sealed together."

"Oh, I see. What did you tell him?"

"I tried to explain it to him, but he's such a rogue. He's a bad boy, you know, not very religious at all. On the other hand, he's the most honest man I've ever known. I trust him completely. He's so good, and I just love that about him."

"I am sure you will work this out. It is obvious that you are meant for each other."

"Well, he isn't too keen on becoming a Mormon. I don't want him to join the church just for me, either. Even if he did want to join the church for himself, what if he leaves on your journey to the stars and never returns? I'll have to wait years for him to return anyway, and when he comes back, I'll be older. What if he doesn't want me anymore?"

Acharya couldn't help but smile. Anchor was so animated. "I see your concerns. Not about wanting you, of course, but I know how much this mission is troubling you. I would suggest that you get married right away and send your missionary friends after him as soon as possible. I am certain he will want to guarantee that you will be together forever in the unlikely event that something did go wrong. Besides, with our project being shut down, it is unlikely that he will be leaving."

"That's my plan exactly," Anchor said with a smile that reminded Acharya of a cat he saw once in a cartoon after it swallowed a mouse.

"I know this must seem terribly mysterious to you. I'm sure as a Hindu that you must know nothing about Mormons. We are Christians, you know. Most people don't know that, and many people think we are a cult."

"As a matter of fact, I do have some knowledge of your Church. I was 'subjected' to the young missionaries myself once." Acharya said.

"You were? How is that possible?"

"Well, as you know, they travel around on their bicycles. I see them when I am walking, and they wave and smile at me. After a while, they rather wear you down. I thought monks where persistent, but we are amateurs compared to those young men. Eventually, I decided to speak with them, and even though I am a Hindu monk, they were anxious to share their message with me. I must say that I was impressed with their knowledge at such a young age. When countries send their young men to war, your Church sends their youth to fight in God's army. Believe me; I was given a first-rate education.

"For example, I know that your Church has created the largest collection of free family history, family tree, and genealogy records in the world. You are pushing the limits in computer technology and web services for history networks. I've even seen the movie *Legacy II,* filmed right here in Kauai, about the early inhabitants on the American continent described in the *Book of Mormon.* I agree with your philosophy that we will have a better future by looking back and understanding our past."

Anchor laughed. "The young missionaries *are* enthusiastic if nothing else. I've been told the same thing about the Hare Krishna at the airport. Are you Hare Krishna?"

"No, I'm not, but there is a famous poem that was written long ago in India that is considered ingenious. It manages to bring together all the various Hindu philosophies in a way that unites us."

"Oh, that sounds interesting. Do you know it by heart?"

Now it was Acharya's time to laugh. "The *Bhagavad-Gita* is the longest poem ever written. To us it is kind of like your bible, but written as a poem."

"That is amazing! I've never heard of this poem," Anchor said as she ran from a wave that was chasing them up the beach.

As they climbed onto some rocks, Acharya reached into his pocket and removed an old and wrinkled piece of paper that contained a poem written by Ralph Waldo Emerson. He knew this poem, but pretended to read it to her.

Maya

Illusion works impenetrable,
Weaving webs innumerable,
Her gay pictures never fail,
Crowds each other, veil on veil,
Charmer who will be believed,
By man who thirsts to be deceived.

"That's beautiful, Acharya, but what does it mean?"

"Emerson was the first great American literary figure to study in depth the philosophic writings from India. One of the greatest writings in the history of the world, the *Bhagavad-Gita*, the poem I told you about, found a place in his heart. Emerson once wrote:

'*I owed a magnificent day to the Bhagavad-Gita. It was the first of books; it was as if an empire spoke to us, nothing small or unworthy, but large, serene, consistent, the voice of an old intelligence which in another age and climate had pondered and thus disposed of the same questions that exercise us.*'

"Would you like me to interpret the poem by Emerson and tell you about the Bhagavad-Gita? It has some bearing on your suffering."

"Yes, please, this is fascinating. How did you remember what Emerson said about your great poem?"

"You might say I am a fan," Acharya said shyly.

"I am sure you will enjoy this. I think a fun place to start would be with the baby god Lord Krishna because he plays an important part. Please remember that what I am about to explain is highly symbolic."

"Oh, wait!" Anchor interrupted, "I remember something that bothered me in the literature they were passing out at the airport, the Hare Krishna I mean. There was both 'Krishna' and 'Krisna,' and I couldn't figure out the difference. I was supposed to be learning about their beliefs, and I became hung up spelling that instead. I asked one of the boys, but he said they were the same name. Surely there must be some difference."

"Have you already heard the story of the baby Lord Krishna?"

"No, I didn't even know he was a baby. I was just confused about the spelling that's all...sorry for the interruption," Anchor said, looking for a place to sit down.

"Not at all, that is an excellent observation. The name comes from Sanskrit, and there are no suitable signs on the English keyboard for some of the symbols. So K R S N A is the spelling used by scholars. But the accepted modern pronunciation is Krishna, and so it is most often spelled the way it sounds."

"Oh, duh, okay, please continue with your story."

"Yes, well, the baby Lord Krishna was supposed to die as an infant because the evil king at the time, King Kamsa, heard a prophecy that the eighth child of his princess cousin Devaki would grow up and slay him. Then, as the story is told, Lord Krishna, the eighth child of course, is secretly exchanged for another child and is raised by cow herdsman. Later, Krishna's safety is put at risk when the evil king learns of his existence and sends a horrible ogress, Putana, to kill the baby."

Anchor and Acharya had found a soft dry location on the edge of the beach under a large tree. Anchor sat with her legs and arms folded, listening to the story.

"Disguised as a beautiful woman, Putana finds the child and seeks to devour him. While his mother is completely taken in by the charm and beauty of Putana, the infant Krishna, even with his eyes closed, immediately recognizes Putana for who she really is. Putana holds the infant Krishna on her lap and offers him her breast to suck on—after smearing it with deadly poison. Grasping the breast, the infant sucks the life out of his attacker as the mountains and hills, and even the entire Earth itself, shake with the horrific screams of Putana."

"There is a message in this early story of Krishna because the evil Putana is allowed to enter into heaven simply because she offered her breast to the infant god—bad intentions and all. The moral is if Putana can enter heaven, then how much better off are those that worship Krishna with *good* intentions.

"You will be able to identify with this next part. When Krishna grows to manhood, all the young maidens in the village are sick with love for the handsome young man and want to marry him, yet Krishna is a bit of a scoundrel. One day, after the maidens have removed their clothing to bathe and play in the river, Krishna comes forth and laughingly steals all their clothes.

"He then climbs a tree and shouts to the maidens, who by now are trying to cover their bareness by sinking lower in the river. Krishna invites the girls to come to him and retrieve their clothing. The girls are filled with love, but shy because they have no clothing. They tell him that they are his slaves, but that he has played a wicked trick on them and they cannot come forth.

"Krishna, unrepentant, taunts them and tells them that if they are truly his slaves then they must obey him. He compels them to bow down to him after placing their hands on their heads and exposing their full nudity to him. The message from this story is that devotees must reveal all to their lord, concealing nothing."

"Some message," Anchor said. "This Lord Krishna is a lot like Skyler, you can believe me about that. They both have the dickens in them, that's for sure. This is fun. Keep going."

"Okay, so now having a glimpse into the nature of Lord Krishna, the important story from the *Bhagavad-Gita* will be even more interesting. But first, let's take a look at the Hindu principle of maya and try to understand the poem by Emerson.

"The word 'maya' is cognate with the English word 'magic.' The original meaning was the magical power by which Brahman created the world, thereby both revealing and concealing itself. When Emerson writes about the impenetrable illusion, he is referring to what we normally think of as the real world. But this real world is in truth nothing but a projection, or what is called maya, from the true reality called Brahman."

"Oh, you mean virtual reality!" Anchor said enthusiastically.

"What?"

"Virtual reality. It's like Brahman is the real world and the Earth, and all that it entails, is virtual."

There was a long silence before Acharya spoke. "That is an interesting observation given that the concept of maya and Brahman are thousands of years old. But yes, that might be one way of looking at it—if the virtual reality creation or illusion was intended to conceal itself. The thing to keep in mind though is that maya is a projection of not just the Earth, but also the universe and all the gods as well. It is easy to believe that everything we experience, see and examine is the ultimate reality because we want to be deceived. So when Emerson talks about the man who thirsts to be deceived, he is capturing the essence of maya.

Anchor was deep in thought. "Okay, then what is the purpose of this maya? Why was it created, and what is reality?"

"The real question is how we find our way back to Brahman," Acharya answered.

"Why would we want to find our way back? If the delusion was created for us to experience, then why not just sit back and enjoy it?"

"That is an excellent question, and the answer is that we can experience this reality as much and as many times as we choose. The trick is to end the cycle and return to heaven, or even better, to join with Brahman. Emerson wrote another famous poem, which coincidently is called 'Brahman.' Somehow, after studying the lengthy *Bhagavad-Gita,* he managed to capture the concept of Brahman into a single short poem. Hindus often quote from this, one of his most famous writings. I can tell it to you if you wish."

"Definitely, I would love to hear it."

Acharya told the poem to Anchor with as much skill as he could.

BRAHMA

If the red slayer think he slays,
Or if the slain think he is slain,
They know not well the subtle ways
I keep, and pass, and turn again.

Far or forgot to me is near,
Shadow and sunlight are the same;
The vanished gods to me appear;
And one to me are shame and fame.

They reckon ill who leave me out;
When me they fly, I am the wings;
I am the doubter and the doubt,
And I the hymn the Brahmin sings.

The strong gods pine for my abode,
And pine in vain the sacred Seven;
But thou, meek lover of the good!
Find me, and turn thy back on heaven.

"That was beautiful Acharya. This concept of maya and Brahman is amazing. But the large poem you mentioned, the Bhagavad-Gita; what's it about?"

"I apologize. I have been talking for a long time. I will try to keep it short and get to my original purpose of introducing this to you."

"Acharya, don't apologize." Anchor was sitting on a solid black slab of lava, splashing her feet in a newly formed pool of water.

"I enjoy our times together. Please continue," Anchor smiled.

"One of the most important stories of the Gita involves two opposing groups of people that are part of a large family. The good guys and the bad guys you could say. The good group was in charge of things for a long time. But then, through treachery, the bad group managed to seize power. As part of the transfer of power there was an agreement in place that after many years the good family would return to power again. So, after years of wandering, the good people returned to take back their kingdom. Unfortunately, the bad group refused to return power, laying the groundwork for a great war between the opposing sides.

"Now, the good people were outnumbered by the bad people, but the good people had a great warrior whose name was Aruna. Aruna's chariot driver just happened to be Krishna, the god I told you about earlier. Aruna had no idea that his chariot driver was a god of course, but he was certain of victory. Because of his confidence in their victory, Aruna decided to ride his chariot through the opposing army just to get a look at the enemy he was about to defeat. As he rode past the people, he found that he recognized them. They were, after all, his relatives. When Aruna saw this he became dejected, confused, and overwhelmed with guilt. So he pulled his chariot over, lay down and refused to fight.

"When Krishna saw what was happening, he told Aruna to get up and fight. Aruna explains the dilemma he is faced with: if he fights and kills his relatives, then their kingdom is ruined, but if he does not fight, the kingdom is also ruined. Then begins the famous symbolic discussion between God and Man as Krishna attempts to convince Aruna to fight.

"Krishna uses various arguments such as how his enemies will brand him as a coward. He tells Aruna about maya and explains how Aruna is deluding himself into believing that he is actually killing anyone. Krishna tells Aruna that there never was a time when the two of them were not alive. 'We have always been and always will be,' he explains.

"All of these arguments fail, and so Krishna tells Aruna to just put his faith in Krishna and do as he says. Eventually, Aruna realizes who he is talking to and begins to see the wisdom in Krishna's arguments. Although there are several yoga paths that can help people break the chain of reincarnation, the one that is most like Christianity is the worship of Lord Krishna. He takes on all the problems and dilemmas mankind is faced with and leads them in the right direction. The interesting thing is that he compelled Aruna to action as opposed to inaction. When Aruna finally does fight, his people are victorious and return to power.

"So you see, we have many things in common, you and I. And, although Skyler is faced with the desire not to hurt you, he also wants to do something that will benefit mankind. I can tell you this from the bottom of my heart, I believe he is necessary to this mission and that he will return to you victorious."

"Oh, Acharya, thank you for telling me how you feel! You have no idea how much that helps." She jumped up and gave him a long hard hug. "Ya see, Acharya, it's all right to hug a monk after all....if he's a dear friend that is. Be at ease, dear Acharya. I come from a people with a long history of sacrifice and adventure. It was the Mormons who conquered the west in pursuit of freedom. It makes sense that we should be part of conquering the galaxy in the quest to free mankind from this lonely globe."

Acharya felt tears come to his eyes. "I agree," was all he could say as he bashfully turned away.

The odd friends, a middle-aged Hindu monk and a beautiful young astronomer, left the ocean shore hand-in-hand. Anchor noticed an enormous woman giving them a non-accepting look as they passed by. The woman's disapproval was so obvious that Anchor couldn't resist cozying up closer. She smiled at the woman, grabbed hold of the monk's arm and said, "So Acharya, any idea yet what caused that strange rainbow?"

SEVENTEEN

On a calm, cool Pacific morning, while all eyes were on the moon, a small, well-lit ball lifted off the surface of the northern-most island of the Hawaiian chain. Traveling at a slow ascent, the craft continued to rise like a bright hot-air balloon. However, unlike a balloon, or any other aircraft to probe the atmosphere, this craft just kept moving upward. *It looks so easy,* James thought to himself as he watched the Babylonian probe with his high-powered binoculars. "On the shoulders of giants," he heard Acharya say.

With no rumbling explosions from massive rockets, with no network televisions, and with no cheering crowd of thousands, the most advanced machine ever built rose smoothly out of the atmosphere into the lonely sea of space. The concept of breaking free from the Earth's gravitational pull at high speeds meant nothing to this craft. There was no deep space injection, simply a constant separation from the planet.

The probe was a larger version of the tiny spheres built and tested inside the research complex. A small energy shield generated from the potacitor protected the craft, which was covered with a completely transparent shell. Swiveling high-powered cameras capable of sight in all directions filled the inside. No spy plane or space probe ever built had better panoramic range or sensory vision.

When Anchor first saw the probe, she said it looked like a big eyeball, and the name stuck with the rest of the team.

"We have visuals from *Eyeball*," Anchor said with excitement in her voice. "Everyone wave, you're on TV."

Skyler looked at the largest monitor, where he could see himself and the other team members standing on the roof of the development center surrounded by dense jungle. The roof was a farrago of equipment—cameras, computers, telescopes, television monitors, and black coax wires running everywhere. Recognizing themselves, people were smiling and waving at *Eyeball* as it transmitted continuous zooming views back from orbital height. Circular orbital speed was unnecessary for *Eyeball* to retain its height. It was hovering with no velocity just on the edge of space.

"All systems are go!" Anchor yelled over the celebration. "We just tested our mini-shield, and it's working as anticipated...standing by for acceleration."

"That's a go, Anchor. Put the pedal to the metal and head for deep space," James said as he toasted her and the other team members with a glass of guava juice.

On the monitor, the building and the people soon panned away while the view widened. As the probe sped farther from the Earth, the entire island came into view. Presently the rest of the islands were visible. Eventually, the full shrinking Earth was visible, along with the small, ostensibly alien-controlled moon.

"Give us a better view of the moon from this angle. Let's see if anything unusual is happening over there," James said.

When the camera zoomed in on the moon, everyone fell silent. "Nothing unusual from this angle, boss," one of the engineers yelled out, gradually lowering the volume of his voice with an embarrassed grin. Obviously, everyone could see what he was looking at.

"Our flight plan calls for a return to Earth in twelve days. We should get a better view then," Anchor said

"Hey, we'll get more than a better view," the same engineer said while he did the mental calculations. "If I'm right, we'll pass right by the moon. But I thought the moon was ordered off-base by the feds."

James stepped to the middle of the team. "We plan to take close-up photos and videos with star mapped time verifications on the way home. You have a right to know that our investors are pulling the plug on the manned mission because of these visitors. I want to see, first-hand, why we have worked so hard for nothing. I'm sure the alien base is visible, but if there is the slightest chance that our visitors are an elaborate fabrication, then we owe it to ourselves, and the entire world, to find out.

"You're right about this being outlawed though. If anyone wants out of this mission, I'll understand, but at the very least, we get to be among the few inhabitants on Earth to see these mysterious aliens." After a few tense moments of silence, everyone spoke at once. This was a team itching for action. They were in unanimous support of the high-tech spy mission.

"Dudes, this is ridiculously crucial!" said Alex, never at a loss for unusual expressions. "I want to see the look on their faces, or whatever they have, as *Eyeball* comes flying in from deep space with all cameras flashing. No way they can catch her...no way!" The brilliant young programmer was laughing as he slapped his partner, Isaac, on the back and accidentally sent him sprawling.

The media buzz was relentless. The major networks were feverously bringing forth experts with rumors of new information about the mysterious aliens. The Earth stood still for a time, but gradually conformed to the demands of the faceless visitors. The constant flow of spin and excitement drowned out the few skeptics. Twenty-four-hour war rooms were set up by the various stations. The coverage, much like the excitement prior to the invasion of Iraq, appeared on all channels. It had become a game.

"I just want proof!" A gray-haired red-faced astronomer was fumbling for the right words on CNN. "Give us just one piece of hard evidence. The government announces UFOs and suddenly everyone is a believer. The government has been spreading UFO disinformation for years. We have nothing to validate any of this. Remember Building 7 of the World Trade Center. Wake up America! If there were aliens..."

The picture suddenly switched to a White House press conference, where the President was preparing to make another announcement. "My fellow Americans, and all people of the Earth, I bring great news. With the hard work of thousands of ambassadors and negotiators worldwide, we are close to forming a unified governing body.

"Let me assure you that our existing governments will function as before, without change. The United States of America is still the United States of America. However, for issues of planetary survival and for issues of war and peace, the new, unified council will have ultimate control. Only this council, representing all the nations of the Earth, will have legal authority to speak for Earth.

"Our friends from the center of the galaxy are pleased with the speed and determination that this governing world council is being formed. Soon, we will enter into negotiations with our adventurous neighbors, and Earth will become the newest member of the galactic array of peaceful worlds."

The president spoke again about the removal of nuclear weapons from individual countries, including the United States; after which he abruptly left the podium, without fielding a single question from the screaming reporters.

჻

Up the stairs, through the door, change shirt, grab wallet, slide the screen door and on to the deck. Just try to relax before leaving, Skyler told himself as he looked out to sea.

The ocean seemed timeless in its slow-motion trek toward the lava rocks below. From his balcony, Skyler could see shiny streaks over the water's surface as if an artist had taken his brush and applied random strokes across a massive canvas.

Take deep breaths and enjoy. It didn't help. He left his condo and drove down the steep winding road to Hanalei's Ching Young Village. Without remembering the drive, Skyler walked toward the small market for a quick snack. It was something he did when he needed a break. His mind was still reeling from the events of this morning.

When *Eyeball* came streaking out of deep space and targeted the far side of the moon, everyone expected a close encounter with the strange and mysterious aliens. Instead, what *Eyeball* saw was a human military base—no alien spacecraft or advanced presence. *Eyeball* zoomed in for a close-up examination. Recording and dating what it saw, *Eyeball* exposed the scam in harsh detail.

There were no alien ships, no alien base camps, and no alien life forms. Instead, there were dozens of grids of Earth-made missiles trying to shoot down the slow moving, yet deceptively swift little sphere. When *Eyeball* had seen enough, it sped away with its recordings. The base missiles could not target the sphere in the sky because it would simply step to the side and the distant explosions were no match for *Eyeball*'s shields.

Skyler had to get away. Anchor was trying to call him on his cell, but Skyler Anderson was in a bad mood. As he walked past the small wooden stage in the middle of the square, he noticed a large and rather muscular man sitting on the edge of the stage laughing at an injured frog. "It's not funny!" his girlfriend was saying. "It's just a poor little old frog."

Suddenly, the man stopped laughing and peered at Skyler. He was off the stage in an instant and approaching fast. "Hey, asshole, I've got you now. No place to hide this time."

What luck, Skyler thought. *Now I have to deal with this prick again.*

The same man who had given him trouble on Na Pali was after him once more. This time Skyler was in no mood to run. Instead, he pretended to be startled, looking for a way out. This gave the bully confidence. He rushed after what looked like a coward turning to flee.

When the large man reached out in an attempt to grab Skyler by the neck, Skyler turned directly into him. Muscle Boy paused for a brief moment. It was a fatal mistake. Skyler threw a solid, angry fist into the man's jaw. His follow through was long and continued in the air above the falling man. Skyler was just breaking bricks. Something was going to give, Skyler's hand or the large man's face.

"Stay away from the frogs, asshole," Skyler heard himself say in one last release of aggression while standing over the man.

Skyler gazed around at the gathering crowd. He was still recovering from the adrenalin rush when he heard a familiar voice behind him.

"Move away, folks," the policeman said. "What's going on here?"

"It was a fight, officer, between Skyler and that big guy," a teenage girl, who recognized Skyler, explained.

The officer turned to Skyler. "Is that right? Who started the fight?"

"No fight, Jeff. Just two hits. I hit him, and he hit the ground." Everyone laughed except the girlfriend, who was now holding her fallen hero's head in her lap while she scowled.

"This is the muscle boy I was having trouble with on Na Pali when I was trying to help that injured tourist."

"Oh, yeah, I remember that," the officer said. "Da dude is just nui kama."

More laughter. Someone whispered in the crowd: "That's Hawaiian for 'big baby.'"

"It wasn't Skyler's fault," the teenage girl was still talking. "This guy just attacked him for no reason."

"That's right," an older man agreed. "I saw everything. This young man was just defending himself and did a pretty good job at that." More laughter.

"I need to leave, Jeff. Do you want anything from me?" Skyler asked.

"No, that's okay. Just come by next week and give us a few more details when you get a chance. I'll take care of it from here unless you want to press charges."

"Nope, just remind him to stay away from me. That's all I ask."

Despite the ruckus, Skyler was still on edge. Earlier he had been witness to the greatest lie in human history. Now officials from the United States government, including the Secretary of Defense, had threatened his team of friends. It hadn't taken long for the government to track them down.

One of the team's engineers had taken it upon himself to paint the words "Kauai rocks! Babylonian science at your service" on the craft. He'd added the artwork just prior to lift off, unaware of their true mission.

The one thing keeping the team from mortal destruction was James' quick thinking. He blasted photos, videos and the other evidence onto the Internet. "Not much point in negotiating with anyone at this stage," he said. "I believe our lives depend on this information getting out there now."

Rumors spread quickly about how a probe from the island of Kauai had managed to circumvent the entire U.S. military and reach the moon. One rumor that seemed most interesting was circulating wildly on the web: a small probe was attached to a secret new version of the Helios high-flying craft to avoid the scrutiny of the spy satellites and aliens looking for launched spacecraft.

After crashing into the ocean, the original Helios airplane had achieved a sort of mythological status among the people of Kauai, especially among the surfers. Its namesake, Helios, was the young Greek god of the sun. According to legend, Helios had drowned in the ocean at the hand of his uncles the Titans, after which he rose to the sky where he became the sun god.

The romantic connection seemed to grab the imagination of the world, even though launching a moon probe from a fragile high-flying solar-powered kite was absurd. But, despite the impractical solution, the talking head experts on the news channels had formulated an amazing set of speculations that were good enough to explain the flight.

James removed the core potacitor technologies from the center. The military and CIA experts scanned the research center, but none had a clue what they were looking for. And, of course, the Babylonian team members were *not* talking.

Isaac and Alex each made copies of the DTK software system on their personal terabyte everlast wands. They destroyed all other copies and hiked eleven miles into the secluded Kalalua Valley on Na Pali where they joined a community. Isaac sent a personal carrier friend to James with a letter explaining where they were. It included an unnecessarily detailed message about Alex. "Alex is no longer a virgin. He believes he has found true love and may never return."

The most important story in the news was the exposure of the alien fabrication. There was a rapid denial and a massive effort to paint the evidence as fake, but it didn't last long.

Once the physical evidence had disbursed through the web, thousands of scientists were explaining why the photos were real. Eventually, the major news networks were on board leading toward a tipping point. Congress impeached the President a mere three months later, and the historic trial for his removal from office began.

A deluge of classified documents soon surfaced, exposing not just the disinformation of this current President but a strategy that began as far back as 1942. The Roswell UFO incident was an expansion of that strategy. The US government had discovered the perfect cover for much of its clandestine aerial activities: mysterious alien visitors from space with flying saucers, and the world had bought into the scheme for decades.

In 1960, after Gary Power's U-2 spy plane was shot down, the CIA's 'Black Operations' pushed for a different kind of spy plane. It started with a secret plane called Silver Bug and grew into a more advanced plane called Black Bird, and later the Stealth. The psychological war with the Soviet Union included UFO cover to help hide the existence of these planes. In fact, the existence of Stealth, a plane capable of avoiding radar detection, remained hidden from 1977 to 1988. And the triangular shaped Stealth was often mistaken for an alien spacecraft—to the delight of the Black Operations people at the CIA.

James agreed to several interviews but refused to talk about the Babylonian technology. He told of his UFO doubts as far back as his college days and his conversations with his professor. On James' recommendation, from notes Feynman had given him, they found the old dusty documents containing interviews of the original Manhattan Project scientists and managers. They revealed a military that was out of control. Instead of closing up shop after World War II, the American military complex grew stronger in weapons and in their willingness to deceive the American people.

For half a century, the UFO strategy had worked well. Ultimately, in a grand scheme for consolidating world control, the president had agreed to go to the UFO well one more time. As outrageous as the plan was, the CIA was confident, from decades of psychological experimentation, that the world would go along with the ruse, especially the Americans. Recent polls taken just prior to the new alien deception found that over 38% of the American people believed the federal government was withholding proof of intelligent life forms on other planets. So 'admitting the truth' was an easy lie. What the government could not anticipate was an *Eyeball* in the sky, watching them from the opposite side of the moon.

In the face of massive political upheaval, the savvy investors managed to get a restraining order against the government. Agents from the various departments were politely escorted from the research vicinity.

After that, the team quickly formed again as parts and pieces of their equipment magically found their way back to the data center from various and unusual hiding places on the island. Alex was the last straggler to return. His true love turned out to be a true believer in community love.

"I told you they would never catch Eyeball," said Alex upon his return. The happy team members gathered around and welcomed him back. James ordered him to take a shower.

With no competitive spaceships from aliens, the investors, brave from their recent legal victory over the government, agreed to allow research for the manned space flight to continue. The world had already experienced a stunning change from the efforts of the Babylonians, however exposure of the biggest facade in human history paled in comparison to what the Babylonians were planning next.

"Looks like we still have some unwanted guests next door." Robert Latier was an electrical engineer on the team who enjoyed espionage. Playing with sleuth and spy equipment was his hobby, so James had put him in charge of security.

"I found a bug and tracked it to our neighbors and then returned the favor with a bug of our own," Robert said with a satisfied grin.

"Which neighbors?" James asked.

"The Devine World Teacher guru place. You know the Adidam guys south of the visitor center."

"Oh sure. What the heck do they do?"

"They teach spiritual stuff and collect tithing. The founder called himself Adi Da Samraj, but he was born Franklin Albert Jones in Jamaica, New York. Our spy goes by the name of Admiral, although I'm not sure why. He used the organization's interest in videographic technology to weasel his way in by giving them some cool technology and money. The guy has basically set up a secret camp over there to spy on us."

James put down the paper clipping he was reading, now interested in what Robert had found. "Any idea who he works for or what his real name is?"

"Nope, but he makes periodic contact with some people that work for him. I followed him yesterday and took these photos. You can keep this set."

James glanced through the photos at a man dressed in a naval shirt with Levis. It was difficult to tell his true rank, if any.

"The bug he planted eliminates amateurs or even corporate spying. His equipment looks like advanced CIA stuff to me. He has no idea we've caught him, and the funny thing is that the Adidam group is going to ask him to leave. They've determined that he's not really interested in their religion," Robert said, still smiling.

"Good work, Bob. Let me know if you find anything more on this so called Admiral."

EIGHTEEN

To the sound of cheers and excitement, James walked into the auditorium room and onto the stage. This was the first formal assembly of the entire team since the government agents had invaded their premises. Yet, despite the jubilant congratulations, James Stevenson, for the first time since taking the helm, was having grave doubts.

Normally, the ultimate optimist, James raised his hands. "We have accomplished nothing."

The room fell silent and Acharya, the humble monk, couldn't believe what he was hearing. "Are you kidding?" he heard himself yell. "We have flown a spacecraft from the Earth to the moon and back. That alone is astounding, but we made it look as easy as floating a balloon."

"Acharya, my skeptical friend, we seem to have reversed roles. We have the engine, but we do not have the basic technology. Our potacitor is a great invention, but without the ability to control its mysterious energies, we cannot reach the stars. I am constantly amazed at the supreme competency of this team.

"You are the Babylonians. However, I need your help more than ever because we are at a standstill. We were able to shunt the energy and deflect the missiles that came for our probe, which must have the U.S. military still scratching their heads." Laughter filled the room as the microphone squeaked from James speaking too close. "But our ability to control the internal g-forces must be solved, and I am beginning to suspect that it may not be possible."

At the back of the auditorium, a timid computer programmer was raising his hand, but went unnoticed as James continued. "We have fought our way past wasted efforts, loose ends, equipment glitches, dubious theories, corrupt data, and impossible goals. I have preached about the possibility of an infinite number of solutions to any problem, and we have dared to know and find those impossible solutions. But I have looked at this problem from every angle, and it seems the very nature of our device precludes the solution we are after. It seems we have an artifact, an artifact that won't go away."

Skyler walked from an aisle to his friend on stage and placed a hand on his shoulder. "Find a way, James. I'm ready to fly." The microphone picked up his words.

"We can do it!" Anchor yelled aloud, glancing back at Acharya as the cheering erupted again.

James raised his hands once more. "All of you need to understand that the forces are basically inverted. Let me try to explain: if you..."

At last, Isaac overcame his bashfulness and interrupted. "Uh, James, I know what you're going to say, but actually the issue that you believe makes this impossible is the inherent solution."

The room fell silent until people repeated what Isaac had said to those who couldn't hear. The entire room turned to see Isaac standing with a guilty look on his red-flushed face. "I've spent the past two weeks working on this problem, and you won't believe this: Einstein was right!" he yelled.

"What are you talking about?" James asked. "Come down here."

"Why bother trying to understand," Acharya said to a man sitting next to him. "Our friend Isaac exists on a different level than the rest of us mortals with IQ's below 180."

James was stunned. What was Isaac saying? James was a rebel and clearly, the most brilliant physicist ever launched from the hardwood classrooms of Caltech. He had spent his life in boredom, trying to deal with the unimaginative thinking of his colleagues and teachers, except Feynman of course. Yet each and every member of this team was his equal or better. Could they have done it again?

As Isaac came forward, James focused on his words. He smiled as the lights in his mind switched on. "Of course, it's counterintuitive. I should have seen it. Energy is released from a *Potential Well* when sufficient energy is added to the system to surmount the local minimum. It's simple quantum physics. The potential energy we need could escape a *Potential Well* without added energy due to the probabilistic characteristics of quantum particles. We use a *Well!* It's not obvious, but it could work. Isaac, *you* are a genius!" James shouted, causing another loud high-pitched squeal from the microphone.

"Is that not what I just said," Acharya nudged the man next to him.

Later that day, a few stragglers gathered to watch the continuing news story about the fall of the American administration. The most interesting residual was that some good was coming from the farce. The countries of the world were still talking and negotiating, still moving forward to rid the Earth of weapons of mass destruction and to build a common organization that would serve all nations. The American President had tried to use these activities in an attempt to justify his actions, but eventually he had resigned.

"So James," Skyler said as they stood together, looking out over the darkening misty jungle through a massive window. "You've solved the secrets of the universe and changed the political landscape of the planet. You will be sending me on a twelve-year journey to another star system. Perhaps now you can tell me what the Babylonians have concluded about my rainbow."

James turned to his young friend. "I'd forgotten about that. An interesting problem indeed. We spent more time on that rainbow than we should have. Our investors would *not* be pleased with the computer time we logged. For several days, everyone on the team worked on it. In the end, even Isaac shrugged his shoulders and threw in the towel. The bottom line is that we don't know what happened. I know there's a logical explanation, but your mystery is still a mystery."

"Okay for now, but when I return in twelve years, I'll be expecting an answer. Call it payback for risking my neck on this harebrained venture."

"That's a deal. Once we launch, I'll make your rainbow a personal quest."

On the other side of the building, Anchor and Acharya had captured Isaac and were quizzing him about what had happened.

"To be honest, we've both studied the designs and computer software used in the production of our potacitor technologies, but we still feel like children. We just don't get it. How does this stuff work, and why was James so concerned today?" Anchor said as she held his arm to prevent escape.

"Yes, Isaac, I would concur with Anchor. We are still not clear on the important principles. We both have technical backgrounds, and yet we have gaps in our knowledge. Perhaps you could take the time to fill in those gaps." Acharya said in his formal style.

"Okay I'll try. We're in the business of stealing energy, so let's start with the definition of potential energy," Isaac said with a sigh. "Because of your technical background, you've been brainwashed by our educational system. A better name for potential energy would be stored energy. Energy is supposedly stored in an object by doing some kind of work against a force such as gravity, or a magnetic field, or even a simple spring." Isaac was definitely going back to basics, and they could see it was difficult for him to rehash such things. It was like watching a little boy wiggling in a tight sweater.

He lifted an empty blue mug from the solid glass coffee table and stared at it. "This heavy mug has more potential energy sitting on this table than the same mug sitting on the floor. When I lift the mug from the floor to the table, I've done work, and that work is now stored in the mug. Can you see my work in the mug?" Isaac smiled and laughed at his own strange joke. When neither Anchor nor Acharya responded, he squirmed and continued. "Anyway, if I push the mug off the table, like so, the mug picks up kinetic energy that is then converted into heat and sound as the mug hits the floor."

Anchor picked up the mug, happy it hadn't broken.

"Okay, that's a straight forward easy concept, taught to us in junior high school. The potential energy is stored in the mug. Simple, would you not both agree?

They both nodded in agreement, ready to move past the basics.

"Okay, but if you really think about it, what I just described is missing something. It doesn't explain anything other than what we already know from common sense. These fancy scientific terms, like potential energy, and our perfect equations, make us believe that we know more than we do. So don't get hung up on the traditional definitions and descriptions, especially when they're flat wrong, as are both of you." Isaac stopped to see their response to that statement.

"Now, the key to the potacitor is not that the energy was stored in the mug when I lifted it up to the table, the important thing to recognize is how that energy was converted to kinetic energy when I pushed it off the table. The kinetic energy came from the gravitational forces between the mug and the Earth. As a simple observer, ask yourself what would happen if the potential energy in the mug was diverted into something like a stored energy stasis shield where it no longer existed until needed."

"Oh, wait, I think I'm beginning to understand. I've been thinking about this all backwards," Anchor blurted. "I *have* been brainwashed."

Isaac perked up. "What do you suppose would happen if we pushed the mug off the table without releasing its stored energy?"

"*We* know what would happen, but only because we have seen it," Acharya answered. "The mug would just float in the air. We can move it down and back up easily, but not past the surface of the table. At that point, it gets heavy again and requires work to lift it above the table."

"Yes, that's right, but has our magic mug changed, or is something outside of the mug changing its behavior. Is the mug's behavior changed on its own or is it changed by the potacitor?" asked Isaac. "So the important question is: does the mug literally hold the additional potential energy as we have all been taught? As a Babylonian, I would have to say that is asking a lot of a simple mug. If you think about it, we somehow believe that every single object in the universe is itself a potacitor. Where else could the energy be? It must be in the mug."

"I'm catching on," Anchor said. "What Euclidians like Newton gave us was an accurate way to measure things, but we're tricking ourselves if we believe that they've also given us an understanding of things. Astronomers know all about stealing energy. If you drop a basketball and a tennis ball, they bounce normally. But if you place the tennis ball on top of the basketball and drop them together, the tennis ball shoots off like a rocket. The tennis ball steals potential energy from the basketball.

"That's how we fling spaceships around the solar system. We steal energy from the planets. What you're saying, if I read you right, is that the potential energy is not actually *in* the mug or the tennis ball. Newton's equations are much simpler if we think of it that way, but that doesn't make it so."

"Exactly right!" Isaac was excited at the breakthrough. "Now you're thinking like Einstein. The mug is made of energy, but the boundless potential energy is *relative* to the mug's own energy, not added to it. That's why the mug looks and feels the same, regardless of its potential energy. I can tell you though, that many great physicists would disagree with you, at least until they had observed for themselves our potacitor in action." Isaac was tempted to diverge into a complicated criticism of present day physics but managed to stop himself.

"With the help of the DTK system, we devised a stasis shield in one of Burkhard's subatomic dimensions. The correct theory, which enabled us to build the potacitor, defined potential energy as a change in energy between masses, a change that is independent of both, a dent in the surface of gravity if you will. Our potacitor acts like a filter between subjects. It intercepts the energy changes, or deltas. That technology is far beyond anything mankind had ever envisioned or would have envisioned for tens of thousands of years, and it is far more complex than this mug."

"Burkhard?" Anchor asked.

"Yes, you know—the theory of everything."

"I'm just an astronomer. I've heard of that stuff, but I have to confess that I still don't follow."

"Burkhard Heim is a little-known German scientist that may have done what Einstein was unable to do: bridge the gap between quantum theory and relativity. Hey, the U.S. government has been working on a Hyperspace engine based on his theories. Their goal is to push the entire spacecraft, people and all, into the same subatomic dimensions that we use to hold potential energy. They will fail, according to DTK. It might be possible someday, but mankind doesn't have the engineering or hardware to pull it off right now.

"Remember, DTK only gives us solutions that we can unequivocally build. Even if we could have built the hyperspace engine, James wasn't interested. He said he didn't want any repeat of that old movie *The Fly*. You know, people in one side and something else out the other. Anyway, Burkhard was right about the subatomic dimensions. He would have been happy to know that we found them and used them to build our potacitor."

"I think I'm beginning to understand the spin device as well," Anchor said. "When NASA launches a spacecraft, they have to lift the craft fast enough to break free of the Earth's gravity. Otherwise, the craft would just convert its potential energy into kinetic energy and fall back to Earth. Their problem is that they have to fight against the gravitational forces in standard real-time. They have to lift the mug up to the table so to speak. Halfway won't work, and the most efficient method for lifting into space is to accelerate the craft at high speeds."

Acharya was eager to enter the conversation. "We spent a month gradually loading our probe's potacitor with enough energy to completely nullify the Earth itself. Is that correct?"

"You have it," Isaac said. "In a way, a potacitor is like having a weightless electric battery capable of holding a potential energy charge, a battery that is 100% efficient. We then divert some of that stored energy to drive the ion engines for propulsion." Isaac's mind wandered away to a complex world, but the sound of Anchor's voice brought him back.

"Well, I still have no clue how the potacitor itself functions, but at least now I understand how it gets us into space. So what was all the excitement about today?" Anchor asked.

"We're loading our craft with much more potential energy than is needed to break free from the Earth because we need energy internally to counterman the g-forces on our astronauts and equipment. We also need energy for our shields.

"Until two days ago, we had no way to do that. We could do amazing things like absorb the mass of our ship as it approached infinity from traveling near light speed, but the simple task of restraining g-forces inside the craft wasn't possible. Everything in our DTK's outside shunt system is eminently intuitive and logical. The solution required, is what you might call reverse intuition, like not thinking about the mug holding its own potential energy. Again, Einstein was the master at that. He's the one who gave me the idea. I thought his approach was wrong in this case, but it was more than brilliant. So I added the necessary countermeasures to the DTK software system, and it quickly spit out the solution for what James called a *Well.*"

The sound of Isaac's voice faded as Acharya gazed out the window. Apparently satisfied, he had lost interest. While he stood by the large window peering into the distance, toward the canyon's edge, he spotted a flash of light move across his angle of view.

"Did you see that?" Anchor half-shouted. "What was that?"

"I do not know," said Acharya.

Off in the distance, and out of sight from the center, an elite team of navy seals moved rapidly toward the complex. Their simple mission was to destroy the main building. One final order from the prior president was still unfinished. Suddenly, an old man in a yellow robe stood before them.

"Move away, old man," their leader ordered. "You are not safe here."

"I am deeply sorry, but this is a mistake," the old man said in a voice that shook the Earth.

"How'd he do that?" one of the soldiers asked.

The leader moved forward, but when the monk turned and flashed a brilliant smile, he stopped. The monk bowed his fragile-looking old head and said, "My most humble apologies, but it is you that must not be here. Go with knowledge." In a blink of an eye, the strike force was gone.

NINETEEN

Skyler made a desperate dive and flew through the air, parallel to the hardwood floor. Too fast, he over-played the ball and couldn't manage a clean shot. As the ball bounced off the back wall, Skyler recognized another slim chance. Swinging his racquet behind his back while still stretched out in the air face down, he executed an acrobatic recovery, sending the ball toward the front wall on the opposite side of the court. He crashed onto the floor, rolled just before striking his head on the side wall, scrambled quickly to his feet and ran back toward the center of the court. *Let's go!* he said to himself. He was in a good position again when James hit a quick and perfect corner pinch shot, driving the ball in the opposite direction of Skyler's momentum and winning the last point and the game 15/3.

"I've only seen one other racquetball player hit that shot before," James said as he shook Skyler's hand. "That was amazing."

"Amazing, but not good enough to win the point," Skyler said dejectedly.

"I was in Phoenix watching a racquetball game with Marty Hogan. Hogan won the national title five consecutive years. Anyway, I was standing close to the back wall when he made that same gymnastic shot. The place went wild. Until today, I've never seen anyone else attempt that shot. You're a great athlete."

"Hey, I'm also a pretty good racquetball player. I didn't want to tell you, but I don't lose here often. I'd heard you were undefeated from some friends, but I didn't honestly expect to lose to an old guy. And I sure didn't expect to get demolished."

"Old guy, huh?" James laughed. "We should have played sooner. Perhaps I'd be getting more respect."

Despite the lopsided score, it was a good game and a large crowd had formed to watch through the transparent wall. As they came out of the court, the spectators clapped and gradually dispersed.

"How did you beat me so easily?" Skyler asked as they sat on a couch, gathering their gear.

"That wasn't easy. You're faster, and you hit the ball harder than I do and with good accuracy. I did use your own speed against you though. I shouldn't tell you this because it'll be a lot tougher for me the next time we play, but I can give you a few basic tips if you'd like," James said reaching for his water bottle.

"Definitely. I'm thinking I should take notes."

"No, this will be easy for you to remember, just not so easy to do in a game for a while. But you're a fast learner, so I'm guessing in a couple weeks, I'll be in big trouble," James said.

"Okay, so what's the secret? Just give it up, and I promise to go easy on you." Skyler smiled.

"First the strategy and then the mental. The most obvious is that when your opponent is in the back-court, kill the ball. When he is in the front-court, hit a pass shot. That sounds obvious, but you need to practice with those thoughts in mind. Now, what do you think you should do when your opponent is in front of you in the middle of the court?" James asked.

"I'm not sure about that. I guess it depends on where you are and how far to the side he is. Am I getting close?"

"Not really. Have you ever noticed how most players hit ceiling shots when they're in the back-court? It's kind of a defensive shot. It's used often because taking the right shot, a kill shot from that far back, can be difficult at times. Hitting a defensive ceiling shot is a good idea, when needed, but good players get past using it as a crutch. Right now though, you should think about using the ceiling as an offensive shot as well. When the player is in front of you in the center court: hit a ceiling shot. Bounce it over his head and make him run backwards.

"If you think about those three simple strategy shots and practice using them in your games, you'll start driving your opponents crazy. I'm not sure why, but it's a lost art. Unlike basketball or football, the racquetball players in the 80's were a more talented bunch."

"Whoa, those tips are so obvious. This is going to be fun. So what did you mean about the mental part of the game?" Skyler asked.

"Yeah, I wanted to find a way to talk to you about that anyway because it's something I want you to keep in mind when you take to the stars. As you know, our team is on a roll. We've solved the problems that would have prevented a launch. This is going to happen, Skyler. I'd still feel better if you would let me find a replacement. I've become too close to you and Anchor. You're like my own children."

"We've been over this. It's going to be okay. I'm the right pilot for this, and you know it. Besides, who's going to take care of Acharya? That goofy monk needs me up there with him."

James leaned over and pretended to be fixing his shoelaces, but Skyler knew he was just thinking.

"Okay," James said with enthusiasm again. "When Marty Hogan turned pro, he was a great athlete, but he was just an average player on the tour. He was emotional, and he hated to lose. He just couldn't get his mental game together. He was coming close to beating the best in the world, but he would choke and find ways to tank. Eventually, he found an ingenious secret for controlling his emotions. I read about it in an obscure article he wrote." James reached for his water bottle again and sat back, looking smug and relaxed.

"So are you going to tell me what he did?" Skyler pleaded. "I feel like a little kid listening to a bedtime story."

"Yep...I'll tell you how Marty Hogan became the greatest racquetball player the world has ever seen. Do you want to get showered and get out of here first?" James said, obviously enjoying the moment with his young friend.

"No! I'm fine. I'm all ears!" Skyler said, clearly not going anywhere.

"Okay, okay...Marty Hogan decided ahead of every game that he wasn't going to be surprised by anything. *Anything can happen*, he would tell himself as he entered the court. Instead of being irate if his opponent made a bunch of obviously lucky shots, he just refused to be surprised. He had the genius to recognize that the game of racquetball has too many variables to be completely predictable. So he embraced the variety and learned to enjoy the game.

"When he made lucky shots, he would smile and accept the gift. When his opponents made lucky or great shots, he would accept the moment for what it was: *anything can happen*. Marty Hogan learned to play without fear and with complete acceptance and focus. He would have made our Hindu friends proud."

"That is probably the best advice I've ever heard," Skyler said. "I can see what happened. By telling himself that anything can happen, he prepared himself for any possibility. How can you get upset or question things when you've already anticipated everything. You're right, it's ingenious."

James looked at Skyler and placed a hand on his shoulder. "Skyler, when you attempt interstellar flight, I guarantee you that anything can happen. You will need to be ready for that. Everything depends on it. Everything depends on your knowing, expecting, and accepting that anything can happen."

As they packed up their bags and prepared to leave, a large young man of obvious Tongan descent, approached them. "James, my man, we have someone for you to play."

"Sorry, Lavaka, I'm beat," James said. "My friend Skyler here just worked me over."

"Yo, we watched the match. That was some amazing shot on the last point he made. Even Denny was clapping. He said he's never seen that before, and Denny over there is a *professional* racquetball player."

The young Tongan pointed to the juice bar, where Denny lifted a glass and smiled. "Denny is a good friend of my cousins. He's ranked number seven in the world, and he wants to play you."

"Wow, why would he be interested in playing an old timer like me?" James asked.

"Because we paid him to come here from San Diego and play you...that's why."

Skyler stopped and put down his gym bag. "Let me get this straight. You hired a professional top-ten racquetball player to come here and play James? Why in the hell would you do that?"

"Oh, that's simple, man, because we want to see what Mr. James does when he loses, and this time he *will* lose."

Denny made his way over to Lavaka. "Hi, my name is Denny. You must be James. I've heard a lot about you."

"Apparently, you have, but this is an obvious mistake. I'm not in your league. I'm just an old amateur who's good at beating a bunch of weekend gym players."

"I just watched you play, and you're better than that. I think it would be fun. What do you say? Best of five to fifteen?"

"How much did they pay you?" Skyler asked. "I'm just curious what the going price is for a hired racquetball gun?"

"Well, that's not really any of your business, now is it?" Denny said. "I'm just looking for a friendly game of racquetball. I think the members would enjoy it. I do exhibitions all the time, so it's no big deal."

James noticed the agitation, so he turned for the locker room and said, "I appreciate the offer, but I'm too old for exhibition racquetball games with world-class players. Thanks, but let's just say you won."

"Hey, hold it, bro," Lavaka said, standing in front of James. "You got a lot of friends here and some not-so-much-friends that don't like you. You walk away, and people are going to say that you're good at playing people you can beat, but playing someone that will kick yo ass, well, then you just chicken shit. Don't expect any friendly local hospitality here no more if you walk away."

"Hey, wait a minute," Skyler said, stepping between James and Lavaka. "This is racquetball, not some local brawl. Just step aside."

As Lavaka reached for Skyler, James reacted, "Oh, what the hell, Skyler. This could actually be fun. Lavaka, lighten up. I'll play your friend. After he makes mince meat out of me, we can sit around and have a good laugh."

"Now that's my man," Lavaka said, grinning from ear to ear and moving Skyler to the side with his belly.

This guy is like a big goofy bear, Skyler thought to himself.

Lavaka rubbed James' shoulders as a crowd formed. "Let's get you ready, bro."

Denny entered the court to warm up as James and Skyler watched. Soon the main room and adjacent café overlooking court number one had filled with spectators. People were running in and out of the gym and within ten minutes, the place was packed. Even the upper weight room area was loaded with people hanging over the railings.

"He's good," James said to Skyler. "I can tell already from watching him warm up."

"Let's just get this over with, so we can appease the restless natives. I'm buying dinner, win or lose," Skyler said, trying to make light of the whole thing.

James put on a dry glove, did some stretches and turned to face the crowd before entering the court. He held up both arms and waved with his racquet. "I go like a lamb to the slaughter," he yelled. Laughter filled the room.

Denny won the first game quickly to Lavaka's delight. He pranced out of the court, drank some water and began chit chatting. It was an obvious stall tactic designed to get James upset while he waited for the next game.

"Oh, I'm sorry," Denny said to James. "Look, you don't need to keep playing if you don't want to."

James had seen this before and just winked at Skyler. "No, that's all right, we might as well finish what we started. I expect more of the same, but this is kind of fun."

"Okay. But if I win the next game that easily, I may have to charge you for a lesson."

Skyler noticed a subtle change in James' attitude. He'd seen it before when James focused on something serious.

James walked to Skyler and said, "I learned a few things in that first game. The next one may not be as easy for him. It'll be interesting to see how he handles the pressure."

The next game was close, with James winning 15/13 to everyone's surprise, especially Denny's. Now it was James' turn to stall as he engaged in small talk with some friends.

"Let's go!" Denny yelled. "I need to get this over with now. I have a date in thirty minutes." Denny was losing points outside the court.

James won the next game easily, 15/6 to the astonishment of everyone, including Skyler. In the next game, Denny was dead serious. He won the hard fought battle 15/10.

James stepped outside the court and spotted Skyler. He could tell by the desperation in his eyes that Skyler was looking for inspiration. James wouldn't let him down. The next game was going to be a war, and the crowded gym of excited spectators had no idea what was metaphorically taking place.

With Denny ahead 9/6 in the final game, James hit four straight service winners to jump into a quick lead 10/9. Denny called time out and stormed from the court, throwing his racquet. "This guy is the luckiest son of a bitch I've ever played."

James smiled at the comment by his rattled opponent who was five points from loosing. James had expected anything to happen. Denny, on the other hand, had expected to win. It was another tight, hard-fought game, but Denny choked twice on critical shots, handing the game to James 15/14.

James tried to shake hands, but Denny ignored him. James calmly retrieved the ball and waved through the large glass window at the stunned crowd.

"This is yours," said James, tossing the ball to Denny. "You're a great player."

"Yo da man, bro," Lavaka said and gave James a big bear hug as he exited the court. "I'll be damned, yo da man."

Denny was still in the court furiously hitting the ball and swearing.

"That boy's as good as anyone I've played," James said. "He should be proud of himself."

"Yeah, but he's not seeing it that way right now, bro."

As James and Skyler were leaving, Denny finally came out of the court and yelled, "James...nice game."

James waved, then turned back and put his arm around the shoulder of his astronaut friend. "Skyler, I want you to take care of Acharya. I'm frightened as hell, but I know you guys will be fine."

Skyler called Anchor and asked her to meet him at his apartment. When he arrived, Anchor was already inside using his computer. *How does she get in?* he asked himself. *I've never given her a key.*

"You should have seen it!" Skyler said as he crashed onto the couch. "A bunch of Tongan racquetball players hired a professional player to come here and beat James. I had no idea he was that good. Who would have thought a fifty-seven-year-old physicist could play racquetball like he does. He's not just good, he's smart and fast. I haven't lost that bad in years. Anyway, he's been cleaning the clocks of these young hotshot players at the club, and so they brought in a hired gun to take him down."

Anchor was listening with a smile, but she wasn't as enthusiastic as Skyler had hoped. "So James beat a professional player? How is that possible?" she asked.

"You've got me, but he won by one point in the fifth game. It was amazing!"

"I got the job today," Anchor said in a sudden change of subject.

Skyler was about to give more details about the game when he stopped in midstream. "Huh? What job?" he asked.

"The House of the Sun. I got the position at the observatory on Maui. Now I can keep an eye on you the whole time you're gone. No chance for any alien space bunny encounters because I'll be watching."

"When do you start?"

"In two weeks. I wanted to start later, but the position is open now, so I need to take it."

"That's great news, Anchor, but I was hoping we could spend more time together before the launch, and James will want to keep you on the team," Skyler said sadly.

"They don't need me any longer, and after the launch, it's just a waiting game, a twelve-year waiting game. I need this job to keep me busy while I'm waiting for you to come back to me."

Skyler knew it was time to have the difficult talk. "Look, Anchor, it's not right for me to expect you to wait that long. You're a young, beautiful girl and..."

"Don't you dare even go there, Skyler Anderson!" she interrupted.

"I love you. Can you understand that? Besides, when you return, we'll both be the same age. No more cradle robbing, and I'll be a lot wiser and prettier."

"I'm sure you will," Skyler said with apprehension.

"What, you don't think I'm pretty and wise enough now?"

"Funny, Anchor, very funny. You're a master at setting these traps. I'm just saying that for me it's just a quick trip into space and back, but for you this is a multi-year expedition. Hey, I think I'll just insist that you go with me."

"If I could, I'd go in a heart beat, darling. Don't worry about me. I'd planned to focus on my career for the next twelve years anyway. You just came along too early and messed things up. Now everything will be as it should."

They heard someone clumping up the stairs to the condo. He knocked on the door briefly and crashed his way in going directly for the fridge.

"Hi guys," Strant said. "What's up?"

They both laughed. "Strant, my friend, you have perfect timing," Skyler said.

"Whoops, why, were you two about to have sex or something?"

"No, Strant, we're just happy to see you—that's all," Anchor said. "Come sit on the couch with us."

She regarded Skyler and he nodded for her to continue. "Skyler is going away for a while, and I'm taking a job at the observatory on Maui."

"What? When? Why?"

"Well, I'm leaving for Maui in two weeks, but Skyler isn't leaving for about two months. I'll try to get back as often as I can."

"Hey, you guys can use my helicopter any time. Don't even bother to ask, Skyler, just take it when you need it."

"Oh thank you, Strant!" Anchor said and kissed him on the cheek.

Skyler glanced at his friend with approval. They had been friends long enough to read each other's body language.

"So where you going, Sky? How long will you be gone?"

"You've *got* to keep this a dead secret, Strant. Can you do that?"

"Sure. You know me by now. They couldn't torture it out of me if it's that important."

"Okay, pal. I have a job as a...test pilot, you could say. I'm flying a spacecraft to Alpha Centauri."

Strant burst into tears of laughter as he slid onto the floor and put his head between his knees. "You guys are good. This is like old times. Seen any more weird rainbows?"

Neither Skyler nor Anchor was laughing. They looked at each other and at Strant on the floor without responding.

"Ah, come on, you can't be serious. Do you have any idea what I have been through trying to figure out that damn rainbow? Now you're telling me that you're going off with aliens, when we know the whole alien thing was a big fraud...it was a fraud, wasn't it?"

"Oh yeah, Strant, it was a fraud. I can guarantee that. We were working with the team of scientists that uncovered that fraud."

"You two were involved with those guys?" Strant jumped to his feet. "I knew it! I just knew it. I even asked Acharya, but couldn't get squat out of him. Okay, so if you aren't flying an alien spaceship, then what are you flying, a rainbow beam?"

"The space probe that uncovered the alien plot wasn't launched from Helios as everyone thinks. It was built with a new technology developed by my friend James and his elite team of scientists and engineers."

"I knew that the Helios theory wasn't possible." Strant said. "That was pathetic—so what you're saying is that the same technology used to uncover the alien plot can also be used to build a manned spacecraft. Is that right?"

"That's exactly right," Anchor said. "Skyler and Acharya have been selected to make the first flight, which will be to Alpha Centauri."

Again, Strant fell silent and looked down with concern. "Oh shit, if that's true, then you'll be gone for a long time. How fast will you be traveling?"

"We'll be traveling near the speed of light," Skyler said. "So we'll be there and back soon, from our perspective, but..."

"I know," Strant said. "To Anchor and me it will be a long time."

"Almost twelve years round trip," Anchor said.

"This is too much. I just stopped by for a beer. What the hell kind of technology can propel a spaceship safely near the speed of light?"

"Trust me, Strant. They've done it. You would not believe the brainpower on that team. They've built the ship. Only a few people on Earth even know about the project. Now, my friend, you are one of them. My job is to take her out and back safely. It's as simple as that."

Strant made a slow whistle and sat back down next to Anchor. "These are amazing times we're living in."

The room fell silent. In time, Strant rolled his eyes and said, "Okay fine, I'll do it. I'll take care of Anchor for you. That's the least I can do. I need a new girlfriend anyway. My last one left for Brazil."

"Oh, that's funny, Strant. Try to understand that when I return, I'll be the same age, and you'll be twelve years older. You try that and I'll just kick your old ass around the block a few times," Skyler said with a wide grin.

They laughed briefly and were again silent. Eventually Strant spoke once more. "So does that rainbow have anything to do with this technology? Is that what happened?"

"Nope. Unfortunately, that isn't the answer. Even these guys, the best physicists ever assembled couldn't figure that one out. It's still a mystery. But James did promise me that he'd find the answer before I return."

"Why Alpha Centauri?" Strant asked.

"That was my idea," Anchor said. "James let me choose. Alpha Centauri is the nearest star system to the sun. That gets Skyler back to me in twelve years. With other star systems, he'd be returning to an old lady or just a memory. Luckily it's also one of the most interesting destinations.

"Alpha Centauri is one of the few places we know of, in the entire Milky Way Galaxy, that may offer terrestrial life conditions. It's is a triple star system: Alpha Centauri A, Alpha Centauri B, and Alpha Centauri C (also called Proxima). Alpha Centauri A is a yellow star with a spectral type of G2, like our sun.

"In other words, its color and temperature match those of the sun. Its diameter is a close match as well, just a little larger. Alpha Centauri B is an orange star with a spectral type of K1. Although slightly smaller and dimmer than the sun, its composition is still similar as well.

"So both Alpha Centauri A and B are stars very much like our sun. The other star in the system is called Proxima. This star is a small and dim red dwarf with a much cooler spectral type of M5. I don't think we'll find much of interest there, but you never know."

Skyler could see Strant focusing on every word, so he sat there and let Anchor continue without interruption. "Acharya knows a lot about star systems that might have life, so we worked on this together. Basically, a star system must pass five tests before it's considered a promising place for terrestrial life.

"Most stars, or star systems, in the entire galaxy fail these tests. But in the case of Alpha Centauri, Alpha Centauri A passes each of the five tests, Alpha Centauri B passes all but one, and poor little Proxima fails completely. The tests applied here are stability, spectral type, brightness variance, age, and enough heavy elements. We already know from the Planet Finder project that there are planets revolving in this star system.

"So when they get there, it's at least possible that we may discover some form of terrestrial life, and that makes the journey even more interesting. We have James' approval to show you around the development center. You'll freak out over the technology these guys have invented. Besides, Skyler wants you there for the launch."

Strant slipped into the last parking space at the park on Hanalei Bay. He jumped out and into a muddy puddle without caring to notice. He grabbed his surfboard from the back of his rusty new truck, tossed his keys under a dirty towel and set out past the rest rooms and onto the park grass.

He paused at the outdoor showers and splashed around, not for any particular reason other than it felt good and gave him a chance to check out the girls of the day. He glanced back toward the parking lot and noticed the large old-style and over extravagant house adjacent to the park.

The well-kept, usually empty house was a curiosity to Strant. According to rumor, a young Steve Jobs had built the house only to lose interest after realizing that he had spent a fortune building a house too near to the public restrooms.

For some reason, the thought made Strant smile. *What a dork*, he thought to himself, not knowing for sure if the rumor was true but not wanting to find out—preferring the tale of stupidity.

"Hi, Strant, what are you smiling about?" The woman entering the opposing shower was in her early twenties, well built and wearing something less than a bikini.

"Uh, oh hi, Becky. I was just thinking how lucky I would be if I could see you today."

"That's sweet, Strant. What were you really smiling about?"

"That big house." Strant gave Becky a quick history lesson.

"That's hilarious. I can't wait to tell my friends."

"Yeah, I guess that's how rumors spread," Strant said.

He watched the sexy girl run away, onto the sand and down the beach.

That's a pleasant sight, he thought as he picked up his board and headed toward the pier.

After a quarter mile, he jumped up onto the wooden boardwalk. A man dressed in partial naval clothing stepped in front of him and blocked his way.

"Do I know you?" Strant asked.

"No, but I know you. In fact, I know everything about you. You're a friend of Skyler Anderson."

"He's no friend of mine." Strant had a habit of throwing people off who approached him too abruptly.

"Isn't your name Mike Stranton?" the Admiral asked.

"Yep, sure is. And to whom do I owe the pleasure of keeping me from my waves?"

"The name's not important, son, but I am in a position to provide you with some extra spending money. All I need is a little cooperation."

"Spending money? Wow, now that's just what I need today."

"Let's cut to the chase. I need you to gather some information for me about the project Skyler is working on. If you cooperate, I give you a carrot. If you don't, I give you a stick."

"Hmmm, okay. Walk with me, and we can talk business," Strant said, jumping off the pier.

"You will be doing both yourself and your country a service," the man said, trying to keep pace.

Strant turned quickly; his surfboard swung close to the Admiral's head. "So how much extra spending money are we talking about, and what is the stick if I don't cooperate?"

"If you deliver the information I need, I'm prepared to pay...twenty thousand dollars, cash."

"And if I don't cooperate?" Strant asked in a soft voice.

"Now, let's not even talk about that. I apologize for putting it that way. I can see we're making progress, so let's just talk about getting you that money."

"Oh, no, that's okay. I like to know my options. So c'mon now, let's have the bad news with the good."

"I have cash in my pocket that I would like to give you right now."

"The question remains," said Strant, "What happens if I fail to cooperate?"

"It's quite simple, Mr. Stranton. If you do not cooperate, you will force us to break both of your legs. That would be bad for your surfing."

"Who is this we?" Strant said looking around. "Well, hey, I believe you. Would you be willing to make it quick? I hate the anticipation of suffering more than the suffering."

The Admiral reached in his pocket and pulled out a weathered brown wallet. "Here's five thousand dollars. Think of this as down payment in good faith. You get the rest when I get some answers."

"Okay, so let me get this straight; I spy on Skyler, and you give me 20K, and you become my friend. Is that about right?"

"Yes, absolutely. I would become your good friend," the Admiral said.

"Cool. Tell ya what, give me your phone number and address, and we can finish this after I get through surfing."

"That is not possible. I contact you, you cannot contact me."

"Well, what the hell kind of friendship is that?" Strant asked in a mock stunned reaction.

"You obviously *do not* understand the seriousness of your situation. I work for people very high in the federal government. I can make people disappear. Nevertheless, if you help us out, you are only serving your country, and no one will be hurt. Are you a patriot, Mr. Stranton?"

"Why are you dressed like that? Are you former navy or something?" Strant asked.

The Admiral seemed puzzled at the sudden change of topic. "I *am* navy, on special assignment to the President. Is that clear enough?"

"Well, my philosophy is why join the navy when you can be a pirate," Strant said, putting the cash in his pocket. *If ever there was a dude in need of vilipending...*

"I don't follow," the Admiral said.

"Do you see that old mangy dog wandering toward the cars?"

The Admiral turned to look. "Yeah, I see him. So what?"

"What I want you to do is—"

The loud public shark-warning-horn interrupted.

"—just follow him out of my sight. Oh, and you were right, Skyler *is* my friend, you insignificant twerp." Strant turned and walked away with the money. *Today I'm a pirate. Take what you can and give nothing back,* Strant said within himself.

The Admiral was furious at first but then he laughed. He was wasting his time with this man. *I will enjoy dealing with this impudence later*, he thought.

Strant reached his spot and dropped his surfboard on the sand. When he leered back, the Admiral was gone. Beyond the beach, in the shade of the trees, he noticed an old homeless-looking man dressed in a yellow robe. Strant crossed the sand and approached the old man, who was sitting with his legs folded and sleeping in an upright position.

The old monk opened his eyes and fell backward, apparently startled to see Strant standing before him.

"Sorry, old timer. I didn't mean to scare you."

Strant kneeled down and pulled open the old man's right hand. He folded in the Admiral's wad of cash and gently closed the wrinkled fingers. "Sleep well tonight," Strant whispered.

The *Keeper* watched as the surfer turned and strolled whistling through the shadows toward the beach. He continued watching with curiosity as the young man paddled out to sea.

TWENTY

The Newport Beach Executive Suite business center was just minutes from the John Wayne Airport. James walked toward the reflective blue class building, still groggy from his all-night flight. Months earlier, while analyzing Skyler's rainbow, he had solicited the help of a few good friends. Mike Shortino was the best scientific investigator James had ever known. James sent him the rainbow photos, but Mike had not responded.

Then, yesterday, Mike had called James in the middle of the night, early morning West Coast time. "How soon can you get here? I've found something we should talk about in private."

"Uh, who is this?" James asked, confused.

"It's Mike. We need to talk about those rainbow photos you sent me. I've found something."

"Let's see...what time is it? Oh, okay, I'll catch a flight tonight," James said, trying to clear his head. "I have too much going on today, but I'll fly out tonight. What did you find?"

"Let's talk when you get here. Can you stay for a day? I'll book you into the old Newport Beach Balboa Inn; I know it's your favorite."

"Yeah, sure, that would be fine. I could use the time off," James said.

❦

When James entered the offices of *Hoover's Research Cell,* a pleasant woman with plump cheeks shuffled him directly into a large, empty meeting room. Moments later, Mike entered the room from the opposite side. His long gray hair was combed straight back, and he was wearing a casual shirt and well-worn Levis. The lights in the room slowly dimmed and a projection screen slid down from the wall.

Mike grabbed James' arm and shook his hand, obviously pleased to see his friend again. "Great to see you, James. I've something to show you."

"It's good to see you again, Mike. What have you got?"

"When I first looked at your photos, I was pretty certain they were contrived. I even put them aside for a while. However, because of my respect for you, I decided to engage in a little investigative research. Your photos are legitimate. There's no doubt that this was an actual event."

"How can you know that?" James asked, surprised at the confidence in Mike's voice.

"It's pretty simple actually. Take a look."

The room darkened and with a couple of console clicks, a presentation started on the screen. An image of the rainbow, in the middle of its transition, displayed clearly. James stared at the slide and noticed the obvious difference. This wasn't one of Skyler's photos. The mountains behind the rainbow weren't those of Kauai's Na Pali coastline.

"Holy Shit! Where and when?" James yelled.

"This is a small island in Thailand's southern Tarutao National Park. Here's another in Scotland, and another in New Zealand."

"So these events are occurring over the entire planet?" James asked.

"No, not occurring anymore. These events happened at the same time, give or take a few hours because of the duration. This was a single global event."

With a slow whistle, James tried to consider what this meant. There was no longer a question of fabrication, but the mystery had expanded.

"Do you have anything else? Any idea what might have caused this?"

"Oh, we have a lot more information. That's why I wanted to talk with you in person. That, and the need for security. Apparently, we, and now you, are the only ones that know about this. I was convinced that it had something to do with the supposed alien visitors, so I was tenacious about secrecy. When the alien scam was exposed I was stumped," Mike said, shaking his head.

"So what caused this? What else do you have?" James asked, unable to quell his enthusiasm.

Mike regarded James for a long time before responding. "I propose we share information. You know damn well that probe you sent to the moon wasn't launched from some glorified high-flying kite. I want to know what's going on."

James plopped down in a chair and put his feet up on the table. "You never cease to surprise me. I remember our days at tech. You were by far the most observant of us all."

"James, you taught me a lesson back then, a lesson I've never forgotten. Do you remember the day professor Warnock laid into you? He said you were the most independent person he had ever met, incapable of teamwork. I took notes that day. I still remember exactly what you wrote on the board. Hell, you walked to the blackboard and wrote: *Can a team player exercise poetic license, or is such a thought just bumptious idiocy?* You challenged the class members to choose. When most of us selected bumptious idiocy, out of fear of reprisal from Warnock, you circled the word *team* and said, 'Without individual poetic license, this team is just a bunch of losers clumped together.' Warnock was furious."

"Yeah, I do remember that day," James said. "He called it the last straw and kicked me out of his business class, saving me the agony of his attempted brainwashing. He had the gull to ask how I felt about being expelled."

"I didn't hear about that. What did you say?"

"I told him the truth. I said he was the dumbest smart person I'd ever met."

Mike chuckled and put his feet up on the table as well. "So what's going on, James? Have you found a poetic team? Have you discovered something?"

"I'd love to tell you, Mike, but this is top secret stuff. The cat will be out of the bag soon enough, but, yes, I do have a poetic team, the best the world has ever assembled. We call ourselves the Babylonians."

Mike understood. "That makes sense. You leaned in that direction from the first day I met you. So what should we do? It seems we have a stalemate."

"Let me think about it. Perhaps I can come up with a solution. Can we start again tomorrow?" James asked.

The next morning, James arose early, grabbed a muffin from the lobby, and walked out the door across the wide sidewalk to the adjacent beach. He stumbled across the deep soft sand, past the volleyball nets, and down to the ocean and the harder wet surface.

After stretching, he set off in a jog with the sunrise to his left. Ten minutes later, his creative subconscious self began to emerge and the difficulty and pain from physical exertion faded. James had discovered long ago that he was discernibly two people: the rational, arrogant, practical, analytical self; and the reclusive, creative, carefree self. Genius finds a way to balance the two. James the Rational, with a little prodding from James the Creative, had decided years before that he needed to be both his own worst critic and his own best friend. For now at least, his rational, practical self was being a best friend to his subconscious creative. "Thanks, buddy," he heard himself say. "This is better. Now, we can think."

Given his workload before launch, why had he made this trip? What was it about the rainbow that interested him so much? The rainbow *had* brought him together with Skyler and Anchor, which was cause enough for him to like the rainbow, but there was something else, something emotional. Why would he like the rainbow? It was something to admire for its natural beauty, but why like it? James the Rational knew that this was the true reason for his success and failure in life: his creative, curious self was definitely strange and unusual.

Thinking about the rainbow again, he considered the obvious. His dog, Data, was a beautiful animal, but he would have liked that goofy creature regardless. How had he known that there was more to this rainbow than an isolated aberration? How had he known it was real?

He made a decision to bring Mike on board and tell him everything about the project. He was prone to risky decisions that could either reward or harm. Decisions of the heart outweighing decisions of the rational: the story of his life. Yet James knew there was something important about the rainbow and he was willing to take a chance for more information.

In the distance, standing in the parking lot near a weathered church, the old monk gazed toward the ocean and the early risers speckled across the beach. He watched

James jogging on the beach with admiration. The *Keeper* of the Gateless Gate knew why James was here. He also knew that the secret of the rainbow was well beyond human knowledge. And yet...even the rainbow was not beyond their scrutiny or understanding if they could gather and interpret enough data.

There was a remote possibility that someone might solve the mystery, and that someone was most likely James. In that case, the answer might disseminate. He would never allow that to happen, of course. No, the mystery of the rainbow would remain a mystery to the continual demise of the most dangerous enemy humankind had ever encountered. However, these curious people, like James, these modern Babylonians: *They are remarkable. No, not remarkable*, the *Keeper* thought to himself in unbreakable quantum-encrypted thoughts. *No, these people are foundational.*

Later that day, James met with Mike again. "Before we start, I just want to let you know that I'm willing to share everything I know about the rainbows—without strings," Mike said.

"I had a hunch you'd say that, and I've decided to bring you on board anyway. If you can come to Kauai next week, you're in for a real treat," James responded with a smile. The two friends laughed and kicked back as the room darkened and the screen came down.

"From what we can determine, these rainbow effects are the result of some kind of storm. We haven't been able to determine the source or the nature of the storm. What we know for sure is that this was a global disruption. Notice how the direction was the same for each of the rainbows.

The patterns were identical across the board. Every rainbow in existence at this moment, as far as we know, was altered. We found that they had to be viewed from the same relative angle and direction across this worldwide grid, and that reduced the total number of rainbows to just a handful."

Mike zoomed in on a diagram with his mouse pointer and then continued. "There were other more subtle disruptions as well."

"Let me guess: there were magnetic disruptions and interference with liquid motions," James said.

"Exactly right, but the changes to the ocean were very quiet and sporadic."

"So what kind of force can cause these changes?" James asked.

"Nothing we currently know of. There are many forces in the universe that we can't explain, though. Now, we have another."

"Here's an odd question," James said. "Is there any way this storm could cause a change in emotion, a calming effect?"

"I don't follow," Mike said.

"There was talk of being able to feel something unusual by some of the witnesses in Kauai. Did you gather anything like that with these other events?"

Mike scanned through his notes. "Actually, we did, from one other source. But with no other reports in hand, we ignored that data. It looks like we have another symptom to deal with."

James stood up and paced in front of the screen as the projector cast a silhouette of his head. "So what kind of storm force can alter light waves, static electricity, ocean activity, *and* human emotions?"

"Hey, wait," Mike said. "There was research done in Russia on the influence of electromagnetic fields on the emotional behavior of rats. If I recall, lower EMR frequency of modulations decreased the emotionally negative reactions such as fear. Higher EMR frequency increased fear."

"So what we have then is just further evidence of the reality of this event," James said softly.

"Apparently," Mike nodded in the affirmative.

"I have one other question. When you look at that video of the rainbow, does it elicit any emotions?"

"It does indeed," Mike said. "I remember now... that's why we ignored our lone witness that said she felt something unusual at the time. Visuals cause various kinds of emotions. It turns out that this particular rainbow effect is enjoyable. People like to watch it. So given the additional electromagnetic changes, we probably have a collection of satisfied witnesses."

"That's helpful to know. So I'm assuming that you have no more shocking information to share with me, is that correct?" James asked.

"That's not entirely correct. According to my physicists, the storm was some kind of aftershock."

"An aftershock? From what?"

"It came from somewhere in our solar system. Given the rapidity of disintegration and the speed of light, we know this was a local event. As to what caused the storm, we have no idea. And that, my friend, is as much as we know at this time."

❦

That evening James called Skyler. "Well, it's great to know I'm not losing my mind," Skyler yelled into his cell phone from the windy beach. "I'm meeting Strant tonight. I'll spread the good news."

"Happy to help, Skyler, but I never had any doubts. I think we should keep this to our friends and family though. We'll be making enough news as it is without stirring up more ideas of mysterious aliens or whatever the heck this is. That could get a lot of people angry with us and question our entire mission, especially after the government's alien debacle. Right now, we're the good guys. I say we keep it that way."

"I couldn't agree more. I need to run. There's a storm coming. Hey, you have a safe trip home — and thanks again," Skyler shouted.

James spent the rest of his time in Newport visiting old sites from his younger days. He had lived in Newport Beach after graduation and worked for a research company in Anaheim. He hated the freeway drive back and forth, but enjoyed living close to the ocean, making the sacrifice bearable.

Now, back in this place of vivid memories, James wandered aimlessly down the pastel beach town. He no longer drank, but for old time's sake, he decided to drop by Blackie's, a beach pub and local hangout. It was amazing that the place was still in business after so many years.

Upon leaving, he noticed an obstreperous group of bikini clad college girls playing on the beach. *It was fun back then.*

His creative self was in full control as he worked his way up the beach toward his hotel. Focusing on what he had learned about the rainbows, his mind explored the vast possibilities. *The rainbows dissolved, as if scattered by random time-delays in the visibility of the reflections. What kind of aftershock would scatter time fragments? Perhaps the initial event occurred sometime in the past. Okay, wait, what am I missing?* Out of his abstract thought, he barely noticed the old man dressed in a yellow robe walking toward him through the encroaching ocean mist. But when the old man smiled, the perfection of his teeth startled James back to the present.

Do I know this man? James thought to himself. He smiled back as the yellow-robed man came directly toward him, paused and bowed. "Most variations are normal and acceptable, but some are not," the old man said. "I will make no change. Please go with wisdom." The monk patted James on the shoulder and continued down the beach.

What did he say? James pondered. After a while he glanced back, but the old man was gone. *Now that was weird.* He remembered the old monk that Anchor had told him about. "He had a perfect smile and the teeth of a young man," she had said. *Well, apparently these Buddhist monks take good care of their teeth,* James mused.

Continuing on, he speculated once more on the impossible. Slowly, an image formed in his mind, an image of a prior event that had altered the future: the now. His mind roamed deeper to an event that was massive, a catastrophe that impacted the very fabric of time. This was no accident, it was the result of an intelligence, a predetermined purpose that either succeeded or went awry.

Perhaps it was the inevitable nature of a man who could crash through the limitations of human understanding, or perhaps it was just a combination of random events that enabled a prodigiously intelligent man to stumble upon the answer. Either way, James had a moment of inspiration. *Best to keep this theory to myself,* he thought.

❧

A heavy downpour made visibility difficult; the plane landed hard on the Lihue airport tarmac. Silvia and Data were waiting for James in their car. As always, Data demanded first attention.

"How was your trip?" Silvia asked. "Did you see any of your old girlfriends?" Data tilted his head and waited for an answer.

"N-no. And you're right, they'd be old by now," James retorted.

"Some military men came to the house asking me questions," Silvia said, obviously troubled.

"What kind of questions?"

"They asked me about your time in Spain, and what I knew about habeas corpus. I heard one of them talking about the military commissions act. Why would they be thinking you're a terrorist?" Silvia seemed scared.

"You cut right to the chase. That's what I love about you. Don't worry, sweetheart. I'm sure it's nothing. Did they say they were coming back?"

"No, but funny you should ask because one of them kicked Data while they were leaving. I had a bad argument with them about that and told them they were not welcome at our home." Data perked up and the hair rose on his back, apparently understanding.

"I'll find out what's going on first thing tomorrow," James said.

Without warning, a half dozen military men stood in the rain surrounding their car. Data growled, then barked frantically as James rolled down the window. In the distance, an airport security guard noticed the noise and commenced walking across the parking lot.

"Hello, sir, are you James Stevenson?" the obvious leader asked.

"What's this about?" James asked abruptly.

"Please follow us to your home. We need to ask you a few questions."

"That's not going to happen, *Admiral*." James stressed the usage of the man's title. "If you want to speak with me then make an appointment." James handed him a business card and spoke in a stern voice. "Now move away, and do *not* follow us."

The Admiral jumped back, surprised, spotted the security guard, and then signaled to his men. As they moved to the side, James nodded to Silvia. Data managed one last angry bark.

As they drove home, James' ancient iPhone woke up and the voice of Yoda rang out repeatedly: *Ahhh, message from the dark side there is.* James fumbled for his phone in the dark before managing to answer. "We just spoke. Do not have the audacity to leave the island again." Before James could respond, the caller hung up.

For the next several days, James worked on tracking down the Admiral and his military squad, but they had disappeared. Eventually he forgot the incident and focused again on the project.

More money poured in from the investors, and the team received explicit instructions to spare no expense. The outside world received glimpses of the project's magnitude and intentions. Security walls and campus police surrounded the complex. Full construction of the *Hispaniola* was underway; humanity was on the precipice of its greatest adventure.

◦♪

Two months later, at a scheduled press conference, James stood before the cameras. "Ladies and gentlemen of the press, thank you for coming today. I believe you will find your time well spent. My name is James Stevenson. For the past two years, I have been in charge of a rare team of scientists, engineers, and programmers. As you may have guessed, this team sent a probe to the backside of the moon and exposed the unfortunate deception perpetrated on the world by the former American administration.

"There has been extensive speculation regarding the technical nature of that probe. I have read reports that suggest the Kauai probe was launched from a high-flying plane. I can tell you today that those articles and reports are in error. The moon probe lifted from the surface of the Earth less than three miles from here.

"There was no large chemical rocket used for launch. That is why the event went unnoticed by the United States military. This has been a privately funded project. With the support of the Hindu Church, a group of far thinking investors, and the team I affectionately refer to as the Babylonians, we have been able to engineer a technology that will enable mankind to achieve interstellar space travel within the next few months.

"You may find it ironic that the fraudulent alien encounter was exposed by a team of humans on the verge of traveling to the stars, and that man's first alien encounter will probably be far from the Earth. The first launch will send a pair of astronauts to our closest neighbor, Alpha Centauri: a star system over four light years away. Alpha Centauri holds much promise for reasons I will not bore you with at this time.

"With the approval of our host nation, the United States, a United Nations task force has been deployed to lock down 450 acres of privately held land for the purpose of protecting this launch site for the people of Earth. We are providing a technical document explaining the core technology behind the spacecraft now under construction. Since launching the moon probe, we have successfully committed three other unmanned craft.

"One of our probes circled Saturn and returned. Its maximum speed was 80% that of the speed of light. An unexpected and interesting result from that experiment is the discovery that Einstein was only partly right in his theory of relativity. Although traveling at 80% of the speed of light, the craft returned to Earth in one forth the expected time, relative to Earth. Traveling that fast presents problems because when an object approaches the speed of light, its mass approaches infinity. Our technology, described in the public document, captures the mass expansion as potential energy in a device we call a 'potacitor.'

"One unexpected by product of this stasis companionship is a relativity advantage. To quote one my most eloquent physicists, 'Strange stuff happens.' It seems that when an object approaches the speed of light without expanding, its original time source changes.

"Time on board the craft was even less, as correctly predicted by Einstein, but capturing the potential energy altered that time as well. What this means, in layman's terms, is that the expected time between round trips will be at least four times *less* for those of us waiting here on Earth. We will send a manned spacecraft on a round trip to Alpha Centauri, and the craft will return to Earth three years later. That's four times the speed of light according to contemporary thinking. Time on board the spacecraft will be in days for the two astronauts.

"There's a useful byproduct from our potacitor solution. The world's scientists will have fun chewing on this. As I mentioned, the potacitor captures the mass expansion in the form of potential energy as we approach the speed of light. When our probe returned from Saturn, it had more stored energy than when it left, resulting in the world's first truly perpetual device. I should note that some of the excess energy was used as a shunt to protect the probe from space debris."

James paused and surveyed the stupefied audience. Taking his time, he smiled and relaxed before continuing. "In honor of an ancestor of mine, Robert Louis Stevenson, we have named our first manned craft the *Hispaniola*. We are going treasure hunting, ladies and gentlemen, and the treasure we seek is an island in the sky.

"We intend to explore the wonder of a vast new star system. Although our first launch is manned by a pair of Americans, our full team, the Babylonians, are from many countries. This is not an American launch, this is an Earth launch, and all the people of our isolated planet should take pride in this accomplishment. Thank you and goodbye for now."

TWENTY-ONE

Skyler studied the instruments again in his mind. The entire ship's controls were committed to memory. He could fly the *Hispaniola* in his sleep. The flight simulators were the best in the world, and he had made good use of them. His confidence was growing in himself, his ship, his support team, and his companion, Acharya.

Acharya was a big part of his new enthusiasm. Together, they were the perfect combination of flying skills and knowledge. It was as if Acharya had been born for this mission. He enjoyed telling Skyler about the great astronauts of the past like Neil Armstrong. The stories gave him inspiration. "Let's light this candle," he had once said to James, an obvious reference to Alan Shepard's remarks while waiting on the launch pad for America's first manned space flight.

Anchor was beside herself with excitement when she found out that Skyler would return in three years instead of twelve. She squealed and jumped up and down. To the men's delight, she ran around kissing the members of the team. "The women in my church wait almost that long for their missionaries to return. Not that you'd qualify, Skyler, unless the missionary sex position counts." Nervous laughter filled the room. Normally restrained around the team, she was buoyant and could care less.

"Anchor," Skyler responded in a soothing tone he reserved for these moments. "Three years is still a long time. I can't ask you to wait that long."

"You said it again!" she snapped. "You are so infuriating! Do you think I'm a child, incapable of making my own decisions? This is not complicated, Skyler. I'm waiting for you."

"You're right, Anchor," Skyler admitted. "I want you to wait for me. If I came back in ten days and you were with someone else...what the hell was I thinking?"

"Make love to me—now!" said Anchor.

"Here?" Skyler replied, glancing around the room for a soft spot.

"No, not here, stupid. At the top of Waialeale canyon. You know, the place you call *poko-point*. I love poko-point."

Somewhere in the room, the sound of a spinning chair remained; the last sign of a room recently occupied with other people.

"Where's Skyler?" James asked the group of men huddled in the kitchen area.

"Just a guess, but he's probably on his way to the top of the grand canyon of the Pacific," Isaac said.

"What the hell is he doing up there? I need to go over these comps with him!" James said abruptly.

"Trust me, boss, you can wait. He's with Anchor."

"Oh," James said, calming down and acknowledging the suppressed humor in the crowd. "I see. Yeah, I can wait," he said with a chuckle.

As he walked away, Acharya followed. "You seem tense, James. What is going on?"

"Oh, nothing, I just want to do everything I can to give you two the best shot at success."

"The awakened sages call a person wise when all his undertakings are free from anxiety about results; all his selfish desires have been consumed in the fire of knowledge."

"The Bhagavad-Gita?" James asked.

"Correct, boss. You know me well. By the way, that was an interesting press conference you gave."

"What did you think of it?"

"Well it was certainly informative, I would say."

"Yeah, a little too informative. I know what you're thinking. I should have dumbed it down, too much technological jargon. I do that sometimes when I'm nervous. I'll do better next time."

"It matters not. You have provided much work for those responsible for translating for the general public," Acharya said with a smile.

"Good point, my friend," James laughed. "Next week, we launch. Any regrets?"

"No regrets, James. I was born for this. And thanks to you and the rest of the members of this amazing team, I can fulfill my destiny."

"You keep an eye on our boy up there. I'll be in a lot of trouble if you don't bring him home," James said.

"I have never seen anyone prepare as he has. I am quite sure that it is Skyler that will be keeping an eye on me. But I was wondering, do you think it is wise to have Anchor handling the CAPCOM during launch? If something happens..."

"She's the best we have, Acharya. I wish she would stay and work the entire flight. I'm confident in our starting team. Besides, having her there will help calm Skyler."

For the first time, the entire world watched an island launch. Unlike prior secluded launches, this was a major event. Press and observation facilities several hundred yards from the *Hispaniola* rumbled with activity. The craft didn't look the way a spacecraft should look to the eyes of the world and that caused no small amount of curiosity and commentary. Instead of a pointed, vertical, rocket-style spacecraft, the *Hispaniola* presented the strange image of a semi flying saucer with a sweptback tail. The design came from engineers spending too much time swimming with black Stingrays but worked perfectly with the potacitor technology.

After several delays caused by a major television network, the two Astronauts fidgeted with anxiety. Skyler couldn't resist the opportunity to quip, "Forget the press, let's light this candle."

Twenty seconds later, Anchor responded. "Countdown has commenced. We now have six minutes and counting for liftoff of the world's first interstellar spacecraft." *That sounded cool*, she thought to herself.

At two minutes, another pause occurred that sent James out of the control room, looking for the investor idiot that authorized a news organization to delay the flight. "Enough of this, gentlemen. I'm taking over the launch from here. We have plenty of cameras ready. If an organization is unprepared they can get copies from the others."

When the countdown started again, Skyler felt a tickle in his stomach. This was it, and he knew it. He turned and gave Acharya a wink. The astronaut monk seemed to like the reaction and returned the biggest smile Skyler had ever seen from his friend.

"Thirty seconds and counting," Anchor said.

"I was thinking about saying something clever when they hook us into the networks. Something like: *to boldly go where no man has gone before*," Skyler said.

"That may not be wise since *to boldly go* is a split infinitive," Acharya cautioned.

"What?"

"You are using a split infinitive, not to mention the obvious impression that women are excluded from such adventures. Since the entire world will be listening, you may want to find a slogan with improved grammar."

"You've *got* to be kidding! You're giving me lessons in speaking. I've heard you talk like a normal person, so I know you have it in you. Besides, if that's a split infinitive, whatever the hell that is, then it's a pretty famous one," Skyler shot back, trying to withhold a smile.

"I was merely suggesting that..."

"Oh, boys, we are now at ten seconds and holding," Anchor interrupted. "Anytime you're ready. I don't want to be rude, but the entire world is waiting while our two greatest explorers bicker over the English language."

"Yeah, good. Well let's go then," Skyler said.

"I do not mean to be disagreeable, but we were hardly bickering," Acharya added.

"I do not mean to be disagreeable? Who the hell talks like that?" Skyler said, getting in the last word.

"I'm going to miss the both of you. God speed, *Hispaniola*. We have ten seconds and counting."

As the countdown ticked off the final seconds, Skyler placed his right hand on the flight stick. Although the craft was set for automatic orbital injection, Skyler was having none of that. He had full authorization to take manual control at anytime, and he was planning to get a feel for his craft as soon as possible.

Anchor announced the anticlimactic launch. The *Hispaniola* lifted slowly from the ground, rising more like a hot air balloon than an explosive rocket-propelled vehicle that thrilled and excited spectators.

"It was an old, weathered fortuneteller," Skyler said to his CAPCOM.

"Repeat again," Anchor said.

"I was just a kid. I snuck off to the circus with some friends. An old fortuneteller grabbed me as we were running past. She offered to tell my fortune at no charge. I was scared at first, but my friends egged me on."

"Okay, sir, is there a problem?" Anchor asked, concerned.

"No problem. Everything is A-OK. Do you remember when we first met? I told you the meaning of your name. The scary wrinkled old woman turned out to be a kind, good-hearted grandma type. She told me that someday I would meet and fall in love with a girl whose name meant 'loved.' I begged her for the name until she told me: *Anchoret*. So you see, I've known you long before we ever met."

"Sir, this is an open communications. The whole world is listening."

"I want the world to know that I'm in love with you and that I will return from the stars to marry you."

There was a long pause before she responded, "Your message has been received and understood…and accepted," Anchor said with a choke in her voice. "Skyler, I love you, and I will love you for all time and all eternity."

"Roger that," Skyler said as he sought to get the feel of his ship.

Skyler flew the *Hispaniola* manually. As they pierced the Earth's atmosphere, their attention was transfixed on the sight of Earth rotating slowly below. "So, my friend, you've achieved your dream. Do you have anything profound to say?" Skyler asked Acharya.

"I believe it was Xenocrates who said, 'I have often regretted my speech, never my silence.'"

"Nice try," Skyler insisted, "let's have it."

"Well, I believed that we were predestined for this journey; then I caught myself looking both ways before crossing the street."

"Good point," Skyler chuckled.

"I was once convinced that traveling to other stars was something that would be gifted to us by an advanced civilization. To be more accurate, I was certain of this because the odds of us succeeding on our own were so low that they were best described as *impossible*."

"So what are your beliefs now?" Skyler asked as he slowed their assent and played with the controls.

"That is simple," Acharya said. "If not now, then when? If not us, then who?"

"Could not have said it better my sel..." Skyler stopped talking as their ship shuddered and warning lights flickered to life. "What the *hell* was that?"

"We have detected a laser beam fired directly at you from China! The beam is not visible from space. According to calculations, they must have partially overshot," Anchor was screaming.

"Line of sight!" Acharya said turning to Skyler.

"Gotcha. We're out of here," Skyler responded without hesitation. He spun the *Hispaniola* around and dove back to Earth at an eastward angle. In a normal craft, the massive g-force would have crushed the two pilots, but their Babylonian-built *Hispaniola* was compensating.

To the observers on Earth, the slow and friendly craft that rose calmly toward orbit had become a spitfire demon, nose-diving straight for Earth and traveling at over 160,000 miles per hour, far faster than any man made object had ever flown this close to the Earth before. An astonished news network immediately reported the catastrophic destruction of man's first starship. Minutes later, the breaking news changed to a heroic maneuver designed to survive a militant attack.

Unable to fire their destructive laser beams around the curvature of the Earth, the Chinese were presently reporting to their superiors a devastating failure, not the well-planned destruction they had expected. The Chinese had designated the Kauai project a direct threat from a *nationless terrorist organization*. They prepared to fire again when the spacecraft orbited back into view.

Flashing across the continental United States at an impossible atmospheric velocity, the *Hispaniola* left no doubt regarding its awesome technology. The inhabitants of Earth had a new story, a new mythical legend about their two, now famous, heroes. As Skyler crossed the eastern shore, he turned the craft upward again. The *Hispaniola* passed through the atmosphere and back into space so fast that the frantic news organizations were unable to report the new launch until much later. Using the Earth itself as a shield, the two heroes were well on their way into deep space, far out of range, before the Earth rotated the Chinese laser complex back into position.

"I must admit that was perhaps the best exhibition of flying the Earth has ever seen. You are magnificently quick on your feet," Acharya said, while trying to gain his breath.

"Whoa, this baby can fly," said Skyler.

Anchor cut in. "James has a big smile on his face, boys. You really put on a show. The whole world is a buzz. It was amazing!"

"Let's hope the worst is behind us. Thanks for the quick thinking down there. We had no idea what was happening," Skyler answered.

"You can thank James' friend Mike for that one. He's been following the activities of those creeps for years."

"A most fortunate addition to our team," Acharya said.

"Oh, how I wish I could be with you. What an adventure. Uh, hold please...James is insisting that I ask if there was any damage."

"No damage here," Skyler said. "All systems have auto reset. The *Hispaniola* is star bound again. Tell James thanks for the Marty Hogan tip, he'll understand."

TWENTY-TWO

This is like looking at space through a fish bowl, Skyler thought to himself. The crew had watched computer simulations, and they had seen the video recording of the Saturn probe. They were prepared for visual changes, but the entire experience of light-speed flight was impossible to simulate. As the *Hispaniola* advanced to its cruising speed, the view port displayed a distorted scene. Distant objects seemed to pull away while closer objects appeared to collapse around them, causing the illusion of moving through a tunnel that was getting longer.

"Any idea if this is normal?" Skyler asked.

Acharya sensed nervousness from Skyler. "I believe what we are seeing, or rather experiencing, is as expected. However, I do not believe the word 'normal' applies to any of this. The aberration is a wonder, is it not?"

"Oh, it's a wonder all right. It makes me wonder what the hell I'm doing out here."

"You are boldly going where no one has gone before," Acharya said, hoping to calm down his pilot.

"Are you feeling anything kind of strange?" Skyler asked with tension in his voice.

"Yes, I am having what could be described as an out-of-body experience. You must be feeling the same thing."

"Exactly, that's what I'm feeling. I wonder if this is something we get used to. I'd rather not spend the next week trying to deal with this."

"I have already discovered that meditation seems to help. I have been able to control the sensation for the most part."

"What?" Skyler asked. "How am I supposed to learn yoga meditation in the next thirty minutes? Just asking, because that's about how long it should take me to go completely insane."

"I can see you are becoming distressed. Let me see if I can help. Try sitting straight up without leaning in any direction. Now think about how much you have already achieved. Think of Anchor, and how much you love her. Allow yourself to breathe in a way that is comfortable."

Acharya watched carefully until Skyler was less anxious. "I want you to experiment and find out what kind of breathing feels best. Once you find a rhythm that feels comfortable, you must ride with that rhythm. You are on a boat and the waves are gently rocking you. Allow yourself to relax and just enjoy the feeling."

"Okay, thanks. The boat idea seems to be working."

"Now, if you start to feel tired or your mind begins to wander, bring yourself back to the boat. You do not want to fall overboard. You want to be completely relaxed and at the same time fully alert. Life is good, and today you are sailing."

After fifteen minutes, Acharya could see that Skyler was improving and that his breathing was regular. "Now I want you to move your awareness outside of your body. First in front, then to the sides, and then behind. Can you see yourself on the boat as you move around yourself? This is your center. Nothing can take your center away if you are not willing to let it."

Skyler drifted on a sailboat, rocking back and forth with the motions of the ocean. He was at home here, relaxed and yet completely aware. He could feel every inch of the boat and his exact location thereon. The waves would sometimes try to knock him off his bearing, but his sailing experience brought him back. He was gaining control. At last, he understood the aberration that was trying to pull him from his position. He understood its intentions. He understood how to push it aside. Someone called his name.

"You have a rare gift, my friend," Acharya said. "You have been in a state of mediation for close to an hour, without a single word."

Skyler glanced around. The strange feeling was gone. He knew how to control it now. He had his sea legs.

"Did you say one hour? That's impossible. What did you drug me with?"

"I did nothing. It was of your own choosing and imagination. Have you been previously trained in meditation?" Acharya asked with serious curiosity.

"No, never gave that kind of thing much thought. It's pretty much like sailing alone though. Thanks for your help. You're good at this stuff. I was starting to freak out, but I'm okay now."

Acharya was impressed. It had taken him months of training to reach the deep meditation state that Skyler had found so easy.

❧

The crew remained awake for more than thirty hours before exhaustion sent them to their sleeping cabins. Eight hours later, they were awake again and checking their heading and distance.

"The thing that gets me," Skyler said, "is how we appear to travel faster than the speed of light to the people back on Earth. It was hard enough for me to come to grips with this Einstein relativity stuff that reduced time for us on the ship, but I just don't understand what that has to do with the people back on Earth."

"You are more complicated than you have led everyone to believe. We thought we were getting a hotshot pilot, but it seems we have a physicist in embryo with unusual powers of meditation. Why the sudden interest in how things work?"

"Hey, it's nothing as deep as you're suggesting. I'm just hoping that this time reduction thing really works as advertised. Perhaps if I understood a little more of the physics, I'd feel less unsure."

"Well, I had a long conversation with our young genius, Isaac," Acharya said. "He told me about a German theoretical physicist named Burkhard Heim who was born in 1925. Burkhard was apparently able to describe Einstein's theory of relativity within the framework of quantum mechanics. Quantum mechanics is the opposite side of Einstein's large view of things involving the four dimensions: width, height, depth, and time.

"According to Relativity, matter deforms space in proportion to its mass; the result is called gravity. This theory successfully describes the behavior of objects in space and time, so long as the material is not subatomic, not smaller than atoms. Objects that are smaller than atoms are better described with quantum mechanics. This theory insists that space is not deformed by the mass of something because space itself is fixed. The two theories are in direct contradiction with each other. Einstein tried to combine the two opposing theories into what is called the 'theory of everything,' but he was unsuccessful."

"Hey, this is getting kind of deep, Acharya. Can you cut to the chase, if that's possible," Skyler pleaded.

"Yes, my apologies, I was getting there. What Burkhard was originally working on was something called a *hyperdrive*. He felt it was possible to build an engine that would locally modify the constants of nature and enable a spacecraft to fly faster than the speed of light through a subatomic dimension.

"It turns out that he was mostly right, not about being able to build a hyperdrive, but about the subatomic dimensions. When we absorb the mass expansion of our ship and store the potential energy in our stasis potacitor, we are literally storing the energy in one of Burkhard's subatomic dimensions.

"One of the lucky benefits of this is a modification of the constants of nature, the spacecraft itself relative to its stationary origin. When the constants change, 'strange stuff happens.' The understanding of this is well beyond my abilities, but you can take comfort in knowing that to Isaac it makes perfect sense, and we know how smart he is."

"I'm almost sorry I asked," Skyler said. "This whole thing reminds me of baseball. There are certain things in baseball that just are the way they are and there's no real explanation."

"I do not understand," Acharya said, puzzled. "What could quantum mechanics have to do with baseball?"

"Well, from what I could understand from your mumbo jumbo, I would say plenty. Baseball has a way of making philosophers out of dumb jocks. I'm sure you've heard of Yogi Berra."

"Well, I've heard of him, but I have never been interested in baseball."

"Yogi Berra played with Mickey Mantle for the New York Yankees. He was their catcher. He was a master at one-liners that would have given Plato plenty to think about.

Yogi Berra, a simple baseball catcher, had a big impact on how I deal with things in my life. My mentor, you might say. For example, he was fond of saying: 'This is like déjà vu all over again.'"

"I think I see what you mean. Why do you suppose baseball caused such a deep perspective?"

Skyler focused on Acharya for a moment, trying to see if he was just playing dumb. "Didn't you find any humor in that? Look, baseball is both serious and funny at the same time. Strange stuff happens in baseball, just like strange stuff happens in physics. It has a way of molding your view of the universe. Something else Yogi Berra said was, 'If you don't know where you are going, you will wind up somewhere else.'"

"Yes, that is funny. I see what you mean but I still do not understand what this has to do with changing the constants of nature, quantum mechanics, or relativity."

"Baseball is all about changing the nature of the universe and altering time. There are great players that are able to block out everything around them and see the game in slow motion. When they learn to defy the laws of nature, it turns them into philosophers. Is this getting too complicated?" asked Skyler.

"I might have thought you were naive about this being complicated, but Isaac told me about your latest chess game. To you, intuition is nothing simple at all."

"Oh, that. Hey, he obviously let up on me...or I was just lucky."

"Not according to Isaac. I asked him how it was that a simple surf bum, like yourself, could possibly win even one game of chess against a software engineer with an IQ of 180."

"Yeah, exactly. He let me win," Skyler said.

"Isaac told me that he won your first three games with ease. But the fourth time you played he said you changed tactics. He said that you would switch at random between an intelligent move and a move based on some kind of intuition. He was no longer able to predict what you would do next, and while trying to do so, you mated him."

"I just slowed the game down a little in my mind and looked at more possibilities. I fly that way sometimes when things get rough. Anyway, what I'm trying to say is that it's just like baseball."

"I am beginning to understand. Please continue."

"Look, players don't dwell on how baseball happens. For example, Yogi spent most of his life in baseball, but once, when asked to explain it, he said, 'In baseball, you don't know nothing.'

"The interesting thing is that he was dead serious. He was probably a fatalist. But most of the time he would use humor to explain things that were intuitively obvious — things that couldn't be explained with mere logic. I'm convinced that emotions help us grasp the impossible better than methods like your relativity theories. It sounds crazy, but it's what makes us smarter than we are — hey, that sounded like something Yogi would have said!"

"I see what you mean," Acharya said. "We are here, traveling through space at an impossible velocity, destined for a star that is not our own. We are not yet intelligent enough to have achieved this, and yet somehow we are here. Our theories of the universe are crude and unrefined. Our politics are self-serving and self-defeating. I can envision advanced races vastly more intelligent than humans. Yet here we are. Something has given us an edge, an edge that has apparently eluded the millions of civilizations that have come and gone throughout the eons of time.

"Perhaps it is us, the players themselves, who have caused the strange stuff to happen. We are unique in the universe. Not because we are so mechanically intelligent, but because we are curious and playful. Apparently, the basis of our genius is much deeper than the superficial measurement of pure intelligence. We must succeed at this journey, Skyler. It is not just the Earth that is depending on us; it is the entire galaxy."

"Oh, we will succeed, Acharya. And we'd better keep our eyes open because a lot of people will want to relive this journey many times over. One last quote from Yogi, and I'll shut that tune out of my head: 'You can observe a lot just by watchin'.'"

"Agreed, and we are well prepared to document this excursion. Now I am getting excited. Now we are having fun."

☙

Hours later, the subtle transition to light speed was having a dangerous impact on the judgment of the crew.

"As you know, I used to teach kids how to sail down at, uh, Nawiliwili Harbor. This astronaut gig has been tough. I miss those simpler days," Skyler said, leaning back in his ergonomic chair. "Damn, those were good times. How did everything get so complicated, so fast?"

"Perhaps we should simplify things," Acharya said.

"Simplify? What did you have in mind?"

"Well look around you my friend. Do you see anyone else? Can anyone hear us? Can anyone see us?"

"Hey, that's a good point. If ever there was a getaway, this is it," Skyler said.

"Just look at that view and feel that aberration. This is one weird ride. I'm thinking we should kick back and enjoy." Acharya reached into a case and pulled out a disc. I would say this occasion calls for some Beach Boys."

"I'm fine with that. Kind of corny, but what the hell? As long as you don't mind if I kick off these shoes and grab a couple beers out of the ice box, then I'm with you."

"How did you get beer onto the ship?" asked Acharya. "Never mind, who cares. I have lived the life of a monk for a long time. I have earned a vacation. Bring on the beer and grab some snacks. Don't worry about making a mess," Acharya said.

An hour later, deep space was alive with strange new sounds of laughter and music:

(Giddy up giddy up 409)
Giddy up 409
(Giddy up giddy up 409)
Giddy up 40...

Nothing can catch her
Nothing can touch my 409
409

"Now we're talking, my friend. Nothing, and I mean nothing, can touch this baby." Skyler laughed over the music, accidentally spilling beer on his shirt when he reached for the manual controls.

"If James could see us now, he would shit!" Acharya said.

"Why mister monk, I don't believe I've ever heard you talk like that before. I'm not sure I approve."

"You have no idea how good that felt. I'm thinking I should have been a baseball player," Acharya said, standing on his head. "This may sound crazy, but I think there is something intoxicating about light speed travel."

"Yeah, what a kick. We've been traveling in a straight line forever," Skyler said with his mouth full of popcorn. "What do you say we do a little zigzagging?"

"Be my guest. That sounds like a great experiment," Acharya said and tried to clap his hands while still standing on his head.

Skyler nudged the craft right and then back. Next he increased the zig time a touch. Suddenly, they were on a roller-coaster ride as the gravitational forces flung them around like rag dolls. Skyler managed to grab the controls again as the forces subsided. He flipped the autopilot back on and strapped himself into his seat. Acharya managed to do the same a few moments later.

As the two half-drunk astronauts looked at each other, Acharya said, "That wasn't supposed to happen. This ship is supposed to dampen all g-forces."

"Wanna try it again?" Skyler said, laughing from the look on Acharya's face.

"Are you nuts? We have to figure out what happened."

"Oh, okay, where do we start?" Skyler said, trying desperately not to laugh again.

With scattered popcorn and spilled beer, the music continued as Acharya examined the computer console:

So take a lesson from a top-notch surfer boy (catch a wave, catch a wave)
Every Saturday boy
But don't treat it like a toy

Just get away from the shady turf
And baby go catch some rays on the sunny surf
And when you catch a wave you'll be sittin on top of the world

Catch a wave and you'll be sittin' on top of the world

"Look at these readings. We have encountered a cluster of objects with a mass twice that of our sun. Wait. I should have noticed this before. We are in the middle of some kind of invisible matter field. It appears splattered around us. While we were traveling in a straight line, our shunt was able to compensate and nudge us aside. When you veered off course, it was too much for the ship to handle." Acharya shook his head, trying to clear the buzz. "We need to get out of here fast. Look how the starlight in that part of the vision tunnel is blocked off, while over there it is normal. I suggest we move away from this stuff. Let me see if I can program a course."

Skyler watched as the computer adjusted their path and the light tunnel returned close to normal; normal, based on what it used to look like. "So what happened?" Skyler asked, beginning to sober up.

"Dark matter," Acharya said with authority. "Most astronomers today believe that all matter in our galaxy is made up of about 90% dark matter. We have no idea what dark matter is, but it looks like the astronomers were right about it being there. I am not able to program the computer to guide us completely out of here. The adjustments are far too complex…I'm sorry. This is a difficult imbroglio we find ourselves in. If we hit a thick spot with no openings, we will not make it through."

The darkness was a looming absence. It was as if a paint program eraser had stroked across a picture of a star field, leaving a swath.

"I'm taking over," Skyler said and reached for the controls. As he wrapped his hand around the stick, he paused and tried to focus. He knew everything there was to know about flying this craft. "Wait, Isaac installed black matter controls. Could that be the same as dark matter?"

"Yes, they are the same thing, but I have no knowledge of what you are talking about."

"Look," Skyler was working the controls rapidly. "I've practiced this before."

"That's it!" Acharya exclaimed. "Someone must have..." Acharya paused. "Yes, Isaac must have written an advisory module for the auto-pilot. It's working!"

The artifacts in the visual quickly disappeared as the spacecraft cleverly maneuvered itself out of the dark matter patch.

"You're right, it was Isaac. He came in late one night when I was alone. He was complaining that the other programmers were giving him some kind of flack about this. He said he didn't have time to explain or go through the red tape to get it approved and pre-installed before the launch. He said the shunt would get overwhelmed in the face of too much black matter congestion. I had no idea what he was talking about, but for some reason I believed him. He taught me how to activate it, probably a dozen times. He became dead serious and said, 'Just activate it and apologize later.' He pleaded with me not to tell anyone, not even James."

"Wait, I do remember something about this," Acharya said. "I did not understand what everyone was arguing about, but Isaac was yelling. I remember now because I had never known him to yell before. He was very upset and yelled at James about poetry or poetic license, I believe he said."

"Yep, that's it. He told me the black matter control wasn't supposed to come with us, and he would lose his job if anyone found out. I'm not sure why, but I trusted him and I wasn't about to get him in trouble. Apparently, the team was certain that the shunt technology could handle the congestion problems and that messing with the autopilot was too risky at such a late date. Looks like our boy Isaac came through for us."

"Did he ever. This is my fault," Acharya said. "The dark matter warnings were displayed on our console, but I was having too much fun to notice. If I had said something, you would have known what to do sooner."

"That was my job as well, Acharya. I knew about the warning icons."

"I believe we should clean up this mess and focus on surviving this incredible and dangerous journey," Acharya said, seeming embarrassed.

"Ah, come on, buddy. Look, we just need to be a little more careful, that's all." Whoa, I'm getting kind of tired. What do you say we clean up this mess in the morning?" Skyler staggered to his cabin and fell asleep without showering.

The next relative morning Acharya had their ship in top shape and was back to his normal self.

"It would seem that I should have taken my own advice, Acharya: *You can observe a lot just by watchin'*. We need to stay alert. I have to tell you though, the combination of the aberration, the weird view, the beer, the junk food, and the 60's music helped me unwind. I slept like a bare-bummed baby."

"I must admit that I slept well myself. Perhaps we have discovered a form of recreation for future space travelers, but we need to remain vigilant from now on—even in the face of light speed temptations."

Six days later, the newly-disciplined crew of the *Hispaniola* prepared for their encounter with Alpha Centauri A. In the last few hours, Skyler had bombarded Acharya with questions about their destination. Skyler decided to brave just one last inquiry: "How can a star system have three stars instead of one like our sun?"

Acharya glanced at Skyler. "Your curiosity is unyielding. In answer to your question, the stars revolve around each other like big planets. The two large stars are about the same distance apart as Saturn and the sun. The universe is filled with systems made of multiple stars and planets."

"Well, I hope we find some planets. That would be cool. Coming all this way for a clump of stars would be kind of boring."

"We should know soon enough. Orbital injection starts in forty-seven minutes."

The starship had been on gradual slowdown for the last two days. It slipped into a high-speed far-distant orbit around the larger star, an alien invader from outer space. The human voyagers were spellbound at what they saw. After staring at the same monotonous view for the past five days, the mysterious and wondrous sight of the bright star was pure eye candy.

The main view screen switched automatically to ultraviolet as the telescopic camera zoomed in on the yellow star. Hanging in the middle of a black background was a burning granular ball of yellow, orange, white and black. Small flares protruding from its outer surface and three white-hot areas contaminated its otherwise consistent grainy texture, like small tears threatening to burst open.

"What do you think?" Skyler asked.

"Of the two large stars, this yellow one is the friendlier; nevertheless, of the three, the orange is the most interesting. It seems to me that the little distant red star, Proxima, does not belong."

"What I meant was, should we move closer to this star?"

Acharya examined his monitor and continued, "That decision seems to have been made by the computer. We are already in orbit around the large yellow star at a distance of 200 million miles. I suggest we go along with the computer for now."

"Okay, but we're slowing down again. I was just getting used to the out-of-body sensations," Skyler said. "This sinking, enclosed feeling is giving me claustrophobia."

"This is most unexpected," Acharya agreed. "I am finding myself missing the mental free-floating. I am wondering if our natural state is the depressed unhealthy state and light-speed euphoria is the preferred way to live."

"Just lock me up in a mental institution and throw the key away. This has been an emotional roller coaster," said Skyler.

The sensors were busy tracking objects near the yellow star as the pre-programming automatically sent them past the orbits of four large planets ranging in size from that of Neptune to a planet larger than Jupiter. Traveling at one forth light speed, they slowed further while approaching a small planet. The numbers on their main monitor spun out evidence of it being near the size of Mars, but they continued past in hot pursuit of something else. The computer had isolated another planet. They came in fast and slowed suddenly, taking orbit around a planet slightly smaller than the Earth.

"This is more than we could have ever hoped for!" Acharya said. He held his breath and fell silent at the scene before them.

"This is worth writing home about," Skyler said as the cameras zoomed in on the surface of the planet. "Whoa, this is cool."

TWENTY-THREE

Residual covert military squads remained from the prior presidential administration. With decades of advance funding to sustain them, they continued in their clandestine duty until congressional oversight found and disbanded them. The most secret of these organizations, *Able Peril*, persisted undetected. Swept from office, along with their president, were the only two Senators aware its existence.

The team's leader called himself Admiral. Other members of the team had their own unique alias. These were men without family or home; their real identities erased from existence. Able Peril was presently on what the Admiral had decided was their most important mission: the removal of James Stevenson, the treacherous traitor.

The Admiral had found an unexpected ally in the Chinese. Threatened by the unimaginable technology wielded by the scientists known to them as the Babylonians, the Chinese found themselves embarrassed by their attempts to shoot down the starship. Following world rebellion, the Chinese issued an apology and a promise to punish those in their military for acting without authorization. In an unusual display of candor, the Chinese state-run news organization criticized its own government.

The newest dark-skinned member of Able Peril, known simply as Joe, was an inconspicuous and seemingly harmless immigrant, just another friendly addition to the melting pot. However, his killing skills were legendary to the Chinese secret police. The perfect eliminator, devoid of human conscience, he was presently on loan to the Admiral. The Chinese would *not* fail a second time.

Joe smiled as he examined his antique bowie knife, a favorite among the martial arts elite. It was a painful way to die. A gift reserved for only the most deserving. As James hiked down from Sleeping Giant Mountain, Joe hid low in the bushes behind a fallen tree. He had picked his spot well. This would be an easy kill. The dog was an unknown, but from Joe's observations, he was willing to take the chance. He would kill them both and feed their remains to the fish.

James was close now, just a few more steps. "Yes, this is perfect," Joe whispered as he crouched to lunge. Unexpectedly he heard James laugh: "Don't get me!"

Joe hesitated. *What is this? Did he see me? Is he mocking me?*

James was gone in a flash as Joe stumbled onto the path. Overwhelmed with anger, he turned to pursue his target. As he flipped his knife around, he found himself knocked off balance by the dog. Stumbling over the large fallen tree that had been his hiding place, he managed to glance up just in time to see the black Labrador recover from their collision and slide around the corner. His foot had snagged itself a root and his momentum brought him face down toward a large black pitted bolder. He tossed the knife forward to free his hands in an effort to soften the blow.

The bowie knife landed, handle first, and wedged perfectly, as luck would have it, between two moss-covered rocks in front of his chest. Unable to slow his fall, the silver shaft pierced cleanly through his heart. The last thing Joe ever heard was the distant laughing and mocking of his victim: "Okay, okay. I give up. You got me!"

Later that day, Able Peril found Joe with a perplexed look on his dead face. Shaken from the loss of the valuable Chinese agent, the Admiral pondered. *What am I up against? I will not underestimate him again.*

◦❧

Accompanied by James, Strant fired up his highly-customized, A-Star 950 helicopter and gently lifted off from his private landing pad. The computer entrepreneur and the physicist found each other's company interesting and amusing. Strant came from the high-tech computer industry, while James was a pure academic. Unlike other computer scientists that James had worked with, Strant was carefree, rich, and informal—a computer programmer who focused exclusively on what he could get from the technologies, not what he could offer.

Strant was fascinated with James's depth and knowledge on just about any subject surrounding the field of physics, including computer science. He couldn't understand why James wasn't one of the wealthiest men on Earth. He certainly could have been with just a little shift in focus.

The Admiral and a handful of his men followed intently with their binoculars as Strant flew north toward Princeville. Each night, for weeks, they had observed Strant's mansion from the nearby hills. Today, well hidden in the deep grass, they watched the two men fly their doomed helicopter over the Princeville golf course toward the steep cliffs of the Na Pali coast.

After weeks of surveillance, and the men's patterns established, the saboteurs had moved in. They placed delayed explosives around the helicopter's fuel lines. The

Admiral knew that if he failed again, the Chinese would take their revenge on him and his men. It had been a mistake to involve the Chinese at the expense of giving up their anonymity.

"A lot's happened since Skyler left," Strant said, adjusting his sunglasses and headset. "Your potacitor technologies are reshaping the entire planet. Soon even this helicopter will be a thing of the past."

"Yes, it has been surprising. Applications are coming on line faster than I thought was possible, especially in the fields of transportation and construction. What I'm excited about is the positive impact frictionless electric cars are having on the environment."

The Admiral watched the chopper fly high and out of sight. Unable to suppress his excitement, he grinned and sent an encrypted text message to his Chinese counterpart: "*Mission accomplished. No chance of survival.*"

Strant banked the helicopter hard around a steep cliff and followed the winding river up the narrow canyon. They approached a large waterfall before aiming skyward; eventually, they swept over the crest of the falls. To get a better view, Strant spun the A-Star completely around and flew back over the edge. Hanging high in the air, Strant smiled and checked to see if James approved.

"Nice flying, buddy. What a view!" James said. A small explosion shook the helicopter. James grabbed desperately for the handrail above his head as alarms flashed across the console. The fuel gauge indicator dropped to empty and the engine came to a gradual stop as the helicopter plunged straight down to its certain destruction in the rocky pool below.

After less than a thirty-yard drop, the fall eerily softened. As if being carefully set down by a large invisible hand from the sky, the helicopter nestled in a grassy patch fifty yards to the side of the waterfall. The two unharmed occupants scrambled out and looked over their stricken craft.

"Some bastard is trying to kill us!" Strant screamed. "Look at this. Explosives have blown away the fuel lines. Thank God for your rescue potacitor. Can't tell you how happy I am that you won the argument and installed that thing. Remind me to buy some stock in that company!"

"That was close, my friend. I think they were after me. You would be wise to stay away for a while. I ran into a squad of bad-looking military types a while back, and I don't think they were there for my protection."

Strant climbed back into the helicopter and notified the authorities. Within two hours, the police had roped off the area and confirmed their suspicions of intentional sabotage.

James and Strant accepted a ride back to Kilauea, where they ordered a late lunch from the local deli. They found a table outside in the nigh empty corridor.

A Chinese operative, sent to keep an eye on the Admiral, happened to walk past the deli and recognized James.

The agent was tempted to move in for the kill, but his well-trained eye noticed the subtle bulge of a sidearm strapped under Strant's shirt. The agent sent a text message to his commander, requesting instructions. The angry commander called the agent back directly. The Admiral had failed twice, cost them the life of one of their own men, and had lied to them. As far as the Chinese were concerned, James was no longer their primary target.

After lunch, the two survivors hiked across the fields toward the ocean boundary hills and northward to Strant's home. Following a tense conversation about the day's events, Strant reluctantly agreed to stay away from James for a few days but vowed to solicit the help of private detectives.

The men shook hands twice before James eventually drove away. After passing through the security gate, James stopped at the main road intersection and turned right. Pausing for a long time at the next deserted intersection, he made the decision to drive toward Secret Beach instead of home to Silvia and Data. He felt compelled to run. He wanted to hear the sounds of crashing waves.

Parking his car near the fenced field above the beach, James climbed down the steep path to the hot sands below. He peered toward the lighthouse on the edge of the distant cliff; its white base, green glass center, and orange cap were familiar sights. He walked past a clump of large black lava boulders. Light and dark green moss on the outer rocks formed a sharp, florescent, contrast with the other boulders in the back.

He started running and ran hard in the direction of the ancient lighthouse. James was deep in reflection as the sand flowed beneath his feet. *That was a close call today. Despite the difficult times, I have lived an exciting and wonderful life. What a hoot this has been.*

As if awakening from a disconnect with reality, he felt strange about his being on the beach. *What am I doing here? I should be checking on Silvia!*

As he approached the south end of the beach, he spotted a woman waving her arms and pointing out to sea. "Help me please!" she yelled. "Lani is in trouble! My daughter, please help!"

James ran forward and the woman grabbed his arm. Beyond the breaking waves and too far out for surfing, a girl was splashing in the waves. Her surfboard had drifted halfway to shore. The protruding fins of tiger sharks encircled the girl. *Where are the dolphins?* James thought.

"It's going to be all right," he said, trying to reassure the woman. "This area is a common playground for large schools of dolphin. They often protect people from the sharks. I'll swim out and return her surfboard to her. She'll be fine."

James had become a strong swimmer since moving to Kauai. He reached the surfboard and then the girl within five minutes. She was panicked by the sharks but apparently unharmed.

"Help me! They won't let me leave!" she screamed.

"Don't be afraid. They're probably just curious," James said, knowing she was lucky to be alive. He pushed forward, ignoring the sharks, until he reached her. "Get on your board, and I'll push you toward shore. Try to keep your hands and feet out of the water. If you hang them out, it will confuse the sharks, and they might mistake you for a turtle."

"I will. Oh, thank you! Thank you so much!"

James pushed the girl until her board's momentum was steady. The girl had been unable to resist and was now paddling as fast as she could toward shore.

Where are those dolphins? I should stop and wait for them, James realized. He felt a hard thump on the back of his neck. *There you are, probably nudging me away from the sharks.*

James felt the need to sleep sweep over him. *Hey, this is no time to be taking a nap*, he told himself and swam harder. He could feel his arms moving, but there was no sensation of resistance from the water. Absurdly, he noticed red coloring filling his vision and realized what had happened.

James Stevenson died that day on Earth. As with everything about his life, even his death was legendary. The shark had bitten clean through his neck in one swift strike just moments before his dolphin friends had arrived.

The girl scrambled to shore and ran crying to her mother. "That man saved me! He saved me from the sharks, and they have him!"

"I know, sweetheart. I know. God bless him. Oh, Lord, please bless that man for saving my daughter."

A crowd gathered as the mother tried to explain what had happened. A large school of dolphins occupied the area, and the sharks were gone. A pair of young surfers swam out to find the dolphins holding James' body above water.

After searching the parking lot, a policeman friend of Strant's recognized James' car and made the call. "Hey, Strant, your racquetball friend, Mr. Stevenson, was killed by sharks at the beach today. Apparently he was helping a girl, saved her life according to witnesses."

A few hours later, Strant and Anchor were with Silvia. "This doesn't surprise me," she sobbed. "He loved children and would never abandon one. I wish I could have given him children of his own." Tears fell from her swollen eyes. Data sat frightened in the corner, unable to understand why Silvia was so upset.

The next day, news of James' death spread throughout the world, hours too late to save the Admiral and his band of Able Peril. James was recognized and given full credit as the creator of the Babylonian team that had built mankind's first starship and the inventor of the now famous potacitor technology.

Silvia asked Mike Stranton to give the eulogy at James' funeral. As the world watched, expecting a long speech with words of heroism, Strant walked to the podium; seeming detached, he offered just one single sentence: "When the universe has long forgotten most of the people we think of as famous today, James Stevenson will be remembered as one of the greatest inventors in the history of the galaxy." He promptly turned and walked away with a quick nod to Silvia.

Company Key Man Insurance provided a generous fund for Silvia. She decided to move to New York, where she could be with her sisters. Unable to care for Data, she gave him to Anchor, who promised to run with him every day until Skyler returned. "Have no fear, my dearest Anchor," Silvia whispered in her ear before boarding the plane. "James is with Skyler and Acharya now."

That evening, Data moved in with Anchor. He was nervous and confused, still waiting for James to return. Anchor cuddled up to him on the floor of her Alii Kai condo and rubbed his ears. "Thank you for coming to live with me, Data. We're orphans, you and I. We'll be traveling to Maui in the morning. I have a wonderful place for us to live."

Data was shaking. He knew something was wrong, so Anchor continued to comfort him. She remembered James telling her that Data had an unusual vocabulary. "We're going to have fun. Tomorrow, we can run together and go swimming in a big river."

That seemed to help. Data perked up and wiggled his tail for the first time since she had taken him. "Skyler will be home in twenty months. He will be so excited to see you. We can play *'don't get me'* together and go sailing. Do you like sailing, Data?"

Data looked up and snuck a wet kiss on Anchor's lips before she could move. She was startled and wiped away the slime. "Oh, yuck, that wasn't funny!" she said. That amused Data, so he tried again, but Anchor ducked and grabbed his head. From that night on, Data and Anchor were the best of friends.

He would insist on going somewhere with her every morning and afterward wait patiently for her to return from work at the observatory. Having Data with her made the days slide by faster. He somehow always knew when she was sad and found ways to cheer her up. Data was normal most of the time, but Anchor had to be careful about mentioning James' name. The slightest slip from her lips, and Data would bark and run to the door. It would take hours to calm him down.

One night, Anchor returned home late from work. Unable to sleep, she walked outside with Data. The sky was clear from a rainstorm that had washed past the islands earlier that day. Anchor decided to drive up to the observatory with Data, not to work, but to get away from the city lights and relax. She walked around to the back of the building and sat on a bench.

Data hopped up on the bench with her, and as if human, tilted his head and stared at her until she laughed. "Oh, Data, I hope they're safe. Our boys are just now approaching that star." Anchor pointed to the brightest star in the south southwestern region of the night by tracing along the almucantar from a dim neighboring star, a method she preferred over direct pointing.

Data followed her finger until it stopped. He wiggled his tail. "That's right, Data. That's where my Skyler is, and

James is watching over him." Data flew from the bench and started barking. He looked back at Anchor to make sure he was barking at the right star. A short while later he stopped, climbed back on the bench and leaned hard against her shoulder. They sat together in silence, enjoying the clear October night. Anchor understood. It was so simple. Apparently Data had just wanted her to tell him where James was.

Anchor would often relive moments with Skyler in her mind. Sitting in the dark with Data, she tried to picture Skyler's face. One of the first things she had found most attractive about Skyler was his unusual ability to express himself effectively without the use of vulgar profanity. He would swear on occasion, but nothing serious. "Oh, Data. How I miss Skyler. He's such a good boy. I wonder what my sweetheart is doing now."

TWENTY-FOUR

"What the f—"

"Impossible!" Acharya interrupted.

"—yeah...what is that?" Skyler asked.

Acharya touched the console in front of him and the camera zoomed closer. "It looks like thousands of trees of some kind growing beyond the planet's atmosphere. There appears to be only one large continent surrounded by ocean. Yes, that is a rainforest, though nothing like any rainforest on Earth. There is evidence to suggest that Earth was something like this before an asteroid wiped out the dinosaurs, but Earth has never grown trees like these monsters."

"Look how they flatten out on top," Skyler said. Their flat tops or heads, or whatever they are, seem to be floating on the edge of the atmosphere. Why would they do that?"

"Wait, Skyler, those are not treetops. They are something else. Yes, look closely. They have attachments. Unless this is just wishful thinking, those treetops could be observatories."

The spacecraft moved in close and took position just above one of the trees. "Nope, that is a natural tree top," Skyler said. "Those attachments are symmetrical, but obviously natural. For some reason, these space-trees like to grow mile wide tops on the edge of the atmosphere. They probably like the unfiltered sunlight or something."

"You are correct. This is a natural phenomenon. It is as if they are trying to reach out and capture the source of their nourishment. I am wondering how they can survive the cold of space."

"What do you say we take a look at the surface?" Skyler said eagerly.

"Very well," Acharya agreed. "Let me take a few more pictures of these 'space-trees' as you call them. We should proceed with caution because this planet is teaming with life. Do not proceed toward anything until we are sure of what we are dealing with."

Skyler could fly the *Hispaniola* from space to the surface of a planet with his eyes closed. His extra hours in the simulator had saved their lives when attacked by the Chinese. He grabbed the controls and initiated his decent.

If ever there was a Garden of Eden this must be it, Acharya thought, sharing his time between the system console and the outside scenery. Suddenly he noticed one of the color graphs rising beyond normal. "Slow down!" Acharya ordered. "We must slow our decent."

"What's wrong now?"

"It is the atmosphere. The humidity level in the atmosphere is off the scale. This atmosphere is somewhere between ocean and air."

"Don't scare me like that," Skyler said, slowing the ship. "Relax, Acharya. It's not liquid, it's air. Moist air is less dense than dry air? Geeze, Acharya, every pilot knows that."

"Yes of course, the ideal gas law—I apologize. I overreacted. I also forgot about our potacitor shunt system. Still, I would feel better if we proceeded with caution."

"No problem, buddy. I'm all for caution," said Skyler in a calm voice.

As they approached within 50,000 feet of the surface, the planet began to reveal its mysteries. A magnificent vista filled the ship's super high-resolution thirty-foot-wide digital view screen. There were forests of endless colors filled with wondrous beasts of assorted shapes and sizes engaging in multifarious activities. Massive flying reptilians with feathers swarmed like sparrows. One of the flying creatures broke from the flock and headed in their direction.

"Uh, hey, Acharya. That thing seems to be getting bigger the closer it gets to us. Probably nothing to worry about, but how big do you think it is?"

"All right, let me see. The computer has made a comparison for us. That, um, thing coming toward us is approximately ten times the size of the *Hispaniola*. I believe it intends to swallow us."

Skyler was flabbergasted. "I've figured it out, Acharya. You must be British. You believe it intends to swallow us? Quick, write this down in the tour guide," Skyler said, shifting their direction. "Avoid being swallowed by the local birdies."

Acharya failed to see the humor.

As they traveled around the planet, it became apparent that industrial life had not yet evolved. If there was intelligent life, it was well hidden and much better at protecting the environment than mankind. It was as if life had existed here for millions of years without a major catastrophe. The planet was a perfect example of life in harmony.

After hours of surveying, they had completely mapped the surface of the planet. The crew of the *Hispaniola* had found their treasure. A treasure beyond any treasure was now theirs.

"What shall we name her?" Acharya asked.

"That's your call my friend. You're the poet on this crew."

"Then we shall name her *Varuna*. In the Vedas, Varuna was the moral overseer of the world. This will remind mankind to protect and not destroy this wonder."

"Varuna it is," Skyler said. You once used the term wonder of wonders. Varuna is truly in that category."

After sleeping and dreaming of their new discovery, the crew awakened and Skyler flew the *Hispaniola* up and away from Varuna in search of other worlds circling Alpha Centauri A. Upon finding no other planets with life, they bridged the wide dark inter-space gap between Alpha Centauri A and the smaller orange sun called Alpha Centauri B.

"You realize," Acharya said after a long silence, "that our days now match those of Earth. Each hour that passes here is one hour on Earth."

"I hadn't thought about that. I guess you're right. That's kind of good to know. Well, any bets on finding life near the orange sun?"

"My guess is that such an infinite possibility will not strike twice on this journey," Acharya answered.

"I would think we can pretty much rule out advanced life in this system. Otherwise, they would have been on Varuna," Skyler said, deep in thought.

"That is a most astute observation. Unless they have reserved Varuna as a retreat for the rich and famous, I am inclined to agree with your theory."

Like alien hunters, they explored the planets of the orange sun. They found five large planets. One fascinating planet was larger than any of those orbiting Varuna's yellow star. Not one of the planets was a true gas giant, but the atmosphere on the mega-planet swirled and exploded as if in disgust at itself for not having become a star.

There were a few small planets with no atmosphere. They had signs of ancient impacts, but nothing recent. From their first cursory examination, no life existed near the orange star, but it was impossible to tell what was really happening below the atmosphere of the monster planet?

Skyler was becoming an expert at forming orbits, swooping in and fishtailing away. "This is just like diving. The large screen is like the faceplate of my diving mask. These planets are just objects in the sea waiting for us. This is the coolest thing I have ever done!"

"Yes, your improved proficiency has not escaped me. I was wondering how you were approaching the task." Acharya said, not looking away from the fourth display monitor to his right. Skyler could tell he was deep into something.

"I have it!" Acharya said, looking up with an awed expression. "I had fallen into the trap of believing that a tri-star system would be littered with debris — I was wrong. The astronomers on Earth were wrong. These two stars and their large planets act as gigantic vacuums, sucking up the smaller objects like dirt. It has long been known that without Jupiter and Saturn, there would have been no life on Earth because too many asteroid impacts would have destroyed any chance. Here, at Alpha Centauri, there is even less debris near the vicinity of Varuna. That is why she has survived so long without impact. It makes you wonder what Earth would be like if it had grown up in the same clean environment."

"I'm guessing that you and I would have scales for skin," Skyler contributed.

"Yes, and we would not be here. We would be frolicking in some jungle."

"Well, I say we skip the dinky red star and head back to Varuna." Skyler was anxious to return. He wanted to walk on the surface but wasn't sure Acharya would agree. Their prime directive was to go EVA in an emergency only. Skyler considered the need to explore Varuna an emergency.

"I agree. Proxima is one half light-year away. It will take us two days to get there, explore the system and return. The plan was to return to Earth directly from Proxima, but that was before we knew about Varuna. Proxima is flaring extensively. It has doubled its brightness and returned several times in just one day. The chance of life existing out there is pretty low indeed."

"Yeah, I was reading about that little twerp. It takes a half million years to orbit the two big suns. The big guys orbit each other every eighty years. We don't even know if Proxima is entirely part of the same system. I'm sure James would want us to head back to Varuna before we leave. I wonder how he's holding up. I wish he were here to see this. We've been gone about a year and a half—Earth time."

Once more, the *Hispaniola* breached the void between the two companion suns and synchronized with the current orbit of Varuna at a distance from the yellow star that would have measured halfway between the Earth and Mars: 115265300.6 miles.

"Let's land and look around," Skyler said casually.

"What? We cannot land. That is forbidden in our flight plan. You know this!"

"What flight plan is that? The one written before we knew about Varuna? Come on, Acharya, you've been dreaming of setting foot on another world your entire life. We can't come this far, discover this amazing planet and not look around a little."

"All right, Skyler...you know me too well. I am willing to land, but first there is something we must consider. I believe there is a strong possibility that intelligent Dinosauroids exist here. I suggest we float above the surface near the base of one of those gigantic trees. I am curious about something."

"You've been holding out on me. What have you found?"

"At the end of Earth's Cretaceous period, a dinosaur killing asteroid hit the Yucatan Peninsula and made way for smaller mammals. I have been reviewing an article I read years ago. In the early 1980's, paleontologist Dale Russell, curator for a museum in Canada, wanted to know what would have happened without the asteroid. His work showed the creatures getting smarter. He speculated that Earth would have become inhabited with smart dinosaurs, sort of reptilian humanoids. He called them 'Dinosauroids.'"

"Look at this." Acharya displayed an image on the main thirty-foot view screen. "Notice the concentric rings around the base of the tree. We were so focused on the tops of the trees that we failed to properly examine the base. From a distance, these circles look like root growth of some kind, but up close these rings look more like the work of social intelligence. I realize nature is good at forming geometric shapes; however, upon closer examination, I am not sure how these rings were formed. I suggest we find out before we land."

"Good thinking. Let's do some real hunting. Plug-in the coordinates of the nearest space-tree and I'll bring us in for a good look."

Ten minutes later, they were in a holding pattern fifty feet above the surface just two hundred yards from the outermost concentric ring. The area outside the last ring was cleared of trees for several miles, like a farmhouse surrounded by fresh tilled land. Acharya was frantically shooting pictures and gathering data when a gleaming projectile targeted their position. Easily deflected by the spacecraft's shunt shield, the object fell to the ground several hundred yards from the ship.

"Okay, that was from no stupid reptile," Skyler said. "That thing came from some kind of cannon. Look, zoom in there. That's the barrel, and those little guys next to it are getting ready to fire again. The spear had a crude rope attached to it. Looks like we broke the rope when it hit our shields."

"This is incredible," Acharya responded. "These rings protect the creatures. They use the space-trees as the center of their habitat. That is most wise because they can climb the trees to any height and monitor their surroundings. A perfect defensive strategy."

Skyler was up and putting on his gear. "Where are those laser knives? I'm going after that spear. See if you can see any animals or birds nearby."

"I do not think that is wise. We still have much to learn."

Skyler ignored the advice and brought the craft down fifty yards from the deflected spear. He used the ship as interference just in case he was wrong about their accuracy. "I need to stretch my legs. I'll just run out there, grab a piece of the spear, and run back. Look, we're in a safe clearing. There's nothing around for miles, and those smart dinos can't see me because our ship is blocking their view."

Acharya made a complete scan of the area. There were several large four legged beasts a few miles away, but nothing else. "Very well then. The planet is oxygen rich, but wear your mask just in case. Do not hesitate. Just grab the spear and return."

Skyler was in full agreement. His voice betrayed his excitement. "I'm not taking any chances on this first EVA. I'll do exactly as you say. Make another scan of the area just to be sure."

At last, Skyler stepped outside and beheld the strange world. With no creatures in sight, he sprinted the fifty yards to the spear and sliced off a part of the rope and a good sized section of the spear. His trophy was heavier than he had expected, so he proceeded back at a lazy walk.

"Wow, it's humid out here," Skyler said as he lifted the mask to wipe sweat from his face.

Inside the craft, Acharya noticed several of the large creatures moving rapidly in their direction. *The scent. We forgot about their sense of smell*, he thought to himself.

"Skyler come back *now*! One of the big creatures is within a mile of us."

"A mile? Hell, I can run forty yards before he can run a mile. I'll pick up the pace."

Acharya stared in disbelief as the creatures advanced toward them. The first was now within half a mile and closing. Skyler was still twenty-five yards from the ship. "Drop the spear, Skyler! Run! Run for your life!"

Skyler ran faster, but held firm to his trophy, not realizing he was already dead. As he approached within twenty yards of the ship, he heard the whistling sound of an object flying through the air, followed by a rumbling explosion. He looked back as the ground shook. A huge, red, reptilian-like creature was tumbling across the surface, felled by one of the smart-dino spears, just three hundred yards away.

In hot pursuit of Skyler, the creature had made the mistake of coming too close to its mortal enemies. Skyler dropped the spear and ran as fast as he could to the ship, but the other two monsters had already turned away after watching the death of their fellow hunter.

"I suggest we stay in the ship from now on," Skyler gasped as he collapsed on the floor near Acharya. "Those bastards are fast."

"You would not have made it back if not for those smart-dinos. You scared the hell out of me. I was certain you were gone."

"Sorry, buddy. Add that to the tour guide list. Don't try to outrun the big red things, and ladies and gentlemen keep your fingers and toes inside the spacecraft at all times."

"For once..." Acharya began with a long pause, "I must disagree."

"You do? So you think we should stick our fingers and toes outside?"

"We need to proceed with caution to obtain physical evidence of life on this planet. It is one thing to convince the inhabitants of Earth that we have been clever enough to manipulate the known laws of physics and travel to another star. Returning with stories and photographs of a world teaming with life would be too much for them to accept without solid proof." "Well, there's the possibility of contamination," said Skyler. "And what about the danger from other creatures that we don't understand? I was nuts to go out there, and now you're nuts for wanting to go again. I say we count our lucky stars and huddle down inside the *Hispaniola*."

"You must know I am right," Acharya said, trying to calm his young companion. "We are here for a reason. It is we who have traveled from another star. Certainly we are capable of outwitting a planet of prehistoric life forms."

"All right, I see your point. They may be faster than us, but we have bigger brains. Let's figure this out."

"Well, actually, some of these dinosaurs have larger... heads," Acharya said with a dumb expression.

"Okay, so they have bigger brains as well. But we're the ones with the spaceship. Let's start by finding a high-tech solution for getting that spear on board."

Ten minutes later, the dinosauroid spear section was magically sliding across the ground toward a small open crack in the door, having been snagged by a jury-rigged rope and hook.

"I've got it!" Skyler yelled, flipping the hydraulic close button and trying to speed the door shut by pushing on it.

"Good job. Now we need to capture one of those droids," Acharya yelled from the pilot's cabin.

"What? Not me!"

Skyler knew he'd been suckered the instant he took the bait. He could hear Acharya trying to contain his laughter. "I think relativity or something is causing us to reverse personalities. That was a good one."

As the crew sat in their cabin, watching the large red beast slowly dragged back to the space-tree city, they both spoke at once: "I have a plan." "I've got a great idea."

"Let's get a piece of one of those teeth," Skyler said first.

"I was thinking of a piece of the long tail, but a tooth would last longer."

The *Hispaniola* lifted up and glided directly in front of the beast, settling down on the drag rope. Skyler grabbed his laser knife and started down toward the hatch.

"Wait, it is my turn," Acharya said, stepping into his path.

"Hold on a minute. I'm the young jock here. That could be dangerous," Skyler said.

"Not really, if you think about it. We know the big creatures are afraid to come this near the city wall, and the droids can't see us. With simple deductive reasoning, we have achieved our prize. Besides, I want a turn outside," Acharya said, proud of himself.

"In that case, let's both go. You hold the bucket, and I'll slice a piece off a tooth. That way we get back faster."

The two thoughtful men opened the hatch and moved quickly the short distance to the creature. Being much larger than they suspected, its size sent adrenaline surging through their veins. They hurried in, clipped off a piece of plant-stained tooth and turned back.

Standing in the entrance to the ship was a lone droid. Startled, Acharya dropped the bucket. "Well, could that thing be any more kenspeckle?"

"What does that mean?"

"Oh, nothing, just trying to make conversation," said Acharya.

"Nice deductive reasoning by the way. Now what do we do?" Skyler asked.

"Try to stay calm. He could have ripped us to shreds already if he had wanted to. Perhaps he is just curious. Look at that expression. He reminds me of a curious puppy," said Acharya.

"Yeah right! A puppy with twelve inch claws."

"He seems to be interested in your knife," Acharya said, forming an idea. "Throw it as far as you can. Now!"

Skyler paused and considered objecting to giving up his only weapon. Instead, looking at the thing standing before them, he shrugged and tossed the knife away from the ship. The droid was after it immediately. Skyler grabbed Acharya and shoved him forward. They stumbled through the entrance and closed the door."

"We need a faster door!" Skyler exclaimed. "On the next trip, let's make sure the doors close faster. And can we get rid of that ugly mascaron of a door latch? Who's big idea was that anyway?"

"I have a list of other things we should bring as well," Acharya gasped, astonished to be alive.

"That was probably a big mistake," Skyler said. "Haven't you heard of the prime directive? When we return, those things will be hunting the big red beasts with laser guns."

"I believe that returning is the key point. Without playing fetch, we might not have been leaving."

To their astonishment, the droid picked up the tooth bucket, placed it at the base of the door and backed away. Seeing that the creature wasn't moving, Skyler cracked open the door and retrieved the bucket.

"Obviously, these droid things are highly intelligent and more curious than aggressive," Acharya said.

"This might sound weird, but for some reason it reminded me of a dolphin. It startled me at first, but I could tell it was non-aggressive. The smart animals on Earth have subtle but definite ways of communicating. I believe that's what we've encountered."

"I want to spend more time studying these beings," Acharya said, "but we are not qualified. I believe we should take the treasures we have and return to Earth. It is tempting to stay and learn more, but what we have learned already is far too valuable."

"You're talking about the treasure hunter's dilemma," Skyler said as he examined the tooth segment. "Upon finding a room full of treasure in the middle of a jungle, the treasure hunters are faced with two choices: take what they can carry in their pockets, or try to haul it all out. Those that make the second choice rarely survive to enjoy their wealth.

"You're right my friend," said Skyler. "It's time to leave Varuna and the stars of Alpha Centauri. Hell, think about it: a couple of amateur bozos that just happened to cross paths with a group of renegade scientists that just happened to be a lot smarter than anyone knew until they got funded. Yeah, let's pack-up and hit the road."

As the *Hispaniola* lifted off slowly, Acharya was able to film several of the droid beings. They stood and watched the spaceship for a while and then moved in unison, like a herd of buffalo, back to the barrier wall enclosing the massive space-tree. Unlike an animal eager to stay with the herd, though, one of the beings remained; still clutching Skyler's laser knife It continued to watch until the spaceship was out of sight.

"I believe we made a friend today," Acharya said as he watched Skyler control their craft with ever-growing skill. "I continue to be amazed with this spacecraft. It attacks the vast distances of space near the speed of light and yet floats slowly above the surface of a planet at your command. Because of the work of James and that remarkable team he assembled, mankind is destined for the Stars. I cannot begin to imagine the adventures that lie ahead. What a marvelous wonder. How I would love to see the future."

"You *have* seen the future, Acharya. It's back there on Varuna, and it's in the galaxy of other incredible worlds man will explore. But for now, I have a wedding to get to, and you're my best man."

"I would be more than honored," Acharya said with a big surprised smile.

TWENTY-FIVE

The *Hispaniola* dropped out of light speed near the orbital plane of Mars. The crew was ready for the dark depression that ripped at the fabric of their minds when slowing after a long period of near light-speed velocity. Approaching Earth's space, they prepared for their first transmission since leaving the solar system.

"Belay that transmission. Earth is in danger!" Acharya announced.

"A...why?" Skyler said, turning to his companion.

"There! I have it on the main view screen now. That asteroid is a planet killer, and it is on a direct collision course with Earth. Take us closer. We need to help."

Within fifteen minutes, Skyler was fast approaching the massive asteroid. As they swung into orbit around the object, they noticed a large, well lit spacecraft on the surface. Presently another was visible, and another. The ships had a stingray look similar to the *Hispaniola*, but much larger.

"Apparently, an Earth saving rescue is already underway," Skyler said.

Acharya was busy evaluating the situation. Eventually, he lifted his head from the space microscope and said, "I do not believe this is a rescue mission. From what I can discern, they are probably extracting iron-nickel ore while pushing the asteroid closer to Earth. Those are asteroid mining ships, and the asteroid is their cargo."

"We have a signal from one of the ships," Skyler said, pointing to the waveform indicator.

"I have it," said Acharya, adjusting his headset.

"This is restricted space. You are trespassing on private AMC property."

"I'll handle it. Pipe me in," Skyler said.

"We are the spaceship *Hispaniola*, returning from a trip to the Alpha Centauri star system."

After a two-minute pause, they received a response: "Welcome home *Hispaniola*! Lot's of cheers on the other end of our channel. We have been ordered to escort you the rest of the way in."

The two spacecrafts landed at the New Kennedy Space Center in Florida. Skyler was determined to fly directly to Kauai, but was convinced to land in Florida after learning that the Kauai project was no longer operational. The *Hispaniola* was legendary and the potacitor technologies had already changed the face of a grateful planet. Upon their arrival, it was obvious that much had changed since they left.

A large assortment of military and civilian dignitaries waited as they exited their ship. "This is weird," Skyler whispered to Acharya. "We've only been gone ten days. This is like a different planet. Look at those hover car things and the people floating in the air using those backpacks. I know how they did it, but it's still weird."

"Welcome home!" A large, jolly-looking man said as he approached. "I am the President of Asteroid Mining Corporation. We are the lucky ones that escorted you back to Earth. I would like to introduce the Director of NASA and the Vice President of the United States. They were both on-site when we received news of your arrival."

Skyler and Acharya shook hands with dozens of important people they had never seen before. As they walked across the tarmac and into a large blue and white building, they received cheers from hundreds of employees lined up for a glimpse at Earth's returning astronauts. The crowd celebrated with hand waves, screams, and other noises.

Because the *Hispaniola* wasn't part of NASA or any government agency, AMC (a subsidiary of a larger conglomerate formed by the Babylonian's original investors) handled the debriefing. Two hours into the briefing, the travelers learned of James.

"Why didn't you tell us about this sooner?" Skyler asked, unable to control his emotions. "Please tell me that Anchor, the girl handling our communications when we left, is all right."

A well-dressed woman nodded to one of the men asking questions and left the room. A few minutes later, she requested to speak directly to Skyler.

"I have just spoken with Miss Mills. She was thrilled to hear of your return. She was rather emotional and it was difficult to understand everything she was saying. She said something about data being with her. I am not sure what kind of data she has, but she felt it was important that I tell you."

"I understand. Thank you, thanks so much."

Skyler glanced at Acharya, who smiled with tears in his eyes. "Forgive us everyone. It has only been ten days for us since we last saw James."

"Thank you for reminding us," the woman said. "We are deeply sorry for your loss. You should take pride in knowing that he too is a hero to the people of Earth."

As the questions continued, Skyler and Acharya told of their journey. Questions about Varuna repeated to the point of monotony. The questions lasted for several hours before the debriefing ended. As the room cleared, two of the men in the back remained. Neither man had asked questions during the session, but it was obvious to Skyler that these men were important decision makers. He had noticed how people would turn to them as if seeking their approval.

"We need to return to Kauai as soon as possible," Skyler said as they approached.

"Naturally, we understand how anxious you must be," one of the men said. "We have a room reserved for you at the Hilton. We were hoping you would agree to a press conference this evening. Then you can get some rest, and we will fly you home in the morning."

"My apologies," Acharya said. "I do not recall being introduced."

"No, no, the fault lies with me," the man said. "My name is Mr. L. Griffin, and my associate here is Mr. Sam Ashcroft. We are owners, you might say, of Asteroid Mining Corporation. I am the Chief Executive Officer of the company and Mr. Ashcroft is the company Secretary. We sat on the board when your project was originally funded. I must confess that I was one of the major skeptics, but you and your team have proven me wrong—very wrong."

"Well, it's just good to be back. I believe I speak for Acharya when I say that we are both more than anxious to return to our homes. Is there any chance we could hold the press conference in Kauai?"

After laughter from both men, the second one spoke. "You obviously do not know how important you are or how big this story is. There are reporters from every news network on the planet gathering this evening for your press conference. I would also like to tell you that you are both extremely wealthy men. We took the liberty of including you in the employee option pool. Your vested shares are now worth in excess of forty million dollars."

Skyler was surprised. "I don't know what to say. Thank you, thanks a lot!"

Acharya remained silent. Skyler knew Acharya well. His silence probably meant there was more to this gift than a magnanimous gesture. Acharya was apparently waiting for the other shoe to drop.

"That is what we wish to speak with you about. You can thank us by letting us manage the depth and timing of information provided to the general public. In other words, we feel that some of the discoveries from Alpha Centauri should be released at the time of our choosing," Mr. Griffin said.

"Do you have any specific discoveries in mind, Mr. Griffin?" Acharya asked.

"Mr. L. Griffin if you don't mind."

"What?" Skyler asked.

"Mr. L. Griffin, I prefer to be addressed as Mr. L. Griffin."

Mr. L. Griffin was a mostly bald man with a round face and small beady eyes. When agitated, as he appeared presently, his face turned bright red. "Yes, we do have specific discoveries in mind. I'm sure you can appreciate the importance of keeping information about your Varuna from the public. The verification and protection of such a resource is of critical importance."

"I must confess that I do not understand the importance of such secrecy. You must certainly control the potacitor technologies. How likely is it that a caravan of tourists would be traveling to Varuna anytime soon?" Acharya responded.

Skyler was impressed with how well Acharya handled the tycoons. *Not bad for a timid monk*, he thought.

Abruptly the tone of the conversation became less cordial. "You do not understand," Mr. Ashcroft said in a clearly threatening voice. "This is not negotiable! We funded this project, and we will decide what information we choose to release to the public." Sam Ashcroft was the younger of the two. His hair was dark with a hint of gray. Unlike his red faced partner, he would look you in the eyes when speaking.

"Now, Sam, there is no need to raise our voices," Mr. L. Griffin said, lifting his hands palms out. "I am sure our heroes have more on their minds than involving themselves in the political workings of a large corporation. We just need to explain to them what is in the best interest of everyone concerned."

"Okay, guys. Let me see if I understand this so we don't have to go through anymore of this good cop/bad cop routine," Skyler interjected. "If we behave ourselves and play along, you will handle the public disclosures, and we will be wealthy beyond our wildest dreams. Do I have it about right?"

"Do not disrespect Mr. Griffin! You do not know who you are dealing with."

"That's Mr. *L.* Griffin," said Skyler.

Mr. L. Griffin's face turned bright red but his voice was calm. "No, it's all right Sammy. I believe Mr. Anderson put it very well. I like his method of cutting through the crap. The question is...do we have an agreement?"

"I was just wondering, Skyler," Acharya said, walking toward the door. "If we wrote a book about our adventures, do you think anyone would buy it?"

Skyler caught on instantly. "Well, I'm not sure. I suppose there is a slim possibility that a few people might be interested."

Skyler let his comment sink in before continuing. "I'm sorry, gentlemen, but we are tired. We've traveled a fair distance and we would like to get this press conference over with so we can go home. Oh, and you clearly don't know who you're dealing with. We are friends of James Stevenson, and we know what he would want us to do. You do remember James Stevenson don't you? He was the wacko scientist that brought down the President of the United States for misleading the world. Sorry dudes, we really don't give a shit what you want kept secret."

Two hours later, following medical examinations, Skyler and Acharya were standing at the podium of a large room filled with reporters and cameras. Acharya began the press conference with: "*Imagine if you can a world...*"

Skyler ended the press conference with: "*Does anyone here know where we can hitch a ride back to Kauai?*"

Later that night, they spread out on a plush airliner owned by CNN. "Any idea how long it's been since we've slept?" Skyler asked.

"Too long, my courageous and stupid friend. We may have just given up a fortune. We could blame it on lack of sleep," Acharya said.

"Hey, I just took your lead. That makes us both stupid."

"Do not forget courageous." Acharya laughed.

Their old-fashioned standard jet, upgraded with a safety potacitor, landed ten hours later at Lihue airport. Acharya woke Skyler and pointed out the window. Standing on the tarmac was a slightly older Anchor, more beautiful than ever.

"She ages well," Skyler said.

"Indeed. An excellent choice for a bride, I would say."

Along with Anchor, a greeting party of several monks, Strant, and three members of the original Babylonian team, including Isaac, were waiting. As Skyler walked down the ramp, Anchor ran toward him. He stepped off the last aluminum stair and caught her as she flew into his arms.

"I can't believe you're back! I worried every day. I didn't believe in my heart that it was possible for you to survive such a mission. You did it! You came home to me."

"Tell me about James," Skyler said.

"I will, Skyler, but haven't you missed me? You've been gone for so long."

"We've been gone for ten days. It's difficult to understand, I know. I love you as much as ever, but I can't miss you the way you've missed me. I can't know all that you've been through."

"I understand, and I know how much it hurts to lose James. I was so sad for months. Forgive me, darling. He died saving the life of a young girl. He wasn't in pain. His wife is living in New York with her sister. Data is waiting for us in the car. I don't believe I could have survived without that goofy dog. We've been helping each other. Should I slow down? Am I talking too fast?"

"Tell me everything," Skyler said. "It just occurred to me that I have no place to live."

"I have a place on Maui, but we can stay at my family's Alii Kai condo for a while. Oh, Skyler, this is wonderful. You have no idea how good it is to hold you. Do I look a lot older? Am I still pretty to you?"

"Anchor, you look terrific. If anything, you're even more beautiful."

The monks and scientists were talking with Acharya and patting him on the shoulder. Skyler spotted Strant again, standing to the side, seeming out of place. He walked toward his friend with Anchor latched to his arm. She jumped to the side as Strant greeted him with a hearty bear hug.

"I was with James the day he died," Strant said. "A team of no-good military bastards tried to kill us that day. He died shortly after he left me."

"Do you think they had something to do with his death?" Skyler asked.

"No, it was just James trying to save a young girl. But there's something I want to talk with you about when we're alone. You look exhausted. Why don't you and Anchor stay at my place tonight? I need to fly to Oahu for a few days, and it would give you some privacy from the press. Anchor needs to be with you now."

"Thanks, buddy. I'll take you up on that. This has been something."

"Yes, thank you, Strant," Anchor said and gave him a kiss on the cheek.

"Just one moment, Anchor. There's someone I need to thank for getting us back here safe and sound." Skyler walked to Isaac and grabbed his hand. They talked for a while as Skyler tried to explain how the unauthorized software program Isaac installed had saved their lives.

Before they left, Acharya pulled Skyler aside and said something to him. At last the party separated. Acharya returned to the monastery with his companions; and with Anchor rambling in a joyful babble, Skyler and Strant accompanied her to the parking lot. A black monster with two bright, anxious eyes stared impatiently at Skyler through the smudged back window of Anchor's car. When Anchor opened the door, Data flew into Skyler's arms.

"Wow, he's happy to see you," Strant said. "I've never seen him do that with anyone else, not even James."

"It's a game we play. James trained him never to jump on anyone, but for some reason, he let us get away with this. Gooood boy. Good old boy," Skyler said just before getting his faced washed with Data's tongue. "Yuck, he got me that time. Damn, I wish James were here. I have so much I wanted to tell him."

"He knows, Skyler. If there's a God in heaven, then he knows," Strant said.

"Hey man, thanks for helping out the team with those stock options. Acharya told me who was responsible."

"No problemo. I managed to get Anchor and myself a few shares as well, so it was mostly greed. I just stirred things up a little with a few things from my Silicon Valley days. Oh, hey, Acharya told me about your little scuffle, and they can't revoke your shares. They were vested over two years, so you've been a wealthy man for over a year now."

"Two years, huh? From my point of view, that's pretty good pay for ten days work."

"Yeah, well I doubt if any attorney is going to argue that position since the shares were invested here on good old Earth."

"This is fun!" Anchor said. "I feel like we're getting away with something. You guys picked up right where you left off. It must be wonderful having such close friends that love each other."

The two men shrugged uncomfortably. "Yeah, whatever," Skyler said, and Strant grudgingly agreed.

"Oh, well excuse me. I didn't mean to embarrass you," Anchor giggled.

The three sat on the balcony of Strant's mansion and talked for hours until Skyler fell asleep in Anchor's arms. Strant helped him to bed, where he slept until the next afternoon. He awoke to Anchor singing in the distant kitchen and to the smell of fresh eggs and sausage.

Strant left for Oahu after the late breakfast. Skyler found Strant's computer and sat down to draft a letter. The words danced off his keyboard in an orchestration of...mediocrity. "What are you doing?" Anchor asked.

"Oh, nothing. I need to call Silvia tomorrow."

They spent the rest of the day making love, walking on the beach with Data, and shopping at the farmer's market in Kilauea where Data stole a piece of goat cheese from one of the vendors and ran like hell. The farmer laughed and accepted a generous payment from Anchor.

"I've never been happier," Anchor said. "I know this isn't that special for you, but it has been so long for me. It's really weird, if you think about it."

"Believe me, Anchor, this is special for me, too. Although we were gone for just ten days, it seems much longer. I've never experienced so much in such a short period of time. With James lost, and the memories of Varuna, it seems like an eternity has passed. Perhaps the universe has a way of making up for lost time or something. Time really is relative. I can tell you this: in all the vastness of space, there is no place I would rather be than home again, here with you."

"Skyler, everything has been changing so fast. For some reason I'm still frightened. I couldn't bear to lose you again. How long will we be together?"

Skyler could feel her trembling in his arms. "I'm not going anywhere, my darling. You're stuck with me for a long, long time."

Somewhere in the depths of her soul Anchor felt otherwise.

"Are we becoming just another version of the arrogant enemy that we used to oppose?" Samuel Ashton asked to the dismay of his powerful boss, Mr. L. Griffin.

"This is bigger, Sammy. With interstellar space travel now at our fingertips, we have a responsibility to mankind, not just our investors.

The two men continued their walk through central park near their company head quarters in New York.

"I agree. But this is a destiny that belongs to all of mankind, not just one company. I have a sinking feeling that we are giving ourselves too much credit."

Sam was a good friend to Mr. L. Griffin. He had served the company and the investors with professionalism, honesty, and loyalty, but he was presently having grave doubts. The company and its board had become too powerful. They believed that the salvation of humanity rested in their hands.

"Sam, those bastard heroes have gone too far. Our disinformation campaign was starting to work when they released that organic evidence to the scientific community. How did they get that material past us in the first place? That's what I would like to know."

"I'll have no part of this, L. If you want to have those boys *eliminated*, as you put it, then you will need to find someone else. I am giving you the best advice I can. Do not go down this road."

L. Griffin had no intention of changing his mind, but he was concerned about Sam. Sam had never refused a direct order before, and they had worked together on some shady projects. *It's best if I keep him out of the loop on this one*, L. Griffin thought to himself. *I should start looking for a replacement. This kitchen is getting too hot for Sammy.*

"Of course, you're right as always. What the hell was I thinking? Do not concern yourself. I was just brainstorming, you know, just exploring the possibilities."

"You had me scared there for a while, boss. I knew this wasn't you. Let's find a way to turn this whole Varuna disclosure to our advantage." Sam was playing along. He knew the two space heroes were as good as dead. It was time for action. He had enough inside information to remove his old errant friend from power. It was time to restore some sanity to the powers that be.

Two weeks later, Sam called together a special meeting of the board of directors. He had secretly garnered support from a majority of the shareholders who were already itching for a way to remove Mr. L. Griffin as CEO. With the transition approved in advance, Sam became the new head of AMC Corp. Unfortunately a prepaid assassin was still in pursuit of Skyler and Acharya.

Once again, evil lurked on the friendly island of Kauai. Sam followed every lead he could find to terminate the corporate assassin contract. On a hunch, he located the contractors in a database that Sam himself had set up. He followed the instructions in the electronic packet and ordered the contract dissolved.

The encrypted text message response read as follows: *Cannot make contact with field until tomorrow. If the targets survive, consider contract altered; otherwise, agreement remains. Do not attempt further communication.*

TWENTY-SIX

Skyler waited with Anchor just outside the health food store in Hanalei's Ching Young Village. It was a perfect morning on the North Shore. The lack of rain for several days meant good footing on the technical trails of Na Pali.

Strant and Acharya were late for the day long hike into Hanakapi'ae Falls. Aware of their destination, Data was anxious to get moving. As he wiggled impatiently, a large, muscular man with long hair walked past and patted him on the head. Skyler gave the man a nonchalant smile, looked away, and looked again. He slowly recognized the man as the Muscle Boy jerk he had dealt with before. The man looked much different—healthier and more natural. His white skin had turned to a Kauai tan, and his brown crew cut had grown out to a length unacceptable by military standards.

"Hey, pal," Skyler said. "Let's not do this again."

The man knelt beside Data, who was enjoying the rubbing, and said, "Relax, Skyler. I mean you no harm. I'm glad I found you. I need to apologize and tell you thanks for putting my lights out years ago. I've spent a lot of time thinking about why I was so angry. I worked at various jobs but landed as yoga instructor, and I've made some great friends. Something about this place has changed me. I was a first rate asshole. I'm truly sorry, man."

At first, Skyler thought he was being set up for a sneak attack, but looking into the man's eyes and watching his relaxed nature, Skyler believed he was sincere. "All right, apology accepted. Do you remember my fiancée, Anchor Mills?"

"I remember her well. My nuts hurt for weeks."

"Oh, I remember now, I'm sorry, too. You don't look like the same person," Anchor said, trying to avoid looking at the man's crotch.

"I hope I'm not disturbing you. This is a great dog you've got here."

"His name is Data," Anchor said with a smile as she shook the man's hand.

"You're one famous dude these days. I wasn't sure if you would give me the time of day to make my peace. Thanks again, man."

"Not so famous. I just wanna fade away from the clatter and the publicity." Skyler paused and looked at the man for a while. "I have to admit, you're much different. I barely recognized you at first. Do you mind if I ask your name?"

"Glen England. I'd just left the military when I came to the islands with my girlfriend. They messed me up bad, made me mean. The funny thing is that before I went in, I never lost my temper. I think I'm finally finding myself again. Shit, I feel bad about that day."

"Which one?" Skyler asked.

"Yeah, good point. Both of them."

"Consider it forgotten, Glen," Skyler said and reached for the man's hand.

"I heard about that scientist. The one that built the spaceship you flew in. I think he died a couple years ago."

"It's been about a year and a half. For me it's only been a month, theory of relativity and all."

"Wow, that's heavy, dude."

"Hey, why don't you come with us today?" Anchor asked. "We're hiking the Na Pali." It was hard to believe the big guy was the same person.

"No, I don't want to impose. You don't need me hanging around."

"It's okay, Glen. We've got a couple friends coming as well. You're more than welcome, if you're not busy."

"Great, count me in then. I'm not working until eight, and I could use the exercise."

A few minutes later, a middle-aged monk and a wild-eyed surfer clamored into the center area, spotted Skyler, and made their approach. They were arguing feverously about something. The scene of a surfer and a monk arguing struck Glen as funny. When he laughed, it caused Data to jump up and bark.

"Calm down, Data. Guys, I'd like you to meet Glen England. This is the big guy I had the fight with the day we learned of the bogus aliens."

Both men looked at Glen in quietude. They suspected something bad was about to happen.

"As I recall," Glen said, "it was no fight. You hit me, and I hit the ground. Isn't that how you described it?"

"Hey, whoa, hold on, pal. Are you a yoga instructor?" Strant asked, as he looked at the man with less than confidence.

"I'm *your* yoga instructor," Glen laughed. "You don't recognize me in my street clothes?"

"It's all right, Strant. We're friends now. Remember what a jerk you were the first time we met?"

"Hey, you were the jerk, dude. That was my girlfriend you were hitting on," Strant responded, forgetting about Glen.

"I want to hear about this," Anchor said.

"Yeah right, you knew the girl for one day and she was all over me. I did you a favor by exposing her," said Skyler.

"You *exposed* her?" Anchor placed her hands on her hips, something she did when her mood darkened.

"No, not that way, I just helped Strant get a better understanding of who she was, that's all."

"I'm sorry you have to see this, Glen," Anchor said, moving away from Skyler.

"So you two aren't about to bust each other up?" Strant asked.

"No, my days of busting up good guys are over," Glen said, still rubbing Data's head for security.

"Glen's coming on the hike with us. He's an ex-military man, so we'll be in good hands," Skyler said.

Interrupting their conversation, a stranger slammed into Acharya's shoulder as he walked past. He had an angry pockmarked face of scarred skin and his head was shaved to a rough stubble. He turned and confronted the monk. "Get the hell out of the way," he said.

"My apologies," Acharya said and bowed.

"Are you screwing with me?" the man continued.

"Where do these people come from?" Skyler asked, glancing at Glen.

"Was I that big of a jerk?" Glen said.

"What did you say?" The hired assassin turned and walked up into Glen's face.

This guy must be nuts. He's about to get his head ripped off, Skyler thought.

"He said he was sorry. We're all sorry. We will be leaving now," Glen said firmly, holding Data's collar.

The assassin smiled a deadly smile. He stood staring at Acharya as they walked away.

Five minutes later, after stopping to pick up Glen's backpack, they turned down highway 560 in route to the trail's head at the end of the road. They gathered on Ke'e Beach to check their equipment, water, and carb-filled snacks. Looking up toward the trail, Skyler noticed a man flying past the nearest visible rim at the peak. He was wearing a personal potacitor kit, a miracle of compact design.

The sight troubled Skyler because he knew that few people on Earth had access to the kits. Not approved for public dissemination, the new United Nations was claiming they would present a risk to world security. Skyler managed a quick look at the flying human and was confident he was the same ugly man that had confronted them in Hanalei. He looked at Glen who nodded in agreement.

"I must object, Strant. I am afraid you are just speaking jabberwocky. None of this makes any sense," Acharya said.

"Acharya, can I break up your spat for a minute? The man that bumped into you earlier just flew around that trail peak wearing one of those potacitor backpack things. Why would an employee of AMC be here?" Skyler said.

"Are you sure it was him?"

"Oh, it was him. Glen saw him as well."

"I would have to speculate that they have people watching us. They are not pleased with our...lack of cooperation. Perhaps they just want us to know that we are being watched."

"I think we should have a more informative chat with him if we get the chance," Skyler said, clearly upset.

Satisfied they were ready, the friends started up Kalalau Trail, a path sliced into the coastline by the ancients. Despite the lack of rain, the trail remained slippery, muddy and steep in numerous places.

"I love this hike," Anchor said. "This is just spectacular. I've never seen anything like it."

Acharya struggled to keep pace with the younger hikers. After two miles, they wandered down the descent to the Hanakapi'ae Beach. Acharya let the others move ahead, knowing that they would be resting at the beach before the climb up to the waterfall. When the others were out of sight, Acharya began whistling as he enjoyed the slower pace. Without warning, the man who had confronted them earlier appeared, standing in the middle of the trail before him.

Acharya stopped. It was a strange and eerie sight to see the angry ugly man standing in the middle of the trail without moving. Acharya reached for his water bottle and sat on a rock. He tried to relax by gazing upon the blue pacific. He glanced periodically at the man who was still standing motionless and staring at him. *This is creepy*, Acharya thought to himself.

Not sure what to do, he decided to risk walking past the man. As he prepared to leave, he heard Strant yelling his name. When he looked up, the mysterious man was gone, and Strant was walking toward him. "Hey, slowpoke! What ya doing? You okay?

"Yes, I am fine. I am not as young as I once was. I was much faster when I was younger."

"Yeah, sure. The older people get, the faster and better looking they were. Let's go, dude."

"Hey, that was very funny, Strant."

As they worked their way down the steep trail to the river and the beach beyond, Acharya told Strant about the strange re-encounter with the man. "What do you think he was going to do?" Strant asked, concerned.

"I do not know. I just know he was blocking my way. It was more frightening than the dinosauroid I encountered on Varuna. He is one strange person."

"That's it!" Skyler said when he found out about Acharya's encounter. "I'm making some calls when we get back. Let's stay together from now on and keep an eye out for this creep. We're going to have to deal with these people once and for all."

Anchor was throwing a stick on the beach for Data. She was happy and having fun. Skyler decided not to concern her with the strange man again. He ran toward her and tried to race Data for the stick. Data thought that was great sport as he managed to reach the stick just ahead of Skyler, taunting him.

They walked to the end of the beach and splashed through an inlet, entering into a small open cave. Skyler held Anchor and kissed her while keeping an eye on Data. Skyler's kisses were intended for Data, not Anchor. The dog became jealous of too much attention to Anchor, and Skyler couldn't resist teasing him. Data barked furiously and nudged his way between them. They both laughed as they leaned over, hugging and rewarding him with a flurry of attention.

Glen was sitting with Strant and Acharya. He told them about his apology and how well Skyler had responded. "You'll never find a better friend if you get Skyler on your side," Strant said.

"There are amazing people on this island. I'd probably be in prison by now if I hadn't found this place."

"According to legend, the islands have a way of keeping the people that should be here and sending the others away," Acharya said. "To have remained here for so many years is an indicator of your enlightenment."

"Thanks, man. Ya know, it was kind of weird seeing Skyler again. I've changed a lot, but he still looks exactly the same. He didn't place me at first, but I recognized him easily."

The group re-assembled at the base of the trail on the river's edge. They washed the sand from their feet and prepared for the two-mile trek to the waterfall. Skyler looked for Data and spotted him running back to the beach. People were screaming and pointing out to sea. A woman was desperately trying to swim back for shore, but the current was pushing her farther away. Another woman panicked on the shore jumping up and down. Skyler knew instantly that the one in the water was in serious trouble. People lost their lives just wading along Hanakapi'ae Beach, one of the most beautiful, yet dangerous, inlets on the islands.

He and Glen were halfway to the beach before the others understood what was happening. When they reached the sand, they kicked off their boots in unison. Data was in the water when Skyler yelled, "No, Data! Come here!" *That was close*, he thought.

Skyler turned to see Glen running toward a large older man with fins sitting on the sand. "I need these," he said, grabbing the fins and running back to Skyler.

"Why don't these people read the signs?" Skyler said, glancing back at the old warning sign on the other side of the river."

> *Hanakapi'ae Beach Warning!*
> *Do not go near the water*
> *Unseen Currents have killed*
> *hundreds of visitors*

"What can we do? Even great swimmers have drowned on this beach, and I'm not a great swimmer."

"She's going to die if we don't do something. I know these waters," Glen said, scanning both directions. "With fins, I believe I can push her down the beach away from the undertow and then back in. I am a great swimmer, but I've never been stupid enough to test these waters."

"You sure you want to do this? That is one hell of a risk, and your chances aren't good."

"I can do this, Skyler. Meet me about a hundred yards down the beach if you can make your way along the cliffs," Glen said, as he ran for the breaking waves, dove in carrying the fins, and disappeared underwater. He rose up like a flying fish. Skyler could see his large muscles rippling through the water in front of the churning fins. With the undertow, he was moving fast toward the desperate woman, who was tiring.

"Is he nuts?" Strant said, sliding to a stop at Skyler's side. "That's suicide! People don't come back from a current this strong."

"Let's go," Skyler said. "He's planning on dragging her sideways away from the current and back to shore. Anchor, you and Acharya wait here, and keep Data with you and out of the water."

Glen reached the woman, who was choking as she splashed to keep her head up, grabbed her, and slung her arms around his neck. "Try to help if you can, but follow my direction."

"Okay, but I can't breathe," she said, coughing.

"Just rest until you're ready, then try helping. We need to get away from this undertow. I'm taking us parallel to the beach."

Glen was swimming hard at a slight angle inward, hoping to counter the current sweeping them out to sea. He noticed Skyler and Strant working their way along the edge of the cliffs, tracking his sideways movement. Fortunately, the current hadn't reached its peak for the day yet. Glen was tiring, but he was making steady progress. The woman had quit choking and was more relaxed.

"Thank you. I didn't think I was going to make it."

"You're right about that, but we're not safe yet. Keep helping if you can."

Twenty minutes later, they were exhausted, but close enough that Skyler and Strant were able to help. While knocked around by the waves, the four managed to climb on to a large lava slab. Thirty minutes later, they were back to where the river met the ocean. As they crossed the creek, dozens of people came to their assistance.

In the commotion, no humans had noticed that Acharya was missing. But Data was on the hunt. Acharya had walked into the bushes to relieve himself and was once again confronted by the same ugly man. This time the man was holding a pistol. He knew he had his mark. With the people huddled around the rescued women, it couldn't be easier. The assassin enjoyed his work and killing a monk was something he had never done before. *Why take the risk of drawing attention from the sound of the gun*, thought the assassin. He smiled at Acharya, who had a stick in his hand for defense.

"Do you intend to fight me with that stick?" the man asked with a mocking laugh. "Very well, we shall do it your way." The man put his gun down on a rock and extracted the knife he had attached to his belt. He casually walked the twenty feet to where Acharya was standing.

"Why are you doing this? If I have offended you, then I am greatly in error. That was never my intention." Acharya knew his words were wasted, but at least it bought him a little more time.

"Oh, it isn't me that you've offended, Acharya. It's the people that hired me. I've enjoyed our conversation, but I really must finish my task now."

The man jolted toward Acharya with his knife held high but stopped abruptly at the sound of a deep, low, and menacing *Wooofffff*. The large black dog stood beside Acharya, all teeth, growling and ready to attack.

The trained assassin considered the situation and realized there was the possibility, though slight, that he might lose to the two of them. He backed up slowly, turned and ran for his gun. By the time he reached it, Acharya and Data were well on their way back to the beach. As they scrambled out of the bushes, Acharya glanced back; to his astonishment, the man was running away, across the river and up the trail back to Ke'e.

Well trained, the assassin knew when to regroup for another attack. He grabbed his hidden flight kit, and when out of sight, flew toward the waterfall, hoping the hikers wouldn't abandon their journey.

Acharya told the others what had happened as they moved away from the crowd. "He ran across the river in the direction of Ke'e. I cannot believe those bastards would resort to this. So much good in this world, and so much evil."

"The police are on their way," Skyler said. "A boy had a short-wave radio and called for help to rescue the woman.

I contacted Jeff and filled him in along with a description of the man. He told us to continue with our hike if we wanted. They're sending a helicopter out just in case he's still around. I'm guessing he's gone for the day, and I'm not in the mood to be intimidated anymore."

"Are you okay to continue, Glen?" Strant said. "You must be exhausted. I'll hike back with you if you're too tired."

"Oh, hell, I forgot. I'm sorry, Glen," Skyler said. "We can head back. I'll tell Jeff we're coming in. This guy saves a woman's life, and all I can do is think about getting to the waterfall."

"It's okay. I recover fast. I'm in a lot better shape than the first time we met. My muscles aren't as big, but I'm in good shape."

"Your muscles aren't as big?" Anchor said, squeezing his arm at the shoulder. "That's hard to imagine."

"So if you're in better shape, does that mean you could take our friend Skyler here now?" Strant loved to stir things up.

"Yeah, I probably could," Glen said with a smile.

"Thanks for the tip," Skyler said. "I'm glad we're on the same team now."

They gathered their gear together and prepared to hike up the trail once again when the rescued woman approached them in her thin green bikini. With her wet brown hair combed back, she was a happy and attractive survivor. She gave Glen a long hard hug and handed him a card with her phone number. "You'd better call me. I live on the South Shore. I would love to fix you dinner sometime." She thanked everyone and walked away.

"Hey, now I know how to attract fine women. We bring Glen along and rescue them. Good thinking, dude. That's a nice looking babe."

"Oh, Strant, don't you ever quit?" said Anchor.

Anchor was worried about Skyler. His determination to continue with the hike was out of character. She decided to dig deeper. As the others started out, she grabbed Skyler's arm. "How are you doing?"

"Great, just happy to be moving again," he said with little thought.

"I'm kind of tired from the excitement. Why don't we just head back and go to a movie tonight. I'm buying."

"You're buying? Are you asking me for a date?"

"Yes, I suppose I am. What do you say? Let's get out of here."

"I'm not in the mood to be intimidated by the strong arm of the AMC. Our mission to Varuna was adventurous and exciting, but I fantasized about making it back and swimming at the waterfall. I need to go behind the blast of the water and scream a great big YEAH! It's a guy thing."

"We could still be at risk, Skyler. We don't know for sure where that killer is."

"Exactly, but he's probably decided we'll give up on the hike and turn back. So I say we do the unexpected, and ignore the bastard."

Skyler ended the conversation by picking up the pace and sliding to the front of the group. At first Anchor was offended. It wasn't in Skyler's nature to walk away while they were talking. She steamed for a while, but her emotions changed to concern and a little fear. She noticed that Acharya and Strant were arguing again, so she moved closer to find out what the spat was about this time.

"One of the most common arguments used to explain Fermi's Paradox is the Rare Earth hypothesis. We destroyed that argument by finding life, and probably intelligent life. So I ask you again: where is everyone?"

"You just made my point," Strant said. "We just need to do a better job of looking."

"I agree with that premise, but it does not explain the paradox; it confirms it. If there is other life, why have they not made contact with us already?"

Strant realized that he was out of his league in this area, but he enjoyed arguing with Acharya and it gave him an excuse for keeping an eye on him. "What does it matter if we find them first? It's not complicated."

"That is impossible. The entire point is that the raw numbers and vast scale make it impossible. We cannot be the first civilization in the vast universe to have achieved interstellar travel."

"Sure, I agree that the odds are against us, but so what?" Strant said emphatically.

"We are not talking about winning the lottery, Strant. I do not mean to be disrespectful, but we are talking about odds that approach impossibility."

"Hell, be disrespectful. How can we argue about this if you continue to be so damn polite? Look, you said the odds approach impossibility. That's not the same as impossible."

Acharya was troubled with Strant's position. Even as he argued the statistics, he had a strange feeling that he had been down this path before. Something was troubling him, something he could not remember. He stumbled on a rock, recovered, and continued the debate.

"Perhaps we've already met them," Anchor said, interrupting the argument.

"What?" Strant asked, turning suddenly and bumping into Anchor. "Sorry, what do you mean?"

"Come on guys, have you forgotten about the old monk. How do we know he wasn't some alien visitor? That old guy saved a man's life. I know that as sure as I know anything. I wish someone else had been there."

"If the old monk is an alien, then why not just tell us? But I see your point," Strant said. "For all we know, they could think of us like ants in an ant box. What about that, Acharya?"

Thinking back, Acharya remembered the old monk, the frail old man with a perfect smile. There was definitely something unusual about him. "Well, I suppose that is a possibility, but I do not believe that aliens would observe us in the form of an old Buddhist monk."

"Why not?" Anchor asked. "They'd have to take on some form. And have you forgotten the rainbow? That's never been explained. It was probably the monk's spaceship that caused the rainbow effect when it landed." Anchor was having fun with this line of speculation.

"Hey, I think she's onto something," Strant said.

Acharya shook his head. "When Skyler and I visited Varuna, we did not disguise ourselves. This does not make sense. You would not travel to another star system and play such games. I met the old monk, and I am sure he is capable of what some might consider miraculous deeds but history is teeming with examples of such people."

As they turned the corner into an open grove area, Anchor noticed the trail that led to the rainhut. "There's the trail," she said. "There's the trail to the rainhut where I spoke with the monk. Let's go see if he's there. We can ask him if he's from another world."

"Skyler and Glen are too far ahead. We'd better keep going," Strant said.

"Where are they going to go? They'll wait for us or continue on to the waterfall. Let's go check it out."

Anchor was already running up the trail in the direction

of the rainhut. Her companions had no choice but to follow. She dashed ahead and disappeared around a corner into the deep jungle brush. She reached the rainhut and stepped inside. Old emotions returned as she remembered the injured tourist and the yellow robed stranger who save him.

Acharya was puffing hard as he and Strant reached the entry. "Anchor, where are you?" he gasped.

There was no answer for ten seconds. Eerily stiff, Anchor walked to the entrance and stared into the distance. The shadows and light formed a strange dance on her features. "You are too late, Earthlings. This body has already been taken. Make no attempt to interfere."

Acharya and Strant felt a chill down their backs as they stared at each other and back to Anchor, who broke into a laugh. "You should have seen your faces. That was the dumbest trick in the book, and you two fell for it."

"Don't be stupid, Anchor. We didn't fall for anything," Strant said, irritated at his own initial reaction.

"Oh, okay...duh. That blank look on your faces was hilarious."

Back down the trail, Data barked as he ran toward them. Having hunted them down, He was delighted with his find. "Come here, boy," Anchor said and wrestled with the squirming dog until he settled down.

"Data does not like it when we get separated. That quirk in his nature most likely saved my life," Acharya said as he joined Anchor in consoling the dog. "Apparently, our monk is not around."

Strant walked into the rainhut and sat on the lone bench. He peered through the other side and into the misty grove. "I kind of like this place. I mean it's old and creepy, but I'll bet it's saved more than a few people from being drenched in a sudden downpour. This would be a good place to crash if you ever found yourself out here at night."

The assassin landed at the top of the waterfall and hid from the helicopter making passes over the area. Later, convinced the search was finished, he began to hatch his devious scheme. He walked near the top edge of the hundred-foot waterfall and surveyed the people swimming in the pool and sitting on the surrounding rocks below.

He gathered boulders from the adjacent fields and assembled a large pile of rocks near the feeding stream. Satisfied with his salvo, he hid in a convenient clump of bushes that gave him a clear view of the domain below. When he saw Skyler working his way toward the pool, the assassin smiled at his own cleverness. One of the others followed, but it was Skyler the assassin wanted. He would take the monk later.

Skyler glanced back to see only Glen following. He assumed that Acharya had been unable to keep up the pace, and the others were with him. He scrambled across the rocks and reached the water's edge. The sound of the waterfall was overwhelming. Skyler loved it. He slid off his shoes and shirt and turned back to see Glen waving at him. With joy, he dove into the ice-cold water. It jolted him and sapped away his breath. Then the familiar numb feeling overcame the unbearable cold.

He enjoyed the way his body felt after swimming in the pristine pool. The swim was painful at first, but well worth the stress. Normally, he would swim around the edge and work his way behind the massive wall of water. However, today he would swim directly through the outer edge of the falls. He had done this before. The water would slam him hard, but Skyler knew where to enter.

The rest of the group was on the trail again; they had the waterfall in sight when Anchor spotted Glen. He waved at the group, obviously waiting for them. *Where's Skyler?* Anchor thought. She had had an uneasy feeling since leaving the rainhut. It was her old fears again. She wished that she had stayed with him.

Skyler lowered his head and swam hard for the waterfall. The blasting sound, the riveting cold, and the pending assault were thrilling. It was just what his young healthy body had yearned for while on the journey to the stars. Skyler was back in his element.

At the top, black boulders slid over the lip and made their direct descent along with the surrounding water molecules. They gained speed and deadly force with every second of their fall. The assassin had released them to impact on the same edge where Skyler was swimming and at the same moment he reached the cascade.

As Skyler felt the force of the falls, he took a deep breath just before the water pushed him under. Explosively, as if shot from a gun, one of the boulders glanced off the side of his head.

Glen heard a woman's scream over the sound of the falls. He turned and saw Skyler floating head down, drifting and bobbing along the wall of water, surrounded by a pool of red blood.

Skyler was dead before Glen reached him. The large man grabbed Skyler's body and pulled him to the pool's edge, lifting him out of the water and carrying him to dry land. The screaming woman was now crying, as people gathered to help.

Anchor and the group could see something was horribly wrong as they approached. Anchor ran and stumbled her way forward. She paused for a moment and spotted someone lying on the ground, covered with a blanket. She recognized Skyler's partially exposed hiking shorts. She stumbled forward again. Her mind was numb, and the water was blasting in her ears...so loud. Slowly the sounds died away, and stillness filled her being.

Acharya and Strant were at her side. Strant grabbed her and kept her from falling. Her legs had become weak when she saw Skyler, wounded and still, with Glen kneeling beside him. Glen gazed up with tears in his eyes. When he shook his head, Anchor went into shock. Nothing seemed real as she fell beside Skyler and grabbed his cold and bloody head in her arms. He still felt alive somehow, but blood was everywhere and he wasn't moving. She gazed around at the gathering crowd, looking for help. Could anyone help?

Minutes later, one of the search helicopters risked landing on the small patch to the west. The rescue workers arrived, pushed through the crowd. They pried Anchor away from Skyler and examined him. "He's gone," the policeman said. "Let's get him into the chopper. Clear a path folks—please."

Acharya was on a nearby bolder, trying to hold back Data, who was struggling to get to Skyler. He looked up and cried as they lifted Skyler onto a stretcher.

Anchor noticed Strant standing on the edge of the pool. What was he doing? He seemed angry, not like the others.

She phased back to reality and the numbness left her. The sound of the waterfall filled her ears again.

Strant turned and peered into her eyes as if trying to summon something from her. He clenched his fist as if to remind her of how strong she was. As their eyes locked, her sorrow changed to rage. Pure rage filled her soul. *Rage*, she said to herself. *Rage against the dying of the light. Do not go quietly.*

She stood up and yelled at the men lifting the stretcher, "Wait! Put him down." She ran to Glen and looked up at him with tears. "I need your help. I need you to bring him with me. Can you do that?"

Glen regarded the rescue workers, who were trying to pull the stretcher away from Strant who held the stretcher with both hands as he glanced back at Glen. Acharya moved in to help Strant, and Data began licking Skyler's face. "Listen to her!" Strant yelled.

Glen grabbed her hands and held them still. "I don't understand. What is it that you want?"

"Pick him up. Pick him up now, and follow me. Please, I beg you."

Glen walked to Skyler and lifted him like a child into his large muscular arms. The workers and the police objected, but Strant and Acharya spoke with them for a moment. They moved away. One of the police officers held back the crowd, preventing them from following after. Glen walked behind Anchor across the shallow waters and onto the ancient trail. Strant, Acharya, and Data soon followed. The police were trying to maintain order. "What the hell do we do now?" one of them asked, confused.

Glen continued to carry Skyler without question. Tears were flowing down his eyes as he drifted down the trail. When they approached a wide opening, Anchor turned left and sped up a thin path on the other side. Data chased after her. She looked back at Glen. "Hurry, this way please!"

Glen continued up the thin trail until he could see Anchor standing by an old hut. "Bring him inside," she sobbed.

Glen placed Skyler on a solid bench and looked around. Anchor stood in the opposite doorway, her eyes searching a grove lit with filtered light. "Where are you?" she yelled.

Strant entered the rainhut along with Data. "What's going on?" Glen asked. "Who's she looking for?"

"The old Buddhist monk," Acharya said, entering the hut as well. "The old monk that she believed saved the life of the tourist the day you first met Skyler."

"So that really happened?" Glen asked.

"Anchor believes that it did," Strant said. "Let's just give her some time and stay with her."

"Where are you?" she screamed again. "Help us please!"

Data was at her side, barking and looking for whatever it was that was out there. She bent down. "My friend to the end," she said.

TWENTY-SEVEN

Skyler found himself inside a structure of unimaginably endless complexity and beauty. Standing to his left, at a vibrating console system, was the old monk. He turned to Skyler and smiled, with his perfect smile. "Welcome home," he said.

"I was in the water," Skyler said. "How did I get here? What is this place?"

"You were on Earth. Your time has ended there. All things will become clear to you in time, but for now you are adjusting. I am here to answer your questions and guide you back. The recovery is best accomplished in this way."

"Guide me back? What's going on? Where's Anchor?"

"Anchor is grieving for you as we speak. From her perspective, you have died."

"What?" Skyler looked down at his body. He grabbed his arms and felt his head. "But I'm still alive, obviously. Where is this place?"

"This place is what we call the Gateless Gate—for sentimental reasons. You are a citizen of the civilization that created this entire Mumonkan."

"I'm still confused. Are you an alien? Have I been abducted?"

"No, Commander, I am not an alien. I am a sentient artificial being. I am the *Keeper* of the Gateless Gate."

Skyler glanced around and walked toward the *Keeper*. There was something familiar about his surroundings, but at the same time strange and difficult to comprehend. He seemed to be experiencing this with more than sight and sound. He seemed able to perceive more, but it was foggy.

"Let's start from the beginning. Am I alive and awake?" Skyler asked.

"Oh yes. You are most assuredly alive."

"Am I in heaven?"

"From your recent understanding, this is much like heaven. But to answer your question accurately, no, you are not in heaven."

Skyler remembered Acharya's night conversation with Anchor in the parking lot at Wailua Falls. "Was Acharya correct then? Was I in a virtual reality system of some kind?"

"Your friend Acharya is too perceptive. I was forced to make adjustments because of his unusual tendency to remember that which he should not remember. In some respects, Acharya was correct. The Earth that you were on is a replicate of the original Earth. But the replicate is not a virtual replicate; it is an actual replicate residing in an alternate universe of our own creation."

"Whoa, hold the phone. What are you saying?"

"Here, in our time, we believe that our future depends on our understanding of the past. Your friend Anchor continues on her sacred journey of enlightenment. Not all the residents of that Earth are...citizens. They live their lives and die just like the inhabitants of the original Earth. Anchor, the name you know her by, is a citizen like yourself."

The direction of this conversation was making Skyler nervous. "What of my friend James? Is he still alive?"

"See for yourself," the monk said. Skyler sensed the presence of another being from behind. He turned to see James standing before him. "James! You're alive?"

"Yes, son. I'm fine."

Skyler reached for his old friend and embraced him. "I can't believe this. How is this possible?"

"Relative to Earth, we are from the future. We have been on an adventure together."

Skyler was happy beyond anything he had ever experienced. His feelings had magnified somehow. It was as if he was able to comprehend more. "I have the feeling that I know you...in a different way. I have the impression of more."

"That's because you are my son. It has been such a great pleasure to learn of Skyler through you—my own son. This journey was your idea. You will soon begin to remember the present, but for now just enjoy your memories of Earth."

"I have so many questions. Am I allowed to ask more questions?"

"I exist for your needs. You may ask any questions," the *Keeper* responded.

"Why Earth? Why did we go to Earth?"

"Earth is of historical importance to our entire Galaxy. Skyler is an enduring legend. He and Acharya were the first inhabitants of any planet to break the stellar barrier, a galactic Columbus, to place it in context."

"But Acharya said that was statistically impossible. How could I, uh, Skyler, be the first?"

"Yes, a statistical impossibility indeed. However, someone had to be the first. Your odds of reliving the life of Skyler, however, is not a statistical impossibility."

"But how could I have actually lived his life if I'm not really him?"

"Your physiological patterns were prepared from our historical knowledge of his personality. You followed in his footsteps with little adjustment. You did live his life in a near replicate of his environment."

"What do you mean by adjustments? What kind of adjustments?"

"I am the *Keeper*. It is my responsibility to maintain the historical accuracy of all sacred journeys for educational purposes."

Skyler's thought processes seemed to be improving as he continued with his questions. "So you, the old monk, are not part of Earth's actual history?"

"The monk, as you see me now, was a mysterious character in Earth's history. Not much is known of him. He was believed to have magical healing skills, and he was seen from time to time. Consequently, he was the personage I chose to monitor and make adjustments with."

"Then what of Anchor? Please tell me she's not my sister."

James laughed and responded. "You met her briefly during the entry ceremony. Selected through a process of qualifications and chance, she became your Anchor. Prior to your journey, you were strangers, like two strangers on a subway, a subway that lasted a lifetime."

"You laughed. So at least there is still humor here in the future," Skyler said, puzzled.

"The ancient body form that you currently inhabit is insufficient to process your entire range of emotions and abilities. You will gradually re-awaken to a form with much greater intelligence, understanding, and emotions. You have lost nothing, including your sense of humor."

"I love Anchor. That hasn't left me. Will I continue to love her?"

"You will remember all that you have experienced. You will be better because of this knowledge. You will need to make adjustments, depending on her feelings. Anchor will return within a week. She died on Earth of apparent heartbreak soon after Skyler died," the *Keeper* said without emotion.

"When you entered the gate, you elected to follow the official guideline," James explained.

"The official guideline?" Skyler asked. "Is there another guideline?"

The *Keeper* stepped closer. "To explain that, I need to tell you that Earth, as you know it, existed over two hundred and thirty thousand years ago—standard Earth time. The stories of Skyler and Anchoret are eternal: the galactic version of Romeo and Juliet. There is the official version, and there is the unofficial version of their lives.

"According to official, preferred documents, Skyler died as you experienced. However, you are in a better position now to decide if that scenario is accurate. The legend has it that Skyler deceived his would-be assassin on that day. We have a digital replicate of a photograph from the era that is most interesting. The authenticity of the photograph has never been disproved. It suggests that the legends of Skyler's survival could be true."

"What's on the photograph?" Skyler asked.

"It is a photograph of Skyler, Anchor, a black dog, and a droid, standing at the base of a Varuna space tree. Clearly, if the photograph is authentic, then Skyler survived and your death experience is not accurate."

"What happened, according to the official records, to Skyler and Anchor's bodies?"

"They were both cremated. Why do you ask?" said the *Keeper*.

"I ask because Anchor was a Mormon. Mormons don't believe in cremation so that couldn't have happened. And when I insisted on continuing the hike, after Acharya's brush with the assassin, I was compelled to do so. I remember that it wasn't my choice. I can't explain why, but it wasn't...correct."

"That is because I was forced to make an adjustment. You were preparing to abandon the hike or make other plans, and that was not acceptable," the *Keeper* explained uneasily.

"I *was* making other plans. I was planning to deceive the bastard. Who authorizes you to make these adjustments?"

"You authorized him," James said. "Think of this as a contract. The *Keeper* does as he is contracted to do."

"A contract you say?"

"Well, that is the easiest way for me to explain it at this time," James responded.

"Then can the contract be re-negotiated?"

The *Keeper* was busy scanning while James seemed concerned. Completing his search, the *Keeper* answered his question. "That would require authorization or approval of the other citizens. We cannot impose a change without authorization or the approval of the other citizens, and we cannot get approval from the other citizens because they are currently engaged."

"Your official rendition of Skyler is...not accurate. Anchor is an intelligent, strong woman. Oh, she would have been heartbroken at the loss of Skyler, but she's no quitter. Anchor is a survivor, not a victim. The Romeo and Juliet scenario, although romantic, just doesn't fit. There's no way she dies soon after Skyler. We have this wrong. How do we correct this mistake?" Skyler demanded.

"Only civilization leaders can adjust contracts, but they do so at the risk of later objections," admitted the *Keeper*.

"Then let's have a talk with one of those leaders. I need to get back to Earth!" Skyler said.

"Son, you *are* one of the leaders. Do you recall the *Keeper* referring to you as Commander? In this time, our true place, you and I are fairly important citizens. We are partly responsible for the security of the Gateless Gate. I would miss you, should you choose to return, but I would understand. Apparently, the woman experiencing Anchor is remarkable, even on Earth."

"How could I return? If Skyler is dead, how can we bring him back to life?"

"We control the environment," said the *Keeper*. "We own the space, matter, and time. Your return is not a technical issue should you make that decision."

"You own the space, matter, and time? Holy shit! Are we immortal?" Skyler asked, astounded.

"Your life expectancy has a limit. However, our knowledge and ability to extend that limit is increasing faster than your duration. So in a word: probably," said the *Keeper* proudly.

"Let's do it! I'll take the responsibility. I'm certain that Anchor would want it this way. I want to finish this the way it should be finished."

Skyler looked at James, who was smiling as if wanting to say something. "What is it?" Skyler asked.

"It's you, son. You're recovering faster than you realize. You're much like yourself already."

"Well then, Father, you owe me something. You made a promise on Earth that you would find an explanation for the rainbow. I would think two hundred thousand years would be enough time for someone to find out what happened."

"You already know the answer. You were involved in the cause. Nevertheless, I will explain it to Skyler.

"As mankind evolved and spread throughout the galaxy, we encountered many strange and wondrous beings. Most were friendly and excited to make contact, but some were aggressive. As we progressed, the combined knowledge and power of the organized galaxy became far too powerful for any individual planet to stop us. Some did rebel, but in the end we were the cause of great good. We, the direct descendants of Earth, have a proud heritage. We explored the galaxy and we created this Gateless Gate for the inhabitants of the Milky Way to experience and learn from.

"As we spread to the most populated regions, near the center of the galaxy, we encountered one race that was evil and deceptive. They were unwilling to accept our existence. This race was far more dangerous than we realized, for they possessed the power of time travel. At first they deceived us by pretending to join the organized galaxy. But once they had obtained some knowledge of our heritage and received our gifts of space travel, they attacked us.

"They sent a weapon back in time to destroy us at our beginning. To be specific, they sent an obliterator back to destroy the third planet from the sun. They were a strange and arrogant race. But that arrogance, and their eagerness to destroy us, was the cause of their downfall. When their obliterator craft found the third planet basking in primitive life, they executed their successful plan.

"The third planet from our star was completely destroyed 400,000 years before it had a chance to achieve agricultural civilization. It sent shockwaves through time, disrupting the very space/time fabrics of the neighboring planets.

"One of those shockwaves struck the Earth, now the third planet from the sun, on the day you were sailing the Na Pali coast. The impact of the shockwave had an instant global effect. Many rainbows were altered, but few were observed. The rainbow transition has come to represent a celebration of our survival and serves as a symbol of our diligence."

James told Skyler about other races they had encountered. It was obvious to Skyler that he could have continued on forever, but Skyler sensed the end was near.

"Wait! Before I return, I have one more question. If Earth, my Earth, is a replicate, then not all people on the planet are from here. Which of my friends are native? What will happen to them?"

"As you have guessed, not all of your close friends are citizens. Established long ago, an immigration policy provides for the sponsorship of native sentient and non-sentient beings. You may choose to sponsor a limited number of natives for citizenship upon your final return. Have a wonderful journey, my son."

"I have just one last simple question," Skyler said, glancing at the *Keeper*.

James shrugged, realizing he'd kept Skyler too long.

"If you can control time, then why tell me about the old photo? Why pretend about your understanding of what really happened?"

There was a long pause before James answered, too long for Skyler's comfort.

"Time travel is forbidden in our own continuum. That, we have learned, is far too dangerous. However, in the worlds that we create for the gateless gateway, we do experiment. That said, we do know more than we have told you about Skyler Anderson. For a hundred thousand years, the stories of Skyler and Anchoret etched their way into the history of our galaxy. When the truth was finally determined, it made little difference.

"Everyone knows historically what happened, of course. The original Skyler and Anchor lived out their lives and died on Varuna. Nevertheless, the alternate story has an emotional life of its own. You, like everyone else, chose the romantic tragedy. The problem we have now is that you and Anchor are exceptionally similar to the originals. The romantic version has failed because you cannot accept the illusion," James said.

"Thank you for that," Skyler said and placed a hand on the shoulder of his father.

James embraced his son, looked to the *Keeper* and nodded. The *Keeper* bowed and waved his hand. The endless room filled with rainbows, both close and distant. It was a magnificent sight beyond description. As Skyler absorbed the hypnotic beauty, the rainbows gradually began to fade. He heard the distant sound of raindrops.

His memory of the rainbows, and James, and the Gateless Gate dissolved into nothingness. He lay on the old bench in the familiar rainhut. As he lifted his head, he saw Anchor standing as a silhouette in the doorway. Rain poured down and the grove beyond was filled with light filtering through the trees. Data was at her side, and she was crying.

"Anchor," he said.

Anchor spun around. "Skyler!"

As she ran forward, she tripped over Data, scrambled to her feet and collapsed into his arms.

"He did it again," she squealed. "That old monk came through again. Where is he?"

"It's not the monk this time, Anchor," Skyler explained. "Strant and I planned this. Strant spotted the assassin crouching at the upper edge of the waterfall. We told Jeff, the police officer, about our plan, but not you and the others. The plan needed reality, and we knew your reactions would provide that. I'm sorry, but it was necessary. I almost blew the cover when Data licked me on the face.

"There was the possibility of another backup assassin, so the best way to survive, we realized, was to let them think they'd succeeded. It's surprising how much blood comes from a small self-inflicted wound on the head. But now we must leave Kauai to protect Acharya."

"Leave for where?" Anchor asked as she brushed away the tears.

TWENTY-EIGHT

The Universe itself takes pause for those who summon her discontinuity

Natalie entered the silent room to find her father gazing out the large bay window at the thousand-foot waterfall—the island's largest.

"The rains of Varuna are coming, Father. We must leave for the cave soon."

"Did you know the name Kauai has no meaning?" Skyler said. "Your mother named this island Kauai after her island on Earth. I wish you could have seen Earth's Kauai. You would have had so many friends."

"Isaac has the s-shield prepared in the cave. Our suspension will last for six months. Please, father, we must go now."

"For what reason? The rains of Varuna are no threat to us. Come here, child, and look at Long Falls with me."

"This time the rains are dangerous, father. A fifty-year storm is approaching. We must leave now," Natalie said, trying to hide her stress.

"Where is Acharya? What does he have to say about this?"

Natalie's heart sank. She could *not* remind her father again that Acharya had died five years earlier. "He's waiting for us in the cave," she said, speaking the partial truth.

Her eyes found the ring on her finger given to her by Acharya on his way to the stasis tomb moments before his death. Acharya was one of the first to volunteer. "I will see you again soon," he whispered. "Please take care of this for me."

"If there's danger, we should take the space ship to a safer location," said Skyler.

"The space craft is no longer operational. Try to remember, Father. We did not have the equipment to salvage her, but we do have Isaac's stasis shield."

Skyler tried to focus. It was difficult for him to keep his memories in sequence since the climbing accident, but he was improving. *How long had they been on Varuna?*

"Yes, I remember now. You're right. We must leave. Is your mother ready?"

"Yes, father. She sent me to bring you."

Natalie led her father across the suspension bridge to the cave in the side of the massive granite mountain. They walked down the worn path and entered the mouth of the cave. The excited chatter of humans and droids echoed in the main chamber. Skyler approached Isaac, who was leaning over a computer console.

"Are you sure this damn thing will work?" Skyler shouted.

Isaac accepted the redundant question and simply nodded to Skyler. "Yes, sir. We've tested for several years now without failure."

"Well, James doesn't like this idea you know. We might come out with fly heads."

Anchor approached Skyler and grabbed his arm. "Come with me, dear. Let Isaac and Natalie finish their work."

"How's it going?" Natalie asked.

"Fine, I'm re-checking the external programs that bring us back. Don't want to get stuck in this thing forever," Isaac chuckled.

Natalie found little humor in Isaac's comment. As brilliant as Isaac was, he was never quite able to figure out what was funny and what was not. Natalie had learned mathematics, physics, astronomy, and programming from Isaac, her mother and the other scientists. No young student in history had the blessing of a better staff of teachers.

Science was her life, but she had learned of adventure and the joy of living from her father. She had his ocean blue eyes that sparkled when she smiled, and she had his perfectly artistic facial lines. From her mother, she was slim, graceful and sensual. Her hair flowed long and dark; the Varuna humidity gave it a soft silkiness that Earth women would have cherished.

Living on a planet with no man made pollutants, she was in perfect health. Her skin glowed with salubriousness. All the children of Varuna were different from their Earth counterparts. The non-toxic food had elevated their intelligence and stamina beyond normal. Nevertheless, with few selections of available men her age, Natalie had spent her youth and her adult life in the abstract world of science, devoid of romance.

She did have droid friends and an assortment of animals that would explore the magnificent planet with her. Her physical activities had kept her relatively happy despite her lack of male companionship; but she longed for something she did not know. Now the people she loved, her parents and her teachers, were getting old and soon they would be gone.

At first, the original inhabitants hid from possible Earth-sent assassins, but after years of isolation, they stopped hiding and prepared beacons. Why humans had not yet returned to Varuna was a mystery. Plans were prepared for a trek back to Earth, but they had waited too long and the spacecraft was no longer safe for travel.

Isaac and the other members of the original Babylonian team began working on an organic stasis shield. For decades, they sought another solution by salvaging potacitor parts and looking deeper into the science behind the potacitor.

Their research turned to the use of alternate dimensional potacitor style fields for transport. Their final solution, though incredible, was a stationary shield: a secure place where time itself suspended; but no displacement in location occurred. The stasis shield was far more complex than the original potacitor technology because of the need to store matter instead of energy, and because of the vastly reduced manufacturing and engineering systems available on the island.

Entering the stasis shield was like walking through a door. There was no feeling of strangeness whatsoever. When you exited the shield, the time dilation would send you to the next day or next week with no memory of where you had been. There was no aging inside a stasis shield because there was nothing that could penetrate the shield to cause aging. Even neutrino particles capable of traveling through a light year of lead deflected away; apparently traveling through lead was much easier than traveling through micro dimensions. From the outside, the shield had the physical form of a shiny, elusive pearl. The ultimate hard-shell, it was impervious to physical change or damage.

Natalie had worked with Isaac and the other original Babylonian scientists for years on the stasis project. Toward the end, her work alone enabled success through a complete redesign. Her colleagues were too old to deal with the complex equations and software solutions. She tried to let them believe that she was still an assistant, but Isaac was well aware of who the true inventor of the stasis shield was, and there were times when she couldn't resist making fun adjustments. Even Isaac was never able to discover how Natalie had managed to place a beautiful Babylonian diaglyph on the surface of every shield. It was impossible of course, and yet there it was. Natalie teased him with the curiosity for years, never giving up her secret.

"As you taught me, we stand on the shoulders of giants," she responded when Isaac had approached her in private and had given her the credit she deserved.

With the community fully assembled, Isaac looked out onto the faces of his friends. His original companions and their children had been isolated from the rest of the human race for half a century. As he prepared for the final lockdown, a thought occurred to him. *If we cannot use the stasis shield to return to Earth, then we could simply wait for Earth to come to us.*

Just before engaging the shield, he instructed the computer to disable the interrupt. Natalie noticed what he was doing and was about to object when she perceived the sadness in the aged eyes of her teacher. She turned and gazed at her father and mother. She saw their master, the old yet sturdy centenarian, standing in the back with his hand on the head of a young droid. Their leader, who many years ago on Earth had refused to believe in aliens, was now standing among aliens. She turned back to Isaac, smiled, kissed him on the cheek, and joined her parents.

The island was devastated, engulfed in a series of perfect storms. The cave had filled, covered with two miles of mud and debris, trapping the occupants of the unbreakable shiny pearl forever.

Discontinuity

The old man with long, tied-back white hair struggled in the dark toward the end of the pier at Hanalei. He slowly crouched down and managed to dangle his legs over the edge.

A crescent moon provided enough light to see the calm waters and white sands. In the distance, a few lights spotted the dark landmass, interrupting the left side of the horizon.

Believing he was alone, his mind wandered back to the days when he would ride the wild reef surf a few hundred yards ahead and to his right. He remembered sitting on the beach for hours waiting for the perfect ebb tide and north swell. He was startled when a young handsome man sat down next to him.

"Pardon me for staring, son, but you look like someone I knew a long time ago."

The young man said nothing but acknowledged the comment with a smile. Unconcerned, the old man went back to his idle thoughts as they sat together in dark silence for several minutes.

"Hey, Strant. Did you see the giant rainbow over the bay today? Rainbows are a celebration of the survival of our species," the young man said, turning to face his old friend.

"Skyler! Is that you?"

"Yep, it's me, dude."

"How is this possible? More space travel? I thought you were going to Varuna?"

"I did Strant. We traveled to Varuna on the backup ship just as we planned. I've been living there for the past forty-six years with Anchor. Now *those* were days of adventure.

I'll tell you about it some time, but right now I'd like you to take a trip with me."

"Hold on. I'm too old. My traveling days are long behind me."

Skyler laughed. "I was hoping you would still be here."

"Hey, Sky, after you left I went back to the rainhut, but I could never find it. Why did you get rid of it?"

"It was never there, Strant. It was never part of Earth's natural history. That's why I want you to come with me. I want to show you the history of the Earth...all of it. Damn, it's good to see you. You're a survivor, buddy."

"A survivor on his last legs, Sky. Not sure why you're still young. The air on Varuna must be pure. I wish I could up and go with you, but I'll be lucky to get to my feet and hobble back down this pier."

"That's just a technical problem, Strant, and not much of one at that." Skyler placed his hand on the shoulder of his old friend.

Strant could hear laughter and barking on the beach to his left. "What the...haven't heard out of that ear for years."

The young Mike Stranton turned to his left to see Anchor and Data playing on the beach. "Don't get me!" Anchor yelled and ran up the beach in a blur.

Data looked toward Strant and Skyler. His black form was difficult to make out in the dark, but his eyes glowed with an apparent happiness as if generating their own light energy. He barked once and was gone in a flash.

"Is that Data? Now I know the air is good on Varuna."

"It's a long story," said Skyler. "A friend of yours came for him."

Strant rose to his feet with astonishing ease. He could feel the island again, as he could in his youth after a hard underestimated the creativity of the original explorers. Given what they accomplished, we should have been more diligent. We've uncovered an advanced neutrino shield with an enigmatic Babylonian diaglyph on the surface. We've found survivors, Strant. Our thirst for knowledge of the past has led us to this unexpected discovery...come with me while I explain."

1184482

Made in the USA

1184482

Made in the USA